BEFORE SHE WENT to join Sam and Mogget downstairs, Lirael paused for a moment to look at herself in the tall silver mirror that hung on the wall of her room. The image that faced her bore little resemblance to the Second Assistant Librarian of the Clayr. She saw a warlike and grim young woman, dark hair bound back with a silver cord rather than hanging free to disguise her face. She no longer wore her librarian's waistcoat, and instead of a library-issue dagger, she had long Nehima at her side. But she couldn't completely let go her former identity. Taking the end of a loose thread from her waistcoat, she drew out a single strand of red silk, wound it around her little finger several times to make a ring, tied it off, and tucked it into the small pouch at her belt with the Dark Mirror. She might not wear the waistcoat any longer, but part of it would always travel with her.

She had become an Abhorsen, Lirael thought. At least on the outside.

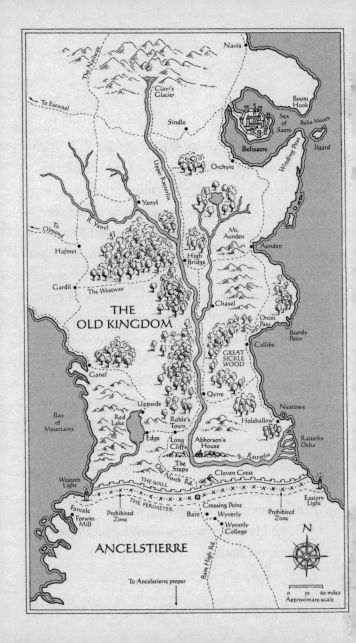

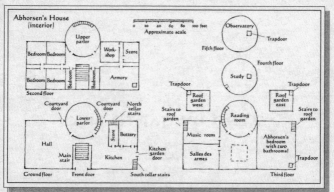

Abhorsen's House (interior)

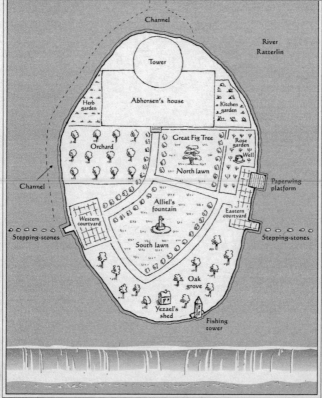

ALSO BY GARTH NIX

Sabriel

Lirael

Shade's Children

The Ragwitch

GARTH NIX

ABHORSEN

An Imprint of HarperCollins*Publishers*

Eos is an imprint of HarperCollins Publishers.

Abhorsen

Library of Congress Cataloging-in-Publication Data
Nix, Garth.
    Abhorsen / Garth Nix. — 1st ed.
        p.   cm.
    Summary: Abhorsen-in-Waiting Lirael and Prince Sameth, a Wallmaker,
must confront and bind the evil spirit Orannis before it can destroy all life.
    ISBN 0-06-027825-0 — ISBN 0-06-027826-9 (lib. bdg.)
    ISBN 0-06-052873-7 (pbk.)
    [1. Fantasy.] I. Title.
PZ7.N647 Ab 2003   2002003151
[Fic]—dc21   CIP
                                                                          AC

Typography by Lizzy Bromley
❖
First paperback edition, 2004
Visit us on the World Wide Web!
www.harpereos.com

18 QGM 30 29 28 27 26 25 24 23

To Anna and Thomas Henry Nix

CONTENTS

PROLOGUE

FOG ROSE FROM the river, great billows of white weaving into the soot and smoke of the city of Corvere, to become the hybrid thing that the more popular newspapers called smog and the *Times* "miasmic fog." Cold, dank, and foul-smelling, it was dangerous by any name. At its thickest, it could smother, and it could transform the faintest hint of a cough into pneumonia.

But the unhealthiness of the fog was not its chief danger. That came from its other primary feature. The Corvere fog was a concealer, a veil that shrouded the city's vaunted gaslights and confused both eyes and ears. When the fog lay on the city, all streets were dark, all echoes strange, and everywhere set for murder and mayhem.

"The fog shows no signs of lifting," reported Damed, principal bodyguard to King Touchstone. His voice showed his dislike of the fog even though he knew it was only a natural phenomenon, a blend of industrial pollution and river-mist. Back in their home, the Old Kingdom, such fogs were often created by Free Magic sorcerers. "Also, the . . . telephone . . . is not working, and the escort is both understrength and new. There is not one of the officers we usually have among them. I don't think you should go, sire."

Touchstone was standing by the window, peering out through the shutters. They'd had to shutter all the windows some days ago, when some of the crowd outside had adopted slingshots. Before that, the demonstrators hadn't been able to throw half bricks far enough, as the mansion that housed the Old Kingdom Embassy was set in a walled park, and a good fifty yards back from the street.

Not for the first time, Touchstone wished that he could reach the Charter and draw upon it for strength and magical assistance. But they were five hundred miles south of the Wall, and the air was still and cold. Only when the wind blew very strongly from the north could he feel even the slightest touch of his magical heritage.

Sabriel felt the lack of the Charter even more, Touchstone knew. He glanced at his wife. She was at her desk, as usual, writing one last letter to an old school friend, a prominent businessman, or a member of the Ancelstierre Moot. Promising gold, or support, or introductions, or perhaps making thinly veiled threats of what would happen if they were stupid enough to support Corolini's attempts to settle hundreds of thousands of Southerling refugees over the Wall, in the Old Kingdom.

Touchstone still found it odd to see Sabriel dressed in Ancelstierran clothes, particularly their court clothes, as she was wearing today. She should be in her blue and silver tabard, with the bells of the Abhorsen across her chest, her sword at her side. Not in a silver dress with a hussar's pelisse worn on one shoulder, and a strange little pillbox hat pinned to her deep-black hair. And the small automatic pistol in her silver mesh purse was no substitute for a sword.

Not that Touchstone felt at ease in his clothes either. An Ancelstierran shirt with its stiff collar and tie was too constricting, and his suit offered no protection at all. A sharp blade would slide through the double-breasted coat of superfine wool as easily as it would through butter, and as for a bullet . . .

"Shall I convey your regrets, sire?" asked Damed.

Touchstone frowned and looked at Sabriel. She had been to school in Ancelstierre, she understood the people and their ruling classes far better than he did. She led their diplomatic efforts south of the Wall, as she had always done.

"No," said Sabriel. She stood up and sealed the last letter with a sharp tap. "The Moot sits tonight,

3

and it is possible Corolini will present his Forced Emigration Bill. Dawforth's bloc may just give us the votes to defeat the motion. We must attend his garden party."

"In this fog?" asked Touchstone. "How can he have a garden party?"

"They will ignore the weather," said Sabriel. "We will all stand around, drinking green absinthe and eating carrots cut into elegant shapes, and pretend we're having a marvelous time."

"Carrots?"

"A fad of Dawforth's, introduced by his swami," replied Sabriel. "According to Sulyn."

"She would know," said Touchstone, making a face—but at the prospect of raw carrots and green absinthe, not Sulyn. She was one of the old school friends who had been so much help to them. Sulyn, like the others at Wyverley College twenty years ago, had seen what happened when Free Magic was stirred up and grew strong enough to cross the Wall and run amok in Ancelstierre.

"We will go, Damed," said Sabriel. "But it would be sensible to put in place the plan we discussed."

"I do beg your pardon, Milady Abhorsen," replied Damed. "But I'm not sure that it will increase your safety. In fact, it may make matters worse."

"But it will be more fun," pronounced Sabriel. "Are the cars ready? I shall just put on my coat and some boots."

Damed nodded reluctantly and left the room. Touchstone picked out a dark overcoat from a number that were draped across the back of a chaise longue and shrugged it on. Sabriel put on another— a man's coat—and sat down to exchange her shoes for boots.

"Damed isn't concerned without reason," Touchstone said as he offered his hand to Sabriel. "And the fog is very thick. If we were at home, I wouldn't doubt it was made with malice afore-thought."

"The fog is natural enough," replied Sabriel. They stood close together and knotted each others' scarves, finishing with a soft, brushing kiss. "But I agree it may well be used against us. Yet I am so close to forming an alliance against Corolini. If Dawforth comes in, and the Sayres stay out of the matter—"

"Little chance of that unless we can show them we haven't made off with their precious son and nephew," growled Touchstone, but his attention was on his pistols. He checked both were loaded and there was a round in the chamber, hammer down and safety on. "I wish we knew more about this guide Nicholas hired. I am sure I have heard the name Hedge before, and not in any positive light. If only we'd met them on the Great South Road."

"I am sure we will hear from Ellimere soon," said Sabriel as she checked her own pistol. "Or perhaps even from Sam. We must leave that matter, at least, to the good sense of our children and deal with what is before us."

Touchstone grimaced at the notion of his children's good sense, handed Sabriel a grey felt hat with a black band, twin to his own, and helped her remove the pillbox and pin her hair up underneath the replacement.

"Ready?" he asked as she belted her coat. With their hats on, collars up, and scarves wound high, they looked indistinguishable from Damed and their other guards. Which was precisely the idea.

There were ten bodyguards waiting outside, not including the drivers of the two heavily armored Hedden-Hare automobiles. Sabriel and Touchstone joined them, and the twelve huddled together for a moment. If any enemies were watching beyond the walls, they would be hard put to make out who was who through the fog.

Two people went into the back of each car, with the remaining eight standing on the running boards. The drivers had kept the engines idling for some time, the exhausts sending a steady stream of warm, lighter emissions into the fog.

At a signal from Damed, the cars started down the drive, sounding their Klaxons. This was the signal for the guards at the gate to throw it open, and for the Ancelstierran police outside to push the crowd apart. There was always a crowd these days, mostly made up of Corolini's supporters: paid thugs and agitators wearing the red armbands of Corolini's Our Country party.

Despite Damed's worries, the police did their job well, separating the throng so that the two cars could speed through. A few bricks and stones were hurled after them, but they missed the riding guards or bounced off the hardened glass and armor plate. Within a minute, the crowd was left behind, just a dark, shouting mass in the fog.

"The escort is not following," said Damed, who was riding the running board next to the front car's driver. A detachment of mounted police had been assigned to accompany King Touchstone and his Abhorsen Queen wherever they went in the city, and up to now they had performed their duty to the expected standards of the Corvere Police Corps. This time the troopers were still standing by their horses.

"Maybe they got their orders mixed up," said the driver through her open quarter window. But there was no conviction in her voice.

"We'd better change the route," ordered Damed. "Take Harald Street. Left up ahead."

The cars sped past two slower automobiles, a heavily laden truck, and a horse and wagon, braked sharply, and curved left into the broad stretch of Harald Street. This was one of the more modern promenades, and better lit, with gas lamps on both sides of the street at regular intervals. Even so, the fog made it unsafe to drive faster than fifteen miles per hour.

"Something up ahead!" reported the driver. Damed looked up and swore. As their headlights pierced the fog, he saw a great mass of people blocking the street. He couldn't make out what was on the banners they held, but it was easy enough to recognize it as an Our Country demonstration. To make it worse, there were no police to keep them in check. Not one blue-helmeted officer in sight.

"Stop! Back up!" said Damed. He waved at the

car behind, a double signal that meant "Trouble!" and "Retreat!"

Both cars started to back up. As they did, the crowd ahead surged forward. They'd been silent till then. Now they started shouting, "Foreigners out!" and "Our Country!" The shouts were accompanied by bricks and stones, which for the moment fell short.

"Back up!" shouted Damed again. He drew his pistol, holding it down by his leg. "Faster!"

The rear car was almost back at the corner when the truck and the wagon they'd passed pulled across, blocking the way. Masked men dropped out of the backs of both vehicles, sending the fog shivering as they ran. Men with guns.

Damed knew even before he saw the guns that this was what he had feared all along.

An ambush.

"Out! Out!" he shouted, pointing at the armed men. "Shoot!"

Around him the other guards were opening car doors for cover. A second later they opened fire, the deeper boom of their pistols accompanied by the sharp tap-tap-tap of the new, compact machine rifles that were so much handier than the Army's old Lewins. None of the guards liked guns, but they had practiced with them constantly since coming south of the Wall.

"Not the crowd!" roared Touchstone. "Only armed targets!"

Their attackers were not so careful. They had gone under their vehicles, behind a post box, and down on the footpath beside a low wall of flower boxes, and were firing wildly.

Bullets ricocheted off the street and the armored cars in mad, zinging screeches. There was noise everywhere, harsh, confused sound, a mixture of screaming and shouting combined with the constant crack and chatter of gunfire. The crowd, so eager to rush forward only seconds before, had become a terrible, tumbling crush of people trying to flee.

Damed rushed to a knot of guards crouched behind the engine of the rear car.

"The river," he shouted. "Go through the square and down the Warden Steps. We have two boats there. You'll lose any pursuit in the fog."

"We can fight our way back to the Embassy!" retorted Touchstone.

"This is too well planned! The police have turned, or enough of them! You must get out of Corvere. Out of Ancelstierre!"

"No!" shouted Sabriel. "We haven't finished—"

She was cut off as Damed violently pushed her and Touchstone over and leaped above them. With his legendary quickness, he intercepted a large black cylinder that was tumbling through the air, trailing smoke behind it.

A bomb.

Damed caught and threw it in one swift motion, but even he was not fast enough.

The bomb exploded while it was still in the air. Packed with high explosive and pieces of metal, it killed Damed instantly. The blast broke every window for half a mile and momentarily deafened and blinded everyone within a hundred yards. But it was the thousands of metal fragments that did the real damage, ripping and screaming through the air, to bounce off stone or metal, or all too often to cut through flesh.

Silence followed the explosion, save for the roar of the burning gas from the shattered lamps. Even the fog had been thrown back by the force of the blast, which had cleared a great circle open to the sky. Rays of weak sunshine filtered through, to illuminate a scene of terrible destruction.

There were bodies strewn all around and under the cars, not one overcoated guard still on his or her feet. Even the car's armored windows were broken, and the occupants were slumped in death.

The surviving assassins waited for a few minutes before they crawled out from behind the low wall and moved forward, laughing and congratulating one another, their weapons cradled casually under their arms or across their shoulders with what they imagined was debonair style.

The talk and laughter were too loud, but they didn't notice. Their senses were battered, their minds in shock. Not only from the explosion or the terrible sights that drew closer and more real with every step, or even with relief at being alive in the midst of so much death and destruction.

The real shock came from the realization that it was three hundred years since a King and a Queen had been slain on the streets of Corvere. Now it had happened again—and they had done the deed.

PART
ONE

CHAPTER ONE

A HOUSE BESIEGED

THERE WAS ANOTHER fog, far away from the smog of Corvere. Six hundred miles to the north, across the Wall that separated Ancelstierre from the Old Kingdom. The Wall where the Old Kingdom's magic really began and Ancelstierre's modern technology failed.

This fog was different from its far-southern cousin. It was not white but the dark grey of a storm cloud, and it was completely unnatural. This fog had been spun from air and Free Magic and was born on a hilltop far from any water. It survived and spread despite the heat of a late-spring afternoon, which should have burned it into nothing.

Ignoring sun and light breezes, the fog spread from the hill and rolled south and east, thin tendrils creeping out in advance of the main body. Half a league on from the hill, one of these tendrils separated into a cloud that rose high in the air and crossed the mighty river Ratterlin. Once across, it sank to sit like a toad on the eastern bank, and new fog began to puff out of it.

Soon the two arms of fog shrouded both western and eastern shores of the Ratterlin, though the sun still shone on the river in between.

Both river and fog sped at their very different paces towards the Long Cliffs. The river dashed along, getting faster and faster as it headed to the great waterfall, where it would plunge down more than a thousand feet. The fog was slow and threatening. It thickened and rose higher as it rolled on.

A few yards before it reached the Long Cliffs, the fog stopped, though it still grew thicker and rose higher, threatening the island that sat in the middle of the river and on the edge of the waterfall. An island with high white walls that enclosed a house and gardens.

The fog did not spread across the river, nor lean in too far as it rose. There were unseen defenses that held it back, that kept the sun shining on the white walls, the gardens, and the red-tiled house. The fog was a weapon, but it was only the first move in a battle, only the beginning of a siege. The battle lines were drawn and the House invested.

For the whole river-circled isle was Abhorsen's House. Home to the Abhorsen, whose birthright and charge was to maintain the borders of Life and Death. The Abhorsen, who used necromantic bells and Free Magic, but who was neither necromancer nor Free Magic sorcerer. The Abhorsen, who sent any Dead who trespassed in Life back to whence they came.

The creator of the fog knew that the Abhorsen was not actually in the House. The Abhorsen and her husband, the King, had been lured across the Wall and would presumably be dealt with there. That was part of her Master's plan, long since laid but only recently begun in earnest.

The plan had many parts, in many countries, though the very heart and reason for it lay in the Old Kingdom. War, assassination, and refugees were elements of the plan, all manipulated by a scheming, subtle mind that had waited generations for everything to come to fruition.

But as with any plan, there had already been complications and problems. Two of them were in the House. One was a young woman, who had been sent south by the witches who lived in the glacier-clad mountain at the Ratterlin's source. The Clayr, who Saw many futures in the ice, and who would certainly try to twist the present to their own ends. The woman was one of their elite mages, easily identified by the colored waistcoat she wore. A red waistcoat, marking her as a Second Assistant Librarian.

The maker of the fog had seen her, black haired and pale skinned, surely no older than twenty, a mere fingernail sliver of an age. She had heard the young woman's name, called out in desperate battle.

Lirael.

The other complication was better known, and possibly more trouble, though the evidence was con-flicting. A young man, hardly more than a boy, curly haired from his father, black eyebrowed from his mother, and tall from both. His name was Sameth, the royal son of King Touchstone and the Abhorsen Sabriel.

Prince Sameth was meant to be the Abhorsen-in-Waiting, heir to the powers of *The Book of the Dead* and the seven bells. But the maker of the fog doubted that now. She was very old, and once she had known a great deal about the strange family and their House in the river. She had fought Sameth barely a night past, and he had not fought like an

Abhorsen; even the way he cast his Charter Magic was strange, reminiscent of neither the royal line nor the Abhorsens.

Sameth and Lirael were not alone. They were supported by two creatures who appeared to be no more than a small bad-tempered white cat and a large black and tan dog of friendly disposition. Yet both were much more than they seemed, though exactly what they were was another slippery piece of information. Most likely they were Free Magic spirits of some kind, bound in service to the Abhorsen and the Clayr. The cat was known to some degree. His name was Mogget, and there was speculation about him in certain books of lore. The Dog was a different matter. She was new, or so old that any book that told of her was long since dust. The creature in the fog thought the latter. Both the young woman and her hound had come from the Great Library of the Clayr. It was likely both of them, like the Library, had hidden depths and contained unknown powers.

Together, these four could be formidable opponents, and they represented a serious threat. But the maker of the fog did not have to fight them directly, nor could she, for the House was too well guarded by both spell and swift water. Her orders were to make sure that they were trapped in the House. The House was to be besieged while matters progressed elsewhere—until it was too late for Lirael, Sam, and their companions to do anything at all.

Chlorr of the Mask hissed as she thought of those orders, and fog billowed around what passed for her head. She had once been a living necromancer, and she took orders from no one. She had made a mistake, a mistake that had led to her servitude and death. But her Master had not let her go to the Ninth Gate and beyond. She had been returned to Life, though not in any living form. She was a Dead creature now, caught by the power of bells, bound by her secret name. She did not like her orders yet had no choice but to obey.

Chlorr lowered her arms. A few feathery tendrils of fog issued from her fingers. There were Dead Hands all around her, hundreds and hundreds of swaying, suppurating corpses. Chlorr had not brought the spirits that inhabited these rotten, half-skeletal bodies out of Death, but she had been given command of them by the one who had. She raised one thin, long arm of shadow and pointed. With sighs and groans and gurgles and the clicking of frozen joints and broken bones, the Dead Hands marched forward, sending the fog swirling all around them.

"There are at least two hundred Dead Hands on the western bank, and fourscore or more to the east," reported Sameth. He straightened up from behind the bronze telescope and swung it down out of the way. "I couldn't see Chlorr, but she must be there somewhere, I guess."

He shivered as he thought of the last time he'd seen Chlorr, a thing of malignant darkness looming above him, her flaming sword about to fall. That had been only the night before, though it already felt much longer ago.

"It's possible some other Free Magic sorcerer could have raised this mist," said Lirael. But she didn't believe it. She could sense the same brooding power out there that she'd felt last night.

"Fog," said the Disreputable Dog, who was delicately balanced on the observer's stool. Apart from the fact that she could talk, and the bright collar made of Charter marks around her neck, she looked just like any other large black and tan mongrel dog. The kind that smiled and wagged their tails more than they barked and growled. "I think it has thickened sufficiently to be called fog."

The Dog; her mistress, Lirael; Prince Sameth; and the Abhorsen's cat-shaped servant, Mogget, were all in the observatory that occupied the top-most floor of the tower on the northern side of Abhorsen's House.

The observatory's walls were entirely transparent, and Lirael found herself taking nervous glances at the ceiling, because it was hard to see if anything was holding it up. The walls were not glass either, or any material she knew, which somehow made it even worse.

But she didn't want her nervousness to show, so Lirael turned her most recent twitch into a nod of agreement as the Dog spoke. Only her hand betrayed her feelings, as she kept it resting on the Dog's neck, for the comfort of warm dog skin and the Charter Magic in the Dog's collar.

Though it was only early afternoon, and the sun still shone directly down on the House, the island, and the river, there was a solid mass of fog on either bank, billowing up in sheer walls that kept on climbing and climbing, though they were already several hundred feet high.

The fog was clearly sorcerous in origin. It had not risen from the river as a normal fog would, or come with lowering cloud. This fog had flowed in from the east and west at the same time, moving swiftly regardless of the wind. Thin at first, it had grown thicker with every passing minute.

A further indication of the fog's strangeness lay directly to the south, where it stopped sharply just before it might mix with the natural mist thrown up by the great waterfall where the river flung itself over the Long Cliffs.

The Dead had come soon after the fog. Lumbering corpses who climbed clumsily along the riverbanks, though they feared the swift-flowing water. Something was driving them on, something hidden farther back in the fog. Almost certainly that something was Chlorr of the Mask, once a necromancer, now herself one of the Greater Dead. A very dangerous combination, Lirael knew, for Chlorr had probably retained much of her old sorcerous knowledge of Free Magic, combined with whatever powers she had gained in Death. Powers that were likely to be dark and strange. Lirael and the Dog had briefly driven Chlorr away in the last night's battle on the riverbank, but it had not been a victory.

Lirael could feel the presence of the Dead and the sorcerous nature of the fog. Though Abhorsen's House was defended by deep running water and many magical wards and guards, she still shivered, as if a cold hand had trailed fingers across her skin.

No one commented on the shiver, though Lirael felt embarrassed at how obvious it had been. No one said anything, but they were all looking at her. Sam, the Dog, and Mogget, all waiting as if she were going to pronounce some great wisdom or insight. For a moment Lirael felt a surge of panic. She wasn't used to taking the lead in conversation, or in anything else. But she was the Abhorsen-in-Waiting now. While Sabriel was across the Wall in Ancelstierre, she was the only Abhorsen. The Dead, the fog, and Chlorr were her problems. And they were only minor problems, compared to the real threat—whatever Hedge and Nicholas were digging up near the Red Lake.

I'll have to pretend, thought Lirael. I'll have to act like an Abhorsen. Maybe if I act well enough, I'll come to believe it myself.

"Apart from the stepping-stones, is there any other way out?" she asked suddenly, turning south to look at the stones that were just visible under the water, leading out to both eastern and western banks. Stepping-stones was not quite the right name, Lirael thought. Jumping-stones would be more appropriate, as they were set at least six feet apart and were very close to the edge of the water-fall. If you missed a jump, the river would snatch you up and the waterfall would throw you down. Down a very long way, under a great weight of crushing water.

"Sam?"

Sam shook his head.

"Mogget?"

The little white cat was curled up on the blue and gold cushion that had briefly been on the observer's stool, before it was knocked off by a paw and put to better use on the floor. Mogget was not actually a cat, though he had the shape of one. The collar of Charter marks with its miniature bell—Ranna, the Sleepbringer—showed that he was much more than any simple talking cat.

Mogget opened one bright-green eye and yawned widely. Ranna tinkled on his collar, and Lirael and Sam found themselves yawning as well.

"Sabriel took the Paperwing, so we cannot fly out," he said. "Even if we could fly, we'd have to get past the Gore Crows. I suppose we could call a boat, but the Dead would follow us along the banks."

Lirael looked out at the walls of fog. She had

been the Abhorsen-in-Waiting for only two hours, and already she didn't know what to do. Except that she had an absolute conviction that they must leave the House and hurry to the Red Lake. They had to find Sam's friend Nicholas and stop him from digging up whatever it was that was imprisoned deep beneath the earth.

"There might be another way," said the Dog. She jumped down from the stool and began to tread a circle near Mogget as she spoke, high-stepping as if she were pressing down grass beneath her paws rather than cool stone. On "way" she suddenly collapsed onto the floor near the cat and slapped a heavy paw near the cat's head. "Though Mogget won't like it."

"What way?" Mogget hissed, arching his back. "I know of no way out but the stepping-stones, or the air above, or the river—and I have been here since the House was built."

"But not when the river was split and the island made," said the Dog calmly. "Before the Wallmakers raised the walls, when the first Abhorsen's tent was pitched where the great fig grows now."

"True," conceded Mogget. "But neither were you."

There was the hint of a question, or doubt, in Mogget's last words, thought Lirael. She watched the Disreputable Dog carefully, but all the hound did was scratch her nose with both forepaws before continuing.

"In any case, there was once another way. If it still exists, it is deep, and it could be dangerous in more ways than one. Some might say it would be safer to cross the stones and fight our way through the Dead."

"But not you?" asked Lirael. "You think there is an alternative?"

Lirael was afraid of the Dead, but not so much that she could not face them if she had to. She was just not entirely confident in her newfound identity. Perhaps an Abhorsen like Sabriel, in the full flower of her years and power, could simply leap across the stepping-stones and put Chlorr, the Shadow Hands, and all the other Dead to rout. Lirael thought if she tried that herself, she would end up retreating back across the stones and quite likely fall into the river and be smashed to pieces in the waterfall.

"I think we should investigate it," pronounced the Dog. She stretched out, almost hitting Mogget again with her paws, then slowly stood up and yawned, revealing many extremely large, very white teeth. All of this, Lirael was sure, was to annoy Mogget.

Mogget looked at the Dog through narrowed eyes.

"Deep?" mewed the cat. "Does that mean what I think it does? We cannot go there!"

"She is long gone," replied the Dog. "Though I suppose something might linger. . . ."

"She?" asked Lirael and Sameth together.

"You know the well in the rose garden?" asked the Dog. Sameth nodded, while Lirael tried to remember if she'd seen a well as they'd crossed the island to the House. She did vaguely recall catching a glimpse of roses, many roses sprawled across trellises that rose up past the eastern side of the lawn closest to the House.

"It is possible to climb down the well," continued the Dog. "Though it is a long climb, and narrow. It will bring us to even deeper caves. There is a way through them to the base of the waterfall. Then we will have to climb back up the cliffs again, but I expect we will be able to do that farther west, bypassing Chlorr and her minions."

"The well is full of water," said Sam. "We'll drown!"

"Are you sure?" asked the Dog. "Have you ever looked in it?"

"Well, no," said Sam. "It's covered, I think. . . ."

"Who is the 'she' you mentioned?" asked Lirael firmly. She knew very well from past experience when the Dog was avoiding an issue.

"Someone once lived down there," replied the Dog. "Someone who had considerable and dangerous powers. There might be some remnant of her there."

"What do you mean, 'someone'?" asked Lirael sternly. "How could someone have lived deep underneath Abhorsen's House?"

"I refuse to go anywhere near that well," interjected Mogget. "I suppose it was Kalliel who thought to dig into forbidden ground. What use to add our bones to his in some dark corner of the depths?"

Lirael's gaze flicked across to Sam for an instant, then back to Mogget. She regretted it instantly, for it showed her own doubts and fears. Now that she was the Abhorsen-in-Waiting, she had to set an example. Sam had been open about his fear of Death and the Dead, and his desire to hide out here in the heavily protected House. But he had overcome his fear, at least for now. How could Sam continue to be brave if she didn't set an example?

Lirael was also his aunt. She didn't feel like an aunt, but she supposed that it carried certain responsibilities towards a nephew, even one who was only a few years younger than herself.

"Dog!" ordered Lirael. "Answer me plainly for once. Who . . . or what . . . is down there?"

"Well, it's difficult to put into words," said the Dog. She shuffled her front paws again. "Particularly since there's probably no one down there at all. If there is, I suppose that you would call her a leftover from the creation of the Charter, as am I, and so many others of varying stature. But if she is there, or some part of her, then it's possible she is as she was, which is dangerous in a very . . . *elemental* . . . way, though it's all so long ago and really I'm only telling you what other people have said or written or thought. . . ."

"Why would she be down there?" asked Sameth. "Why under Abhorsen's House?"

"She's not exactly anywhere," replied the Dog, who was now scratching at her nose with one paw and totally failing to meet anybody's eyes. "Part of her power is invested here, so if she were to be anywhere, it's likely to be here, and that's where if she were anywhere she'd be."

29

"Mogget?" asked Lirael. "Can you translate anything the Dog has said?"

Mogget didn't answer. His eyes were shut. Somewhere in the space of the Dog's answer he had curled up and gone to sleep.

"Mogget!" repeated Lirael.

"He sleeps," said the Dog. "Ranna has called him into slumber."

"I think he only listens to Ranna when he feels like it," said Sam. "I hope Kerrigor sleeps more soundly."

"We can look, if you like," said the Dog. "But I am sure we would know if he had woken. Ranna has a lighter hand than Saraneth, but she holds tightly when she must. Besides, Kerrigor's power lay in his followers. His art was to draw upon them, and his downfall was to depend upon it."

"What do you mean?" asked Lirael. "I thought he was a Free Magic sorcerer who became one of the Greater Dead?"

"He was more than that," said the Dog. "For he had the royal blood. Mastery of others ran deep in him. Somewhere in Death, Kerrigor found the means to use the strength of those who swore allegiance to him, through the brand he burned upon their flesh. If Sabriel had not accidentally used a

30

most ancient charm that severed him from this power, I think Kerrigor would have triumphed. For a time, at least."

"Why only for a time?" asked Sam. He wished he had never mentioned Kerrigor in the first place.

"I think he would eventually have done what your friend Nicholas is doing now," said the Dog. "And dug up something best left alone."

No one said anything to that.

"We're wasting time," Lirael said finally.

She looked out at the fog on the western bank again. She could feel many Dead Hands there, more than could be seen, though there were plenty enough of those. Rotting sentries, wreathed in fog. Waiting for their enemy to come out.

Lirael took a deep breath and made her decision.

"If you think we should climb down the well, Dog, then that is the way we will go. Hopefully we will not encounter whatever remnant of power lurks below. Or perhaps she will be friendly, and we can talk—"

"No!" barked the Dog, surprising everyone. Even Mogget opened an eye but, seeing Sam looking at him, hastily shut it again.

"What?" asked Lirael.

"If she is there, which is very unlikely, you musn't speak to her," said the Dog. "You must not listen to her or touch her in any way."

"Has anyone ever heard or touched her?" asked Sam.

"No mortal," said Mogget, raising his head. "Nor passed through her halls, I would guess. It is madness to try. I always wondered what happened to Kalliel."

"I thought you were asleep," said Lirael. "Besides, she might ignore us as we ignore her."

"It is not her ill will I am afraid of," said Mogget. "I fear her paying us any attention at all."

"Perhaps we should—" said Sam.

"What?" asked Mogget nastily. "Stay here all nice and safe?"

"No," replied Sam quietly. "If this woman's voice is so dangerous, then perhaps we should make earplugs before we go. Out of wax, or something."

"It wouldn't help," said Mogget. "If she speaks, you will hear her through your very bones. If she sings . . . We had best hope she will not sing."

"We will avoid her," said the Dog. "Trust to my nose. We will find our path."

"Can you tell us who Kalliel was?" asked Sam.

"Kalliel was the twelfth Abhorsen," replied

Mogget. "A most untrusting individual. He kept me locked up for years. The well must have been dug then. His grandson released me when Kalliel disappeared, and he inherited his grandsire's bells and title. I do not wish to share Kalliel's doom. Particularly down a well."

Lirael twitched as she suddenly felt some shift out in the fog. The brooding presence that had been lurking farther back was moving. She could sense it, a being far more powerful than the Shadow Hands who were beginning to flicker in and out of the edge of the fog.

Chlorr was coming closer, almost down to the riverbank. Or if not Chlorr, someone of equal or greater power. Perhaps it was even the necromancer she had encountered in Death.

Hedge. The same necromancer who had burned Sam. Lirael could still see the scars on Sam's wrists, through the slits in the sleeves of his surcoat.

That surcoat was another mystery—for another day, Lirael thought wearily. A surcoat that quartered the royal towers with a device that had not been seen for millennia. The trowel of the Wallmakers.

Sam caught her glance and picked at the heavy golden thread where the Wallmakers' symbol was woven through the linen. It was only slowly entering his head that the sendings hadn't made a mistake with the surcoat. For a start, it was new made, not some old thing they'd dragged out of a musty cupboard or centuries-old laundry basket. So he probably was entitled to wear it for some reason. He was a Wallmaker as well as a royal Prince. But what did that mean? The Wallmakers had disappeared millennia ago, putting themselves into the creation of the Wall and the Great Charter Stones. Quite literally, as far as Sam knew.

For a moment, he wondered if that would be his destiny, too. Would he have to make something that would end his life, at least as a living, breathing man? For the Wallmakers weren't exactly dead, Sam thought, remembering the Great Charter Stones and the Wall. They were more transformed or transfigured.

Not that he fancied that, either. In any case, he was far more likely to simply get killed, he thought, as he looked out to the fog and felt the cold presence of the Dead within it.

Sam touched the gold thread on his chest again and took comfort from it, his fear of the Dead receding. He had never wanted to be an Abhorsen. A Wallmaker was much more interesting, even if he didn't know what it meant to be one. It would have the added benefit of driving his sister, Ellimere, crazy, since she would never believe he didn't know and couldn't, rather than wouldn't, explain what it was to be a Wallmaker.

Presuming he ever saw Ellimere again . . .

"We'd best be moving," said the Dog, startling both Lirael and Sam. Lirael had been staring out into the fog again, too, lost in her own thoughts.

"Yes," said Lirael, tearing her gaze away. Not for the first time, she wished she were back in the Great Library of the Clayr. But that, like her lifelong wish to wear the white robes and the silver-and-moonstone crown of a fully fledged Daughter of the Clayr, had to be pushed away and buried deep. She was an Abhorsen now, and there was a great and momentous task ahead of her.

"Yes," she repeated. "We'd best be moving. We will go by way of the well."

CHAPTER TWO

INTO THE DEEP

IT TOOK LITTLE more than an hour to prepare for their departure, once the decision had been made. Lirael found herself wearing armor for the first time since her Fighting Arts lessons many years before—but the coat the sendings brought her was much lighter than the mail hauberks the Clayr kept in their schoolroom armory. It was made of tiny overlapping scales or plates of some material Lirael didn't recognize, and despite its length to her knees and its long, swallow-tailed sleeves, it was quite light and comfortable. It also didn't have the characteristic odor of well-oiled steel, for which Lirael was grateful.

The Disreputable Dog told her the scales were a ceramic called "gethre," made with Charter Magic but not magic in itself, though it was stronger and lighter than any metal. The secret of its making was long lost, and no new coat had been made in a thousand years. Lirael felt one of the scales and was surprised to find herself thinking, "Sam could make this," though she had no real reason to suppose that he could.

Over the armored coat, Lirael wore the surcoat of golden stars and silver keys. The bell-bandolier would lie across that, but Lirael had yet to put it on. Sam had reluctantly taken the panpipes, but Lirael kept the Dark Mirror in her pouch. She knew it was very likely that she would need to look into the past again.

Her sword, Nehima, her bow and quiver from the Clayr, and a light pack cleverly filled by the sendings with all manner of things that she hadn't had a chance to look at completed her equipment.

Before she went to join Sam and Mogget downstairs, Lirael paused for a moment to look at herself in the tall silver mirror that hung on the wall of her room. The image that faced her bore little resemblance to the Second Assistant Librarian of the Clayr. She saw a warlike and grim young woman, dark hair bound back with a silver cord rather than hanging free to disguise her face. She no longer wore her librarian's waistcoat, and instead of a library-issue dagger, she had long Nehima at her side. But she couldn't completely let go her former identity. Taking the end of a loose thread from her waistcoat, she drew out a single strand of red silk, wound it around her little finger several times to make a ring, tied it off, and tucked it into the small pouch at her belt with the Dark Mirror. She might not wear the waistcoat any longer, but part of it would always travel with her.

She had become an Abhorsen, Lirael thought. At least on the outside.

The most visible sign of both her new identity and her power as the Abhorsen-in-Waiting was the bell-bandolier. The one Sabriel had given to Sam after it had mysteriously appeared in the House the previous winter. Lirael loosened the leather pouches one by one, slipping her fingers in to feel the cool silver and the mahogany, and the delicate balance between Free Magic and Charter marks in both metal and wood. Lirael was careful not to let the bells sound, but even the touch of her finger on a bell rim was enough to summon something of the voice and nature of each bell.

The smallest bell was Ranna. Sleeper, some called it, its voice a sweet lullaby calling those who heard it into slumber.

The second bell was Mosrael, the Waker. Lirael

38

touched it ever so lightly, for Mosrael balanced Life with Death. Wielded properly, it would bring the Dead back into Life and send the wielder from Life into Death.

Kibeth was the third bell, the Walker. It granted freedom of movement to the Dead, or it could be used to make them walk where the wielder chose. Yet it could also turn on a bell-ringer and make her march, usually somewhere she would not wish to go.

The fourth bell was called Dyrim, the Speaker. This was the most musical bell, according to *The Book of the Dead*, and one of the most difficult to use as well. Dyrim could return the power of speech to long-silent Dead. It could also reveal secrets, or even allow the reading of minds. It had darker powers, too, favored by necromancers, for Dyrim could still a speaking tongue forever.

Belgaer was the name of the fifth bell. The Thinker. Belgaer could mend the erosion of mind that often occurred in Death, restoring the thoughts and memory of the Dead. It could also erase those thoughts, in Life as well as in Death, and in necromancers' hands had been used to splinter the minds of enemies. Sometimes it splintered the mind of the necromancer, for Belgaer liked the sound of its own voice and would try to steal the chance to sing of its own accord.

The sixth bell was Saraneth, also known as Binder. Saraneth was the favorite bell of all Abhorsens. Large and trustworthy, it was powerful and true. Saraneth was used to dominate and bind the Dead, to make them obey the wishes and directions of the wielder.

Lirael was reluctant to touch the seventh bell, but she felt it would not be diplomatic to ignore the most powerful of all the bells, though it was cold and frightening to her touch.

Astarael, the Sorrowful. The bell that sent all who heard it into Death.

Lirael withdrew her finger and methodically checked every pouch, making sure the leather tongues were in place and the straps tight but also able to be undone with one hand. Then she put the bandolier on. The bells were hers, and she had accepted the armament of the Abhorsens.

Sam was waiting for her outside the front door, sitting on the steps. He was similarly armored and equipped, though he did not have a bow or a bell-bandolier.

"I found this in the armory," he said, holding up a sword and tilting the blade so that Lirael could see the Charter marks etched into the steel. "It isn't one of the named swords, but it is spelled for the destruction of the Dead."

"Better late than never," remarked Mogget, who was sitting on the front step looking sour.

Sam ignored the cat, pulled out a sheet of paper from inside his sleeve, and handed it to Lirael.

"This is the message I've sent by message-hawk to Barhedrin. The Guard post there will send it on to the Wall, and it will be passed through to the Ancelstierrans, who will . . . um . . . send it by a device called a telegraph to my parents in Corvere. That's why it's written in telegraphese, which is pretty strange if you're not used to it. There were four hawks in the mews—not counting the one from Ellimere, which won't fly again for a week or two—so I've sent two to Belisaere for Ellimere and two to Barhedrin."

Lirael looked down at the paper and the words printed in Sam's neat hand.

TO   KING TOUCHSTONE AND
        ABHORSEN SABRIEL
        OLD KINGDOM EMBASSY
        CORVERE   ANCELSTIERRE
COPY   ELLIMERE VIA MESSAGEHAWK

HOUSE SURROUNDED DEAD PLUS CHLORR
NOW GREATER DEAD STOP HEDGE IS NECRO-
MANCER STOP NICK WITH HEDGE STOP THEY
EVIL UPDUG NEAR EDGE STOP GOING EDGE
SELF PLUS AUNT LIRAEL FORMER CLAYR NOW
ABHORSENINWAITING STOP PLUS MOGGET
PLUS LIRAEL APOSTROPHE ESS CHARTER DOG
STOP WILL DO WHAT CAN STOP SEND HELP
COME SELVES EXPRESS URGENT STOP SENT
TWO WEEKS PRIOR MIDSUMMER DAY
SAMETH END

The message was indeed written strangely, but
it made sense, thought Lirael. Given the limitations
of the message-hawks' small minds, "telegraphese" was probably a good form of communication
even when a telegraph was not involved.

"I hope the hawks make it," she said as Sam
took the paper back. Somewhere out in the fog
lurked Gore Crows, a swarm of corpse birds ani-
mated by a single Dead spirit. The message-hawks
would have to get past them, and perhaps other dangers as well, before they could speed on to Barhedrin
and Belisaere.

"We cannot count on it," said the Dog. "Are

you ready to go down the well?"

Lirael walked down the steps and took a few paces along the redbrick path. She shrugged her pack higher up her back and tightened the straps. Then she looked up at the sunny sky, now only a very small patch of blue, the walls of fog hemming it in on three sides and the mist from the waterfall on the fourth.

"I guess I'm ready," she said.

Sam picked up his pack, but before he could put it on, Mogget leaped onto it and slid under the top flap. All that could be seen of him were his green eyes and one white-furred ear.

"Remember I advised against this way," he instructed. "Wake me when whatever terrible thing is about to happen happens, or if it appears I might get wet."

Before anyone could answer, Mogget wriggled deeper into the pack, and even his eyes and that one ear disappeared.

"How come I get to carry him?" asked Sam aggrievedly. "He's supposed to be the Abhorsen's servant."

A paw came back out of the pack, and a claw pricked into the back of Sam's neck, though it didn't break the skin. Sam flinched and swore.

The Dog jumped up at the pack and braced her forepaws on it. Sam staggered forward and swore again as the Dog said, "No one will carry you if you don't behave, Mogget."

"And you won't get any fish, either," muttered Sam as he rubbed his neck.

Either one or both of these threats worked, or else Mogget had subsided into sleep. In any case, there was no reappearance of the claw or the cat's sarcastic voice. The Dog dropped down, Sam finished adjusting the straps on his pack, and they set off along the brick path.

As the front door shut behind them, Lirael turned back and saw that every window was crowded with sendings. Hundreds of them, pressed close together against the glass, so their hooded robes looked like the skin of some giant creature, their faintly glowing hands like many eyes. They did not wave or move at all, but Lirael had the uncomfortable feeling that they were saying goodbye. As if they did not expect to see this particular Abhorsen-in-Waiting return.

The well was only thirty yards from the front door, hidden beneath a tangled network of wild roses that Lirael and Sam had to tear away, pausing every few minutes to suck their thorn-pierced fingers. The thorns were unusually long and sharp, Lirael thought, but she had limited experience with flowers. The Clayr had underground gardens and vast greenhouses lit by Charter marks, but most were dedicated to vegetables and fruit, and there was only one rose garden.

Once the rose vines were cleared away, Lirael saw a circular wooden cover of thick oak planks, about eight feet in diameter, set securely inside a low ring of pale white stones. The cover was chained in four places with bronze chains, the links set directly into the stones and bolted to the wood, so there was no need for padlocks.

Charter marks of locking and closing drifted across both wood and bronze, gleaming marks only just visible in the sunlight, till Sam touched the cover and they flared into sudden brightness.

Sam laid his hand on one of the bronze chains, feeling the marks within it and studying the spell. Lirael looked over his shoulder. She didn't know even half of the marks, but she could hear Sam muttering names to himself as if they were familiar to him.

"Can you open it?" asked Lirael. She knew scores of spells for opening doors and gates, and had practical experience of opening ways into many places she wasn't supposed to have entered in the Great Library of the Clayr. But she instinctively knew none of them would work here.

"I think so," Sam replied hesitantly. "It's an unusual spell, and there are a lot of marks I don't know. As far as I can work out, there are two ways it can be opened. One I don't understand at all. But the other . . ."

His voice trailed off as he touched the chain again and Charter Marks left the bronze to drift across his skin and then flow into the wood.

"I think we're supposed to breathe on the chains . . . or kiss them . . . only it has to be the right person. The spell says 'my children's breath.' But I can't work out whose children or what that means. Any Abhorsen's children, I guess."

"Try it," suggested Lirael. "A breath first, just in case."

Sam looked doubtful but bent his head, took a deep breath, and blew on the chain.

The bronze fogged from the breath and lost its shine. Charter marks glittered and moved. Lirael held her breath. Sam stood up and edged away, while the Disreputable Dog came closer and sniffed.

Suddenly the chain groaned aloud, and everyone jumped back. Then a new link came out of the seemingly solid stone, followed by another and another, the chain rattling as it coiled to the ground. In a few seconds there was an extra six or seven feet of chain piled up, enough to allow that corner of the well cover to be lifted free.

"Good," said the Disreputable Dog. "You do the next one, Mistress."

Lirael bent over the next chain and breathed lightly upon it. Nothing happened for a moment, and she felt a stab of uncertainty. Her identity as an Abhorsen was so new, and so precarious, that it could be easily doubted.

Then the chain frosted, the marks shone, and the links came pouring out of the stone with the sharp rattle of metal. The sound was echoed almost immediately from the other side, as Sam breathed on the third chain.

Lirael breathed on the last chain, touching it for a moment as she took in a breath. She felt the marks shiver under her fingers, the lively reaction of a Charter-spell that knew its time had come. Like a person tensing muscles in that frozen instant before the beginning of a race.

With the loosening of the chains, Lirael and Sam were able to lift one end of the cover and slide it away. It was very heavy, so they didn't drag it completely off, just making an opening large enough for them to climb down with their packs on.

Lirael had expected a wet, dank smell to come up from the open well, even though the Dog had said it wasn't full of water. There was a smell, strong enough to overcome the scent of the roses, but it wasn't of old standing water. It was a pleasant herbal odor that Lirael couldn't identify.

"What can I smell?" she asked the Dog, whose nose had often picked up scents and odors that Lirael could neither smell, spell, or imagine.

"Very little," replied the Dog. "Unless you've improved recently."

"No," said Lirael patiently. "There's a particular smell coming out of the well. A plant, or an herb. But I can't place it."

Sam sniffed the air and his forehead furrowed in thought.

"It's something used in cooking," he said. "Not that I'm much of a cook. But I've smelled this in the Palace kitchens, when they were roasting lamb, I think."

"It's rosemary," said the Dog shortly. "And there is amaranth, too, though you probably cannot smell it."

"Fidelity in love," said a small voice from Sam's backpack. "With the flower that never fades. And you still say she is not there?"

The Dog didn't answer Mogget but stuck her snout down the well. She sniffed around for at least a minute, pushing her snout farther and farther down the well. When she pulled back, she sneezed twice and shook her head.

"Old smells, old spells," she said. "The scent is already fading."

Lirael sniffed experimentally, but the Dog was right. She could smell only the roses now.

"There is a ladder," said Sam, who was also looking into the well, a Charter-conjured light bobbing above his head. "Bronze, like the chains. I wonder why. I can't see the bottom, though—or any water."

"I'll go first," said Lirael. Sam seemed about to protest but stepped away. Lirael didn't know whether this was because he was afraid or because he was acquiescing—to the familial authority of Lirael as his newfound aunt or because she was now the Abhorsen-in-Waiting.

She looked into the well. The bronze ladder gleamed near the top, disappearing down into darkness. Lirael had climbed up, down, and through many dark and dangerous tunnels and passages in the Great Library of the Clayr. But that had been in more innocent times, even though she had experienced her share of danger. Now she felt a sense of great and evil powers at work in the world, of a terrible fate already in motion. The Dead surrounding the House were only a small and visible part of that. She remembered the vision the Clayr had shown her, of the pit near the Red Lake, and the terrible stench of Free Magic from whatever was being unearthed there.

Climbing down this dark hole was only the beginning, Lirael thought. Her first step onto the bronze ladder would be the first real step of her new identity, the first step of an Abhorsen.

She took one last look at the sun, ignoring the climbing walls of fog to either side. Then she knelt down and gingerly lowered herself into the well, her feet finding secure footholds on the ladder.

After her came the Disreputable Dog, her paws elongating to form stubby fingers that gripped the ladder better than any human fingers could. Her tail brushed in Lirael's face every few rungs, sweeping across with greater enthusiasm than Lirael could have mustered if she'd had a tail of her own.

Sam came last, his Charter light still hovering above his head, Mogget securely fastened in his backpack.

As Sam's hobnailed boots clanged on the rungs, there was an answering clatter above as the chains suddenly contracted. He barely had time to bring in his hands before the cover was dragged across and slammed into place with a rattle and a deafening crash.

"Well, we won't be going back that way," said Sam, with forced cheerfulness.

"If at all," whispered Mogget, his voice so low that it was possible no one heard him. But Sam hesitated for a moment, and the Dog let out a low growl, while Lirael continued to climb down, cherishing that last memory of the sun as they descended farther into the dark recesses of the earth.

CHAPTER THREE

AMARANTH, ROSEMARY, AND TEARS

THE LADDER WENT down and down and down. At first Lirael counted the rungs, but when she got to 996, she gave up. Still they climbed down. Lirael had conjured a Charter light herself. It hovered about her feet, to complement the one Sam had dancing above his head. In the light of these two glowing balls, with the shadows of the rungs flickering on the wall of the well, Lirael found it easy to imagine that they were somehow stuck on the ladder, repeating the same section time after time.

A treadmill that they could never leave. This fancy grew on her, and she started to think it real, when suddenly her foot met stone instead of bronze, and her Charter light rebounded as high as her knee.

They had reached the bottom of the well. Lirael

pronounced a Charter mark, and her light flew up to join the spoken word, circling her head. In its light she saw that they had come to a rectangular chamber, roughly hewn from the rich red rock. A passage led off from the chamber into darkness. There was an iron bucket next to the passage, filled with what looked like torches, simple lengths of wood topped with oil-soaked rags.

Lirael walked forward as the Disreputable Dog jumped down behind her, closely followed by Sam.

"I suppose this is the way," Lirael whispered, indicating the passage. Somehow she felt that it was safer not to raise her voice.

The Dog sniffed at the air and nodded.

"I wonder if I should take—" Lirael said, reaching out for one of the torches. But even before her hand could close on it, the torch puffed into dust. Lirael flinched, almost falling over the Dog, who stepped back into Sam.

"Watch it!" Sam called out. His voice echoed in the well shaft and reverberated past Lirael down the corridor.

Lirael reached out again, more gingerly, but the other torches also simply fell into dust. When she touched the bucket, it collapsed in on itself, becoming a pile of rusted shards.

"Time never truly falters," said the Dog enigmatically.

"I guess we have to go on," said Lirael, but she was really only speaking to herself. They didn't need the torches, but she would have felt better with one.

"The faster the better," said the Dog. She was sniffing the air again. "We do not want to tarry anywhere under here."

Lirael nodded. She took one step forward, then hesitated and drew her sword. Charter marks burned brightly on the blade as it came free of the scabbard, and the name of the sword rippled down the steel, briefly changing into the inscription Lirael had seen before. Or was it different? She couldn't remember, and the words rippled away too quickly for her to be sure.

"The Clayr Saw a sword and so I was. Remember the Wallmakers. Remember Me."

Whatever it said, the extra light reassured Lirael, or perhaps it was just the feel of Nehima in her hand.

She heard Sam draw his sword behind her. He waited for a few seconds as she started on again. Obviously he did not want to trip and impale the Dog or Lirael from behind, a precaution Lirael thoroughly approved.

For the first hundred paces or so, the passageway was of worked stone. Then that suddenly ended and they came to a tunnel that was not the work of any tool. The red rock gave way to a pallid greenish-white stone that reflected the Charter lights, making Lirael hood her eyes. The tunnel seemed to have been eroded rather than worked, and there were the patterns of many swirls and eddies upon the ceiling, floor, and walls. Yet even these seemed strange, contrary to what they ought to be, though Lirael didn't know why. She just felt their strangeness.

"No water ever cut this way," said Sam. He was whispering, too, now. "Unless it flowed back and forth at the same time on different levels. And I have never seen this kind of stone."

"We must hurry," said the Dog. There was something in her voice that made Lirael move more quickly. An anxiety she had not heard before. Perhaps it was even fear.

They began to walk more swiftly, as fast as they could without risk of tripping over or falling into some unsuspected hole. The strange, glowing tunnel continued on for what felt like several miles, then opened into a cavern, again carved by unknown means out of the same reflective stone. There were three tunnels off this, and Lirael and Sam stopped while the Dog sniffed carefully at each entrance.

There was a pile of what Lirael thought was stone in one corner of the cavern, but when she looked at it more closely, she realized it was actually a mound of old, powdery bones mixed with pieces of metal. Touching the mound with the corner of her boot, she separated out several shards of tarnished silver and the fragment of a human jaw, still showing one unbroken tooth.

"Don't touch it," Sam warned in a hasty whisper, as Lirael bent to inspect the metal fragments.

Lirael stopped, her hand still outstretched.

"Why not?"

"I don't know," replied Sam, an unconscious shiver rippling across his neck. "But that's bell metal, I think. Best to leave it alone."

"Yes," agreed Lirael. She stood up and couldn't help shivering herself. Human bones and bell metal. They had found Kalliel. What was this place? And why was the Dog taking so long to decide which way to go?

When she voiced the question, the Disreputable Dog stopped her sniffing and pointed her right paw to the center tunnel.

"This one," she said, but Lirael noted a certain

lack of enthusiasm in the Dog. The hound had not spoken with total confidence, and even her pointing had wavered. If she had been in a pointing competition, she would have lost points.

The tunnel was significantly wider than the previous one, and the ceiling higher. It also felt different to Lirael, and not because there was more room to move. At first she couldn't place what it was; then she realized the air around her was growing colder. And she had a strange sensation around her feet and ankles, almost as if there were something rushing around her heels. A current that swished one way and then the other, but there was no water there.

Or was there? When she looked directly in front or down, Lirael saw stone. But when she looked out of the corners of her eyes, she could see dark water flowing. Coming from behind them, pushing past, and then curling back, like a wave falling upon the shore. A wave that was trying to knock them down and sweep them back the way they'd come.

In a very unsettling way, it reminded her of the river of Death. But she did not feel they were in Death, and apart from the growing cold and the peripheral view of the river, all her senses told her that she was firmly in Life, though in a very strange tunnel, far underground.

Then she smelled rosemary again, with something sweeter, and at that moment the bells in the bandolier across her chest began to vibrate in their pouches. Their clappers stilled by leather tongues, they could not sound, but she could feel them moving and shaking, as if they were trying to break free.

"The bells!" she gasped. "They're shaking. . . . I don't know what . . ."

"The pipes!" cried Sam, and Lirael heard a brief cacophany as the panpipes sounded with the voices of all seven bells, before they were suddenly cut off.

"No!" shouted a voice that was not instantly recognizable as Mogget's. "No!"

"Run!" roared the Dog.

Amidst the shouts and yells and roaring, the Charter light above Lirael's head suddenly dimmed to little more than a faint glow.

Then it went out.

Lirael stopped. There was some light from the marks on Nehima's blade, but these were fading too, and the sword was twisting strangely in her hand. Undulating in a way that no thing of steel could ever move, it had become alive, not so much a sword anymore as an eel-like creature, writhing and growing in her grasp. The green stone on the pommel had become a bright, lidless eye, and the silver wire on the hilt had become a row of shining teeth.

Lirael shut her eyes and sheathed the sword, ramming it hard into the scabbard before she let go with relief. Then she opened her eyes and looked around. Or tried to. All the golden Charter light was gone, and it was dark. The total darkness of the deep earth.

In the black void Lirael heard cloth tear and rip, and Sam cried out.

"Sam!" she cried. "Over here! Dog!"

There was no answer, but she heard the Dog growl, and then there was a soft, low laugh. A horrible, gloating chuckle that set the hair on the back of her neck on edge. It was made worse because there was something familiar in it. Mogget's laugh, twisted and made more sinister.

Desperately Lirael tried to reach for the Charter, to summon a new light spell. But there was nothing there. Instead of the Charter she felt a terrible, cold presence that she knew at once. Death. That was all she could feel.

The Charter was gone, or she could not reach it.

Panic began to flower in her as the gloating chuckle deepened and the darkness pressed upon her. Then Lirael's eyes registered a faint change. She became aware of subtle greys in the darkness, and she felt a momentary hope that there would be light. Then she saw the barest fingernail scraping of illumination spark and fizz and steadily grow till it became a pool of fierce, bright, white light. With the light came the hot metal stench of Free Magic, a smell that rolled across in waves, each one causing a reflex gag as the bile rose in Lirael's throat.

Sam moved with the light, appearing at Lirael's side as if he'd flown there. His backpack was open at the top, ragged edges showing where something had cut free. His sword was sheathed, and he was holding the panpipes with both hands, fingers jammed on the holes. The pipes were vibrating, sending out a low hum that Sam was desperately trying to stifle. Lirael had her own arm pressed along the bell-bandolier, to try to still the bells.

The Dog stood between the pool of white fire and Lirael, but it was not the Dog as Lirael knew her. She still had a dog shape, but the collar of Charter marks was gone, and she was once more a creature of intense darkness outlined with silver fire. The Dog looked back and opened her mouth.

"She is here!" boomed a voice that was the Dog's and yet not the Dog's, for it penetrated Lirael's ears and sent sharp pains coursing through her jaw. "The Mogget is free! Run!"

Lirael and Sam stood frozen as the echoes of the Dog's voice rolled past them. The pool of white fire was sparking and crackling, spinning counterclockwise as it rose up to form the shape of a spindly, too-thin humanoid.

But beyond the thing that was Mogget unbound, an even brighter light shone. Something so bright that Lirael realized she had shut her eyes and was seeing it through her eyelids, eyelids seared through with the image of a woman. An impossibly tall woman, her head bowed even in this high tunnel, reaching out her arms to sweep up the Mogget creature, the Dog, Lirael, and Sam.

A river flowed around and in front of the shining woman. A cold river that Lirael knew at once. This was the river of Death, and this creature was bringing it to them. They would not cross into it but be swamped and taken away. Thrown down and taken up, carried in a rush to the First Gate and beyond. They would never be able to make their way back.

Lirael had time to think only a few final, awful thoughts.

They had failed so soon.

So many depended on them.

All was lost.

Then the Disreputable Dog shouted, "Flee!" and barked.

The bark was infused with Free Magic. Without opening her eyes, without conscious thought, Lirael swung around and suddenly found herself running, running headlong, running as she had never run before. She ran without care, into the unknown, away from the well and the House, her feet finding the twists and turns of the tunnel even though they left the white light behind and in the darkness Lirael couldn't tell whether her eyes were open or not.

Through caverns and chambers and narrow ways she ran, not knowing whether Sam ran with her or whether she was pursued. It was not fear that drove her, for she didn't feel afraid. She was somewhere else, locked away inside her own body, a machine that drove on and on without feeling, acting on directions that had not come from her.

Then, as suddenly as it began, the compulsion to run stopped. Lirael fell to the floor, shuddering, trying to draw breath into her starved lungs. Pain shot through every muscle, and she curled into a ball of cramps, frantically massaging her calf muscles as she bit back cries of pain.

Someone was near her doing the same thing, and as reason returned, Lirael saw that it was Sam. There was a dim light falling from somewhere ahead, enough to make him out. A natural light, though much diffused.

Hesitantly Lirael touched the bell-bandolier. It was still, the bells quiescent. Her hand fell to Nehima's hilt, and she was relieved to feel the solidity of the green stone in the pommel, and the silver wire no more than silver wire.

Sam groaned and stood up. He leaned against the wall with his left hand and stowed the pan-pipes away with his right. Lirael watched that hand flicker in a careful movement, and a Charter light blossomed in his palm.

"It was gone, you know," he said, sliding back down the wall to sit facing Lirael. He seemed calm but was obviously in shock. Lirael realized she was, too, when she tried to stand up and simply couldn't.

"Yes," she replied. "The Charter."

"Wherever that was," continued Sam, "the Charter wasn't. And who was *she*?"

Lirael shook her head, as much to clear it as to indicate her inability to answer. She shook it again immediately, trying to force her thoughts back into action.

"We'd better . . . better go back," she said, thinking of the Dog facing both Mogget and that shining woman alone in the darkness. "I can't leave the Dog."

"What about *her*?" asked Sam, and Lirael knew who he meant. "And Mogget?"

"You need not go back," said a voice from the dark reaches of the passage. Lirael and Sam instantly leapt up, finding new strength and purpose. Their swords were out and Lirael found she had one hand on Saraneth, though she had no idea what she was going to do with the bell. No wisdom from *The Book of the Dead* or *The Book of Remembrance and Forgetting* came unbidden into her head.

"It's me," said the voice in an aggrieved tone, and the Disreputable Dog slowly walked into the light, her tail between her legs and her head bowed. Apart from this uncharacteristic pose, she seemed back to normal—or what was normal for her—with the deep, rich glow of many Charter Marks once more around her neck, and her short hair dusty and golden save for her back, where it was black.

Lirael didn't hesitate. She put Nehima down and flung herself on the Dog, burying her face in her friend's neck. The Dog licked Lirael's ear without her usual enthusiasm, and she didn't try even one affectionate nip.

Sam hung back, his sword still in his hand.

"Where is Mogget?" he asked.

"She wished to speak to him," replied the Dog, throwing herself sorrowfully across Lirael's feet. "I was wrong. I put you in terrible danger, Mistress."

"I don't understand," Lirael replied. She felt incredibly tired all of a sudden. "What happened? The Charter . . . the Charter seemed to suddenly . . . not be."

"It was her coming," said the Dog. "It is her fate, that her knowing self will be forever outside what she chose to make, the Charter that her unknowing self is part of. Yet she stayed her hand when she could so easily have taken you to her embrace. I do not know why, or what it may mean. I believed her to be past any interest in the things of this world, and so I thought to pass here unscathed. Yet when ancient forces stir, many things are woken. I should have guessed it would be so. Forgive me."

Lirael had never seen the Dog so humbled, and it scared her more than anything that had happened. She scratched her around the ears and along the jaw, seeking to give as much comfort as she took. But her hands shook, and she felt that at any moment she would shudder into tears. To try to stop them, she took slow breaths, counting them in, and counting them out.

"But . . . what will happen to Mogget?" asked Sam, his voice unsteady. "He was unbound! He'll try to kill the Abhorsen . . . Mother . . . or Lirael! We haven't got the ring to bind him again!"

"Mogget has long avoided her," mumbled the Dog. She hesitated, then quietly said, "I don't think we need to worry about Mogget anymore."

Lirael let out her breath and didn't take another. How could Mogget not be coming back?

"What?" asked Sam. "But he's . . . well, I don't know, but powerful . . . a Free Magic spirit. . . ."

"Who is she?" asked Lirael. She spoke very sternly as she took the Disreputable Dog by the jaw and stared into her deep, dark eyes. The Dog tried to turn away, but Lirael held her fast. The hound shut her eyes hopefully, only to be foiled as Lirael blew on her nose and they snapped open again.

"It won't help you to know, because you can't understand," said the Dog, her voice filled with great weariness. "She doesn't really exist anymore, except every now and then and here and there, in small ways and small things. If we had not come this way, she would not have been, and now that we have passed, she will not be."

"Tell me!"

"You know who she is, at least in some degree," said the Dog. She tapped her nose against Lirael's bell-bandolier, leaving a wet mark on the leather of the seventh bell, and a single slow tear rolled down her snout to dampen Lirael's hand.

"Astarael?" whispered Sam in disbelief. The most frightening bell of them all, the one he had never even touched in his brief time as custodian of that set of bells. "The Weeper?"

Lirael let the Dog go, and the hound promptly pushed her head farther into Lirael's lap and let out a long sigh.

Lirael scratched the Dog's ears again, but even with the feel of warm dog skin under her hand, she could not help asking a question she had asked before.

"What are you, then? Why did Astarael let you go?"

The Dog looked up at her and said simply, "I am the Disreputable Dog. A true servant of the Charter, and your friend. Always your friend."

Lirael did weep then, but she wiped the tears

away as she lifted the Dog by her collar and moved her away so she could stand up. Sam picked up Nehima and silently handed the sword to her. The Charter marks on the blade rippled as Lirael touched the hilt, but no inscription became visible.

"If you are sure Mogget will not be coming, bound or unbound, then we must go on," said Lirael.

"I suppose so," said Sam doubtfully. "Though I feel . . . feel sort of strange. I got kind of used to Mogget, and now he's just . . . just gone? I mean, has she . . . has she killed him?"

"No!" answered the Dog. She seemed surprised at the suggestion. "No."

"What then?" asked Sam.

"It is not for us to know," said the Disreputable Dog. "Our task lies ahead, and Mogget lies behind us now."

"You're absolutely sure he won't come after Mother or Lirael?" asked Sam. He knew Mogget's recent history well and had been warned since he was a toddler of the danger of removing Mogget's collar.

"I am sure that your mother is safe from Mogget across the Wall," replied the Dog, only half-answering Sam's question.

Sam did not look entirely convinced, but he slowly nodded in reluctant acceptance of the Dog's assurance.

"We haven't got off to a good start," muttered Sam. "I hope it gets better."

"There is sunlight ahead, and a way out," said the Dog. "You will be happier under the sun."

"It should be dark by now," said Sam. "How long have we been underground?"

"Four or five hours, at least," replied Lirael with a frown. "Maybe more, so that can't be sunshine."

She led the way across the cavern, but as they drew closer to the entrance, it was clear that it *was* sunshine. Soon they could see a narrow cleft ahead, and through it a clear blue sky, misted with spray from the great waterfall.

Once through the cleft, they found themselves several hundred yards to the west of the waterfall, at the base of the Long Cliffs. The sun was halfway up the sky to the west, the sunshine making rainbows in the huge cloud of spray that hung above the falls.

"It's afternoon," said Sam, shielding his eyes to look near the sun. He looked along the line of the cliffs, then held up his hand to gauge how many fingers the sun was above the horizon. "Not past four o'clock."

"We've lost practically a whole day!" exclaimed Lirael. Every delay meant a greater chance of failure, and her heart sank at this further setback. How could they have spent almost twenty-four hours underground?

"No," said the Disreputable Dog, who was watching the sun and sniffing the air. "We have not lost a day."

"Not more?" whispered Lirael. Surely not. If they had somehow spent weeks or more underground, it would be too late to do anything. . . .

"No," continued the Dog. "It is the same day we left the House. Perhaps an hour since we climbed down the well. Maybe less."

"But—" Sam started to say something, then stopped. He shook his head and looked back at the cleft in the cliff.

"Time and Death sleep side by side," said the Dog. "Both are in Astarael's domain. She has helped us, in her own way."

Lirael nodded, though she didn't feel as if she'd been helped. She felt shocked and tired, and her legs hurt. She wanted to curl up in the sun and wake up

70

in the Great Library of the Clayr with a sore neck from sleeping at her desk and a vague memory of disturbing nightmares.

"I can't sense any Dead down here," she said, after dismissing her daydream. "Since we've been given the gift of an afternoon, I guess we'd better use it. How do we get back up the cliffs?"

"There is a path about a league and a half to the west," said Sam. "It's narrow and mostly steps, so it's not often used. The top of that should be well clear of the fog and Chlorr's minions. Beyond that, the Western Cut is at least twelve or so leagues farther on. That's where the road goes through."

"What is the stepped path called?" asked the Dog.

"I don't know. Mother just called it the Steps, I think. It's quite strange really. The path is only wide enough for one, and the steps are low and deep."

"I know it," said the Dog. "Three thousand steps, and all for the sweet water at the foot."

Sam nodded. "There is a spring there, and the water is good. You mean someone built the whole path just to get a drink of good water?"

"Water, yes, but not to drink," said the Dog. "I am glad the path is still there. Let us go to it."

With that, the hound sprang forward, jumping

over the sprawl of boulders that helped conceal the cleft and the caves beyond.

Lirael and Sam followed more sedately, clambering between the stones. Both were still sore, and they had many things to think about. Lirael in particular was thinking of the Dog's words: "When ancient forces stir, many things are woken." She knew that whatever Nicholas was digging up was both powerful and evil, and it was clear that its emergence had set many things in motion, including a rising of the Dead across the whole Kingdom. But she had not considered that other powers might also be woken, and how that might affect their plans.

Not that they really had a plan, Lirael thought. They were simply rushing headlong to try to stop Hedge and save Nicholas and keep whatever it was safely buried in the ground.

"We should have a proper plan," she whispered to herself. But no brilliant thoughts or strategies came to mind, and she had to concentrate on climbing between and over stones as she followed the Disreputable Dog along the base of the Long Cliffs, with Sam close behind.

CHAPTER FOUR

BREAKFAST OF RAVENS

THE SUN HAD almost set by the time Lirael, Sam, and the Dog arrived at the foot of the Steps, and the shadow of the Long Cliffs stretched far across the Ratterlin plain. Lirael easily found the spring—a clear, bubbling pool ten yards wide—but it took longer to find the beginning of the steps, as the path was narrow, cut deeply into the face of the cliff, and disguised by many overhangs and jutting buttresses of jagged stone.

"Can we climb it by night?" asked Lirael uncertainly, looking up at the shadowed cliff above them and the last faint touch of sun a thousand feet above. The cliff stretched up even farther than that, and she couldn't see the top. Lirael had climbed many stairs and narrow ways in the Clayr's Glacier, but she had little experience of traveling in the open under sun and moon.

"We shouldn't risk a light," replied the Dog, who had been uncharacteristically silent. Her tail still hung limply, without its usual wag or spring. "I could lead you, though it will be dangerous in the dark if any steps have fallen away."

"The moon will be bright," said Sam. "It was in its third quarter last night, and the sky is reasonably clear. But it will not rise till the early morning. An hour after midnight at least. We should wait till then, if not overnight."

"I don't want to wait," Lirael muttered. "I have this feeling . . . an anxiety I can't describe. The vision the Clayr told me about, me with Nicholas, on the Red Lake . . . I feel it slipping away, as if I'll somehow miss the moment. That it will become the past rather than a possible future."

"Falling off the Long Cliffs in the dark won't get us there any faster," said Sam. "And I could do with a bite to eat and a few hours' rest before we get climbing."

Lirael nodded. She was tired, too. Her calves ached, and her shoulders were sore from the weight of the pack. But there was another weariness, too, one that she was sure Sam shared. It was a weariness of the spirit. It came from the shock of losing Mogget, and she really just wanted to lie down by the cool spring and go to sleep in the vain hope that the new day would be brighter. It was a feeling she recognized from her younger days. Then it had been the vain hope that she would sleep and in the morning awake with the Sight. Now she knew that the new day could bring nothing good. They needed to rest, but not for too long. Hedge and Nicholas would not rest, nor would Chlorr and her Dead Hands.

"We'll wait for the moon to rise," she said, slipping the pack off her shoulders and sitting down next to it on a convenient boulder.

The next instant she was back on her feet, sword in hand even before she realized she'd drawn it, as the Dog catapulted past her with a sudden bark. It took Lirael a moment to hear that the bark had no magical resonance, then another to spot the target of the Dog's attack.

A rabbit zigzagged between the fallen stones, desperately trying to evade the pursuing Dog. The chase ended some distance away, but it was not clear with what result. Then a great plume of dirt, dust, and stones flew up, and Lirael knew the rabbit had gone to ground and the Dog had begun to dig.

Sam was still sitting next to his pack. He had half-risen several seconds after Lirael, had caught on what was happening, and had sat back down. Now he was looking at the torn hole in the top flap of his pack.

"At least we're alive," said Lirael, mistaking his silent scrutiny of the tear for remorse at the loss of Mogget.

Sam looked up, surprised. He had a sewing kit in his hand and was about to open it.

"Oh, I wasn't thinking about Mogget. At least not right then. I was wondering how best to sew up this hole. I'll have to patch it, I think."

Lirael laughed, a peculiar half-hearted sort of laugh that just escaped her.

"I'm glad you can think of patches," she said. "I . . . I can't help thinking of what happened. The bells trying to sound, the white lady . . . Astarael . . . the presence of Death."

Sam selected a large needle and bit off a length of black thread from a bobbin. He frowned as he threaded the needle, then spoke off to the setting sun, not directly to Lirael.

"It's strange, you know. Since I learned that you were the Abhorsen-in-Waiting, not me, I haven't felt afraid. I mean I've been scared, but it wasn't the same. I'm not responsible now. I mean, I am responsible because I'm a Prince of the Kingdom, but it's normal things I'm responsible for now. Not necromancers and Death and Free Magic creatures."

He paused to knot the end of the thread, and this time he did look at Lirael.

"And the sendings gave me this surcoat. With the trowel. The Wallmakers' trowel. They gave it to me, and I've been thinking that it's as if my ancestors are saying it's all right to make things. That's what I'm meant to do. Make things, and help the Abhorsen and the King. So I'll do that, and I'll do my best, and if my best isn't good enough, at least I will have done everything I could, everything that is in me. I don't have to try to be someone else, someone I could never be."

Lirael didn't answer. Instead, she looked away, back to where the Dog was returning, a limp rabbit in her jaws.

"Dimsher," pronounced the Dog, repeating herself more clearly after she dropped the rabbit at Lirael's feet. Her tail had started to wag again, just at the tip. "Dinner. I'll get another one."

Lirael picked up the rabbit. The Dog had broken its neck, killing it instantly. Lirael could feel its spirit close by in Death, but she walled it out. It hung heavy in her hand, and she wished that they could simply have eaten the bread and cheese the sendings had packed for them. But dogs will be dogs, she thought, and if rabbits beckon . . .

"I'll skin it," offered Sam.

"How will we cook it?" asked Lirael, gladly handing over the rabbit. She had eaten rabbits before, but only either raw, in her Charter-skin of a barking owl, or cooked and served in the refectories of the Clayr.

"A small fire under one of these boulders should be all right," replied Sam. "In a little while, anyway. The smoke won't be visible, and we can shield the flame well."

"I'll leave it to you," said Lirael. "The Dog will eat hers raw, I'm sure."

"You should sleep," said Sam as he tested the blade of a short knife with his thumb. "You can get an hour while I prepare the rabbit."

"Looking after your old aunt," said Lirael with a smile. She was only two years older than Sameth, but she had once told him she was much older, and he had believed her.

"Helping the Abhorsen-in-Waiting," said Sameth, and he bowed, not entirely in jest. Then he bent down and, with a practiced move, made a cut and pulled the skin off the rabbit in one piece, like taking the cover off a pillow.

Lirael watched him for a moment, then turned away and lay down on the stony ground with her head on her pack. It wasn't at all comfortable, particularly since she was still in armor and kept her boots on. But it didn't matter. She lay on her back and looked up at the sky, watching the last blue fade away, the black creep in, and the stars begin to twinkle. She could not feel any Dead creatures close, or sense any hint of Free Magic, and the weariness that had been in her came back a hundredfold. She blinked twice, three times; then her eyes would stay open no more, and she sank into a deep and instant sleep.

When she awoke, it was dark, save for the starlight and the dim red glow of a well-hidden fire. She saw the silhouette of the Dog sitting nearby, but there was no sign of Sam at first, till she saw a man-sized lump of darkness stretched along the ground.

"What time is it?" she whispered, and the Dog stirred and padded over to her.

"Close to midnight," replied the Dog quietly. "We thought it best to let you sleep, and then I convinced Sam it would be safe for him to sleep, too, leaving me on guard."

"I bet that wasn't easy," said Lirael, levering herself up and groaning at her stiffened muscles.

"Has anything happened?"

"No. It is quiet, save for the usual things of the night. I expect Chlorr and the Dead still watch the House, and will do so for many days yet."

Lirael nodded as she groped between the boulders and trod gingerly over to the spring. It was the only patch of brightness in the calm, dark night, its silver surface picking up the starlight. Lirael washed her face and hands, the cold shock of the water bringing her fully awake.

"Did you eat my share of the rabbit?" Lirael whispered as she made her way back to her pack.

"No, I did not!" exclaimed the Dog. "As if I would! Besides, Sameth kept it in the pot. With the lid on."

Not that this would have stopped the Dog, thought Lirael as she found the small cast-iron traveling pot by the side of the dying fire. The pieces of rabbit inside had been simmered overlong, but the stew was still warm and tasted very good. Either Sam had found herbs or the sendings had packed them, though Lirael was glad that there was no hint of rosemary. She did not want to smell that herb.

By the time she'd finished the rabbit and washed her hands and scrubbed the pot clean with a handful of grit at the spring, the moon had begun to rise. As Sam had said, it was somewhat past three quarters, well on its way to the full, and the sky was clear. Under its light Lirael could clearly make out details on the ground. It would be enough to climb the Steps.

Sam woke quickly when she shook him, his hand going to his sword. They didn't speak—something about the quiet of the night forestalled any conversation. Lirael covered the fire as Sam splashed water on his face, and they helped each other shoulder their packs. The Dog loped backwards and forwards as they got ready, her tail wagging, all eagerness to be off again.

The Steps began in a deep cut that went straight into the cliff for twenty yards, so at first it seemed it would become a tunnel. But it was open to the sky, and it soon turned to run along and up the cliff, striking westward. Each step was exactly the same size, in height and breadth and depth, so the climb was regular and relatively easy, though still exhausting.

As they climbed, Lirael came to understand that the cliff was not, as she had thought, a single almost vertical face of rough stone. It was actually composed of hundreds of faces of slipped rock, as if a sheaf of paper had been propped up and many individual pages had slipped down. The stepped path was mainly built between and on top of the faces, running along till it had to turn and be cut back deeper into the cliff in order to reach the next higher face.

The moon rose higher as they climbed, and the sky became much lighter. There was moon shadow now, and whenever they stopped for a rest, Lirael looked out to the lands beyond, to the distant hills to the south and the silver-brushed trail of the Ratterlin to the east. She had often flown in owl shape above the Clayr's Glacier and the twin mountains of Starmount and Sunfall, but that was different. Owl senses were not the same, and back there she had always known that come the dawn, she would be safely tucked in bed, secure in the fastness of the Clayr. Those flights had been pure adventure. This was something much more serious, and she could not simply enjoy the cool of the night and the bright moon.

☀

Sam looked out, too. He couldn't see the Wall to the south—it was over the horizon—but he recognized the hills. Barhedrin was one, Cloven Crest of old, where there was a Charter Stone and, since the

Restoration, a tower that was the Guard's south-ernmost headquarters. Beyond the Wall was the country of Ancelstierre. A strange country, even to Sameth, who had gone to school there. A country without the Charter, or Free Magic, save for its northern regions, close to the Old Kingdom. Sameth thought of his mother and father there, far off to the south. They were trying to find a diplomatic solution to stop the Ancelstierrans from sending Southerling refugees across the Wall, to their certain deaths and, after that, to serve at the command of the necromancer Hedge. It could be no coincidence, Sam thought grimly, that this Southerling refugee problem had arisen at the same time that Hedge was masterminding the digging up of the ancient evil that was imprisoned near the Red Lake. It all smacked of a long-term, well-laid plan, on both sides of the Wall. Which was extremely unusual and did not bode well. What could a necromancer of the Old Kingdom really hope to gain from the world beyond the Wall? Sabriel and Touchstone thought their Enemy's plan was to bring hundreds of thousands of the Southerlings across the Wall, kill them by poison or spell, and make them into an army of the Dead. But the more Sam thought about it, the more he wondered. If that was the Enemy's sole intention, what was being dug up? And what part did his friend Nicholas have to play in it all?

The rests became more frequent as the moon slowly drifted down the sky. Though the steps were regular and well made, it was a steep climb, and they were tired to begin with. The Dog kept loping ahead, occasionally doubling back to make sure her mistress was keeping up, but Lirael and Sam were faltering. They trod with mechanical regularity, and their heads were bowed. Even the sight of a nest full of cliff owl chicks near the path attracted only a brief look from Lirael and not even a glance from Sameth.

They were still climbing when a red glow started to the east, coloring the moon's cold light. Soon it became bright enough to make the moon fade, and birds began to sing. Tiny swifts issued from cracks all along the cliff, flying out to chase insects rising with the morning wind.

"We must be close to the top," said Sam as they paused to rest, the three of them strung out along the narrow way: the Dog at the top, as high as Lirael's head, and Sameth below her, his head at about her knee level.

Sam leaned against the cliff face as he spoke,

only to recoil with a cry as an unnoticed thorn tree pricked him in the legs.

For a moment Lirael thought he would fall, but he recovered his balance and twisted himself around to pick out the thorns.

The Steps were considerably scarier in daylight, Lirael thought, as she looked down. All it would take was a step to the left and she would fall, if not the whole way down, at least to the next rock slip. That was twenty yards below them here, enough to break bones if it didn't kill immediately.

"I never realized!" said Sam, who had stopped pulling out thorns and was kneeling down to brush away the dust and fragments of stone on the steps in front of him. "The steps are made of brick! But they would have had to cut into the stone anyway, so why face the stone with brick?"

"I don't know," replied Lirael, before she caught on that Sam had actually been asking himself. "Does it matter?"

Sam stood up and brushed his knees.

"No, I suppose not. It's just odd. It must have been an enormous job, particularly as I can't see any sign of magical assistance. I suppose sendings could have been used, though they do tend to shed the odd mark here and there. . . ."

"Come on," said Lirael. "Let's get to the top. Perhaps there will be some clue to the Steps' making there."

But well before they came to the top of the Steps, Lirael had lost all interest in plaques or builder's monuments. A terrible foreboding that had been lurking in the back of her mind grew stronger as they climbed the last few hundred feet, and slowly it became more and more concrete. She could feel a coldness in her gut, and she knew that what awaited them at the top would be a place of death. Not recent death, not within the day, but death nonetheless.

She knew Sam felt it, too. They exchanged bleak looks as the Steps widened at last near the top. Without needing to talk about it, they moved from single file to a line abreast. The Dog grew slightly larger and stayed close to Lirael's side.

Lirael's sense of death was confirmed by the breeze that hit them on the last few steps. A breeze that carried with it a terrible smell, giving a few moments' warning before they reached the top of the Steps, to look out on a barren field strewn with the bodies of many men and mules. A great gathering of ravens clustered around and on the corpses, tearing at flesh with their sharp beaks and squabbling amongst themselves.

Fortunately, it was immediately clear the ravens were normal birds. They flew away as soon as the Disreputable Dog ran forward, croaking their displeasure at the interruption to their breakfast. Lirael could not sense any Dead among them, or nearby, but she still drew Saraneth and her sword, Nehima. Even from a distance, her necromantic senses told her the bodies had been there for days, though the smell could have told her just as much.

The Dog ran back to Lirael and tilted her head in question. Lirael nodded, and the hound loped off, sniffing the ground around the bodies in wider and wider circles till she disappeared out of sight behind a particularly large clump of thorn trees. There was a body hanging from the tallest tree, tossed there by some great wind or a creature far stronger than any man.

Sam came up next to Lirael, his sword in hand, the Charter marks on the blade glowing palely in the sun. It was full dawn now, the light rich and strong. It seemed wrong for this field of death, Lirael thought. How could good sunshine play across such a place? There should be fog and darkness.

"A merchant party by the look of them," said

Sam as they advanced closer. "I wonder what . . ."

It was clear from the way the bodies lay that they had been fleeing something. All the merchants' bodies, distinguishable by their richer clothes and lack of weapons, lay closer to the Steps. The guards had fallen defending their employers, in a line some twenty yards farther back. A last stand, turning to face an enemy they could not outrun.

"A week or more ago," said Lirael as she walked towards the bodies. "Their spirits will be long gone. Into Death, I hope, though I am not sure they have not been . . . harvested for use in Life."

"But why leave the bodies?" asked Sam. "And what could have made these wounds?"

He pointed at a dead guardsman, whose mail hauberk had been pierced in two places. The holes were about the size of Sam's fists and were scorched around the edges, the steel rings and the leather underneath blackened as if by fire.

Lirael carefully returned Saraneth to its pouch and walked over to take a closer look at the body and the strange wounds. She tried not to breathe as she got closer, but a few paces away she suddenly stopped and gasped. With that gasp the awful stench entered her nose and lungs. It was too much, and she began to gag and had to turn away and throw up. As soon as she did, Sam immediately followed suit, and they both emptied their stomachs of rabbit and bread.

"Sorry," said Sam. "Can't stand other people being sick. Are you all right?"

"I knew him," said Lirael, glancing back at the guardsman. Her voice trembled until she took a deep breath.

"I knew him. He came to the Glacier years ago, and he talked to me in the Lower Refectory. His hauberk didn't fit him then."

She took the bottle Sam offered her, poured some water into her hands, and rinsed out her mouth.

"His name was . . . I can't quite remember. Larrow, or Harrow. Something like that. He asked me my name, and I never answered—"

She hesitated, about to say more, but stopped as Sam suddenly whipped around.

"What was that?"

"What?"

"A noise, somewhere over there," replied Sam, pointing to a dead mule that was lying on the lip of a shallow erosion gully that led down to the cliffs. Its head hung over the gully and was out of sight.

As they watched, the mule shifted slightly; then with a jerk, it slid over the edge and into the gully.

They could still see its hindquarters, but most of it was hidden. Then the mule's rump and back legs began to shake and shiver.

"Something's eating it!" exclaimed Lirael in disgust. She could see drag marks on the ground now, all leading to the gully. There had been more bodies of mules and men. Someone . . . or something had dragged them to the narrow ditch.

"I can't sense anything Dead," said Sam anxiously. "Can you?"

Lirael shook her head. She slipped off her pack and took up her bow, strung it, and nocked an arrow. Sam drew his sword again.

They advanced slowly on the gully while more and more of the mule disappeared from sight. Closer, they could hear a dry gulping noise, rather like the sound of someone shoveling sand. Every now and then it would be accompanied by a more liquid gurgle.

But they still couldn't see anything. The gully was deep and only three or four feet wide, and whatever was in it lay directly under the mule. Lirael still couldn't sense anything Dead, but there was a faint tang of something in the air.

Both of them recognized what it was at the same time. The acrid, metallic odor characteristic of Free

Magic. But it was very faint, and it was impossible to tell where it was coming from. Perhaps the gully, or possibly blowing in on the faint breeze.

When they were only a few paces from the edge of the gully, the rear legs of the mule disappeared with a final shake, its hooves flying in a grim parody of life. The same liquid gurgle accompanied the disappearance.

Lirael stopped at the edge and looked down, her bow drawn, a Charter-spelled arrow ready to fly. But there was nothing to shoot. Just a long streak of dark mud at the bottom of the gully, with a single hoof sinking under the surface. The smell of Free Magic was stronger, but it was not the corrosive stench she had encountered from the Stilken or other lesser Free Magic elementals.

"What is it?" whispered Sam. His left hand was crooked in a spell-casting gesture, and a slim golden flame burned at the end of each finger, ready to be thrown.

"I don't know," said Lirael. "A Free Magic thing of some kind. Not anything I've ever read about. I wonder how—"

As she spoke, the mud bubbled and peeled back, to reveal a deep maw that was neither earth nor flesh but pure darkness, lit by a long, forked tongue of silver fire. With the open maw came a rolling stench of Free Magic and rotten meat, an almost physical assault that sent Lirael and Sam staggering back even as the tongue of silver fire rose into the air and struck down where Lirael had stood a moment before. Then a great snake head of mud followed the tongue, rearing out of the gully, looming high above them.

Lirael loosed her arrow as she stumbled back, and Sam thrust out his hand, shouting the activating marks that sent a roaring, crackling fountain of fire towards the thing of mud and blood and darkness that was rising up. Fire met silver tongue, and sparks exploded in all directions, setting the grass alight. Neither arrow nor Charter fire seemed to affect the creature, but it did recoil, and Lirael and Sam had no hesitation in running farther back.

"Who dares disturb my feasting!" roared a voice that was many voices and one, mixed with the braying of mules and the cries of dying men. "My feast so long since due!"

In answer Lirael dropped her bow and and drew Nehima. Sam muttered marks and drew them into the air with his sword and hand, knitting together many complex symbols. Lirael took a half step forward to guard Sam while he completed the spell.

Sam finished with a master mark that wreathed his hand in golden flames as he drew it in the air. It was a mark that Lirael knew could easily immolate an unready caster, and she flinched slightly as it appeared. But it left Sam's hand easily, and the spell hung in the air, a glowing tracery of linked marks, rather like a belt of shining stars. He took one end gingerly, swung the whole thing round his head, and let it fly at the creature, simultaneously shouting out, "Look away!"

There was a blinding flash, a sound like a choir screaming, and silence. When they looked back, there was no sign of the creature. Just small fires burning in the grass, coils of smoke twining together to cast a pall across the field.

"What was that?" asked Lirael.

"A spell for binding something," replied Sam. "I was never quite sure what, though. Do you think it worked?"

"No," said the Dog, her sudden appearance making Lirael and Sam jump. "Though it was quite bright enough to let every Dead thing between here and the Red Lake know where we are."

"If it didn't work, then where is that thing?" asked Sam. He looked around nervously as he spoke. Lirael looked, too. She could still smell the

Free Magic, though once more only faintly, and it was impossible to tell where it was coming from amidst the eddying smoke.

"It's probably under our feet," said the Dog. She suddenly thrust her nose into a small hole and snorted. The snort sent a gout of dirt flying into the air. Lirael and Sam jumped away, hesitated on the brink of flight, then slowly stood back-to-back, their weapons ready.

CHAPTER FIVE

BLOW WIND, COME RAIN!

"EXACTLY WHERE UNDER our feet!?" exclaimed Sam. He looked down anxiously, his sword and spell-casting hand ready.

"What can we do?" asked Lirael quickly. "Do you know what that was? How do we fight it?"

The Dog sniffed scornfully at the ground.

"We will not need to fight. That was a Ferenk, a scavenger. Ferenks are all show and bluster. This one lies under several ells of earth and stone now. It will not come out till dark, perhaps not even till dark tomorrow."

Sam scanned the ground, not trusting the Dog's opinion, while Lirael bent down to talk to the hound.

"I've never read anything about Free Magic creatures called Ferenks," said Lirael. "Not in any of the books I went through to find out about the Stilken."

"There should be no Ferenk here," said the Dog. "They are elemental creatures, spirits of stone and mud. They became nothing more than stone and mud when the Charter was made. A few would have been missed, but not here . . . not in a place so traveled. . . ."

"If it was just a scavenger, what killed these poor people?" asked Lirael. She'd been wondering about the wounds she'd seen and not liking the direction her thoughts were going in. Most of the corpses had, like the guardsman, two holes bored right through them, holes where clothing and skin were scorched around the edges.

"Certainly a Free Magic creature, or creatures," said the Dog. "But not a Ferenk. Something akin to a Stilken, I think. Perhaps a Jerreq or a Hish. There were many thousands of Free Magic creatures who evaded the making of the Charter, though most were later imprisoned or made to serve after a fashion. There were entire breeds, and others of a singular nature, so I cannot speak with absolute certainty. It is complicated by the fact that there was a forge here long ago, inside the ring of thorns. There was a creature bound inside the stone anvil of that forge, yet I can find neither anvil nor any other remnants.

Possibly whatever was bound here killed these people, but I think not. . . ."

The Dog paused to sniff the ground again, wandered in a circle, absently snapped at her own tail, and then sat down to offer her conclusion.

"It might have been a twinned Jerreq, but I am inclined to think the killing here was done by two Hish. Whatever did the deed, it was done in the service of a necromancer."

"How do you know that?" asked Sam. He'd stopped circling when the Dog started, though he still kept on looking at the ground. Now he was looking for signs of a stone anvil as well as an erupting Ferenk. Not that he'd ever seen an anvil here.

"Tracks and signs," replied the Dog. "The wounds, the smells that remain, a three-toed impression in soft soil, the body hung in the tree, the thorns stripped from seven branches in celebration . . . all this tells me what walked here, up to a point. As to the necromancer, no Jerreq or Hish or any of the other truly dangerous creatures of Free Magic has woken in a thousand years save to the sound of Mosrael and Saraneth, or by a direct summons using their secret names."

"Hedge was here," whispered Lirael. Sam

flinched at the name, and the burn scars on his wrists darkened. But he did not look at the scars or turn away.

"Perhaps," said the Dog. "Not Chlorr, anyway. One of the Greater Dead would leave different signs."

"They died eight days ago," continued Lirael. She did not question how she knew this. Now that she had seen the corpses more closely, she just knew. It was part of her being an Abhorsen. "Their spirits were not taken. According to *The Book of the Dead*, they should not be past the Fourth Gate. I could go into Death and find one. . . ."

She stopped as both the Dog and Sam shook their heads.

"I don't think that's a good idea," said Sam. "What could you learn? We know that there are bands of the Dead and necromancers and who knows what else roaming around."

"Sam is right," said the Dog. "There is nothing useful to learn from their deaths. And since Sam has already announced our presence with Charter Magic, let us give these poor people the cleansing fire, so that their bodies may not be used. But we should be quick."

Lirael looked across the field, blinking as the

sun cut across her eyes, over to where the young man who had once been Barra lay. The name came to her as she looked. She had thought of finding Barra in Death, and telling his spirit that the girl he had probably forgotten years ago had always wished she had talked to him, kissed him even, done anything other than hide behind her hair and weep. But even if she could find Barra in Death, she knew he would be long past any concerns of the living world. It would not be for him that she sought his spirit, but for herself, and she could not afford the luxury.

All three of them stood together over the closest body. Sam drew the Charter mark for fire, the Disreputable Dog barked one for cleansing, and Lirael drew those for peace and sleep and pulled all the marks together. The marks met and sparked on the man's chest, became leaping golden flames, and a second later exploded to immolate the entire body. Then the fire died as quickly as it had come, leaving only ash and lumps of melted metal that had once been belt buckle and knife blade.

"Farewell," said Sam.

"Go safely," said Lirael.

"Do not come back," said the Dog.

After that, they did the ritual individually,

moving as quickly as they could among the bodies. Lirael noticed that Sam was at first surprised, then obviously relieved, that the Disreputable Dog could cast the Charter marks and perform a rite that no necromancer or pure Free Magic creature could do, because of the rite's inherent opposition to the forces they wielded.

Even with the three of them performing the rite, the sun was high and the morning almost gone by the time they finished. Not counting the unknown number of people taken by the Ferenk to its muddy lair, thirty-eight men and women had died in the field of thorn trees. Now they were only piles of ash in a field of rotting mules and ravens, who had come back, croaking their dissatisfaction at the diminution of their feast.

It was Lirael who first noticed that one of the ravens was not actually alive. It sat on the head of a mule, pretending to pick at it, but its black eyes were firmly fixed on Lirael. She had sensed its presence before seeing it, but hadn't been sure whether it was the deaths of eight days ago she felt, or the presence of the Dead. As soon as she met its gaze, she knew. The bird's spirit was long gone, and something festering and evil lived inside the feathered body. Something once human, transformed by ages spent in Death, years misspent in an endless struggle to return to Life.

It was not a Gore Crow. Though it wore a raven's body, this was a much stronger spirit than was ever used to animate a flock of just-killed crows. It was out in the glare of the full sun, and so must be a Fourth or Fifth Gate Rester at least. The raven body it used had to be fresh, for such a spirit would corrode the flesh of whatever it inhabited within a day.

Lirael's hand flew to Saraneth, but even as she drew the bell, the Dead creature shot into the air and flew swiftly west, hugging the ground and twisting among the thorn trees. Feathers and bits of dead flesh dropped as it flew. It would be a skeleton before it went much farther, Lirael realized, but then it did not need feathers to fly. Free Magic propelled it, not living sinew.

"You should have got it," criticized the Dog. "It could still hear the bell, even past those thorn trees. Let's hope it was an independent spirit; otherwise we'll have Gore Crows—at the least—all over us."

Lirael returned Saraneth to its pouch, carefully holding the clapper till the leather tongue slipped into place to keep the bell still.

"I was surprised," she said quietly. "I'll be quicker next time."

"We'd better move on," said Sam. He looked at the sky and sighed. "Though I had hoped to have a bit of a rest. It's too hot to walk."

"Where are we going?" asked Lirael. "Is there a wood or anything nearby that will hide us from the Gore Crows?"

"I'm not sure," said Sam. He pointed north, where the ground rose up to a low hill, the thorn trees giving way to a field that once must have been cultivated, though it was now home to weeds and saplings. "We can take a look from that rise. We have to head roughly northwest anyway."

They did not look back as they left what had become a funerary ground. Lirael tried to look everywhere else, her sight and sense of Death alert for any slight indication of the Dead. The Dog loped along next to her, and Sam walked to her left, a few steps behind.

They followed the remnants of a low stone wall up the hill. Once it would have separated two fields, and there might have been sheep on the higher pasture and crops below. But that was long ago, and the wall had not been mended for decades.

Somewhere, less than a league or so away, there would be a ruined farmhouse, ruined yards, a choked well. The telltale signs that people had once lived there and had not fared well.

From their high point they could see the Long Cliffs stretching out to the east and west, and the undulating hills of the plateau. They could see the Ratterlin stretching from north to south, and the plume of the waterfall. Abhorsen's House was hidden by the hills, but the tops of the fog banks that still surrounded it were eerily visible.

Several hundred years ago, before Kerrigor's rise, they would also have seen farms and villages and cultivated fields. Now, even twenty years after King Touchstone's Restoration, this part of the Kingdom was still largely deserted. Small forests had joined to become larger ones, single trees had become small forests, and drained marshes had returned happily to swamps. There were villages out there somewhere, Lirael knew, but none she could see. They were few and far between, because just a handful of Charter Stones had been replaced or restored. Only Charter Mages of the royal line could make or mend a Charter Stone—though the blood of any Charter Mage could break a normal stone. Too many Charter Stones had been broken in the two hundred years of the Interregnum for even twenty years of hard work to fix.

"It's at least two, maybe three days' solid march to Edge," said Sam, pointing nor-norwest. "The Red Lake is behind those mountains. Which we pass to the south, I'm glad to say."

Lirael shielded her eyes against the sun with her hand and squinted. She could just make out the peaks of a distant mountain range.

"We may as well get started then," she said. Still shading her eyes, she gradually turned a full circle, looking up into the sky. It was a beautiful, clear blue, but Lirael knew that all too soon she would see telltale black blots—distant flocks of Gore Crows.

"We could head for Roble's Town first," suggested Sam, who was also looking up at the sky. "I mean, Hedge is going to know where we are anyway soon, and we might be able to get some help in Roble's Town. There'll be a Guard post there."

"No," said Lirael thoughtfully. She could see a line of puffy, black-streaked clouds far to the north, and it had given her an idea. "We'd just be getting other people into trouble. Besides, I think I know how to get rid of the Gore Crows, or hide from them at least—though it won't be pleasant. We'll try it a bit later on. Closer to nightfall."

"What do you plan, Mistress?" asked the Dog. She had collapsed near Lirael's feet, her tongue lolling out as she panted to cool down after the climb. This was a difficult task, since the sky was clear and the day was getting hotter and hotter as the sun climbed.

"We'll whistle down those rain clouds," replied Lirael, pointing at the distant cushion of dark cloud. "Good heavy rain and wind will blow away the Gore Crows, make us hard to find, and cover our tracks as well. What do you think?"

"An excellent plan!" exclaimed the Dog with approval.

"Do you think we can bring that rain down here?" asked Sam dubiously. "I reckon that cloud is about as far away as High Bridge."

"We can try," said Lirael. "Though there is more cloud to the west. . . ."

Her voice trailed off as she really focused on the blacker cloud beyond the hills, close to the western mountains. Even from this far away she could sense a wrongness in it, and as she stared, she saw the sheen of lightning within the cloud.

"I guess not that cloud."

"No," growled the Dog, her voice very deep, rumbling in her chest. "That is where Hedge and

Nicholas are digging. I fear that they may have already uncovered what they seek."

"I'm sure Nick doesn't know he's doing anything bad," said Sam quickly. "He's a good man. He wouldn't do anything that would hurt anyone intentionally."

"I hope so," said Lirael. She was wondering once again what they would do when they got there. Why did Hedge need Nicholas? What was being dug up? What was their Enemy's ultimate plan?

"We'd better keep moving, anyway," she said, tearing her gaze away from the distant dark cloud and its flickering lightnings to look at the rolling land to the west. "What if we follow that valley? It goes in the right direction, and there's quite a lot of tree cover and a stream."

"That should be practically a small river," said Sam. "I don't know what's happened to the spring rains down here."

"Weather can be worked two ways," said the Dog absently. She was still looking towards the mountains. "It may be no accident that the rain clouds hug the north. It would be good to bring them south for several reasons. I would like it even more if we could stop that lightning storm."

"I guess we could try," said Sam doubtfully,

but the Dog shook her head.

"That storm would not answer to any weather magic," she said. "There is too much lightning, and that confirms a fear I had hoped to lay to rest. I had not thought they would find it so quickly, or that it could be so easily untombed. I should have known. Astarael does not lightly tread the earth, and a Ferenk released already . . ."

"What is *it*?" asked Lirael nervously.

"The thing that Hedge is digging up," said the Dog. "I will tell you more when needs must. I do not wish to fill your bones with fear, or tell ancient tales for no purpose. There are still several possible explanations and ancient safeguards that might yet hold even if the worst is true. But we must hurry!"

With that, the Dog leapt up and shot off down the hill, grinning as she zigzagged around white-barked saplings with silver-green leaves and shot over yet another ruined stone wall.

Lirael and Sam looked at each other and then at the lightning storm.

"I wish she wouldn't do that," complained Lirael, who had opened her mouth to ask another question. Then she went down after the Dog, at a considerably slower pace. Magical dogs might not tire, but Lirael was already very weary. It would be a long and exhausting afternoon, if no worse, for there was always the chance the Gore Crows would find them.

"What have you done, Nick?" whispered Sam. Then he followed Lirael, already pursing his lips and thinking about the Charter marks that would be needed to shunt a rain cloud two hundred miles across the sky.

❋

They walked steadily all afternoon, with only short breaks, following a stream that flowed through a shallow valley between two roughly parallel lines of hills. The valley was lightly wooded, the shade saving them from the sun, which Lirael was finding particularly troubling. She was already sunburnt a little on the nose and cheekbones, and had neither the time nor the energy to soothe her skin with a spell. This was also a niggling reminder of the differences that had plagued her all her life. Proper Clayr were brown skinned, and they never burnt—exposure to sun simply made them darker.

By the time the sun had begun its slow fall behind the western mountains, only the Dog was still moving with any grace. Lirael and Sam had been awake for nearly eighteen hours, most of it climbing up the Long Cliffs or walking. They were stumbling, and falling asleep on their feet, no matter how they tried to stay alert. Finally Lirael decided that they had to rest, and they would stop as soon as they saw somewhere defensible, preferably with running water on at least one side.

Half an hour later, as they kept stumbling on and the valley began to narrow and the ground to rise, Lirael was prepared to settle for anywhere they could simply fall down, with or without running water to help defend against the Dead. The trees were also thinning out, giving way to low shrubs and weedy grass as they climbed. Another field that was returning to the wild, and totally indefensible.

Just when Lirael and Sam could hardly take another step, they found the perfect place. The soft gurgle of a waterfall announced it, and there was a shepherd's hut, built on stilts across the swift water at the foot of a long but not very high waterfall. The hut was both shelter and bridge, so solidly built of ironwood that it showed little sign of decay, save for some of the shingles missing from the roof.

The Dog sniffed around outside the river hut, pronounced it dirty but habitable, and got in the way as Lirael and Sam tried to climb the steps and enter.

It was filthy inside, having at some time been

subject to a flood that had deposited a great deal of dirt on the floor. But Lirael and Sam were past caring about that. Whether they slept on dirt outdoors or in, it was all one.

"Dog, can you take the first watch?" asked Lirael, as she gratefully shrugged off her pack and settled it in one corner.

"I can watch," protested Sam, belying his words with a mighty yawn.

"I will watch," said the Disreputable Dog. "Though there may be rabbits. . . ."

"Don't chase them out of sight," warned Lirael. She drew Nehima and laid the sword across her pack, ready for quick use, then did the same with the bell-bandolier. She kept her boots on, choosing not to speculate on the state of her feet after two days' hard traveling.

"Wake us in four hours, please," Lirael added as she slumped down and leant back against the wall. "We have to call the rain clouds down."

"Yes, Mistress," replied the Dog. She had not come in but sat near the rushing water, her ears pricked to catch some distant sound. Rabbits, perhaps. "Do you want me to bring you a boiled egg and toast as well?"

There was no answer. When the Dog looked in

a moment later, both Lirael and Sam were sound asleep, slumped against their packs. The Dog let out a long sigh and slumped down herself, but her ears stayed upright and her eyes were keen, gazing out long after the summer twilight faded into the night.

Near midnight, the Dog shook herself and woke Lirael with a lick on her face and Sam with paw pressed heavily on his chest. Each woke with a start, and both reached for their swords before their eyes adjusted to the dim light from the glow of the Charter marks in the Dog's collar.

Cold water from the stream woke them a little more, followed by necessary ablutions slightly farther afield. When they came back, a quick meal of dried meat, compressed dry biscuits, and dried fruit was eaten heartily by all three, though the Dog regretted the absence of rabbit or even a nice bit of lizard.

They couldn't see the rain clouds in the night, even with a star-filled sky and the moon beginning its rise. But they knew the clouds were there, far to the north.

"We will have to go as soon as the spell is done," warned the Dog, as Lirael and Sam stood under the stars quietly discussing how they would call the clouds and rain. "Such Charter Magic will call anything Dead within miles, or any Free Magic creatures."

"We should press on anyway," said Lirael. The sleep had revived her to some degree, but she still wished for the comfort of the sleeping chair in her little room in the Great Library of the Clayr. "Are you ready, Sam?"

Sam stopped humming and said, "Yes. Um, I was wondering whether you might consider a slight variation on the usual spell? I think that we will need a stronger casting to bring the clouds so far."

"Sure," said Lirael. "What do you want to do?"

Sam explained quickly, then went through it again slowly as Lirael made certain she knew what he planned to do. Usually both of them would whistle the same marks at the same time. What Sam wanted to do was whistle different but complementary marks, in effect weaving together two different weather-working spells. They would end and activate the spell by speaking two master marks at the same time, when one was normally all that would be used.

"Will this work?" asked Lirael anxiously. She had no experience of working with another Charter Mage on such a complex spell.

"It will be much stronger," said Sam confidently.

Lirael looked at the Dog for confirmation, but the hound wasn't paying attention. She was staring back towards the south, intent on something Lirael and Sam couldn't see or sense.

"What is it?"

"I don't know," replied the Dog, turning her head to the side, her pricked ears quivering as she listened to the night. "I think something is following us, but it is still distant. . . ."

She looked back at Lirael and Sam.

"Do your weather magic and let us be gone!"

A league or more downstream of the shepherd's hut, a very short man—almost a dwarf—was paddling in the shallows. His skin was as white as bone, and the hair on his head and beard was whiter still, so white it shone in the darkness, even under the shadow of the trees where they overhung the water.

"I'll show her," muttered the albino, though no one was there to hear his angry speech. "Two thousand years of servitude already, and then to—"

He stopped mid word and swooped into the stream, one knobby-fingered hand plunging into the water. It emerged a moment later holding a struggling fish, which he immediately bit behind its eyes, severing the spinal cord. His teeth, bright in the starlight, were sharper by far than any human's.

The dwarf tore at the fish again, blood dribbling down his beard. In a few minutes he'd eaten the whole thing, spitting out the bones with curses and grumbling between bites over the fact that he'd wanted a trout and had got a redjack.

When he finished, he carefully cleaned his face and beard and dried his feet, though he left the bloodstains on the simple robe he wore. But as he walked along the bank of the stream, the stains faded and the cloth was once again clean and white and new.

The robe was fastened around the little man's waist with a red leather belt, and where the buckle should have been there was a tiny bell. All this time the albino had held it, using only one hand to catch the fish and clean himself. But his caution failed when he stumbled on a slippery patch of grass. The bell sang out as he fell to one knee, a bright sound that paradoxically made the man yawn. For a moment it seemed he might lie down there and then, but with an obvious effort he shook his head and stood up.

"No, no, sister," he muttered, clutching the bell even more fiercely. "I have work to do, you see. I cannot sleep, not now. There are miles to go, and

I must make the most of two legs and two hands while I still have them."

A night bird called nearby and the man's head flashed around, instantly spotting it. Still holding the bell, he licked his lips and, taking one slow step after the other, began to stalk it. But the bird was wary, and before the albino could pounce, it flew away, calling plaintively into the night.

"I never get dessert," complained the man. He turned back to the stream and began to follow it westwards once again, still holding the bell and muttering complaints.

CHAPTER SIX

THE SILVER HEMISPHERES

ONE HUNDRED AND twenty miles to the northwest of Abhorsen's House, the eastern shores of the Red Lake lay in darkness, even though a new day had dawned. For it was not the dark of night but of storm, the sky heavy with black clouds, that stretched for several leagues in all directions. The darkness had already lasted for more than a week. What little sunlight came through the cloud was weak and pale, and the days were lit by a strange twilight that did no favor to any living thing. Only at the epicenter of this immovable cluster of storm clouds was there any other light, and that was sudden, harsh and white, from the constant assault of lightning.

Nicholas Sayre had grown used to the twilight, as he had grown used to many other things, and he no longer thought it strange. But his body still rebelled, even when his mind did not. He coughed and held his handkerchief against his nose and mouth. Hedge's Night Crew were sterling workers, but they did smell awful, as if the flesh were rotting on their bones. Generally he didn't like to get too close—in case whatever they had was contagious—but he'd had to this time, to check out what was happening.

"You see, Master," Hedge explained, "we cannot move the two hemispheres any closer together. There is a force that keeps them apart, no matter what methods we employ. Almost as if they are identical poles of a magnet."

Nick nodded, absorbing this information. As he'd dreamt, there had been two silver hemispheres hidden deep underground, and his excavation had found them. But his sense of triumph at their discovery was soon dispelled by the logistical problems of getting them out. Each hemisphere was seven feet in diameter, and the strange metal it was made of was much heavier than it should be, weighing even more than gold.

The hemispheres had been buried some twenty feet apart, separated by a strange barrier made of seven different materials, including bone. Now that they were being raised, it was clear that this barrier had helped negate the repulsive force, for the hemispheres simply could not be brought within fifty feet of each other.

Using rollers, ropes, and over two hundred of the Night Crew, one of the hemispheres had been dragged up the spiral ramp and over the lip of the pit. The other lay abandoned a good distance down the ramp. The last time they had tried to drag and push up the lower hemisphere, the repulsive force had been so great it was hurled back down, crushing many of the workers beneath it.

In addition to this strange repulsive force, Nick noted, there were other effects around the hemispheres. They seemed to generate an acrid, hot-metal smell that cut through even the fetid, rotting odor of the Night Crew. The smell made him sick, though it did not seem to affect either Hedge or his peculiar laborers.

Then there was the lightning. Nick flinched as yet another bolt struck down, momentarily blinding him, deafening thunder coming an instant later. The lightning was striking even more frequently than before, and now both hemispheres were exposed, Nick could see a pattern. Each hemisphere was struck eight times in a row, but the ninth bolt would invariably miss, often striking one of the workers.

Not that this seemed to affect them, part of Nick's mind observed. If they didn't catch alight or get completely dismembered, they kept on working. But this information didn't stay in his head, as Nick's thoughts always came back to his primary goal with an intense focus that banished all extraneous thoughts.

"We will have to move the first hemisphere on," he said, fighting the shortness of breath that came with the nausea he suffered whenever he went too close to the silver metal. "And we will need an additional barge. The two hemispheres won't fit on the one we've got, not with a fifty-foot separation. I hope the import license I have will allow two shipments. . . . In any case, we have no choice. There must be no delay."

"As you say, Master," replied Hedge, but he kept staring at Nick as if he expected something else.

"I meant to ask if you'd found a crew," Nick said at last, when the silence became uncomfortable. "For the barges."

"Yes," replied Hedge. "They gather at the lakeside. Men like me, Master. Those who served in the Army of Ancelstierre, down in the trenches of the

Perimeter. At least till the night drew them from their pickets and listening posts and made them cross the Wall."

"You mean deserters? Are they trustworthy?" Nick asked sharply. The last thing he wanted was to lose a hemisphere through human stupidity, or to introduce some additional complication for when they crossed back into Ancelstierre. That simply could not be allowed to happen.

"Not deserters, sir, oh, no," replied Hedge, smiling. "Simply missing in action, and too far from home. They are quite trustworthy. I have made certain of that."

"And the second barge?" Nick asked.

Hedge suddenly looked up, nostrils flaring to sniff the air, and he didn't answer. Nick looked up, too, and a heavy drop of rain splashed upon his mouth. He licked his lips, then quickly spat as a strange, numbing sensation spread down his throat.

"This should not be," Hedge whispered to himself, as the rain came heavier and a wind sprang up around them. "Summoned rain, coming from the northeast. I had best investigate, Master."

Nick shrugged, uncertain what Hedge was talking about. The rain made him feel peculiar, recalling him to some other sense of himself. Everything around him had assumed a dreamlike quality, and for the first time he wondered what on earth he was doing.

Then a strange pain struck him in the chest and he doubled over. Hedge caught him and laid him down onto earth that was rapidly turning into mud.

"What is it, Master?" asked Hedge, but his tone was inquisitive rather than sympathetic.

Nick groaned and clutched at his chest, his legs writhing. He tried to speak, but only spittle came from his lips. His eyes flickered wildly from side to side, then rolled back.

Hedge knelt by him, waiting. Rain continued to fall on Nick's face, but now it sizzled as it hit, steam wafting off his skin. A few moments later, thick white smoke began to coil out of the young man's nose and mouth, hissing as it met the rain.

"What is it, Master?" repeated Hedge, his voice suddenly nervous.

Nick's mouth opened, and more smoke puffed out. Then his hand moved, quicker than Hedge could see, fingers clutching at the necromancer's leg with terrible force. Hedge clenched his teeth, fighting back the pain, and asked again, "Master?"

"Fool!" said the thing that used Nick as its voice. "Now is not the time to seek our enemies.

They will find this pit soon enough, but by then we will be gone. You must procure an additional barge at once, and load the hemispheres. And get this body out of the rain, for it is already too fragile, and much remains to be done. Too much for my servants to laze and chatter!"

The last words were said with venom, and Hedge screamed as the fingers on his leg dug in like a steel-toothed mantrap. Then he was released, to fall back into the mud.

"Hurry," whispered the voice. "Be swift, Hedge. Be swift."

Hedge bowed where he was, not trusting himself to speak. He wanted to edge out of reach of the grasping, inhuman power of those hands, but he feared to move.

The rain grew heavier, and the white smoke began to sink back into Nick's nose and mouth. After a few seconds it disappeared completely, and he went totally limp.

Hedge caught his head just before it splashed back into a puddle. Then he lifted him up and carefully arranged him over his shoulders in a fireman's lift. A normal man's leg would have been broken by the force exerted through Nick's hand, but Hedge was no normal man. He lifted Nick easily, merely grimacing at the pain in his leg.

He'd carried Nick halfway back to his tent before the inert body on his shoulders twitched and the young man began to cough.

"Easy, Master," said Hedge, increasing his pace. "I'll soon have you out of the rain."

"What happened?" asked Nick, his voice rasping. His throat felt as if he'd just smoked half a dozen cigars and drunk a bottle of brandy.

"You fainted," replied Hedge, pushing through the flaps of the tent door. "Are you able to dry yourself and get to bed?"

"Yes, yes, of course," snapped Nick, but his legs trembled as Hedge put him down, and he had to balance himself against a traveling chest. Overhead, the rain beat out a steady rhythm on the canvas, accentuated every few minutes by the dull bass boom of thunder.

"Good," replied Hedge, handing him a towel. "I must go and give the Night Crew their instructions; then I have to go and . . . acquire another barge. It would probably be best if you rested here, sir. I will make sure someone—not one of the afflicted—brings your meals and empties the necessaries and so forth."

"I'm quite able to look after myself," replied

Nick, though he couldn't stop shivering as he stripped off his shirt and began to weakly towel his chest and arms. "Including overseeing the Night Crew."

"That will not be required," said Hedge. He leaned over Nick, and his eyes appeared to grow larger and fill with a flickering red light, as if they were windows to a great furnace somehow burning inside his skull.

"It would be best if you rested here," he repeated, his breath hot and metallic on Nick's face. "You do not need to supervise the work."

"Yes," agreed Nick dully, the towel frozen in mid motion. "It would be best for me to rest . . . here."

"You will await my return," commanded Hedge. His usual subordinate tone was completely gone, and he loomed over Nick like a headmaster about to cane a pupil.

"I will await your return," Nick repeated.

"Good," said Hedge. He smiled and turned on his heel, striding back out into the rain. It evaporated instantly into steam as it touched his bare head, wreathing him with a strange white halo. A few steps later, the steam wafted away, and the rain simply plastered down his hair.

Back in his tent, Nick suddenly started drying himself again. That done, he put on a pair of badly repaired pajamas and went to his bed of piled furs. His camp bed from Ancelstierre had broken days before, the springs collapsing into rust and the canvas crumbling with mildew.

Sleep came quickly, but not rest. He dreamed of the two silver hemispheres, and his Lightning Farm that was being set up across the Wall. He saw the hemispheres absorbing power from a thousand lightning strikes and, as they drew power, overcoming the force that kept them apart. He saw them finally hurtle together, charged with the strength of ten thousand storms . . . but then the dream began again from the beginning, so he couldn't see what happened when the hemispheres met.

Outside, the rain came down in sheets and the lightning struck again and again into and around the pit. Thunder rumbled and shook as the Dead Hands of the Night Crew strained at the ropes, slowly dragging the first silver hemisphere towards the Red Lake and the second hemisphere up and out of the pit.

CHAPTER SEVEN

A LAST REQUEST

IT WAS STILL raining two days after Lirael and Sam's all-too-successful weather working. Despite the oilskin coats thoughtfully packed by the sendings back at the House, they were completely, and seemingly permanently, sodden. Fortunately the spell was finally weakening, particularly the wind-summoning aspect, so the rain had lessened and was no longer driving horizontally into their faces, and they weren't being assaulted by sticks, leaves, and other wind-borne debris.

On the positive side, as Lirael had to remind herself every few hours, the rain had made it absolutely impossible for any Gore Crows to find them. Though that was somehow not as cheering as it should have been.

It also wasn't cold, which was another positive. They would have frozen to death otherwise, or exhausted themselves into immobility by using Charter Magic to stay alive. Both the wind and the rain were warm, and if there had been even an hour or two without them, Lirael would have thought their weather working a great success. As it was, misery rather tainted any pride in the spell.

They were getting close to the Red Lake now, climbing up through the lush forested foothills of Mount Abed and her sisters. The trees grew close here, forming a canopy overhead, interspersed with many ferns and plants Lirael knew only from books. The leaf litter from all of them was thick on the ground, making a carpet over the mud. Because of the rain, there were thousands of tiny rivulets of water everywhere, cascading among tree roots, down stone, and around Lirael's ankles. When she could see her ankles, because most of the time her legs were buried up to the shins in a mixture of wet leaves and mud.

It was very hard going, and Lirael was more tired than she had thought possible. The rests, when they had them, consisted of finding the largest tree with the thickest foliage to keep out the rain, and the highest roots to sit on, to keep out of the mud. Lirael had found that she could sleep even in these conditions, though more than once she awoke, after the scant two hours they allowed themselves, to find herself lying in the mud rather than sitting above it.

Of course, once they got back out in the rain, the mud soon washed off. Lirael wasn't sure which was worse. Mud or rain. Or the middle course: the first ten minutes after moving out of shelter, when the mud was getting washed off and running down her face, hands, and legs.

It was at exactly that time after a rest, with her total attention on getting the mud out of her eyes as they climbed up yet another gully, that they found a dying Royal Guard, propped up against the trunk of a sheltering tree. Or rather, the Disreputable Dog found her, sniffing her out as she scrabbled ahead of Lirael and Sam.

The Guardswoman was unconscious, her red and gold surcoat stained black with blood, her mail hauberk ripped and torn in several places. She still held a notched and blunted sword firmly in her right hand, while her left was frozen in a spell-casting gesture she would never complete.

Both Lirael and Sam knew that she was almost gone, her spirit already stepping across the border into Death. Quickly Sam bent down, calling up the most powerful healing spell he knew. But even as the first Charter mark flowered brightly in his mind, she was dead. The faint sheen of life in her eyes disappeared, replaced by a dull, unseeing gaze. Sam let the healing mark go and brushed her eyelids gently shut.

"One of Father's Guards," he said heavily. "I don't know her, though. She was probably from the Guard tower at Roble's Town or Uppside. I wonder what she was doing . . ."

Lirael nodded, but she couldn't tear her gaze away from the corpse. She felt so useless. She kept on being too late, too slow. The Southerling in the river, after the battle with Chlorr. Barra and the merchants. Now this woman. It was so unfair that she should die alone, with only a few minutes between death and rescue. If only they'd been quicker climbing the hill, or if they hadn't stopped for that last rest . . .

"She was a few days dying," said the Disreputable Dog, sniffing around the body. "But she can't have come far, Mistress. Not with those wounds."

"We must be close to Hedge and Nick then," said Sam, straightening up to cast a wary eye around. "It's so hard to tell under all these trees. We could be near the top of the ridge or still have miles to go."

"I guess I'd better find out," said Lirael slowly. She was still looking down at the dead body of the Guard. "What killed her, and where the enemy are."

"We must hurry then," said the Dog, jumping up on her hind legs with sudden excitement. "The river will have taken her some distance."

"You're going into Death?" asked Sam. "Is that wise? I mean, Hedge could be nearby—or even waiting in Death!"

"I know," said Lirael. She had been thinking exactly the same thing. "But I think it's worth the risk. We need to find out exactly where Nick's diggings are, and what happened to this Guard. We can't just keep blindly marching on."

"I suppose so," said Sam, biting his lip with unconscious anxiety. "What will I do?"

"Watch over my body while I'm gone, please," said Lirael.

"But don't use any Charter Magic unless you have to," added the Dog. "Someone like Hedge can smell it from miles away. Even with this rain."

"I know that," replied Sam. He betrayed his nervousness by drawing his sword, as his eyes kept moving, checking out every tree and shrub. He even looked up, just in time to receive a trickle of rain that had made it through the thick branches over-head. It ran down his neck and under the oilskin, to make him even less comfortable. But nothing lurked in the branches of the tree, and from what little he could see of the sky, it seemed empty of anything but rain and clouds.

Lirael drew her sword, too. She hesitated over which bell to choose for a moment, her hand flat against the bandolier. She had entered Death only once before, when she had been so nearly defeated and enslaved by Hedge. This time, she told herself, she would be stronger and better prepared. Part of that meant choosing the right bell. Her fingers lightly touched each pouch till the sixth one, which she carefully opened. She took out the bell, holding it inside its mouth so the clapper couldn't sound. She had chosen Saraneth, the Binder. Strongest of all the bells save Astarael.

"I am coming, too, aren't I?" asked the Dog eagerly, jumping around Lirael's feet, her tail wagging at high speed.

Lirael nodded her acquiescence and began to reach out for Death. It was easy here, for the Guard's passing had created a door that would link Life and Death at this spot for many days. A door that could work both ways.

The cold came quickly, banishing the humidity of the warm rain. Lirael shivered but kept forcing herself forward into Death, till the rain and the wind and the scent of wet leaves and Sam's watching face were all gone, replaced by the chill, grey light of Death.

The river tugged at Lirael's knees, willing her onwards. For a moment she resisted, reluctant to give up the feel of Life at her back. All she had to do was take one step backwards, reach out to Life, and be back in the forest. But she would have learned nothing. . . .

"I am the Abhorsen-in-Waiting," she whispered, and she felt the river's tug lessen. Or perhaps she just imagined it. Either way, she felt better. She had a right to be here.

She took her first slow step forward, and then another and another, until she was walking steadily forward, the Disreputable Dog plunging along at her side.

If she was lucky, Lirael thought, the Guard would still be on this side of the First Gate. But nothing was moving anywhere she could see, not even drifting on the surface, caught by the current. In the far distance was the roar of the Gate.

She listened carefully to that—for the roar would stop if the woman went through—and kept walking, careful to feel for potholes or sudden dips. It was much easier going with the current, and she relaxed a little, but not so much that she lowered sword or bell.

"She is just ahead, Mistress," whispered the Dog, her nose twitching only an inch above the surface of the river. "To the left."

Lirael followed the Dog's pointing paw and saw that there was a dim shape under the water, drifting with the current towards the First Gate. Instinctively, she stepped forward, thinking to physically grab the Guard. Then she realized her mistake and stopped.

Even the newly Dead could be dangerous, and a friend in Life would not necessarily be so here. It was safer not to touch. Instead she sheathed her sword and, keeping Saraneth stilled with her left hand, transferred her right to grasp the bell's mahogany handle. Lirael knew she should have flipped it one-handed and begun to ring it at the same time, and she knew she could if she had to, but it seemed sensible to be more cautious. After all, she had never used the bells before. Only the panpipes, and they were a lesser instrument of power.

"Saraneth will be heard by many, and afar,"

whispered the Dog. "Why don't I run up and grab her by the ankle?"

"No." Lirael frowned. "She's a Royal Guard, Dead or not, and we have to treat her with respect. I'll just get her attention. We won't be waiting around anyway."

She rang the bell with a simple arcing motion, one of the easiest peals described in *The Book of the Dead* for Saraneth. At the same time, she exerted her will into the sound of the bell, directing it at the submerged body floating away ahead.

The bell was very loud, eclipsing the faint roar of the First Gate. It echoed everywhere, seeming to grow louder rather than fainter, the deep tone creating ripples on the water in a great ring around Lirael and the Dog, ripples that moved even against the current.

Then the sound wrapped around the spirit of the Guard, and Lirael felt her twist and wriggle against her will like a fresh-hooked fish. Through the echo of the bell, she heard a name, and she knew that Saraneth had found it out and was giving it to her. Sometimes it was necessary to use a Charter-spell to discover a name, but this Guard had no defenses against any of the bells.

"Mareyn," said the echo of Saraneth, an echo

that sounded only inside Lirael's head. The Guard's name was Mareyn.

"Stay, Mareyn," she said in a commanding tone. "Stand, for I would speak with you."

Lirael felt resistance from the Guard then, but it was weak. A moment later the cold river frothed and bubbled, and the spirit of Mareyn stood up and turned to face the bell wielder who had bound her.

The Guard was too newly dead for Death to have changed her, so her spirit looked the same as her body out in Life. A tall, strongly built woman, the rents in her armor and the wounds in her body as clear here in the strange light of Death as they had been under the sun.

"Speak, if you are able," ordered Lirael. Again, being newly Dead, Mareyn could probably talk if she chose. Many who dwelled long in Death lost the power of speech, which could only then be restored by Dyrim, the speaking bell.

"I . . . am . . . able," croaked Mareyn. "What do you want of me, Mistress?"

"I am the Abhorsen-in-Waiting," declared Lirael, and those words seemed to echo out into Death, drowning the small still voice inside her that wanted to say, "I am a Daughter of the Clayr."

"I would ask the manner of your death and

what you know of a man called Nicholas and the pit he has dug," she continued.

"You have bound me with your bell and I must answer," said Mareyn, her voice devoid of all emotion. "But I would ask a boon, if I may."

"Ask," said Lirael, flicking her glance to the Disreputable Dog, who was circling behind Mareyn like a wolf after a sheep. The Dog saw her looking, wagged her tail, and started to circle back. She was obviously just playing, though Lirael didn't understand how she could be so lighthearted here in Death.

"The necromancer of the pit, whose name I dare not speak," said Mareyn. "He killed my companions, but he laughed and let me crawl away, wounded as I was, with the promise that his servants would find me in Death and bind me to his service. I feel that this is so, and my body also lies unburnt behind me. I do not wish to return, Mistress, or to serve such a one as he. I ask you to send me on, where no power can turn me back."

"Of course I will," said Lirael, but Mareyn's words sent a stab of fear through her. If Hedge had let Mareyn go, he had probably had her followed and knew where her body was. It might be under observation at this moment, and it would be easy enough to set a watch in Death for Mareyn's spirit when it came. Hedge—or his servants—might be approaching in both Life and Death, right now.

Even as she thought that, the Dog's ears pricked up and she growled. A second later Lirael heard the roar of the First Gate falter and become still.

"Something comes," warned the Dog, nose snuffling at the river. "Something bad."

"Quickly then," Lirael said. She replaced Saraneth and drew Kibeth, transferring the bell to her left hand so she could also unsheath Nehima. "Mareyn, tell me where the pit is, in relation to your body."

"The pit lies in the next valley, over the ridge," replied Mareyn calmly. "There are many Dead there, under constant cloud and lightning. They have made a road, too, along the valley floor to the lake. The young man Nicholas lives in a patch-work tent to the east of the pit. . . . Something comes for me, Mistress. Please, I beg you to send me on."

Lirael felt the fear within Mareyn's spirit, even though her voice had the steady, uninflected tone of the Dead. She heard it and responded instantly, ringing Kibeth above her head in a figure-eight pattern.

"Go, Mareyn," she said sternly, her words weaving into the toll of the bell. "Walk deep into Death and do not tarry, or let any bar your path. I command thee to walk to the Ninth Gate and go beyond, for you have earned your final rest. Go!"

Mareyn jerked completely around at that last word and began to march, her head high and arms swinging, as she must once have marched in Life on the parade ground at the barracks at Belisaere. Straight as an arrow she marched, off towards the First Gate. Lirael saw her falter for a moment in the distance, as if something had tried to waylay her, but then she marched on, till the roar of the First Gate stilled to mark her passage.

"She's gone," remarked the Dog. "But whatever came through is here somewhere. I can smell it."

"I can feel it, too," whispered Lirael. She swapped bells again, taking up Saraneth. She liked the security of the big bell, and the deep authority of its voice.

"We should go back," said the Dog, her head slowly moving from side to side as she tried to locate the creature. "I don't like it when they're clever."

"Do you know what it is?" whispered Lirael as they began to trudge back to Life, zigzagging so her back was never truly turned. As on her first trip, it was much harder going against the current, and it seemed colder than ever, too, leaching away at her spirit.

"Some sneaker from beyond the Fifth Gate, I think," said the Dog. "Small, and long since whittled down from its original—There!"

She barked and dashed through the water. Lirael saw something like a long, spindle-thin rat—with burning coals for eyes—leap aside as the Dog struck. Then it was coming straight at her, and she felt its cold and powerful spirit rise against her, out of all proportion to its rat-like form.

She screamed and struck at it with her sword, blue-white sparks streaming everywhere. But it was too quick. The blow glanced off, and it snapped at her left wrist, at the hand that held the bell. Its jaws met her armored sleeve, and black-red flames burst out between its needle-like teeth.

Then the Dog fastened her own jaws on the creature's middle and twisted it off Lirael's arm, the hound's bloodcurdling growl adding to the sound of the thing squealing and Lirael's scream.

A moment later all were drowned in the deep sound of Saraneth as Lirael stepped back, flipped the bell, caught the handle, and rang it, all in one smooth motion.

CHAPTER EIGHT

THE TESTING OF SAMETH

SAM WALKED AROUND his small perimeter again, checking to make sure nothing was approaching. Not that he could see much through the rain and the foliage. Or hear anything, for that matter, till it would be too close for him to do anything but fight.

He checked Lirael again for any sign of change, but she remained in Death, her body still as a statue, rimed with ice, cold billowing out to freeze the puddles at her feet. Sam thought about breaking off a piece of ice to cool himself down but decided against it. There were several large Dog footprints in the middle of the frozen puddle, for the Disreputable Dog—unlike her mistress—was able to bodily cross into Death, confirming Sam's guess that her physical form was entirely magical.

The Guard's body was still propped up against

the tree as well. Sam had considered laying her out properly, but that seemed stupid when it meant putting her body down into the mud. He wanted to give her body a proper ending, too, but didn't dare use the Charter Magic required. Not until Lirael came back, at least.

Sam sighed at that thought and wished he could shelter out of the rain against the tree until Lirael did return. But he was acutely aware that he was responsible for Lirael's safety. He was alone again, in effect, now without even the dubious companionship of Mogget. It made him nervous, but the fear that had been with him all through his flight from Belisaere was gone. This time he simply didn't want to let Aunt Lirael down. So he hefted his sword and began once again to walk around the tight ring of trees he'd selected as his patrol route.

He was halfway around when he heard something above the steady sound of the rain. The soggy snap of wet twigs breaking underfoot, or something like it. A sound out of keeping for the forest.

Immediately, Sam knelt down behind the checkered trunk of a large fern and froze, so he could hear better.

At first, all he heard was the rain and his own beating heart. Then he caught the sound again. A

soft footfall, leaves crushed underfoot. Someone—
or something—was trying to sneak up on him. The
sounds were about twenty feet away, lower down
the slope, hidden by all the green undergrowth.
Coming closer very slowly, just a single pace every
minute or so.

Sam glanced back at Lirael. There was no sign
of her returning from Death. For a moment, he
thought he should run and tap her on the shoulder,
to alert her to come back. It was very tempting,
because then she could take charge.

He dismissed the thought. Lirael had a task to
do, and so did he. There would be time enough to
call her back if he had to. Perhaps it was only a big
lizard crawling up between the ferns, or a wild dog,
or one of those large black flightless birds that he
knew lived in these mountains. He couldn't remember what they were called.

It wasn't anything Dead. He would have sensed
it for sure, he thought. A Free Magic creature
would be sizzling from the rain, and he'd smell it.
Probably . . .

It moved again, but not uphill. It was circling
around, Sam realized. Perhaps trying to work its
way past them to attack down the slope. That would
be a human trick.

It could be a necromancer, said a fearful part of Sam's mind.

Not Dead, so you couldn't sense it. Wielding Free Magic, but not of it, so you couldn't smell anything. It could even be *him*. It could be Hedge.

Sam's sword hand began to tremble. He gripped the hilt tighter, made the trembling stop. The burn scars on his wrists grew livid, bright with the effort.

This is it, he told himself. This was the test. If he didn't face whatever was out there now, he would know he was a coward forever. Lirael didn't think he was, nor the Dog. He had run from Astarael, but not out of fear. He had been made to by magic, and Lirael had run, too. There was no shame in that.

It moved again, slinking closer. Sam still couldn't see it, but he was sure he knew where it was.

He reached into the Charter and felt his heart slow from a frantic pace as he was embraced by the familiar calm of the magic that linked all living things. Drawing in the air with his free hand, Sam called forth four bright Charter marks. The fifth he spoke under his breath, into his cupped hand. When the marks joined, Sam held a dagger that was like a sunbeam caught in his hand. Too bright to look at directly, but golden at a glance.

"For the Charter!"

Sun dagger in one hand, sword in the other, Sam roared a battle cry and leapt forward, crashing through the ferns, slipping in the mud, half-falling down the slope. He saw a flash of movement behind a tree and changed direction, still roaring, his father's berserker blood beating in his temples. There was the enemy, a strange pallid little man—

Who disappeared.

Sam tried to stop. He dug his heels in, but his feet skidded in the mud and he ran straight into a tree trunk, rebounded into a fern, and fell flat on his back. Down in the mud, he remembered his arms master telling him, "Most who go down in a battle never get up again. So don't bloody well fall down!"

Sam dropped the sun dagger, which was extinguished immediately, the individual marks melting into the ground, and pushed himself up. He had been down for only a second or two, he thought, as he stared wildly around. But there was no sign of the . . . whatever it was. . . .

Lirael.

The thought struck him like a blow, and instantly he was running up the slope he'd just careered down, grabbing at ferns and branches and anything that could make him go faster. He had to get back! What if Lirael was attacked while she was still in Death? Struck from behind with a dagger, or a knife? She wouldn't have a chance.

He made it back to the small clearing. Lirael still stood there. Icicles made from raindrops hung from her outstretched arms. The frozen pool around her feet had spread, so strange in this warm forest. She was unharmed.

"Lucky I was here," said a voice behind Sam. A familiar voice.

Mogget's voice.

Sam whirled around.

"Mogget? Is that you? Where are you?"

"Here, and regretting it as per usual," replied Mogget, and a small white cat sauntered out from behind a fern tree.

Sam did not relax his guard. He could see that Mogget still wore his collar, and there was a bell on it. But it could be a trick. And where . . . or who . . . was that strange pale man?

"I saw a man," said Sam. "His hair and skin were white, white as snow. White as your fur . . ."

"Yes," yawned Mogget. "That was me. But that shape was forbidden to me by Jerizael, who was . . . let me see . . . she was the forty-eighth Abhorsen. I cannot use it in the presence of an

Abhorsen, even an apprentice, without prior permission. Your mother does not generally give me permission, though her father was more flexible. Lirael cannot currently say yea or nay, so once again you see me as I am."

"The Dog said that she . . . Astarael . . . wasn't going to let you go," said Sam. He had not lowered his sword.

Mogget yawned again, and the bell rang on his neck. It *was* Ranna—Sam recognized both the voice and his own reaction: he couldn't help yawning himself.

"Is that what that hound said?" remarked the cat as he padded over to Sam's pack and delicately sliced open half the stitches on the patch with one sharp claw so he could climb in. "Astarael? Is that who it was? It's been so long, I can't really remember who was who. In any case, she said what she wanted to say, and then I left. Wake me up when we're somewhere dry and comfortable, Prince Sameth. With civilized food."

Sam slowly lowered his sword and sighed in exasperation. It clearly was Mogget. Sam just wasn't sure if he was pleased or not that the cat had returned. He kept remembering that gloating chuckle in the tunnel below the House, and the stench and dazzle of Free Magic. . . .

Ice cracked. Sam whirled about again, his heart hammering. With the cracking of the ice, he heard the echo of a distant bell. So distant it might have been a memory, or an imagined <u>sound</u>.

More ice cracked, and Lirael fell to one knee, ice flaking off her like a miniature snowstorm. Then there was a bright flash, and the Dog appeared, jumping around anxiously and growling deep in her chest.

"What happened?" asked Sam. "Are you hurt?"

"Not really," said Lirael, with a grimace that showed there was something wrong, and she held up her left wrist. "Some horrible little Fifth Gate Rester tried to bite my arm. But it didn't get through the coat—it's only bruised."

"What did you do to it?" asked Sam. The Dog was still running around as if the Dead creature might suddenly appear.

"The Dog bit it in half," said Lirael, forcing herself to take several long, slow breaths. "Though that didn't stop it. But I made it obey me in the end. It's on its way to the Ninth Gate—and it won't be coming back."

"You really are the Abhorsen-in-Waiting now,"

said Sam, admiration showing in his voice.

"I guess I am," replied Lirael slowly. She felt as if she'd claimed something when she'd announced herself as such in Death. And lost something, too. It was one thing to take up the bells at the House. It was another to actually use the bells in Death. Her old life seemed so far away now. Gone forever, and she did not yet know what her new life would be, or even what she was. She felt uncomfortable in her own skin, and it had nothing to do with the melting ice, or the rain and mud.

"I can smell something," announced the Dog.

Lirael looked up and for the first time noticed that Sam was much muddier than he had been, and was bleeding from a scratch across the back of his hand, though he didn't appear to have noticed it.

"What happened to you?" she asked sharply.

"Mogget came back," replied Sam. "At least I think it's Mogget. He's in my pack. Only at first he was a sort of really short albino man and I thought he was an enemy—"

He stopped talking as the Dog prowled over to his pack and sniffed at it. A white paw flashed out, and the Dog jerked back just in time to avoid a clawed nose. She settled back on her haunches, and her forehead furrowed in puzzlement.

"It is the Mogget," she confirmed. "But I don't understand—"

"She gave me what she chooses to call another chance," said a voice from inside the pack. "More than you've ever done."

"Another chance at what?" growled the Dog. "This is no time for your games! Do you know what is being dug up four leagues from here?"

Mogget thrust his head out of the pack. Ranna jangled, sending a wave of weariness across all who heard the bell.

"I know!" spat the little cat. "I didn't care then and I don't care now. It is the Destroyer! The Unmaker! The Unraveler—"

Mogget paused for breath. Just as he was about to speak again, the Dog suddenly barked, a short, sharp bark infused with power. Mogget yowled as if his tail had been trodden on and sank hissing back into the pack.

"Do not speak Its name," ordered the Dog. "Not in anger, not when we are so close."

Mogget was silent. Lirael, Sam, and the Dog looked at the pack.

"We have to get away from here." Lirael sighed,

wiping the most recent raindrops off her forehead before they could get into her eyes. "But first I want to get something straight."

She approached Sam's pack and leaned over it, careful to stay out of striking distance of a paw.

"Mogget. You are still bound to be a servant of the Abhorsens, aren't you?"

"Yes," came the grudging reply. "Worse luck."

"So you will help me, help us, won't you?"

There was no answer.

"I'll find you some fish," interjected Sam. "I mean, when we're somewhere where there are fish."

"And a couple of mice," added Lirael. "If you like mice, that is."

Mice chewed books. All librarians disliked mice, and Lirael was no exception. She was quite pleased to discover that becoming an Abhorsen had not removed that essential part of the librarian in her. She still hated silverfish as well.

"There is no point bargaining with the creature," said the Dog. "He will do as he is told."

"Fish when available, and mice, and a songbird," said Mogget, emerging from the pack, his little pink tongue tasting the air as if the fish were even now in front of him.

"No songbird," said Lirael firmly.

"Very well," agreed Mogget. He cast a disdainful glance at the Dog. "A civilized agreement, and in keeping with my current form. Food and lodging in return for what help I care to offer. Better than being a slave."

"You are a—" the Dog began hotly, but Lirael grabbed her collar and she subsided, growling.

"There's no time for bickering," said Lirael. "Hedge let Mareyn—the Guard—go, intending to enslave her spirit later—a slow death makes for a more powerful spirit. He knows roughly where she died, and he may have had other servants in Death who will report my presence. So we need to get going."

"We should . . ." Sam began as Lirael started to walk off. "We have to give her a proper ending."

Lirael shook her head, a diagonal motion that was neither agreement nor refusal, but simply weariness.

"I must be tired," she said, wiping her brow again. "I promised her I would."

Like the bodies of the merchant party, Mareyn's body, if left here, could become inhabited by another Dead spirit, or Hedge might be able to use it for even worse things.

"Can you do it, Sam?" Lirael asked, rubbing her wrist. "I'm a bit worn out, to be honest."

"Hedge may smell the magic," warned the Dog. "As may any Dead creatures that are close enough. Though the rain will help."

"I've already cast a spell," said Sam apologetically. "I thought we were being attacked—"

"Don't worry," interrupted Lirael. "But hurry."

Sam went over to the body and drew the Charter marks in the air. A few seconds later, a white-hot shroud of fire enveloped the body, and soon there was nothing left for any necromancer save the blackened rings of mail.

Sam turned to go then, but Lirael stepped forward, and three simple Charter marks fell from her open hand into the bark of the tree above the ashes. She spoke to the marks, placing her words there for any Charter Mage to hear in the years ahead, for as long as the tree might stand.

"Mareyn died here, far from home and friends. She was a Royal Guard. A brave woman, who fought against a foe too strong for her. But even in Death she did her duty and more. She will be remembered. Farewell, Mareyn."

"A fitting gesture," said the Dog. "And a—"

"Fairly stupid one," interrupted Mogget, from

behind Sam's head. "We'll have the Dead down on us in minutes if you keep doing all this magic."

"Thank you, Mogget," said Lirael. "I'm glad you're helping us already. We are leaving now, so you can go back to sleep. Dog—please scout ahead. Sam—follow me."

Without waiting for an answer, she struck off up towards the ridgeline, heading for a point where the trees clustered more thickly together. The Dog ran up behind her, then slipped around to get ahead, her tail wagging.

"Bossy, isn't she?" remarked Mogget to Sam, who was following more slowly. "Reminds me of your mother."

"Shut up," said Sam, pushing aside a branch that threatened to slap him in the face.

"You do know that we should be running as fast as we can in the other direction," said Mogget. "Don't you?"

"You told me before, back at the House, that's there's no point running away or trying to hide," snapped Sam. "Didn't you?"

Mogget didn't answer, but Sam knew he hadn't fallen asleep. He could feel the cat moving around in his pack. Sam didn't repeat his question, because the slope was becoming steeper and he needed all his breath. Any thoughts of conversation quickly slipped away as they climbed farther, weaving between the trees and over fallen logs, torn out of the hillside by the wind and their inability to set deep roots.

At last they reached the ridge, sodden despite their oilskins, and wretchedly tired from the climb. The sun, lost somewhere in cloud, was not far off setting, and it was clear they couldn't go much farther before nightfall.

Lirael thought of calling a rest, but when she gestured at the Dog, the hound ignored her, pretending she couldn't see the frantic hand signals. Lirael sighed and followed, thankful that the Dog had turned to the west and was following the ridge now, instead of climbing down. They kept on for another thirty minutes or so, though it felt like hours, till at last they came to a point where a landslide had carved out a great swathe of open ground down the northern face of the ridge.

The Dog stopped there, choosing a stand of ferns that would shelter them. Lirael sat down next to her, and Sam staggered in a minute later and collapsed like a broken concertina. As he sat, Mogget climbed out of his pack and stood on his hind legs, using Sam's head as a rest for his two front paws.

The four of them looked down through the clearing, out and along the valley, all the way to the Red Lake, a dull expanse of water in the distance, lit by flashes of lightning and what little of the setting sun made it through the cloud.

Nick's pit was clearly visible, too, an ugly wound of red dirt and yellow clay in the green of the valley. The land around it was constantly struck by lightning, the boom of the thunder rolling back to the four watchers, a constant background noise. Hundreds of figures, made tiny by the distance, toiled around the pit. Even from a few miles away, Lirael and Sam could feel that they were the Dead.

"What are the Hands doing?" whispered Lirael. Though they were hidden high on the ridge amongst the trees and ferns, she still felt that they were on the verge of detection by Hedge and his servants.

"I can't tell," replied Sam. "Moving something—that glittering thing—I think. Towards the lake."

"Yes," said the Dog, who was standing absolutely stiff next to Lirael. "They are dragging two silver hemispheres, three hundred paces apart."

Behind Sam's ear, Mogget hissed, and Sam felt a shudder run down his spine.

"Each hemisphere imprisons one half of an

ancient spirit," said the Dog. Her voice was very low. "A spirit from the Beginning, from before the Charter was made."

"The one you said to Mogget not to name," whispered Lirael. "The Destroyer."

"Yes," said the Dog. "It was imprisoned long ago, and trapped within the silver hemispheres; and the hemispheres were buried deep beneath wards of silver, gold, and lead; rowan, ash, and oak; and the seventh ward was bone."

"So it's still bound?" whispered Sam urgently. "I mean, they might have dug up the hemispheres, but it's still bound inside them, isn't it?"

"For now," said the Dog. "But where the prison fails, little hope can be placed in the bonds. Someone must have found a way to join the hemispheres, though I cannot guess how, and where they are taking them. . . ."

"I am sorry to have failed you, Mistress," she added, sinking down on her belly, her chin digging into the ground with misery.

"What?" asked Lirael, looking down at the dejected Dog. For a moment she couldn't think of anything to say. Then she felt a little voice inside her ask, "What would an Abhorsen do?" and she knew that she must be what she was supposed to be. Undaunted, even though she felt exactly the opposite.

"What are you talking about? It's not your fault."

Her voice trembled for a second, but she disguised it with a cough before continuing.

"Besides, the . . . the Destroyer is still bound. We'll just have to stop those hemispheres joining or whatever it is Hedge plans to do with them."

"We should rescue Nick," said Sam. He swallowed audibly, then added, "Though there's an awful lot of Dead down there."

"That's it!" exclaimed Lirael. "That's what we can do to start with, anyway. Nick will know exactly where they plan to take the hemispheres."

"She plans like your mother, too," said Mogget. "What are we supposed to do? Walk down there and ask Hedge to hand over the boy?"

"Mogget—" Sam started to say, and the Dog growled, but Lirael spoke over them. A plan of sorts had come to mind, and she wanted to get it out before it started to sound hopeless even to her.

"Don't be silly, Mogget. We'll rest for a while; then I'll put on the Charter-skin I made on the boat and fly down as an owl. The Dog can fly down, too, and between both of us, we'll find Nick and sneak him away. You and Sam can follow us down, and we'll rendezvous near running water—that stream over there. By then we'll have daylight and running water, and we can find out what's happening from Nick. What do you think?"

"That is only the fourth-most stupid plan I have ever heard from an Abhorsen," replied Mogget. "I like the part about sleeping for a while, though you neglected to mention dinner."

"I'm not sure you should be the one to fly down," said Sam uncomfortably. "I'm sure I could get the hang of the owl shape, and I might be better able to convince Nick to come with us. And how can the Dog fly?"

"There won't be any convincing required," growled the Dog. "Your friend Nick must be largely a creature of the Destroyer. He will have to be compelled—and we must be wary of him and any powers he may have been granted. As to flying, I just make myself smaller and grow some wings."

"Oh," said Sam. "Of course. Grow some wings."

"We'll have to watch out for Hedge, too," added Lirael, who was belatedly wondering if perhaps there wasn't a better plan after all. "But it will have to be me who uses the Charter-skin. I made it to my size—it wouldn't fit you. I hope it isn't too crumpled in my pack."

"It'll take me at least two hours to get down to that creek—since I can't fly," said Sam, looking down the ridge. "Perhaps we should all go on later tonight; then you can fly from there. That way I'll be closer and ready immediately if there's any trouble. And you could lend me your bow, so I can spell some arrows while I'm waiting."

"Good idea," said Lirael. "We should go on. But the bow won't be much use if it keeps raining—and I don't think we can risk any more weather magic to stop it. That will give us away for sure."

"It'll stop before dawn," said the Dog with great authority.

"Humph," replied Mogget. "Anyone could have told them that. It's stopping now, for that matter."

Sam and Lirael looked up through the canopy of the trees, and sure enough, though the storm to the northwest was constant, the clouds above and to the east were parting to show the fading red wash of the sun and the first star of the night. It was Uallus, the red star that showed the way north. Lirael was heartened to see it, though she knew it was only a shepherd's tale that said Uallus granted luck if it was the first star in the sky.

"Good," said Lirael. "I hate flying in the rain. Wet feathers are a pain."

Sam didn't answer. It was getting dark, but the lightning around the pit made it possible to make out some things down in the valley in a sort of stop-start way. There was a square-shaped blob that could easily be a tent. Presumably Nick's tent, for there were no others visible.

"Hang on, Nick," whispered Sam. "We'll save you."

FIRST INTERLUDE

TOUCHSTONE'S HAND CLASPED Sabriel's shoulder as they lay under the car. Neither of them could hear after the explosion, and they were dazed from the shock. Many of their guards were dead around them, and their eyes could not process the dreadful human wreckage that surrounded them. In any case, they were intent on their would-be assassins. They could see their feet approaching, and their laughter sounded muffled and distant, like noisy neighbors on the other side of a wall.

Touchstone and Sabriel crawled forward, their pistols in their hands. The two guards who had also made it under the car crawled forward, too. One was Veran, Sabriel saw, still clutching her pistol despite the blood that ran down her hands. The other survivor was the oldest of all the guards,

Barlest, his grizzled hair stained and no longer white. He had a machine rifle and was readying it to fire.

The assassins saw the movement, but it was too late. The four survivors fired almost at the same time, and the laughter was drowned in an assault of sudden gunfire. Empty brass cartridges rattled on the underside of the car, and acrid smoke billowed out between the wheels.

"To the boat!" shouted Barlest to Sabriel, gesturing behind him. She couldn't hear him properly at first, till he had shouted it three times: "Boat! Boat! Boat!"

Touchstone heard it, too. He looked at Sabriel, and she saw the fear in his eyes. But it was fear for her, she knew, not for himself. She gestured back towards the lane that ran between the houses behind them. That would take them to Larnery Square and the Warden Steps. They had boats there, and more guards disguised as river traders. Damed had carefully prepared several escape routes, but this was the closest. As in everything, he had thought only of the safety of his King and Queen.

"Go!" shouted Barlest. He had changed the drum on his automatic rifle, and he began firing short bursts to the right and left, forcing any of their attackers who had made it back to cover to keep their heads down.

Touchstone gripped Barlest's shoulder for a brief, final moment, then wriggled around and moved across to the other side of the car. Sabriel crawled next to him, and they briefly touched hands. Veran, next to her, took a deep breath and hurled herself out, leaping to her feet and running the second she was clear of the car. She got to the lane, crouched behind a fire hydrant, and covered Sabriel and Touchstone as they followed. But for the moment there were no shots apart from the disciplined bursts from Barlest, still under the car.

"Come on!" roared Touchstone, turning at the entrance to the lane. But Barlest did not come, and Veran grabbed Touchstone and Sabriel and pushed them down the lane, shouting, "Go! Go!"

They heard Barlest shout a battle cry behind them, heard his footsteps as he charged out from under the car on the opposite side. There was one long shuddering burst of automatic fire and several louder, single shots. Then there was silence, save for the clattering of their own boots on the cobbles, the pant of their labored breaths, and the beating of their hearts.

Larnery Square was empty. The central garden,

usually the habitat of nannies and babies, was completely devoid of life. The explosion had probably happened only a few minutes ago, but that was enough. There had been plenty of trouble in Corvere since the rise of Corolini and his Our Country thugs, and the ordinary citizens had learned when to retreat quickly from the streets.

Touchstone, Sabriel, and Veran ran grimly through the square and clattered down the Warden Steps on the far side. A drunken bargeman saw them, three gun-wielding figures splattered in blood and worse, and was not so drunk that he got in the way. He cowered to one side, hunching himself into as small a ball as possible.

The Sethem River flowed dirtily past the short quay at the end of the steps. A man dressed in the oilskin thigh boots and assorted rags of a tide dredger stood there, his hands inside a barrel that he'd presumably just salvaged from the muddy river flats. As he heard the clatter on the stairs, his hands came out holding a sawed-off shotgun, the hammers cocked.

"Querel! A rescue!" shouted Veran.

The man carefully decocked the shotgun, pulled a whistle out from under his many-patched shirt and blew it several times. There was an answering whistle, and several more Royal Guards leapt up from a boat that was out of sight beneath the quay, the river being at low tide. All the guards were armed and expecting trouble, but from their expressions none expected what they saw.

"An ambush," exclaimed Touchstone quickly as they approached. "We must be away at once."

Before he could say any more, many hands grabbed him and Sabriel and practically threw them onto the deck of the waiting boat, Veran jumping on after them. The craft, a converted river tramp, was six or seven feet below the quay, but there were more hands to catch them. Even as they were hustled into the heavily sandbagged cabin, the engine was going from a slow idle to a heavy throb and the boat was shuddering into motion.

Sabriel and Touchstone looked at each other, reassuring themselves that they were still alive and relatively unhurt, though they were both bleeding from small shrapnel cuts.

"That is it," said Touchstone quietly, setting his pistol down on the deck. "I am done with Ancelstierre."

"Yes," said Sabriel. "Or it is done with us. We will not find any help here now."

Touchstone sighed and, taking up a cloth, wiped

the blood from Sabriel's face. She did the same for him; then they stood and briefly embraced. Both were shaking, and they did not try to disguise it.

"We had best see to Veran's wounds," said Sabriel as they let go of each other. "And plot a course to take us home."

"Home!" confirmed Touchstone, but even that word wasn't said without both of them feeling an unspoken fear. Close as they had come to death today, they feared their children would face even greater dangers, and as both of them knew so well, there were far worse fates than simple death.

PART
TWO

CHAPTER NINE

A DREAM OF OWLS
AND FLYING DOGS

NICK WAS DREAMING the dream again, of the Lightning Farm, and the hemispheres coming together. Then the dream suddenly changed, and he seemed to be lying on a bed of furs in a tent. There was the slow beat of rain on the canvas above his head, and the sound of thunder, and the whole tent was lit by the constant flicker of lightning.

Nick sat up and saw an owl perched on his traveling chest, looking at him with huge, golden eyes. And there was a dog sitting next to his bed. A black and tan dog not much bigger than a terrier, with huge feathery wings growing out of its shoulders.

At least it's a different dream, part of him thought. He had to be almost awake, and this was one of those dream fragments that precede total wakefulness, where reality and fantasy mix. It was his tent, he knew, but an owl and a winged dog!

I wonder what that means, Nick thought, blinking his dream eyes.

Lirael and the Disreputable Dog watched him look at them, his eyes sleepy but still full of a fevered brightness. His hand clutched at his chest, fingers curled as if to scratch at his heart. He blinked twice, then shut his eyes and lay back on the furs.

"He really is sick," whispered Lirael. "He looks terrible. And there's something else about him . . . I can't tell properly in this shape. A wrongness."

"There is something of the Destroyer in him," growled the Dog softly. "A sliver of one of the silver hemispheres, most like, infused with a fragment of its power. It is eating away at him, body and spirit. He is being used as the Destroyer's avatar. A mouthpiece. We must not awaken this force inside him."

"How do we get him out without doing that?" asked Lirael. "He doesn't even look strong enough to leave his bed, let alone walk."

"I can walk," protested Nick, opening his eyes and sitting up again. Since this was his dream, surely he could participate in the conversation between the winged dog and the talking owl. "Who is the Destroyer, and what's this about eating away at me? I just have a bad influenza or something.

"Makes me hallucinate," he added. "And have vivid dreams. A winged dog! Hah!"

"He thinks he's dreaming," said the Dog. "That's good. The Destroyer will not rise in him unless it feels threatened or there is Charter Magic close. Be careful not to touch him with your Charter-skin, Mistress!"

"Can't have an owl sit on my head," giggled Nick dreamily. "Or a dog, neither."

"I bet he can't get up and get dressed," Lirael said archly.

"I can so," replied Nick, immediately swiveling his legs across and sliding out of bed. "I can do anything in a dream. Anything at all."

Staggering a little, he took off his pajamas, unconscious of any need for modesty in front of his dream creatures, and stood there, stark naked. He looked very thin, Lirael thought, and was surprised to feel a pang of concern. You could see his ribs—and everything else for that matter. "See?" he said. "Up and dressed."

"You need some more clothes," suggested Lirael. "It might rain again."

"I've got an umbrella," declared Nick. Then his face clouded. "No—it broke. I'll get my coat."

Humming to himself, he crossed to the chest

and reached for the lid. Lirael, surprised, flew away just in time and went to perch on the vacated bed.

"The Owl and the Pussycat went . . ." sang Nick as he pulled out underwear, trousers, and a long coat and put them on, bypassing a shirt. "Except I've got it wrong in my dream . . . because you're not a pussycat. You're . . . a . . .

"A winged dog," he finished, reaching out to touch the Disreputable Dog on the nose. The solidity of that touch seemed to surprise him, and the fever flush deepened on his face.

"Am I dreaming?" he said suddenly, slapping himself in the face. "I'm not, am I? I'm . . . only . . . going . . . mad."

"You're not mad," soothed Lirael. "But you are sick. You have a fever."

"Yes, yes, I do," agreed Nick fretfully, feeling his sweaty forehead with the back of his hand. "Must go back to bed. Hedge said, before he went to get the other barge."

"No," Lirael commanded, her voice strangely loud from the owl's small beak. Hearing that Hedge was absent made her certain they must seize this opportunity. "You need fresh air. Dog—can you make him walk? Like you did the crossbowman?"

"Perhaps," growled the Dog. "I feel several forces at work within him, and even a fragment of the bound Destroyer is a power to be reckoned with. It will also alert the Dead."

"They're still dragging the hemispheres to the lake," said Lirael. "They'll take a while to get here. So I think you'd better do it."

"I'm going back to bed," declared Nick, holding his head in his hands. "And the sooner I get home to Ancelstierre, the better."

"You're not going back to bed," growled the Dog, advancing upon him. "You're coming for a walk!"

With that word, she barked, a bark so deep and loud that the tent shook, poles quivering in resonance. Lirael felt the force of it strike her, ruffling her feathers. It sent sparks flying off her, too, as the Free Magic fought the Charter marks of her altered shape.

"Follow me!" ordered the Dog as she turned and left the tent. Nick took three steps after her but paused at the entrance, clutching at a canvas flap.

"No, no, I can't," he muttered, his muscles moving in weird spasms under the skin of his neck and hands. "Hedge told me to stay. It's best I stay."

The Dog barked again, louder, the noise carrying even above the constant thunder. A corona of sparks flared about Lirael, and the discarded pajamas under her claws suddenly caught fire, forcing her to fly out of the tent.

Nick shuddered and twisted as the force of the bark hit him. He fell to his knees and began to crawl out of the tent, groaning and calling out to Hedge. Lirael circled above him, looking to the west.

"Stand," commanded the Dog. "Walk. Follow me."

Nick stood, took several steps, then froze in place. His eyes rolled back, and tendrils of white smoke began to drift out of his open mouth.

"Mistress!" shouted the Dog. "The fragment wakes within him! You must resume your form and quell it with the bells!"

Lirael dropped like a stone, instantly calling up the Charter marks to unravel the owl skin she wore. But not before her huge golden owl eyes had cut through the lightning-laced night to where the Dead toiled to move the silver hemispheres. Hundreds of Dead Hands were already throwing down their ropes and turning towards the tent. A moment later they began to run, the massed sound of hundreds of dried-out joints clicking in a ghastly undercurrent to the thunder. The Hands at the front fought one another to get past, as they were drawn by the lure of magic and the promise of a rich life for the taking. Life to assuage their eternal hunger.

The Dog barked again as the smoke rose from Nick's nose, but it seemed to have little effect. Lirael could only watch the white smoke coil, as she was momentarily caught within a shining tornado of light, while the Charter-skin spun back into its component marks.

Then she was there in her own form, hands reaching for Saraneth and Nehima. But something else was there, too, some presence that burned inside Nick, filling him with an internal glow that set the raindrops sizzling as they touched his skin. The hot-metal stench of Free Magic rolled off him in a wave as a voice that was not Nicholas's came out of his mouth, accompanied by puffs of white smoke.

"How dare— Ah . . . I should have expected you, meddler, and one of your sister's get—"

"Quick, Lirael," shouted the Dog. "Ranna and Saraneth together, with my bark!"

"To me, my servants!" shouted the voice from

Nick, a voice far louder and more horrible than could come from any human throat. It carried even over the thunder, rolling out across the valley. All the Dead heard, even those who still labored stupidly on the ropes, and they all hurried, a tide of rotten flesh that flowed around both sides of the pit, rushing towards the beacon of the burning tent, where their ultimate Master called.

Others heard it, too, though they were farther away than any sound could carry. Hedge cursed and turned aside to slay an unlucky horse, so that he could make a mount that would not shy to carry him. Many leagues to the east, Chlorr turned away from the riverbank near Abhorsen's House and began to run, a great shape of fire and darkness that moved faster than any human legs could take her.

Lirael dropped her sword and drew Ranna, so hastily the bell tinkled briefly and a wave of tiredness washed across her. Her wrist still hurt from her encounter in Death, but neither pain nor Ranna's protest were enough to stop her. The relevant pages from *The Book of the Dead* shone in her mind, showing her what to do. So she did it, joining Ranna's gentle sound with Saraneth's deep strength, and with them the imperative sharp bark of the Dog.

The sound wrapped around Nick, and the voice that spoke from him was dampened. But a raging will fought against the spell, a will that Lirael could feel pushing against her, fighting against the combined powers of bell and bark. Then suddenly that resistance snapped, and Nick fell to the ground, the white smoke retreating rapidly back into his nose and throat.

"Hurry! Hurry! Get him up!" urged the Dog. "Cut south and head for the rendezvous. I'll hold them off here!"

"But—Ranna and Saraneth—he'll be asleep," protested Lirael as she put the bells away and hauled Nick upright. He was much lighter than she expected, even lighter than he looked. Obviously he was worn to the bone.

"No, only the shard within him sleeps," said the Dog rapidly. She had absorbed her wings and was growing to her combat size. "Slap him—and run!"

Lirael obeyed, though she felt cruel. The slap stung her palm, but it certainly woke Nick up. He yelped, looked around wildly, and struggled against

Lirael's grip on his arm.

"Run!" she commanded, dragging him along, with a momentary pause to pick up Nehima. "Run—or I'll stick you with this."

Nick looked at her, the burning tent, the Dog, and the onrushing horde of what he thought of as diseased workers, his face blank with shock and amazement. Then he started running, obeying Lirael's push on his arm to make him head south.

Behind them, the Dog stood in the light of the fire, a grim shadow now easily five feet tall at the shoulder. The Charter marks that ran in her collar glowed eerily with their own colors, stronger than the red and yellow blaze of the burning tent. Free Magic pulsed under the collar, and red flames dripped like saliva from her mouth.

The first mass of Dead Hands saw her and slowed, uncertain of what she was and how dangerous she might be.

Then the Disreputable Dog barked, and the Dead Hands shrieked and howled as a power they knew and feared gripped them, a Free Magic assault that made them shuck their putrescent bodies . . . and forced them to walk back into Death.

But for every one that fell, there were another dozen charging forward, their grasping, skeletal hands ready to grip and tear, their broken, grave-bleached teeth anxious to bite into any flesh, magical or not.

CHAPTER TEN

PRINCE SAMETH AND HEDGE

LIRAEL WAS HALFWAY back to the rendezvous with Sam when Nick fell and could not get up. His face was blotched with fever and exertion, and he could not get his breath. He lay on the ground looking up at her dumbly, as if waiting for execution.

Which was probably what it looked like, she realized, since she was standing above him with a naked sword held high. Lirael sheathed Nehima and stopped frowning, but she saw that he was too ill and tired to understand that she was trying to reassure him.

"Looks like I'm going to have to carry you," she said, her voice mixed with equal parts of exhaustion and desperation. He wasn't at all heavy, but it was at least half a mile to the stream. And she didn't know how long the shard of the Destroyer or whatever it was in him would stay subdued.

"Why . . . why are you doing this?" croaked Nick as she levered him across her shoulders. "The experiment will go on without me, you know."

Lirael had been taught how to do a fireman's carry back in the Great Library of the Clayr, though she hadn't practiced it in several years. Not since Kemmeru's illicit still had caught fire when Lirael was doing her turn on the librarians' fire brigade. She was pleased she hadn't forgotten the technique, and that Nick was a lot lighter than Kemmeru. Not that it was a fair comparison, as Kemmeru had insisted on being carried out with her favorite books.

"Your friend Sam can explain," puffed Lirael. She could still hear the Dog barking somewhere behind her, which was good, but it was hard to see where she was going, since there was only the soft predawn light, not even strong enough to cast a shadow. It had been much easier crossing this stretch of valley as an owl.

"Sam?" asked Nick. "What's Sam got to do with this?"

"He'll explain," Lirael said shortly, saving her

breath. She looked up, trying to fix her position by Uallus again. But they were still too close to the pit, and all she could see was thunderclouds and lightning. At least it had stopped raining, and the more natural clouds were slowly blowing away.

Lirael kept on going, but with a growing suspicion that she'd somehow veered off the track and was no longer heading in the right direction. She should have paid more attention when she was flying, Lirael thought, when everything had been laid out below her in a beautiful patchwork.

"Hedge will rescue me," Nick whispered weakly, his voice hoarse and strange, particularly since it was coming from somewhere near her belt buckle, as he was draped over her back.

Lirael ignored him. She couldn't hear the Dog anymore, and the ground was getting boggy under her feet, which couldn't be right. But there was a dim mass of something ahead. Bushes perhaps. Maybe the ones that lined the stream where Sam was waiting.

Lirael pressed forward, Nick's extra weight pushing her feet deep into the soggy ground. She could see what lay ahead, now she was close enough and more light trickled in from the rising sun. It was reeds, not bushes. Tall rushes with red flowering heads, the rushes that gave the Red Lake its name, from their pollen that colored the lakeshores with a brilliant scarlet wash.

She'd gone completely the wrong way, Lirael realized. Somehow she must have turned west. Now she was on the shore of the lake, and the Gore Crows would soon find her. Unless, she thought, they couldn't see her. She shifted Nick higher and bent over a little more to balance the load. He groaned in pain, but Lirael ignored him and pressed on into the reeds.

Soon the mud gave way to water, up to her shins. The reeds grew closer together, their flowery heads towering over her. But there was a narrow path where the reeds were beaten down, allowing passage through them. She took the path, winding deeper and deeper into the reedy marsh.

Sam drew another mark out of the endless flow of the Charter and forced it into the arrow he was holding across his knees, watching it spread like oil over the sharp steel of the head. It was the final mark for this arrow. He had already put marks of accuracy and strength into the shaft, marks for flight and luck into the fletching, and marks for unraveling and banishment into the head.

It was the last arrow of twenty, all now spelled to be weapons of great use against the Lesser Dead, at the least. It had taken Sam two hours to do all twenty, and he was a little weary. He was unaware that it would have taken most Charter Mages the better part of a day. Working magic on inanimate objects had always come easily to Sam.

He was doing his work while sitting on the dry end of a half-submerged log that stuck out of the stream. It was a good stream from Sam's point of view, because it was at least fifteen yards wide, very deep, and fast. It could be crossed via the log and jumping across a couple of big stones, but Sam didn't think the Dead would do that.

Sam put the finished arrow back into the quiver built into Lirael's pack and slung that on his back. His own pack was pushed up against the stream bank, with Mogget asleep in the top of it. Though not anymore, Sam noticed, as he bent down to see it more clearly in the predawn light. The patch on the flap had gone completely, and there was no sign of the cat in the top pocket.

Sam looked around carefully, but he couldn't see anything moving, and the light wasn't good enough to see anything standing still or hiding. He couldn't hear anything suspicious either—just the burble of the stream and the distant thunder from the lightning storm around the pit.

Mogget had never slipped off like this before, and Sam trusted the little white cat thing even less than he had before their experience in the strange tunnels under the House. Slowly he took Lirael's bow from its cover and nocked an arrow. His sword was at his side, but with the dawn, it was just light enough to shoot a little way with accuracy. At least across the stream, which Sam had no intention of crossing.

Something moved on the other side. A small, white shape, slinking near the water. It was probably Mogget, Sam thought, peering into the gloom. Probably.

It came closer, and his fingers twitched on the string.

"Mogget?" he whispered, nerves strung as taut as the bow.

"Of course it is, stupid!" said the white shape, leaping nimbly from rock to rock and then to the log. "Save your arrows—you'll need them. There's about two hundred Dead Hands headed this way!"

"What!" exclaimed Sam. "What about Lirael

and Nick? Are they all right?"

"No idea," said Mogget calmly. "I went to see what was happening when our canine companion started to bark. She's heading this way—hotly pursued—but I couldn't see Lirael or your troublesome friend. Ah—I think that's the Disgusting Dog now."

Mogget's words were followed by an enormous splash as the Dog suddenly appeared on the opposite bank and dived into the stream, sending a cascade of water in all directions, but mostly over Mogget.

Then the Dog was next to them, shaking herself so vigorously that Sam had to hold his bow out of the way.

"Quick," she panted. "We need to get out of here! Stay on this side and head downstream!"

As soon as she'd spoken, the Dog was off again, loping easily along beside the stream. Sam leapt off the log, swooped upon his pack, picked it up, and stumbled after the Dog, questions falling out of his mouth as he ran. With Lirael's pack on his back, the bow and an arrow in one hand, and his own pack in the other hand, it took most of his concentration not to fall over and into the stream.

"Lirael . . . and Nick? What . . . can't we

stop . . . got to rearrange all this . . ."

"Lirael went into the reeds, but the necromancer suddenly showed up so I couldn't follow without leading him to her," said the Dog, turning her head back as she ran. "*That's* why we can't wait!"

Sam looked back, too, and immediately fell over his pack and dropped both bow and arrow. As he stumbled to his feet, he saw a wall of Dead Hands lurch to a stop on the other side of the stream, back up near the sunken log. There were hundreds of them, a great dark mass of writhing figures that immediately started to parallel the dog's course on the opposite bank.

In the midst of the Dead Hands, one figure stood out. A man cloaked in red flame, riding a horse that was mostly skeleton, though some flesh still hung on its neck and withers.

Hedge. Sam felt his presence like a shock of cold water, and a sharp pain in his wrists. Hedge was shouting something—perhaps a spell—but Sam didn't hear it because he was scrabbling to pick up the bow and get another arrow. It was still quite dark, and a fair distance, he thought, but not too far for a lucky shot, in the stillness before the dawn.

As quick as that thought, he nocked an arrow and drew. For an instant, his whole concentration was on a line between himself and that shape of fire and darkness.

Then he loosed, and the spelled arrow flew like a blue spark from him. Sam watched it, filled with hope as it sped as true as he could wish, and arrow met necromancer with a blaze of white fire against the red. Hedge fell from his skeleton horse, which reared and then dived forward, smashing through several ranks of Dead Hands to plunge into the water in an explosion of white sparks and high-pitched screaming. Instinctively, it had known how to free itself and die the final death.

"That'll annoy him," said Mogget from somewhere near Sam's feet.

Sam's sudden hope died as he saw Hedge stand up, pluck the arrow from his throat, and throw it on the ground.

"Don't waste another on him," said the Dog. "He cannot be slain by any arrow, no matter the spells laid upon it."

Sam nodded grimly, threw the bow aside, and drew his sword. Though the stream might hold the Dead Hands back, he knew that it would not stop Hedge.

Hedge drew his own sword and walked forward, his Dead Hands parting to make a corridor.

At the edge of the stream the necromancer smiled an open smile, and red fire licked about his teeth. He put one boot in the stream—and smiled again as the water burst into steam.

"Go and help Lirael," Sam ordered the Dog. "I'll hold off Hedge as long as I can. Mogget—will you help me?"

Mogget didn't answer, and he was nowhere to be seen.

"Good luck," said the Dog. Then she was gone, racing along the bank to the west.

Sam took a deep breath and crouched into a defensive stance. This was his worst fear, come into terrible reality. Alone again, and facing Hedge.

Sam reached into the Charter, as much for comfort as to be ready to cast a spell. His breathing steadied as he felt its familiar flow all around him, and almost without thinking he began to draw out Charter marks, whispering their names quietly as they fell into his open hand.

Hedge took another step. He was wreathed in steam now and almost completely obscured, the stream bubbling and roiling both upstream and down. With a shrinking feeling, Sam saw that the necromancer was actually boiling the stream dry. There was already significantly less water below him, the streambed was becoming visible, and the Dead Hands were starting to move.

Hedge wouldn't even have to fight him, Sam thought. All he had to do was stand in the stream, and his Dead Hands would cross and finish Sam off. Though he had the panpipes, Sam didn't know how to use them properly, and there were simply too many Hands.

There was only one thing he could do. Sam would have to attack Hedge in the stream and kill him before the Hands could cross. If he could kill Hedge, a little nagging voice said from deep inside his mind. Wouldn't it be better to run away? Run away before you are burnt again, and your spirit ripped out of your flesh and taken by the necromancer. . . .

Sam buried that thought away, sending the nagging voice so far into the recesses of his mind that it was just a meaningless squeak. Then he let the Charter marks he already held in his hand fall into nothingness, reached into the Charter again, and drew out a whole new string of marks. As he summoned them, Sam hurriedly traced the marks on his legs with a finger. Marks of protection, of reflection, of diversion. They joined and shimmered there, wrapping his legs in Charter Magic armor that would resist the steam and boiling water.

He looked down for only ten, or perhaps fifteen seconds. But when he looked back up, Hedge was gone. The steam was dissipating, and the water was flowing again. The Dead Hands were turning their backs to him and lumbering away, leaving the ground churned up and littered with pieces of rotting flesh and splintered bone.

"Either you were born to a different death, Prince," remarked Mogget, who had appeared at Sam's feet like a newly sprung plant, "or Hedge just found something more important to do."

"Where were you?" asked Sam. He felt strangely deflated. He'd been all ready to plunge into the stream, to fight it out, and now all of a sudden it was just a quiet morning again. The sun was even up, and the birds had resumed their singing. Though only on his side of the stream, Sam noticed.

"Hiding, like any sensible person would when confronted by a necromancer as powerful as Hedge," replied Mogget.

"Is he that powerful?" asked Sam. "You must have encountered many necromancers, serving my mother and the other Abhorsens."

"They didn't have help from the Destroyer,"

said Mogget. "I must say I'm impressed with what it can do, even bound as it is. A lesson for us all, that even trapped inside a lump of silver metal—"

"Where do you think Hedge went?" interrupted Sam, who wasn't really listening.

"Back to those lumps of metal, of course," yawned Mogget. "Or after Lirael. Time for me to have a nap, I think."

Mogget yawned again, then yelped in surprise as Sam grabbed him and shook him, setting Ranna jangling on his collar.

"You have to track the Dog! We have to go and help Lirael!"

"That's no way to ask me." Mogget yawned again, as waves of sleep from Ranna washed over both of them. Sam suddenly found that he was sitting down, and the ground felt so comfortable. All he had to do was lie back and put his hands behind his head. . . .

"No! No!" he protested. Staggering to his feet, he plunged into the stream and pushed his face into the water.

When he climbed out, Mogget was back in his pack. Fast asleep, a wicked grin on his little face.

Sam stared down at him and ran his hands through his dripping hair. The Dog had run off downstream. What had she said? "Lirael went into the reeds."

So if Sam followed the stream to the Red Lake, there was a good chance he'd find Lirael. Or some sign of her, or the Dog. Or Mogget might wake up.

Or Hedge might come back. . . .

Sam didn't want to just sit where he was. Lirael might need his help. Nicholas might need his help. He had to find them. Together, they might survive long enough to do something about this Destroyer trapped in the silver hemispheres. Alone, they could only fail and fall.

Sam packed away Lirael's bow and the dropped arrow. Then he balanced the two packs using a single strap on each shoulder, made sure Mogget would not fall out even though the cat deserved to, and started west, the stream burbling along beside him.

CHAPTER ELEVEN

HIDDEN IN THE REEDS

LIRAEL MORE THAN half-expected to find a boat made of woven reeds, since the Clayr had Seen her and Nicholas in it on the Red Lake. Even so, she was very much relieved when she did stumble across the strange craft, because the water was now well above her thighs. If it had got any deeper, she would have had to turn back or risk Nick's drowning, since she couldn't carry him any other way than the fireman's lift, which put his head about two feet lower than hers.

Carefully, she unloaded him into the center of the canoe-like boat, quickly grabbing the sides as it tipped. The boat was about twice as long as she was tall, but very narrow apart from its midsection—so there would be only just enough room for both of them.

Nick was semiconscious, but he rallied as they

sat quietly in the boat, and Lirael considered her options. The reeds leaned over them, creating a secret bower, and small waterbirds called plaintively nearby, with the occasional splash as one dived after some fishy treat.

Lirael sat with her sword across her lap and a hand on the bell-bandolier, listening. The marsh birds would be happily piping and fishing, then they would suddenly go silent and hide deeper in the reeds. Lirael knew it was because Gore Crows were flying low overhead. She could feel the cold spirit that inhabited them, single-mindedly following the orders of its necromancer master. Searching for her.

The boat was exactly as the Clayr had said it would be, but Lirael felt a strange new fear as she sat rocking in it. This was the limit of the Clayr's vision. They had Seen her here with Nicholas, but no further, and they had not Seen what Nicholas was. Was their Sight limited because this was the end? Was Hedge about to appear through the reeds? Or would the Destroyer emerge from within the slight young man opposite her?

"What are you waiting for?" Nick asked suddenly, showing himself to be more recovered than she'd thought. Lirael jumped as he spoke, setting the boat rocking more violently. Nick's voice was loud, strange in the quiet world of the reeds.

"Silence!" ordered Lirael in a stern whisper.

"Or what?" asked Nick with some bravado. But he spoke more softly, and his eyes were on her sword.

A few seconds passed, then Lirael said, "We're waiting for noon, when the sun is brightest and the Dead are weak. Then we'll head along the lakeshore and, hopefully, make it to a meeting place where your friend Sameth will be."

"The Dead," said Nick with a superior smile. "Some local spirits to appease, I take it? And you mentioned Sam before. What's he got to do with this? Did you kidnap him, too?"

"The Dead . . . are the Dead," replied Lirael, frowning. Sam had mentioned that Nick didn't understand, or even try to comprehend, the Old Kingdom, but this blindness to reality could not be natural. "You have them working in your pit. Hedge's Dead Hands. And no, Sam is working with me to rescue you. You obviously don't understand the danger."

"Don't tell me Sam has fallen back into all this superstition," said Nick. "The Dead, as you call them, are simply poor unfortunates who suffer from something like leprosy. And far from rescuing me, you have taken me away from an important scientific experiment."

"You saw me as an owl," said Lirael, curious to find exactly how blinkered he was. "With the winged dog."

"Hypnosis . . . or hallucinations," replied Nick. "As you can see, I'm not well. Which is another reason I shouldn't be in this . . . this compost heap of a craft."

"Curious," said Lirael thoughtfully. "It must be the thing inside you that has closed your mind. I wonder what purpose that serves."

Nick didn't reply, but he rolled his eyes eloquently enough, obviously dismissing whatever Lirael had to say.

"Hedge will rescue me, you know," he said. "He's a very resourceful chap, and he's just as keen to stay on schedule as I am. So whatever mad belief has seized you, you should give it up and go home. In fact, I'm sure there would be some sort of reward if you returned me."

"A reward?" Lirael laughed, but with bitterness. "A horrible death and eternal servitude? That's the 'reward' for anyone living who goes near Hedge. But tell me—what is your 'experiment' all about?"

"Will you let me go if I tell you?" asked Nick. "Not that it's terribly secret. After all, you won't be publishing in Ancelstierran scientific journals, will you?"

Lirael didn't answer either question. She just looked at him, waiting for him to talk. He met her gaze at first, then faltered and looked away. There was something unnerving about her eyes. A toughness he had never seen in the young women he knew from the debutante parties in Corvere. It was partly this that made him talk, and partly a desire to impress her with his knowledge and intelligence.

"The hemispheres are a previously unknown metal that I postulate has an almost infinite capacity to absorb electrical energy for later discharge," he said, arching his fingers together. "They also create some sort of ionized field that attracts the thunderstorms, which in turn create lightning that is drawn down by the metal. Unfortunately, that ionized field also prevents working of the metal, as steel or iron tools cannot be brought close.

"It is my intention to connect the hemispheres to a Lightning Farm, which a trusted associate of mine is building in Ancelstierre even as we speak.

The Lightning Farm will be composed of a thousand connected lightning rods that will draw down the full electrical force of an entire storm—rather than just a number of strikes—and feed it into the hemispheres. This power will . . . ah . . . repolarize . . . or demagnetize . . . the two hemispheres so they can be brought together as one. This is the ultimate goal. They must be brought together, you see. It is absolutely essential!"

He collapsed back with the last word, his breath coming in ragged gasps.

"How do you know?" asked Lirael. To her it sounded like the sort of waffle used by false seers and charlatan mages, as much to convince themselves as anything.

"I just know," whispered Nick. "I am a scientist. When the hemispheres are in Ancelstierre, I will be able to prove my theories, with proper instruments and proper help."

"Why do the hemispheres have to be brought together?" asked Lirael. That seemed to be the weakest point of his belief, and the most dangerous, for bringing the hemispheres together would make whatever was trapped inside them whole. It was only as she asked it that she realized there was a more important question.

"They have to be," replied Nick, puzzlement showing clearly on his face. Obviously he couldn't think clearly about it at all. "That should be obvious."

"Yes, of course," said Lirael, soothingly. "But I'm curious about how you will get the hemispheres to Ancelstierre. And where exactly is your Lightning Farm? It must be hard to set something like that up. I mean, it would take an awful lot of space."

"Oh, it's not as difficult as you might think," said Nick. He seemed relieved to be moving away from the subject of bringing the hemispheres together. "We'll take the metal down to the sea in barges, and then follow the coast south. Apparently the waters are too disturbed and the weather too foggy as a rule to go all the way by sea. We'll take them ashore just north of the Wall, drag them over that, and then it's only a matter of ten or twelve miles to Forwin Mill, where my Lightning Farm is being built. It should be just about completed by the time we arrive, all being well."

"But . . ." Lirael said, "how will you get them over the Wall? It is a barrier to the Dead and all such things. You won't be able to get the hemi-spheres across the Wall."

"Rubbish!" exclaimed Nick. "You're as bad as Hedge. Except that he at least is prepared to try, provided I let him do some mumbo jumbo first."

"Oh," said Lirael. Obviously Hedge—or more likely his ultimate Master—had found a way to get the hemispheres across the Wall. It had been a vain hope anyway, because Lirael knew Hedge had crossed more than once, and Kerrigor and his army had crossed years ago. She'd just hoped the hemi-spheres would be prevented.

"Won't . . . ah . . . won't you have difficulties with the authorities in Ancelstierre?" Lirael asked hopefully. Sam had told her about the Perimeter the Ancelstierrans had built to stop anything from entering their country from the north. She had no idea what she could do if the hemispheres were taken out of the Old Kingdom.

"No," said Nick. "Hedge says there won't be any trouble he can't handle, but I think he was a bit of a smuggler in the past, and he does have rather unconventional ways. I prefer to work within the law, so I got all the usual customs permits and approvals and so on. Though I admit that they're not for things from the Old Kingdom, because officially there is no Old Kingdom, so there are no forms. I also have a letter from my uncle, granting approval for me to bring across whatever I need for my experiment."

"Your uncle?"

"He's the Chief Minister," Nick replied proudly. "Seventeen years as CM this year—with a three-year break in the middle when the Moderate Reform lot got it. The most successful CM the country has ever had, though of course he's having trouble now, with the continental wars and all the Southerling refugees pouring in. Still, I don't think Corolini and his ragtag bunch will get the numbers to unseat him. He's my mother's oldest brother, and a damn good chap. Always happy to help a deserving nephew."

"Those papers would have burned in your tent," suggested Lirael, clutching at another hope.

"No," said Nick. "Thanks to Hedge again. He suggested I leave them with the fellow who's meeting us over the Wall. Said they'd rot, which in hindsight is absolutely true. Now—are you going to let me go?"

"No," said Lirael. "You're being rescued, whether you like it or not."

"In that case I shan't tell you any more," Nick proclaimed petulantly. He laid himself back down again, rustling against the rushes.

Lirael watched him, thoughts churning in her head. She hoped Ellimere had received Sam's message, and at this moment there might be a strong force of Guards riding to the rescue. Sabriel and Touchstone might also be rushing north from Corvere. They could even be about to cross the Wall.

But all of them would be heading for Edge, while the hemispheres that held the bound thing slipped away—into Ancelstierre, where the ancient spirit of destruction could gain its freedom, free from interference by the only people who understood the danger.

Nick was watching her, too, she realized, as those thoughts clamored in her mind. But not with puzzlement or enmity. He was just looking, tilting his head on the side, with one eye partly closed.

"Pardon me," he said. "I was wondering how you knew Sam. Are you a . . . um . . . a princess? Only, if you're his fiancée or something, I thought I should know. To . . . ah . . . offer my congratulations, as it were. And I don't even know your name."

"Lirael," Lirael replied shortly. "I'm Sam's aunt.

I'm the Ab— Well, let's say I sort of work with Sam's mother, and I also . . . was . . . a Second Assistant Librarian and a Daughter of the Clayr, though I don't expect you know what those titles mean. I'm not at all sure myself at the moment."

"His aunt!" exclaimed Nick, a flush of embarrassment rather than fever coloring his face. "How can you be—I mean, I had no idea. I apologize, ma'am."

"And I'm . . . I'm much older than I look," Lirael added. "In case you were going to ask."

She was a little embarrassed herself, though she couldn't think why. She still didn't know how to talk about her mother. In some ways it was more painful thinking about her now that she knew about her father and how she had come to be conceived. One day, she thought, she would find out exactly what had happened to Arielle, and why she had chosen to go away.

"Wouldn't dream of it," replied Nick. "You know, this sounds stupid, but I feel much better here than I have for weeks. Never would have thought a swamp could be a tonic. I haven't even fainted today."

"You did once," said Lirael. "When we first took you from the tent."

"Did I?" asked Nick. "How embarrassing. I seem to be fainting a lot. Fortunately it tends to be when Hedge is there to catch me."

"Can you tell when you're about to faint?" asked Lirael. She hadn't forgotten the Dog's warning about how long the fragment would be subdued, and she was fairly certain she could not quell it again by herself.

"Usually," said Nick. "I get nauseous first and my eyesight goes peculiar—everything goes red. And something happens to my sense of smell, so I get the sensation of something burning, like an electric motor fusing. But I do feel much better now. Perhaps the fever's broken."

"It isn't a fever," Lirael said wearily. "Though I hope it is better, for both our sakes. Sit still now—I'm going to paddle us out a bit farther. We'll stay in the reeds, but I want to see what's happening on the lake. And please keep quiet."

"Sure," said Nick. "I don't really have a choice, do I?"

Lirael almost apologized, but she held it back. She did feel sorry for Nick. It wasn't his fault he had been chosen by an ancient spirit of evil to be its avatar. She even felt sort of maternal to him. He needed to be tucked in bed and fed willow-bark tea.

That thought led to the idle speculation of what he might look like if he were well. He could be quite handsome, Lirael thought, and then instantly banished the notion. He might be an unwitting enemy, but he was still an enemy.

The reed boat was light, but even so it was hard work paddling with just her hands. Particularly since she also had to keep an eye on Nicholas in case of trouble. But he seemed content to lie back on the high prow of the reed boat. Lirael did catch him looking at her surreptitiously, but he didn't try to escape or call out.

After about twenty minutes of difficult paddling, the reeds began to thin out, the red water paled into pink, and Lirael could see the muddy lake bottom. The sun was well and truly up, so Lirael chanced pushing the boat to the very fringe of the reed marsh so she could look out on the lake but keep hidden.

They were still covered overhead because of the way the reeds leaned into one another. Even so, Lirael was relieved to discover that she couldn't sense any Gore Crows about. Probably because there was a strong current beyond the reedy shores, combined with the bright sun of morning.

Though there were no Gore Crows in sight,

there was something moving out on the surface of the lake. For a second Lirael's heart lifted as she thought it might be Sam, or a force of Guards. Then she realized what it was, just as Nick spoke.

"Look—my barges!" he called, sitting up and waving. "Hedge must have got the other one—and loaded already!"

"Quiet!" hissed Lirael, reaching out to drag him down.

He offered no resistance but suddenly frowned and clutched his chest. "I think . . . I think I was counting my chickens before—"

"Fight it!" interrupted Lirael urgently. "Nick—you have to fight it!"

"I'll try—" Nick began, but he didn't finish his sentence, his head falling back with a dull, reedy thud. His eyes showed white, and Lirael saw a thin tendril of smoke begin to trickle from his nose and mouth.

She slapped him hard across the face.

"Fight it! You're Nicholas Sayre! Tell me who you are!"

Nick's eyes rolled back, though smoke still trickled from his nose.

"I'm . . . I'm Nicholas John Andrew Sayre," he whispered. "I'm Nicholas . . . Nicholas . . ."

"Yes!" urged Lirael. She put her sword down by her side and took his hands, shuddering as she felt the Free Magic coursing in the blood under his cold skin. "Tell me more about yourself, Nicholas John Andrew Sayre! Where were you born?"

"I was born at Amberne, my family home," whispered Nick. His voice grew stronger and the smoke receded. "In the billiard room. No, that's a joke. Mother would kill me for that. I was born all proper for a Sayre, doctor and midwives in attendance. Two midwives, no less, and the society doctor . . ."

Nick closed his eyes, and Lirael gripped his hands tighter.

"Tell me . . . anything!" she demanded.

"The specific gravity of orbilite suspended in quicksilver is . . . I don't know what it is. . . . The snow in Korrovia is confined to the southern Alps, and the major passes are Kriskadt, Jorstschi, and Korbuk. . . . The average blue-tailed plover lays twenty-six eggs in the course of its fifty-four-year lifespan. . . . More than a hundred thousand Southerlings landed illegally in the last year. . . . The chocolate tree is an invention of—"

He stopped suddenly, took a deep breath, and opened his eyes. Lirael kept holding his hands for a moment, but when she saw no sign of smoke or strangeness in his gaze, she dropped them and took up her sword again, resting the blade across her thighs.

"I'm in trouble, aren't I?" said Nick. His voice was unsteady. He looked down at the bottom of the boat, hiding his face, taking very controlled breaths.

"Yes," said Lirael. "But Sameth and I, and the . . . our friends . . . will do the best we can to save you."

"But you don't think you can," said Nicholas softly. "This . . . thing . . . inside me. What is it?"

"I don't know," replied Lirael. "But it is part of some great and ancient evil, and you are helping it to be free. To wreak destruction."

Nick nodded slowly. Then he looked up and met Lirael's gaze.

"It's been like a dream," he said simply. "Most of the time I don't really know whether I'm awake or not. I can't remember things from one minute to the next. I can't think of anything except the hemi—"

He stopped talking. Fear flashed in his eyes and he reached out for Lirael. She took his left hand but kept hold of her sword. If the thing inside him took over and wouldn't let her go, she knew she would have to cut her way free.

"It's okay, it's okay, it's okay," Nick repeated to himself, rocking backwards and forwards as he spoke. "I've got it under control. Tell me what I have to do."

"Keep fighting," Lirael instructed, but she didn't know what else to tell him. "If we can't keep you, then when the time comes, you must do whatever you can to stop . . . to stop it. Promise me you will!"

"I promise," groaned Nick through clenched teeth. "Word of a Sayre. I'll stop it! I will! Talk to me, please, Lirael. I have to think about something else. Tell me . . . tell me . . . where were you born?"

"In the Clayr's Glacier," said Lirael nervously. Nick's grip was tightening, and she didn't like it. "In the Birthing Rooms of the Infirmary. Though some Clayr have their babies in their own rooms, most of us . . . them . . . have their children in the Birthing Rooms because everyone's there and it's more communal and fun."

"Your parents," gasped Nick. He shuddered and started to speak very quickly. "Tell me about them. Nothing to tell about mine. Father's a bad politician, though enthusiastic with it. His older brother is the success. Mother goes to parties and drinks too much. How is it you are Sameth's aunt? I don't understand how you could be Touchstone's or Sabriel's sister. I've met them. Much older than you. Ancient. Must be forty, if a day. . . . Speak to me, please, speak to me—"

"I'm Sabriel's sister," said Lirael, though the words felt strange on her tongue. "Sabriel's sister. But not by the same mother. Her . . . my father was . . . . um . . . with my mother only for a little while, before he died. I didn't even know who he was till quite recently. My mother . . . my mother went away when I was five. So I didn't know my father was the Abhorsen— Oh no!"

"Abhorsen!" cried Nick. His body convulsed, and Lirael felt his skin suddenly grow even colder. She hurriedly wrenched her hand free and backed as far away as she could, cursing herself for saying "Abhorsen" aloud when Nicholas was already on the edge of losing control. Of course it would set off the Free Magic inside him.

White smoke began to pour out of Nick's nose and mouth. White sparks flickered behind his tongue as he desperately tried to speak. He mouthed it, but only smoke came out, and it took a moment for Lirael to work out what it was he was trying to say.

"No!" Or perhaps "Go!"

CHAPTER TWELVE

THE DESTROYER IN NICHOLAS

FOR A MOMENT, Lirael was caught in indecision, unable to decide whether to simply jump overboard and flee, or to reach for her bells. Then she acted, drawing Ranna and Saraneth, a difficult operation while sitting with a sword across her thighs.

Nick still hadn't moved, but the white smoke was billowing out in slow, deliberate tendrils that reached this way and that, as if they had a life of their own. The nauseating stench of Free Magic came with them, biting at Lirael's nose, bile rising in her throat in response.

She didn't wait to see more but rang the bells together, focusing her will into a sharp command directed at the figure in front of her and the drifting smoke.

Sleep, Lirael thought, her whole body tense with the effort of concentrating the power of the two bells. She could feel Ranna's lullaby and Saraneth's compulsion, loud as they echoed across the water. Together they wreathed Nicholas with magic and sound, sending the Free Magic spirit inside him back into its parasitic sleep.

Or not, Lirael saw, as the white smoke only recoiled, and the bells began to glow with a strange red heat, their voices losing pitch and clarity. Then Nick sat up, his eyes still rolled back and unseeing, and the Destroyer spoke through his mouth.

Its words struck at Lirael with physical force, the marrow in her bones suddenly burning and her ears pierced with a sudden, sharp ache.

"Fool! Your powers are thin hand-me-downs to pit against me! I almost sorrow that Saraneth and Ranna live on only in you and your trinkets. Be still!"

The last two words were spoken with such force that Lirael screamed with sudden pain. But the scream became a choking gurgle as she ran out of air. The thing inside Nick—the fragment—had bound her so fast that even her lungs were frozen. Desperately she tried to breathe, but it was no use. Her entire body was paralyzed, inside and out, held by a force she could not even begin to combat.

"Farewell," said the Destroyer. Then it stood Nick's body up, carefully balancing as the reed boat swayed, and waved at the barges. At the same time, it shouted a name that echoed through the whole lake valley.

"Hedge!"

Panicking, Lirael tried to breathe again and again. But her chest remained frozen, and the bells lay lifeless in her still hands. Wildly, she ran through Charter marks in her head, trying to think of something that might free her before she died of asphyxiation.

Nothing came to her, nothing at all, till she suddenly noticed she did have some sensation. In her thighs, where Nehima lay across her legs. She could only just see it there—being unable to move her eyes—but Charter marks were burning on the blade and flowing from there into her, fighting the Free Magic spell that held her in its deathly grip.

But the marks were only slowly defeating the spell. She would have do something herself, because at this rate, she would asphyxiate before her lungs were freed.

Desperate to do anything, she found she could twist her calves from side to side, trying to rock the boat. It wasn't very stable, so perhaps if it went over and distracted the Free Magic spirit . . . it might break the spell.

She rocked again, and water slopped into the craft, soaking into the tightly corded reeds. Still Nick's body didn't turn, his legs unconsciously adapting to the swaying motion. The thing inside him was clearly intent on the approaching barges and the hemispheres that held its greater self.

Then Lirael blacked out, her body starving for air. She came to in an instant, more panicked adrenaline flooding through her veins, and rocked again as hard as she could.

The reed boat rolled—but it didn't go over. Lirael screamed inside and rocked for what she knew would be the last time, using every muscle that had been freed by her sword.

Water sloshed in like a tide, and for a brief moment, the boat seemed about to capsize. But the lakefolk had woven it too well, and it righted. Nick's body, surprised by the violence of the roll, didn't. He swayed one way, made a grab at the prow, swung back the other—and fell into the lake.

Instantly, Lirael took a breath. Her lungs stayed frozen for a moment, then inflated with a shudder she felt through her entire body. The spell had broken with Nick's fall. Sobbing and panting, she thrust the bells back into their pouches and grabbed her sword, the Charter marks in the hilt pulsing with warmth and encouragement.

All the time, she was looking for the Nick creature. At first there was no sign of anything moving in the water. Then she saw a great steaming and bubbling a few yards away, as if the lake were boiling. A hand—Nick's hand—reached up and gripped the side of the boat, tearing away a whole section of the woven reeds with impossible strength; his mouth cleared the water, and a high-pitched scream of anger sent every marsh bird within a mile into panicked flight.

It sent Lirael, too. Instinctively, she jumped straight off the other side of the boat as far as she could, smashing into the reeds and water and starting off at a wading run. The terrible scream came again, followed by a violent splashing. For a moment Lirael thought that Nick was right behind her; but instead there was a violent explosion of water and broken reeds: Nick had picked up the entire boat and thrown it at her. If she had been a little slower, it would have been the boat that struck her back, rather than spray and some harmless bits of reed.

Before he could do anything else, Lirael redoubled her efforts to get away. The water wasn't as deep as she expected—only up to her chest—but it slowed her down, so every second she thought the creature would catch her, or strike her with a spell. Desperately, she headed back towards shallower water, hacking at the reeds with Nehima to speed the way.

She didn't look back, because she couldn't face what she might see, and she didn't stop, not even when she was lost in the rushes with no idea where she was going, and her lungs and muscles ached and burned with the effort of moving.

Finally, she was forced to a halt when the cramp in her side became impossible to ignore, and her legs were unable to hold her up out of the water. Fortunately, it was only knee-deep now, so Lirael sat down, crushing reeds into a wet and muddy seat.

All her senses were attuned to pursuit, but there didn't seem to be anything behind her—at least nothing she could hear over the pounding of her heart echoing through every blood vessel in her entire body.

She rested there, in the muddy water, for what seemed like a long time. Finally, when she felt as if she could move without bursting into tears or vomiting, she got up and sloshed forward again.

As she waded, she thought about what she'd done—or hadn't done. Over and over the scene played through her head. She should have been quicker with the bells, she thought, remembering her hesitation and clumsiness. Maybe she should have stabbed Nick—though that didn't seem right, since he had no idea what lurked within him, awaiting the chance to manifest itself. It probably wouldn't even have helped, since the fragment could probably inhabit a Dead Nick as easily as it did while he lived. Perhaps it could even have got inside her. . . .

The Clayr's vision of a world destroyed was also prominent in her mind. Had she missed her chance to stop the Destroyer? Were those few minutes with Nick in the reed boat some great cusp of destiny? A vital chance that she could have grasped but failed to?

She was still thinking about that when the water she was racing through turned to actual mostly solid mud, instead of muddy water. The reed clumps started to thin out, too, so clearly she was coming to the edge of the marsh. But as this particular marsh stretched in patches for a good twenty miles along the eastern shore of the Red Lake, Lirael still didn't really know where she was.

She took a guess at south from the position of the sun and the length of a tall reed's shadow, and started to head that way, keeping to the fringe of the marsh. It was harder going than dry ground, but safer if there were Dead about, forced out into the sun by Hedge.

Two hours later Lirael was wetter and more miserable than ever, thanks to an unexpectedly deep hole along the way. She was almost completely covered in a sticky and revolting mixture of red reed pollen and black mud. It stank, and she stank, and there seemed no end to the marsh, and no sign of her friends, either.

Doubts began to assail her even more strongly, and Lirael began to fear for her companions, particularly the Disreputable Dog. Perhaps she had been overcome by the sheer numbers of the Dead, or had been overmastered by Hedge, in the same way even the fragment in Nick had swatted her magic aside as if it didn't exist.

Or perhaps they were wounded, or still fighting, she thought, forcing herself to greater speed. Without her and the bells, they would be much weaker against the Dead. Sam hadn't even finished reading *The Book of the Dead*. He wasn't an Abhorsen. What if there was a Mordicant pursuing them, or some other creature that was strong enough to endure the sun at noon?

Thinking about that made her leave the rushes and start alternately running and walking along firmer ground. Run a hundred paces, walk a hundred paces—all the while keeping an eye out for Gore Crows, other Dead, or the human servants of Hedge.

Once she saw—and felt—Dead nearby, but they were Dead Hands fleeing in the distance, seeking some refuge from the harsh sun that was eating into them, flesh and spirit, the sun that would send them back into Death if they could not find a cave or unoccupied grave.

Soon she felt like an animal that is both hunter and hunted—like a fox or a wolf. All she could concentrate on was getting to the stream as quickly as possible, to search along its length to find either her friends or—as she feared—some evidence of what had happened to them. At the same time, she had the unpleasant sensation that some enemy was about to appear from behind every slight rise or shrunken tree, or dive down from the sky.

At least it was much easier to see where she was going, Lirael thought, as she noted the line of trees and bushes that marked the stream. It was less than a half mile away, so she redoubled her running, doing two hundred paces at a stretch instead of one.

She was up to 173 running paces when something burst out of the line of trees, straight towards her.

Instinctively Lirael reached for her bow—which wasn't there. She changed that movement to a swing across her body to draw her sword and kept on running.

She was just about to scream and turn the run into a charge when she recognized the Disreputable Dog and let out a glad cry instead, a cry that was met by the Dog's happy yelp.

A few minutes later they met in a tangle of jumping, licking, and dancing around (on the Dog's part) and hugging, kissing, and keeping her sword out of the way (on Lirael's part).

"It's you, it's you, it's you!" woofed the Dog, wiggling her hindquarters and squeaking.

Lirael didn't say anything. She knelt and put her head against the Dog's warm neck and sighed, a sigh that held all her troubles in it.

"You smell worse than I usually do," observed the Dog, after the initial excitement had worn off and she had had a chance to sniff Lirael's mud-covered body. "You'd better get up. We have to get back to the stream. There are still plenty of Dead about—Hedge seems to have abandoned them to do what they will. At least so we suppose, since the lightning storm—presumably following the hemispheres—has moved out over the lake."

"Yes," said Lirael, after they'd started walking back. "Hedge is there. Nick . . . the thing inside . . . called out to him from the reeds. They have two barges, and they're taking the hemispheres to Ancelstierre."

"It rose again in Nick," mused the Dog. "That didn't take long. Even the fragment must be stronger than I would have thought."

"It was a lot stronger than I ever imagined," replied Lirael, shivering. They were almost at the stream, and there was Sam waiting in the shadow of the trees, with an arrow nocked ready to fire. How was she going to explain to him that she'd rescued Nicholas—and lost him again?

Suddenly, Sam moved, and Lirael stopped in

surprise. It looked as if he was going to shoot her—or the Dog. She just had time to duck as his bow twanged, and an arrow leapt out—straight at her head.

CHAPTER THIRTEEN

DETAILS FROM THE
DISREPUTABLE DOG

AS SHE DUCKED, Lirael suddenly sensed a Gore Crow's cold presence directly above her. An instant later its dive was arrested, and it smacked into the ground, transfixed by Sam's arrow, the Charter Magic he'd set in the sharp point sparking as it ate into the splinter of Dead Spirit that was trying to crawl away.

Lirael found herself instinctively with a bell in hand, looking up for more Gore Crows. There was another, diving down, but an arrow lofted up and met it, too. This missile punched straight through the ball of feathers and dried bone and kept on going—but the Gore Crow didn't, and another fragment of Dead Spirit writhed on the ground near the first, suffering in the sunshine.

Lirael looked at the bell in her hand, and the

spirit fragments, pools of inky darkness that were already creeping together, seeking to join for greater strength. The bell was Kibeth, which was appropriate, so she rang it in a quick S shape, producing a clear and joyful tune that made her left foot break out into a little jig.

It had a more inimicable effect upon the remnant spirit fragments of the Gore Crows. The two blots reared up like salted leeches and almost somersaulted as they sought to evade the sound. But there was nowhere for them to go, nowhere they could escape Kibeth's peremptory call. Except the one place the spirit never wished to see again. But it had no choice. Shrieking inside, the spirit obeyed the bell, and the two blots vanished into Death.

Lirael cast her eye around the sky again and smiled in satisfaction as three more distant black dots fell earthwards: Gore Crows destroyed when the first two banished fragments sucked the rest of the shared spirit back into Death. Then she put the bell away and walked forward to greet Sam, the Disreputable Dog taking a quick side trip to sniff at the crow feathers, to make absolutely sure the spirit was gone and there was nothing worth eating.

Sam, like the Dog, also seemed extremely happy

to see Lirael, and was even about to give her a welcoming hug—till he smelled the mud. That made him change his open arms into an expansive welcoming gesture. Even so, Lirael noticed that he was looking behind her for someone else.

"Thanks for shooting the crows," she said. Then she added, "I lost Nick, Sam."

"Lost him!"

"There's a fragment of the Destroyer inside him, and it took him over. I couldn't stop it. It almost killed me when I tried."

"What do you mean a fragment of the Destroyer? Inside him how?"

"I don't know!" snapped Lirael. She took a deep breath before continuing. "Sorry. The Dog says that there's a sliver of the metal from one of the hemispheres inside Nicholas. I don't know any more than that, though it does explain why he's working with Hedge."

"So where is he?" asked Sam. "And what . . . what are we going to do now?"

"He's almost certainly on the barges Hedge is using to transport the hemispheres," replied Lirael. "To Ancelstierre."

"Ancelstierre!" exclaimed Sam, his surprise

echoed by Mogget, who emerged from Sam's pack. The little cat took several steps towards Lirael; then his nose wrinkled and he backed away.

"Yes," said Lirael heavily, ignoring Mogget's reaction. "Apparently Hedge—or the Destroyer itself, I suppose—knows some way to get across the Wall. They're taking the hemispheres by barge as close as they can. Then they'll cross the Wall and go to a place called Forwin Mill, where Nick will use a thousand lightning rods to funnel the entire power of a storm into the hemispheres. This will somehow help them come together, and then, I imagine, whatever it is will be whole again, and unbound. Charter knows what will happen then."

"Total destruction," said the Dog bleakly. "The end of all Life."

Silence greeted her words. The Dog looked up to see Sam and Lirael staring at her. Only Mogget was unmoved, choosing that moment to clean his paws.

"I suppose it is time to tell you exactly what we face," said the Dog. "But we should find somewhere defensible first. All the Dead that Hedge used to dig the pit are still about, and those strong enough to face the day will be hungry for life."

"There's an island at the mouth of the stream,"

said Sam slowly. "It's not much, but it would be better than nothing."

"Lead on," said Lirael wearily. She wanted to collapse on the spot and block her ears from whatever the Dog was going to tell them. But this wouldn't help. They had to know.

The island was a tumbled patch of rocks and stunted trees. It had once been a low hillock on the edge of the lake, with the stream on one side, but centuries ago the lake had risen or the streambed split. Now the island stood in the broad mouth of the stream, surrounded by swift water to the north, south, and east, and the deep waters of the lake to the west.

They waded across, Mogget clinging to Sam's shoulder and the Dog swimming in the middle. Unlike most dogs, Lirael noticed, her friend actually stuck her whole head underwater, ears and all. And whatever power fast-moving water had over the Dead and some Free Magic creatures clearly didn't apply to the Disreputable Dog.

"How come you like to swim but hate baths?" asked Lirael curiously as they reached dry ground and found a sandy patch between the rocks to set up a makeshift camp.

"Swimming is swimming, and the smells stay the same," said the Dog. "Baths involve soap."

"Soap! I would love some soap!" exclaimed Lirael. Some of the mud and reed pollen had come off in the stream, but not enough. She felt so filthy that she couldn't think straight. But she knew from long experience that any delay would only encourage the Dog to avoid telling them anything. She sat down on her pack and looked expectantly at the Dog. Sam sat down, too, and Mogget leapt down and stretched for a moment before settling comfortably into the warm sand.

"Tell us," ordered Lirael. "What is the thing bound in the hemispheres?"

"I suppose the sun is high enough," said the Dog. "We will not be bothered for a few hours yet. Though it might perhaps—"

"Tell us!"

"I am telling you," protested the Dog with great dignity. "It's just finding the best words. The Destroyer was known by many names, but the most common is one that I will write here. Do not speak it unless you must, for even the name has power, now that the silver hemispheres have been brought out under the sky."

The Dog flexed her paw, and a single sharp claw

popped out. She scratched seven letters in the sand, using the modern version of the alphabet favored by Charter Mages for nonmagical communication about magical topics.

The letters she wrote spelled out a single word. ORANNIS.

"Who . . . or what . . . is this thing?" asked Lirael when she'd silently read the name. She already had a feeling that it would be worse than she expected. There was a great but subtle tension in the way Mogget was crouched, his green eyes fixed on the letters, and the Dog wouldn't meet her eyes.

The Dog didn't answer at first but shuffled her paws and coughed.

"Please," said Lirael gently. "We have to know."

"It is the Ninth Bright Shiner, the most powerful Free Magic being of them all, the one who fought the Seven in the Beginning, when the Charter was made," said the Dog. "It is the Destroyer of worlds, whose nature is to oppose creation with annihilation. Long ago, beyond counting in years, It was defeated. Broken in two, each half bound within a silver hemisphere, and those hemispheres secured with seven bonds and buried deep beneath the earth. Never to be released, or so it was thought."

Lirael nervously tugged at her hair, wishing she

could disappear behind it forever. She felt a nervous desire to laugh or scream or fall to the ground weeping. She looked at Sam, who was biting his lip, unconscious of the fact that he had really bitten it and blood was trickling down his chin.

The Dog did not say anything more, and Mogget just kept staring at the letters.

ORANNIS.

"How can we defeat something like that?" burst out Lirael. "I'm not even a proper Abhorsen yet!"

Sam shook his head as she spoke, but whether it was in negation or agreement, Lirael couldn't tell. He kept on shaking it, and she realized it was simply that he couldn't fully grasp what the Dog had told them.

"It is still bound," said the Dog gently, giving Lirael an encouraging lick to her hand. "While the hemispheres are separate, the Destroyer can use only a small portion of Its power, and none of Its most destructive attributes."

"Why didn't you tell me this before!"

"Because you were not strong enough in yourself," explained the Dog. "You did not know who you are. Now you do, and you are ready to know fully what we face. Besides, I was not sure myself until I saw the lightning storm."

"I knew," said Mogget. He stood up and stretched out to a surprising length before sitting back and inspecting his right paw. "Ages ago."

The Dog wrinkled her nose in obvious disbelief and kept talking.

"The most disturbing aspect of this is that Hedge is taking the hemispheres to Ancelstierre. Once they are across the Wall, I do not know what is possible. Perhaps these massed lightning rods of Nick's will enable the Destroyer to join the hemispheres and become whole. If It does, then everyone . . . and everything is doomed, on both sides of the Wall."

"It was always the most powerful and cunning of the Nine," mused Mogget. "It must have worked out that the only place It could come back together was somewhere It had never existed. And then somehow It must have learned that we infringed upon a world beyond our own, for the Destroyer was bound long before the Wall was made. Clever, clever!"

"You sound like you admire It," said Sam somewhat bitterly. "Which is not the right attitude for a servant of the Abhorsens, Mogget."

"Oh, I do admire the Destroyer," replied

Mogget dreamily, his pink tongue licking the corners of his white-toothed mouth. "But only from a distance. It would have no qualms about annihilating me, you know—since I refused to ally with It against the Seven when It gathered Its host all those long-lost dreams ago."

"Only sensible thing you ever did," growled the Dog. "Though not as sensible as you could have been."

"Neither for nor against," said Mogget. "I would have lost myself either way. Not that it helped me any in the end, choosing the middle road, for I've lost most of myself anyway. Well, lackaday. Life goes on, there are fish in the river, and the Destroyer heads for Ancelstierre and freedom. I am curious to hear your next plan, Mistress Abhorsen-in-Waiting."

"I'm not sure I have one," replied Lirael. Her brain was saturated with danger. She couldn't even begin to comprehend the threat the Destroyer posed. That left room for tiredness, hunger, and a fierce loathing for her muddy, stinking body to become uppermost in her thoughts. "I think I have to get clean and eat something. Only I do have one question first. Or two questions, I guess.

"First of all, if the Destroyer does join Itself

back together in Ancelstierre, can It do anything? I mean, both Charter and Free Magic don't work on the other side of the Wall, do they?"

"Magic fades," answered Sam. "I could do Charter Magic at school, thirty miles south of the Wall, but none at all in Corvere. It also depends on whether the wind blows from the north or not."

"In any case, the Destroyer is a source of Free Magic in Itself," said the Dog, her brow wrinkled in thought. "Should It become whole and free, It could range wherever It wills, though I do not know how It would manifest Itself beyond the Kingdom. The Wall alone could not stop It, for the stones carry the power of only two of the Seven, and it took all of them to bind the Destroyer in the long ago."

"That leads to my next question," said Lirael wearily. "Do either of you know—or remember—exactly *how* It was split in two by the Seven and bound into the hemispheres?"

"I was already bound, like so many others," sniffed Mogget. "Besides, I am not really who I was even one millennium ago, let alone what I was in the Beginning."

"In a way I was present," said the Dog after a long pause. "But I, too, am only a shadow of what I once was, and my clear memories all stem from a later time. I do not know the answer to your question."

Lirael thought of a particular passage in *The Book of Remembrance and Forgetting* and sighed. She had heard the term "the Beginning" before but only now could place it as coming from that book.

"I think I know how to find out, though I don't know whether I'll be able to do it. But first of all I have to wash before this mud eats through my clothes!"

"And think of a plan?" Sam asked hopefully. "I guess we'll have to try to stop the hemispheres crossing the Wall, won't we?"

"Yes," said Lirael. "Keep watch, will you?"

She walked carefully down to the stream proper, thankful that it was another unseasonably hot day. She had considered stripping off for a complete wash but decided against it. Whatever the scales of her armored coat were called or made of, they weren't metal, so there was no danger of rust. And she didn't like the idea of being surprised by the Dead while seminaked. Besides, it was hot, the rain had long gone, and she would dry off quickly.

She put her sword on the bank, close at hand, and the bell-bandolier next to it. Both would need serious cleaning, too, and the bandolier rewaxing.

Her surcoat almost had to be scraped off, there was so much mud in and under it. She rolled it up and carried it into a convenient pool, out of the main current.

A sound made her look around, but it was only the Disreputable Dog, carefully sliding down the bank with something bright and yellow in her mouth. She spat it out as she reached Lirael, followed by a mixture of dog spit and bubbles.

"Yeerch," said the Dog. "Soap. See how much I love you?"

Lirael smiled and caught the soap, let the stream take the coating of dog saliva off, and started to lather herself and her clothes. Soon she was entirely covered in soapy foam but wasn't much cleaner, since the mud and the red pollen were very resistant, even to soap and water. Her surcoat looked as if it would be permanently stained until she had the time and energy to do some laundry magic.

Washing it without the help of magic gave her something to do while she thought about their next step. The more she considered it, the more it became clear that they couldn't stop Hedge from transporting the hemispheres through the Old Kingdom. Their only real chance was to stop him and the hemispheres at the Wall. That meant going into

Ancelstierre, to enlist whatever help they could get there.

If despite their efforts Hedge did get the hemispheres over the Wall, then there would still be one last chance: to stop Nick's Lightning Farm from being used to make the Destroyer whole.

And if that failed . . . Lirael didn't want to think about any last resorts beyond that.

When she judged herself to be about as clean as possible without entirely new clothes, Lirael waded back out to take care of her equipment. She carefully wiped the bandolier and waxed it with a lump of lovely-smelling beeswax, and went over Nehima with goose grease and a cloth. Then she put surcoat, bell-bandolier, and sword baldric back on, over her armor.

Sam and the Disreputable Dog stood on the largest of the rocks, watching both the lakeshore and the sky above. There was no sign of Mogget, though he could easily be back in Sam's pack. Lirael climbed up to the rock to join Sam and the Dog. She chose a small patch of sunshine between the two, sat down, and ate a cinnamon biscuit to satisfy her immediate pangs of hunger.

Sam watched her eat, but it was obvious he couldn't wait for her to finish and start talking.

Lirael ignored him at first, till he pulled a gold coin out of his sleeve and tossed it in the air. It spun up and up, but just when Lirael thought it would come down, it hovered, still spinning. Sam watched it for a while, sighed, and clicked his fingers. Instantly, the coin dropped into his waiting hand.

He repeated this process several times till Lirael snapped.

"What is that?"

"Oh, you're finished," said Sam innocently. "This? It's a feather-coin. I made it."

"What is it for?"

"It isn't for anything. It's a toy."

"It's for annoying people," said Mogget from Sam's pack. "If you don't put it away, I shall eat it."

Sam's hand closed on the coin, and it went back up his sleeve.

"I suppose it does annoy people," he said. "This is the fourth one I've made. Mother broke two, and Ellimere caught the last one and hammered it flat, so it could only wobble about close to the ground. Anyway, now that you've finished eating—"

"What!" asked Lirael.

"Oh, nothing," Sam replied brightly. "Only I

was hoping we could discuss what . . . what we're going to do."

"What do you think we should do?" asked Lirael, suppressing the irritation that the feather-coin had created. Despite everything, Sam appeared to be less tense and nervous than she'd expected. Perhaps he had become fatalistic, she thought, and wondered if she had as well. Faced by an Enemy that was so clearly beyond them, they were just resigned to doing whatever they could before they got killed or enslaved. But she didn't feel fatalistic. Now that she was clean, Lirael felt curiously hope-ful, as if they actually could do something.

"It seems to me," Sam said, pausing to chew his lip thoughtfully again. "It seems to me that we should try to get to this Torwin Mill—"

"Forwin Mill," interrupted Lirael.

"Forwin, then," continued Sam. "We should try to get there first, with whatever help we can muster from the Ancelstierrans. I mean, they don't like anyone bringing anything in from the Old Kingdom, let alone something magical they don't understand. So if we can get there first and get help, we could have Nick's Lightning Farm dismantled or destroyed before Hedge and Nick arrive with the hemispheres. Without the Lightning Farm, Nick won't be able to feed power into the hemispheres, so It will stay bound."

"That's a good plan," said Lirael. "Though I think we should work on stopping the hemispheres before they can cross the Wall."

"There is another problem that makes both plans a bit iffy," said Sam hesitantly. "I think those Edge sailing barges do the journey from Edge to the Redmouth in under two days. Faster with a spelled wind. It's not far from there to the Wall, maybe half a day depending on how fast they can drag the hemispheres. It'll take us at least four or five days to walk there. Even if we manage to find some horses today, we'll be at least a day behind."

"Or more," said Lirael. "I can't ride a horse."

"Oh," said Sam. "I keep forgetting you're a Clayr. Never seen one of them on a horse. . . . I guess we'll have to hope that the Ancelstierrans won't let them cross. Though I'm not sure they could stop even Hedge by himself, unless there were a lot of Crossing Point Scouts—"

Lirael shook her head. "Your friend Nick has a letter from his uncle. I don't know what a Chief Minister is, but Nick seemed to think that it would force the Ancelstierrans to allow him to bring the hemispheres across the Wall."

"How come he's always 'your friend Nick' when he makes things difficult?" protested Sam. "He *is* my friend, but it's the Destroyer and Hedge making him do all this stuff. It's not his fault."

"Sorry," sighed Lirael. "I know it's not his fault, and I won't call him 'your friend Nick' anymore. But he does have that letter. Or actually, someone on the other side of the Wall has it, who will be meeting them."

Sam scratched his head and frowned in exasperation.

"It depends on where they cross and who is in charge," he said despondently. "I guess they'll be intercepted at the Perimeter by a patrol, who will probably be all regular Army and not Scouts, and only the Scouts are Charter Mages. So they might let Nick and Hedge and everyone go through the Perimeter. I don't think any of the normal patrols could stop Hedge anyway, even if they wanted to. If only we could get there first! I know General Tindall well—he commands the Perimeter. And we would be able to wire my parents at the embassy in Corvere. If they're still there."

"Can we sail ourselves?" asked Lirael. "Where could we get a boat that's faster than the barges?"

"Edge would be the closest," replied Sam. "At least a day north, so we'd lose as much time as we gained. If Edge is still there. I don't want to think about how Hedge got his barges."

"Well, what about downstream?" asked Lirael. "Is there a fishing village or something?"

Sam shook his head absently. There was an answer, he knew. He could feel an idea just lurking out of reach. How could they reach the Wall faster than Hedge and Nick?

Land, sea . . . and air.

"Fly!" he exclaimed, jumping up and throwing his arms in the air. "We can fly! Your owl Charter-skin!"

It was Lirael's turn to shake her head.

"It would take me at least twelve hours to make two Charter-skins. Maybe more, since I need some sort of rest first. And it takes weeks to learn how to fly properly."

"But I won't need to," said Sam excitedly. "Look—I watched you making the barking owl skin before and I noticed that there's only a few key Charter marks that set how big it is, right?"

"Maybe," said Lirael dubiously.

"Well, my idea is that you make a really big

owl, big enough to carry me and Mogget in your claws," continued Sam, gesturing wildly. "It wouldn't take any longer than it usually does. Then we fly to the Wall . . . um, cross it . . . and take it from there."

"An excellent idea," said the Dog, her expression a mixture of surprise and approval.

"I don't know," said Lirael. "I'm not sure a giant Charter-skin would work."

"It will," said Sam confidently.

"I don't suppose there's much else we can do," Lirael said quietly. "So I guess I'd better give it a go. Where's Mogget? I'm curious to see what he thinks of your plan."

"It stinks," said Mogget's muffled voice from the shade below the boulder. "But there's no reason why it won't work."

"There's one other thing I guess I might have to do later," Lirael said hesitantly. "Is it possible to enter Death on the other side of the Wall?"

"Sure, depending how far into Ancelstierre you go, just like with magic," Sam replied, his voice suddenly very serious. "What . . . . what is it you might have to do?"

"Use the Dark Mirror and look back into the

past," Lirael said, her voice unconsciously taking on some of the timbre of a Clayr's prophecy. "Back to the Beginning, to see how the Seven defeated the Destroyer."

CHAPTER FOURTEEN

FLIGHT TO THE WALL

"IT WAS HUGE," sobbed the man, panic in his eyes and voice. "Bigger than a horse, with wings . . . wings that blocked the sky. And it had a man in its claws, dangling . . . horrible . . . horrible! The screeching . . . you must have heard the screeching?"

The other members of the small band of Travelers nodded, many of them looking up into the fading light of the evening sky.

"And something else was flying with it," whispered the man. "A dog. A dog with wings!"

His listeners exchanged glances of disbelief. A giant owl they could accept, after the screeching they'd heard. This was the Borderlands, after all, and in troubled times. Many things they had thought never to see had walked the earth in the last few days. But a winged dog?

248

"We'd best move along," said the leader, a tough-looking woman who bore the Charter mark on her forehead. She sniffed the air and added, "There's something odd about, all right. We'll go on to the Hogrest, unless anyone has a better idea. Somebody help Elluf, too. Give him some wine."

Quickly, the Travelers broke their camp and unhobbled their horses. Soon, they were headed north, with the unfortunate Elluf swigging from a wineskin as if it were water.

South of the Travelers, Lirael flew with gradually slowing wing beats. It was much, much harder to fly as a twenty-times-sized barking owl than as a normal one, particularly carrying Sam, Mogget, and both packs. Sam had helped along the way by casting Charter marks of strength and endurance into her, but a large part of the sustaining magic had been absorbed by the Charter-skin itself.

"I have to set down," she called to the Disreputable Dog, who was flying behind her, as pain coursed through her wings again. She picked a clear glade amongst the mass of trees and started to glide in for a landing.

Then she suddenly saw their destination. There, beyond the forest—a long grey line snaking along the crest of a low hill, going from east to west as far as she could see. The Wall that separated the Old Kingdom from Ancelstierre.

And on the far side of the Wall, darkness. The full dark, near midnight of an Ancelstierran early spring, spreading up to the Wall, where it suddenly met the warmth of an Old Kingdom summer evening. It gave Lirael an instant headache, her owl eyes unable to adjust to the contradiction—sunset here and night over there.

But there was the Wall, and buoyed up by this sighting, she forgot her pain and the intended landing site. With a push of her wings she lofted up again, heading straight for the Wall, a triumphant screech splitting the night.

"Don't try to cross!" Sam called urgently from below, as he swung in the makeshift harness of sword baldrics and pack straps that was held tight by her claws. "We have to land on this side, remember!"

Lirael heard him, recalled his warnings about the Perimeter on the Ancelstierran side, and dropped one wing. Immediately this became a diving turn, followed by frenzied flapping as Lirael realized she'd misjudged their airspeed and was about to plow Sam, Mogget, and herself into the ground at a painful velocity.

The flapping worked, after a fashion. Sam picked himself off the ground, checked that his bruised knees still functioned, and went over to the enormous owl who lay next to him, apparently stunned.

"Are you all right?" he asked anxiously, uncertain how he could check. How did you feel an owl's pulse, particularly an owl that was twenty feet long?

Lirael didn't answer, but faint lines of golden light began to run in hairline cracks through the giant owl shape. The lines ran together till Sam could see individual Charter marks; then the whole thing began to blaze so brightly that Sam had to back off, shielding his eyes against the brilliance.

Then there was only soft twilight in his eyes, as the sun slowly set on the Old Kingdom side. And there was Lirael, lying spread-eagled on her stomach, groaning.

"Ow! Every muscle in my entire body hurts," she muttered, slowly pushing herself up with her hands. "And I feel absolutely disgusting! Worse than the mud, that Charter-skin. Where's the Dog?"

"Here, Mistress," answered the Disreputable Dog, rushing over to surprise Lirael with a lick to her open mouth. "That was fun. Particularly flying over that man."

"That wasn't intentional," said Lirael, using the Dog as a crutch to help herself up. "I was just as surprised as he was. Let's just hope that we've saved enough time to make it worthwhile."

"If we can get across the Wall—and the Perimeter—tonight, we have to be ahead of Hedge," said Sam. "How fast can a barge go, after all?"

It was a rhetorical question, but it was answered.

"With a spelled wind, they could sail more than sixty leagues in a day and night," said Mogget, a hidden voice of authority from inside Sam's pack. "I would presume they reached the Redmouth around noon today. From there, who knows? It depends how quickly they can move the hemispheres. They may even have crossed, and time is disjointed between the Old Kingdom and Ancelstierre. Hedge—aided by the Destroyer—may even be able to manipulate that difference to gain a day . . . or more."

"Ever cheerful, aren't you, Mogget?" said Lirael. She actually felt surprisingly cheerful herself, and not as tired as she'd thought she was. She felt quietly proud that the giant owl Charter-skin had worked, and she was sure that they had got ahead of Hedge and his barges.

"I suppose we should push on," she said. Better not to count her apples before the tree grew. "Sam, I hadn't actually thought of this, but how will we get into Ancelstierre? How do we get across the Wall?"

"The Wall is the easy part," replied Sam. "There are lots of old gates. They'll be locked and warded, except for the one at the current Crossing Point, but I think I can open them."

"I'm sure you can," said Lirael encouragingly.

"The Perimeter is more difficult in some ways. They shoot on sight over there, though most of the troops are around the Crossing Point, so there will only be a chance of a patrol this far west. To be on the safe side, I was thinking we might take on the semblance of an officer and a sergeant from the Crossing Point Scouts. You can be the sergeant, with a head wound—so you can't talk and get us into trouble. They might believe that—enough not to shoot us straightaway."

"What about the Dog and Mogget?" asked Lirael.

"Mogget can stay in my pack," said Sam. With a backwards glance towards the cat, he added, "But you have to promise to be quiet, Mogget. A talking pack will get us killed for sure."

Mogget didn't answer. Sam and Lirael took this to be a surly agreement, since he didn't protest.

"We can disguise the Dog with a glamour as well," continued Sam. "To make her look like she's got a collar and breastplate like the Army sniffer dogs."

"What do they sniff?" asked the Disreputable Dog with interest.

"Oh, bombs and other . . . um . . . exploding devices—like the blasting marks we use, only made from chemicals, not magic," explained Sam. "Down south, that is. But they have special dogs on the Perimeter that sniff out the Dead or Free Magic. The dogs are much better than ordinary Ancelstierrans at detecting such things."

"Naturally," said the Disreputable Dog. "I take it I'm not allowed to talk, either?"

"No," confirmed Sam. "We'll have to give you a name and number, like a real sniffer dog. How about Woppet? I knew a dog called that. And you can have my old service number from the cadet corps at school. Two Eight Two Nine Seven Three. Or Nine Seven Three Woppet for short."

"Nine Seven Three Woppet," mused the Dog, rolling the words around in her mouth as if they were something potentially edible. "A curious name."

"We'd better cast the illusions here for us to take on," said Sam. "Before we try to cross the Wall."

He looked at the full dark of the Ancelstierran night beyond the Wall and said, "We need to cross before dawn, which can't be too far away. We're less likely to run into a patrol at night."

"I've never cast a glamour before," said Lirael doubtfully.

"I have to do them anyway," replied Sam. "Since you don't know what we want to look like. They're not that hard—a lot easier than your Charter-skins. I can do three easily enough."

"Thank you," said Lirael. She sat down next to the Dog, easing her aching muscles, and scratched the hound under the collar. Sam walked a few paces away and began to reach into the Charter, gathering the marks that he needed for casting the spells of disguise.

"Funny to think he's my nephew," whispered Lirael to the Dog. "It feels very strange. An actual family, not just a great clan of cousins, like the Clayr. To be an aunt, as well as having one. To have a sister, too . . ."

"Is it good as well as strange?" asked the Dog.

"I haven't had a chance to think about it," replied Lirael, after a moment of thoughtful silence. "It's sort of good and sort of sad. Good, because I am . . . I am an Abhorsen, blood and bone, so I have found where I belong. Sad, because all my life before was about not belonging, not being properly one of the Clayr. I spent so many years wanting to be something I wasn't. Now I think if I could have become a Clayr, would it have been enough for me? Or would I simply be unable to imagine being anything else?"

She hesitated, then quietly added, "I wonder if my mother knew what my childhood would be. But then Arielle was a Clayr, too, and probably couldn't comprehend what it would be like growing up at the Glacier without the Sight."

"That reminds me," Mogget said, unexpectedly emerging from the pack, his left ear crumpled by his rapid exit. "Arielle. Your mother. She left a message with me when she was at the House."

"What!" exclaimed Lirael, jumping over to grab Mogget by the scruff of the neck, ignoring Ranna's call to sleep and the unpleasant interchange of Free Magic under cat skin and the Charter-spelled collar. "What message? Why didn't you give it to me before?"

"Hmmm," replied Mogget. He pulled himself free, catching his collar against Lirael's hand. She let go just before he could slip out of the leather band, and Ranna's warning chime made the cat stop wriggling. "If you listen, I'll tell you—"

"Mogget!" growled the Dog, stalking over to breathe in the cat's face.

"Arielle Saw me with you, near the Wall," said Mogget quickly. "She was sitting in her Paperwing, and I was handing her a package—I had a different form in those days, you understand. In fact, I probably wouldn't have remembered this if I hadn't taken that shape again after my forced conversation under the House. It's funny how in man shape I remember things differently. I suppose I had to forget in order to not remember until I was where she Saw me—"

"Mogget! The message!" pleaded Lirael.

Mogget nodded and licked his mouth. Clearly he would proceed only in his own time.

"I handed her the package," he continued. "She was looking into the mist above the waterfall. There was a rainbow there that day, but she did not see it. I saw her eyes cloud with the Sight, and she said, 'You will stand by my daughter near the Wall. You will see her grown, as I will not. Tell Lirael that . . . that my going will be . . . will have been . . . no choice of mine. I have linked her life and mine to the Abhorsen, and put the feet of both mother and daughter on a path that will limit our own choosing. Tell her also that I love her, and will always love her, and that leaving her will be the death of my heart.'"

Lirael listened intently, but it was not Mogget's voice she heard. It was her mother's. When the cat finished, she looked up at the red-washed sky above and the glittering stars beyond the Wall, and a single tear ran down her cheek, leaving a trail of silver, caught by the last moments of evening light.

"I've made your glamour," said Sam, who had been so intent on his spells that he had totally missed what Mogget said. "You just need to step into it. Make sure you keep your eyes closed."

Lirael turned to see the glowing outline hanging in the air and stumbled towards it. She had her eyes closed well before she walked into the spell. The golden fire spread across her face like warm, welcoming hands and brushed away her tears.

CHAPTER FIFTEEN

THE PERIMETER

"SARGE—THERE'S DEFINITELY something moving out there," whispered Lance Corporal Horrocks, as he looked out over the sights of his Lewin machine-gun. "Should I let 'em have a few rounds?"

"No bloody fear!" Sergeant Evans whispered back. "Don't you know anything? If it's a haunt or a Ghlim or something, it'll just come over here and suck your guts out! Scazlo—get back and tell the Lieutenant something's up. The rest of you, pass the word to fix bayonets, quiet like. And don't nobody do nothing unless I say so."

Evans looked again himself as Scazlo hurried back down the communications trench behind them. All along the main fighting trench there was the click of bayonets being fixed as quietly as possible. Evans himself strung his bow and loaded a flare pistol with a red cartridge. Red was the sign for an incursion from across the Wall. At least it would be the sign if it worked, he thought. There was a warm, northerly wind blowing in from the Old Kingdom. It was good for taking the chill out of the icy mud of the trenches, for spring had yet to fully banish the past winter, but it also meant that guns, planes, trip flares, mines, and everything else technological might not work.

"There's two of them—and something, looks like a dog," whispered Horrocks again, his trigger finger slowly curling back from its orthodox position held straight against the trigger guard.

Evans peered into the darkness, trying to make something out himself. Horrocks wasn't too bright, but he did have extraordinary night vision. A lot better than Evans. He couldn't see anything, but there were tin cans tinkling together on the wire. Someone . . . or something . . . was slowly coming through.

Horrocks's finger was inside the trigger guard now, the safety off, a full drum of ammunition on top, a round in the chamber. All he needed was the word, and maybe the wind to change.

Then he suddenly sighed, his trigger finger came out again, and he leaned back from the stock.

"Looks like some of our mob," he said, no longer whispering. "Scouts. An officer and some poor bastard with a bandaged head. And one of them . . . you know . . . smeller dogs."

"Sniffer dogs," corrected Evans automatically. "Shut up."

Evans was thinking about what to do. He'd never heard of Old Kingdom creatures taking the shape of an Ancelstierran officer or an Army dog. Practically invisible shadows, yes. Ordinary-looking Old Kingdom folk, yes. Flying horrors, yes. But there was always a first time—

"What's up, Evans?" asked a voice behind him, and he felt an internal relief he would never show. Lieutenant Tindall might be a General's son, but he wasn't a good-for-nothing staff officer. He knew what was what on the Perimeter—and he had the Charter mark on his forehead to prove it.

"Movement in front, about fifty yards out," he reported. "Horrocks thinks he can see a couple of Scouts, one wounded."

"And a smell . . . sniffer dog," added Horrocks.

Tindall ignored him, stepping up to peer over the parapet himself. Two dim shapes were definitely closing, whoever they were. But he could sense no inimicable force or dangerous magic. There was something . . . but if they were Crossing Point Scouts, they would both be Charter Mages as well.

"Have you tried a flare?" he asked. "White?"

"No, sir," said Evans. "Wind's northerly. Didn't think it would work."

"Very well," said the Lieutenant. "Warn the men that I'm going to cast a light out in front. Everyone to stand ready for my orders."

"Yes, sir!" confirmed Evans. He turned to the man at his side and said quietly, "Stand to the step! Light in front! Pass it on."

As the word rippled down the line, the men stood up on the firing step, tension evident in their postures. Evans couldn't see all the platoon—it was too dark—but he knew his corporals at each end would sort them out.

"Casting now," said Lieutenant Tindall. A faint Charter mark for light appeared in his cupped hand. As it began to brighten, he threw it overarm like a cricket ball, directly out in front.

The white spark became brighter as it flew through the air, till it became a miniature sun, hovering unnaturally over No Man's Land. In its harsh light all shadows were banished, and two figures could clearly be seen following the narrow zigzagged trail through the wire entanglements. As Horrocks had said, they had a sniffer dog with them, and both wore the khaki uniforms of the Ancelstierran Army under the mail coats that were peculiar to the Perimeter Forces. Some indefinable unorthodoxy about their webbing gear and weapons also proclaimed them to be members of the Northern Perimeter Reconnaissance Unit, or as they were better known, the Crossing Point Scouts.

As the light fell on them, one of the two men put up his hands. The other, who was bandaged around the head, followed suit more slowly.

"Friendly forces! Don't shoot!" shouted Sameth as the Charter light slowly faded above him. "Lieutenant Stone and Sergeant Clare coming in. With a sniffer dog!"

"Keep your hands up and come in single file!" shouted Tindall. Aside to his sergeant, he said, "Lieutenant Stone? Sergeant Clare?"

Evans shook his head. "Never heard of 'em, sir. But you know the Scouts. Keep themselves to themselves. The Lieutenant does look sort of familiar."

"Yes," murmured Tindall, frowning. The approaching officer did look vaguely familiar. The wounded sergeant was moving with the shuffling gait of someone forcing himself into action despite constant pain. And the sniffer dog had the correct khaki breastplate with its number stenciled on in white, and a broad, spiked leather collar. All together, they looked authentic.

"Stop there!" Tindall called as Sameth trod down a piece of unsupported concertina wire, only ten yards from the trench. "I'm coming out to test your Charter marks.

"Cover me," he whispered aside to Evans. "You know the drill if they're not what they seem."

Evans nodded, stuck four silver-tipped arrows in the mud between the duckboards for quick use, and nocked another. The Army didn't issue or even recognize the use of bows and silver arrows, but like a lot of such things on the Perimeter, every unit had them. Many of the men were practiced archers, and Evans was one of the best.

Lieutenant Tindall looked at the two figures, dim shapes again now that his spell was fading. He'd kept one eye closed against the light, as taught, to preserve his night vision. Now he opened it, noting once again that it didn't seem to make that much of a difference.

He drew his sword, the silver streaks on it shining even with the dim starlight, and climbed out of the trench, his heart thumping so loud, it seemed to be echoing inside his stomach.

Lieutenant Stone stood waiting, his hands held high. Tindall approached him carefully, all his senses open to any sensation, any hint or scent of Free Magic or the Dead. But all he could feel was Charter Magic, some fuzzy, blurring magic that wrapped both men and the dog. Some protective charm, he presumed.

At arm's length, he gently placed his sword point against the stranger Lieutenant's throat, an inch above where the mail coat laced. Then he reached forward and touched the Charter mark on the man's forehead with the index finger of his left hand.

Golden fire burst from the mark as he touched it, and Tindall felt himself fall into the familiar, never-ending swirl of the Charter. It was an unsullied mark, and Tindall felt relief as strongly as he felt the Charter.

"Francis Tindall, isn't it?" asked Sam, thankful that he'd made a luxurious mustache part of the glamour that disguised him with the uniform and accoutrements of a Scout officer. He'd met the young officer several times the year before at the regular official functions he always attended in term time. The Lieutenant was only a few years older than Sam. Francis's father, General Tindall, commanded the entire Perimeter Garrison.

"Yes," replied Francis, surprised. "Though I don't recall?"

"Sam Stone," said Sameth. But he kept his hands up and jerked his head back. "You'd better check Sergeant Clare. But be careful of his head. Arrow wound on the left side. He's pretty groggy."

Tindall nodded, stepped past, and repeated the procedure with sword and hand on the wounded sergeant. Most of the man's head was roughly bandaged, but the Charter mark was clear, so he touched it. Once again he found it uncorrupted. This time he also realized that the power within the Sergeant was very, very strong—as had been Lieutenant Stone's. Both these soldiers were enormously powerful Charter Mages, the strongest he'd ever encountered.

"They're clear!" he shouted back to Sergeant Evans. "Stand the men down and get the listening posts back out!"

"Ah," said Sam. "I wondered how you picked us up. I didn't expect the trenches here to be manned."

"There's some sort of emergency farther west," explained Tindall, as he led the way back to the trench. "We were ordered out only an hour ago. It's lucky we were still here, in fact, since the rest of the battalion is halfway to Bain. Called out in support of the civil authorities. Probably trouble with the Southerling camps again, or Our Country demonstrations. Our company was the rear party."

"An emergency west of here?" asked Sam anxiously. "What kind of emergency?"

"I haven't had word," replied Tindall. "Do you know something?"

"I hope not," replied Sam. "But I need to get in touch with HQ as quickly as possible. Do you have a field telephone with you?"

"Yes," replied Tindall. "But it's not working. The wind from across the Wall, I expect. The one at the Company CP might just work, I suppose, but otherwise you'll have to go all the way back to the road."

"Damn!" exclaimed Sam as they climbed down into the trench. An emergency to the west. That had to have something to do with Hedge and Nicholas. Absently, he returned Evans's salute and noted all the white faces staring at him out of the darkness of the trench, faces that showed their relief that he was not a creature of the Old Kingdom.

The Dog jumped down beside him, and the

closest soldiers flinched. Lirael climbed down slowly after the hound, her muscles still sore from flying. It was strange, this Perimeter, and frightening, too. She could feel the vast weight of many deaths here, everywhere about her. There were many Dead pressing against the border with Life, prevented from crossing only by the wind flutes that sang their silent song out in No Man's Land. Sabriel had made them, she knew, for wind flutes would stand only as long as the current Abhorsen lived. When she passed on, the wind flutes would fail with the next full moon, and the Dead would rise, till they were bound again by the new Abhorsen. Which, Lirael realized, would be herself.

Lieutenant Tindall noticed her shiver and looked at her with concern.

"Shouldn't we get your Sergeant to the regimental aid post?" he asked. There was something peculiar about the Sergeant, something that made him difficult to look at directly. If he looked out of the corners of his eyes, Tindall could see a fuzzy aura that didn't quite match the outline he was expecting. That bandolier was odd, too. Since when did the Scouts carry bandoliers of rifle ammunition? Particularly when neither of them was carrying a rifle?

"No," said Sam quickly. "He'll be all right. We have to get to a phone as fast as possible and contact Colonel Dwyer."

Tindall nodded but didn't say anything. The nod hid a flash of concern across his face, and the thoughts that were racing through his head. Lieutenant Colonel Dwyer, who commanded the Crossing Point Scouts, had been on leave for the last two months. Tindall had even seen him off, following a memorable dinner at his father's headquarters.

"You'd better come with me to the Company CP," he said finally. "Major Greene will want to have a word."

"I must telephone," Sam insisted. "There's no time for talking!"

"Major Greene's telephone may be operational," said Tindall, trying to keep his voice as even as possible. "Sergeant Evans—take charge of the platoon. Byatt and Emerson . . . follow on. Keep those bayonets fixed. Oh, Evans—send a runner for Lieutenant Gotley to join me at the CP. I think we might need his signals expertise."

He led the way off down the communications trench, Sam, Lirael, and the Dog following. Evans, who had caught his Lieutenant's eye and call for the only other Charter Mage in the company besides Major Greene, held Byatt and Emerson back for a few moments, whispering, "Something funny's up, lads. If the boss gives the word, or there's any sign of trouble, stick those two in the back!"

CHAPTER SIXTEEN

A MAJOR'S DECISION

SAMETH'S HEART FELL as Lieutenant Tindall led them into a deep dugout about a hundred yards behind the fighting trench. Even in the dim light of an oil lamp, he could see it looked too much like the abode of a lazy and comfort-loving officer—who probably wouldn't even listen, let alone understand what they needed to do.

There was a woodstove burning fiercely in one corner, an open bottle of whisky on the map table, and a comfortable armchair wedged in one corner. Major Greene, in turn, was wedged in the chair, looking red faced and cantankerous. But he did have his boots on, Sam noted, a sword next to his chair, and a holstered revolver that hung by its lanyard from a nearby peg.

"What's this?" bellowed the Major, creakily rising up as they ducked under the lintel and spread out around the map table. He was old for a major, Sam thought. Pushing fifty at least, and imminent retirement.

Before he could speak, Lieutenant Tindall—who'd moved around behind them—said, "Imposters, sir. Only I'm not sure what kind. They do bear uncorrupted Charter marks."

Sam stiffened at the word "imposters," and he saw Lirael grab the Dog's collar as she growled, deep and angrily.

"Imposters, hey?" said Major Greene. He looked at Sam, and for the first time Sam realized the old officer had a Charter mark on his forehead. "What do you have to say for yourselves?"

"I'm Lieutenant Stone of the NPRU," said Sam stiffly. "That is Sergeant Clare and the Sniffer Dog Woppet. I need to phone Perimeter HQ urgently—"

"Rubbish!" roared the Major, without any anger. "I know all the officers of the Scouts, the NCOs, too. I was one for long enough! And I'm pretty familiar with the sniffer dogs, and that one ain't of the breed. I'd be surprised if it could smell a cow pat in a kitchen."

"I could so," said the Dog indignantly. Her words were met by a hushed silence; then the Major had his sword out and leveled at them, and

Lieutenant Tindall and his men had moved forward, sword and bayonet points only inches behind Sam's and Lirael's unprotected necks.

"Oops," said the Dog, sitting down and resting her head on her paws. "Sorry, Mistress."

"Mistress?" exclaimed Greene, his face going even redder. "Who are you two? And what is that?"

Sam sighed and said, "I am Prince Sameth of the Old Kingdom, and my companion is Lirael, the Abhorsen-in-Waiting. The Dog is a friend. We are all under a glamour. Do I have your permission to remove it? We'll glow a bit, but it isn't dangerous."

The Major looked redder-faced than ever, but he nodded.

A few minutes later Sam and Lirael stood in front of Major Greene wearing their own clothes and faces. Both were obviously very tired, and clearly had suffered much in recent times. The Major looked at them carefully, then down at the Dog. Her breastplate had disappeared and her collar changed, and she looked larger than before. She met his gaze with a sorrowful eye, then spoiled it by winking.

"It is Prince Sameth," declared Lieutenant Tindall, who'd edged around to see their faces.

There was a strange expression on his face. A sympathetic look, and he nodded twice at Sameth, who looked surprised. "And she looks . . . I beg your pardon, ma'am. I mean to say you look very like Sabriel, I mean the Abhorsen."

"Yes, I am Prince Sameth," said Sam slowly, with little expectation that this overweight, soon-to-be-retired Major would be much help. "I urgently need to contact Colonel Dwyer."

"The phone doesn't work," replied the Major. "Besides, Colonel Dwyer is on leave. What's this urgent need to communicate?"

Lirael answered him, her voice cracked and croaking from the onset of a cold, caused by the sudden transition from a warm Old Kingdom summer to the Ancelstierran spring. The oil lamp flared as she spoke, sending her shadow flickering and dancing across the table.

"An ancient and terrible evil is being brought into Ancelstierre. We need help to find It and stop It—before It destroys your country and then our own."

The Major looked at her, his red face set in a frown. But it wasn't a frown of disbelief, as Sam had feared.

"If I didn't know what your title signified, and recognize the bells you wear," the Major said slowly, "I would suspect you of overstatement. I don't think I have ever heard of an evil so powerful it could destroy my entire country. I wish I weren't hearing about it now."

"It is called the Destroyer," said Lirael, her voice soft, but charged with the fear that had been growing since they had left the Red Lake. "It is one of the Nine Bright Shiners, the Free Spirits of the Beginning. It was bound and broken by the Seven and buried deep beneath the ground. Only now the two metal hemispheres that hold It prisoner have been dug up by a necromancer called Hedge, and even as we talk here, he could be bringing them across the Wall."

"So that's what it is," said the Major, but there was no satisfaction in his voice. "I had a carrier pigeon from Brigade about trouble to the west and a defense alert, but there's been nothing since. Hedge, you say? I knew a sergeant of that name, in the Scouts when I first joined. Couldn't be him, though—that was thirty-five years ago and he was fifty if he was a day—"

"Major, I have to get to a telephone!" interrupted Sameth.

"At once!" declared the Major. He seemed to be recalled to a more vigorous and perhaps younger version of himself. "Mister Tindall, pull your platoon in and tell Edward and CSM Porrit to organize a move. I'm going to take these two—"

"Three," said the Dog.

"Four," interrupted Mogget, poking his head out of Sam's pack. "I'm tired of keeping quiet."

"He's a friend, too," Lirael assured the soldiers hastily, as hands once more went for swords and bayonets swung back. "Mogget is the cat and the Disreputable Dog is the . . . um . . . dog. They are . . . er . . . servants of the Clayr and the Abhorsen."

"Just like the Perimeter! It never rains but it pours," declared the Major. "Now, I'm going to take you four back to the reserve line road, and we'll try the phone there. Francis, follow to the transport rendezvous as fast as you can."

He paused and added, "I don't suppose you know where this Hedge is going, if they've got across the Perimeter?"

"Forwin Mill, where there is something called a Lightning Farm that they will use to free the Destroyer," said Lirael. "They may have no difficulty getting across the Perimeter. Hedge has the

Chief Minister's nephew with him, Nicholas Sayre, and they're being met by someone who has a letter from the Chief Minister allowing them to bring the hemispheres in."

"That wouldn't be sufficient," declared the Major. "I suppose it might work at the Crossing Point, but there'd be hours of to and fro with Garrison at Bain and even Corvere. No one in their right mind would fall for it on the real Perimeter. They'll have to fight their way through, though if an alert was sounded an hour ago, they probably already have. Orderly!"

A corporal, a burning cigarette disguised in one cupped hand, poked his head into the dugout entrance.

"Get me a map that covers Forwin Mill, somewhere west of here! I've never heard of the bloody place."

"It's about thirty miles down the coast from here, sir," volunteered Tindall, stopping in mid rush for the exit. "I've been fishing there—there's a loch with quite good salmon. It is a few miles outside the Perimeter Zone, sir."

"Is it? Humph!" remarked Greene, his face once again turning a deeper shade of red. "What else is there?"

"There was an abandoned sawmill, a broken-down dock, and what's left of the railway they once used to bring the trees down from the hills," said Tindall. "I don't know what this Lightning Farm might be, but there is—"

"Nicholas had the Lightning Farm built there," interrupted Lirael. "Quite recently, I think."

"Any people about the place?" asked the Major.

"There are now," replied Lieutenant Tindall. "Two Southerling refugee camps were built there late last year. Norris and Erimton they're called, in the hills immediately above the loch valley. There might be fifty thousand refugees there, I suppose, under police guard."

"If the Destroyer is made whole, they will be among the first to die," said the Dog. "And Hedge will reap their spirits as they cross into Death, and they will serve him."

"We'll have to get them out of there, then," said the Major. "Though being outside the Perimeter makes it difficult for us to do anything. General Tindall will understand. I only hope General Kingswold has gone home. He's an Our Country supporter through and through—"

"We must hurry!" Lirael suddenly interrupted. There was no time for more talk. A terrible sense of foreboding gripped her, as if every second they spent here was a grain of sand lost from a nearly empty hourglass. "We have to get to Forwin Mill before Hedge and the hemispheres!"

"Right!" shouted Major Greene, suddenly energized again. He seemed to need spurring along every now and then. He snatched up his helmet, threw it on his head, and snagged his revolver by the lanyard with the return motion. "Carry on, Mister Tindall. Quickly now!"

Everything did happen very quickly then. Lieutenant Tindall disappeared into the night, and the Major led them at a trot down another communications trench. Eventually it rose out of the ground and became a simple track, identified every few yards with a white-painted rock that shone faintly in the starlight. There was no moon, though one had risen on the Old Kingdom side, and it was much colder here.

Twenty minutes later, the wheezing—but surprisingly fit—Major slowed to a walk, and the track joined a wide asphalt road that stretched as far as they could see by starlight, due east and west. Telephone poles lined the road, part of the network that connected the full length of the Perimeter.

A low, concrete blockhouse brooded on the other side of the road, fed from the telegraph poles with a spaghetti-like pile of telephone wires.

Major Greene led the way inside like some corpulent missile, shouting to wake the unfortunate soldier who was slumped over a switchboard desk, his head nestled in a web of lines and plugs.

"Get me Perimeter HQ!" ordered the Major. The semiconscious soldier obeyed him, plugging in lines with the dumb expertise of the highly trained. "General Tindall in person! Wake him up if necessary!"

"Yes sir, yes, sir, yes," mumbled the telephone orderly, wishing that he had chosen a different night to drink his secret hoard of rum. He kept one hand over his mouth to try to keep the smell from the ferocious Major and his strange companions.

When the call went through, Greene grabbed the handset and spoke quickly. Obviously he was talking to various unhelpful in-between people, because his face kept getting redder and redder, till Lirael thought his skin would set his mustache on fire. Finally he reached someone who he listened to for a minute, without interruption. Then he slowly put the handset back in its cradle.

"There is an incursion happening at the

western end of the Perimeter right now," he said. "There were reports of red distress rockets, but we've lost communication from Mile One to Mile Nine, so it's a broad attack. No one knows what's going on. General Tindall has already ordered out a flying column, but apparently he's gone to some other trouble at the Crossing Point. The shiny-bum staff colonel on the other end has ordered me to stay here."

"Stay here! Can't we go west and try and stop Hedge at the Wall?" asked Lirael.

"We lost communication an hour ago," said Major Greene. "It hasn't been re-established. No more rockets have been seen. That means there is no one left alive to fire any. Or else they've run away. In either case, your Hedge and his hemispheres will already be over the Wall and past the Perimeter."

"I don't understand how they could have caught up with us," said Lirael.

"Time plays tricks between here and home," said Mogget sepulchrally, frightening the life out of the telephone operator. The little cat jumped out of Sam's pack, ignored the soldier, and added, "Though I expect it will be slow going, dragging the hemispheres to this Forwin Mill. We may have time to get *there* first."

"I'd better get in touch with my parents," said Sam. "Can you patch into the civilian telephone system?"

"Ah," said the Major. He rubbed his nose and seemed unsure of what he was going to say. "I thought you would have known. It happened almost a week ago. . . ."

"What?"

"I'm sorry, son," said the Major. He braced himself to attention and said, "Your parents are dead. They were murdered in Corvere by Corolini's radicals. A bomb. Their car was totally destroyed."

Sam listened blank faced to the Major's words. Then he slid down the wall and put his head in his hands.

Lirael touched Sam's left shoulder, and the Dog rested her nose on his right. Only Mogget seemed unaffected by the news. He sat next to the switchboard operator, his green eyes sparkling.

Lirael spent the next few seconds walling off the news, pushing it down to where she had always pushed her distress, somewhere that allowed her to keep on going. If she lived, she would weep for the sister she had never known, as she would weep for Touchstone, and her mother, and so many other things that had gone wrong in the world. But now there was no time for weeping, since many other sisters, brothers, mothers, fathers, and others depended on them doing what must be done.

"Don't think about it," said Lirael, squeezing Sam's shoulder. "It's up to us now. We have to get to Forwin Mill before Hedge does!"

"We can't," said Sam. "We might as well give up—"

He stopped himself in mid sentence, let his hands fall from his face, and stood up, but hunched over as if there were a pain in his gut. He stood there silently for almost a minute. Then he took the feather-coin out of his sleeve and flipped it. It spun up to the ceiling of the blockhouse and hung there. Sam leaned against the wall to watch it, his body still crooked but his head craned back.

Eventually he stopped looking at the spinning coin and straightened up, until he was standing at attention opposite Lirael. He didn't snap his fingers to recall the coin.

"I'm sorry," he whispered. There were tears in his eyes, but he blinked them back. "I'm . . . I'm all right now."

He bent his head to Lirael and added, "Abhorsen."

Lirael shut her eyes for a moment. That single word brought it all home. She was the Abhorsen. No longer in waiting.

"Yes," she said, accepting the title and everything that went with it. "I am the Abhorsen, and as such, I need all the help I can get."

"I'll come with you," said Major Greene. "But I can't legally order the company to follow. Though most of 'em would probably volunteer."

"I don't understand!" protested Lirael. "Who cares what's legal? Your whole country could be destroyed! Everybody killed everywhere! Don't you understand?"

"I understand. It's just not that simple . . ." the Major began. Then he paused, and his red face went blotchy and pale at the temples. Lirael watched his brow furrow up as if a strange thought were trying to break free. Then it cleared. Carefully he put his hand into his pocket, then suddenly withdrew it and punched his newly brass-knuckled fist into the Bakelite exchange board, its delicate internal mechanisms exploding with a rush of sparks and smoke.

"Damn it! It is that simple! I'll order the company to go. After all, the politicos can only shoot me for it later if we win. As for you, Private, if you mention a word of this to anyone, I'll feed you to the cat thing here. Understand?"

"Yum," said Mogget.

"Yes, sir!" mumbled the telephone operator, his hands shaking as he tried to smother the burning wreckage of his switchboard with a fire blanket.

But the Major hadn't paused for his answer. He was already out the door, shouting at some poor subordinate outside to "Hurry up and get the trucks going!"

"Trucks?" asked Lirael as they rushed out after him.

"Um . . . horseless wagons," said Sam mechanically. The words came out of his mouth slowly, as if he had to remember what they were. "They'll . . . they'll get us to Forwin Mill much faster. If they work."

"They might well do so," said the Dog, lifting her nose and sniffing. "The wind is veering to the southwest and it's getting colder. But look to the west!"

They looked. The western horizon was lit by bright flashes of lightning, and there was the dull rumble of distant thunder.

Mogget watched, too, from his post back on top of Sam's pack. His green eyes were calculating, and Lirael noticed he was counting quietly aloud.

Then he sniffed with a disgruntled tone.

"How far did that boy say Forwin Mill was?" he asked, noting Lirael's look.

"About thirty miles," said Sam.

"About five leagues," said Lirael at the same time.

"That lightning is due west, and six or seven leagues away. Hedge and his cargo must still be crossing the Wall!"

SECOND INTERLUDE

THE BLUE POSTAL Service van crunched its gears as it slowed to take the turnoff from the road into the bricked drive. Then it had to slow even more and judder to a stop, because the gates that were normally open were closed. There were also people with guns and swords on the other side. Armed schoolgirls in white tennis dresses or hockey tunics, who looked as if they should be holding racquets or hockey sticks rather than weapons. Two of them kept their rifles trained on the driver while another two came through the little postern gate in the wall, the naked blades they held at the ready catching the light of the late-afternoon sun.

The driver of the van looked up at the gilt, mock-Gothic letters above the gate that read "Wyverley College" and the smaller inscription below, which said, "Established in 1652 for Young Ladies of Quality."

"Peculiar bloody quality," he muttered. He

didn't like to feel afraid of schoolgirls. He looked back into the interior of the van and said more loudly, "We're here. Wyverley College."

There was a faint rustle from the back, which grew into a series of thumps and muffled exclamations. The driver watched for a second, as the mailbags stood up and hands reached out from the inside to open the drawstrings at the top. Then he turned his attention back to the front. Two of the schoolgirls were coming to his window, which he immediately wound down.

"Special delivery," he said, with a wink. "I'm supposed to say Ellie's dad and mum and that'll mean something to you, so you don't go sticking me with a sword or shooting me neither."

The closer girl, who could be no more than seventeen, turned to the other—who was even younger—and said, "Go and get Magistrix Coelle.

"You stay where you are and keep your hands on the wheel," she added to the driver. "Tell your passengers to keep still, too."

"We can hear you," said a voice from the back. A woman's voice, strong and vibrant. "Is that Felicity?"

The girl started back. Then, keeping her sword on guard in front of her, she peered through the window, past the driver.

"Yes, it's me, ma'am," said the girl cautiously. She stepped back and made a signal to the rifle girls, who relaxed slightly but did not lower their weapons, much to the driver's discomfort. "Do you mind waiting till Magistrix Coelle comes down? We can't be too careful today. There is a wind from the north, and reports of other trouble. How many of you are there?"

"We'll wait," said the voice. "Two. There's myself, and . . . Ellimere's father."

"Um, hello," said Felicity. "We had news . . . that you . . . though Magistrix Coelle did not believe it. . . ."

"Do not speak of that for now," said Sabriel. She had climbed out of the mailbag and was now crouched behind the driver. Felicity peered in again, reassuring herself that the woman she saw was in fact Ellimere's mother. Even though Sabriel was wearing blue Postal Service overalls and a watch cap pulled low over her night-black hair, she was recognizable. But Felicity was still wary. The true test would come when Magistrix Coelle tested these people's Charter marks.

"Here is your payment, as agreed," said Sabriel, passing a thick envelope to the driver. He took it and immediately looked inside, a slight smile touching his mouth and eyes.

"Much obliged," he said. "And I'll keep my mouth shut, too, as I promised."

"You'd better," muttered Touchstone.

The driver was clearly offended by this remark. He sniffed and said, "I live near Bain and always have, and I know what's what. I didn't help you for the money. That's just a sweetener."

"We appreciate your help," said Sabriel, with a quelling glance at Touchstone. Being cooped up in a mailbag for several hours had not done anything for his temper, nor did waiting, now that they were so close to the Wall and home. Wyverley College was only forty miles south of the border.

"Here, I'll bloody well give it back," said the driver. He dragged out the envelope and thrust it towards Touchstone.

"No, no, consider it a just reward," Sabriel said calmly, and pushed the envelope back. The driver resisted for a moment, then shrugged and replaced the money somewhere inside his jacket and settled sulkily down in his seat.

"Here is the magistrix," said Felicity with relief, as she looked back at an older woman and several students who were coming down the drive. They appeared to have emerged out of nowhere, for the main school building was out of sight around the bend, cloaked by a line of closely hugging poplars.

Once Magistrix Coelle arrived, it was only a matter of minutes before Sabriel and Touchstone had the Charter marks on their foreheads assessed for purity and they were all on their way to the school, and the postal van on its way back to Bain.

"I knew the news was false," said Magistrix Coelle as they walked quickly—almost at a trot—up to the huge, gate-like doors of the main building. "The *Corvere Times* ran a photo of two burnt-out cars and some bodies but had little else to say. It seemed very much a put-up job."

"It was real enough," said Sabriel grimly. "Damed and eleven others were killed in that attack, and two more of our people outside Hennen. Perhaps more have been killed. We split up after Hennen, to lay false trails. None of our people have beaten us here?"

Coelle shook her head.

"Damed won't be forgotten," said Touchstone. "Or Barlest, or any of them. We will not forget our enemies, either."

"These are terrible times," sighed Coelle. She shook her head several times again as they went inside, past more armed schoolgirls, who looked on in awe at the legendary Sabriel and her consort, even if he was only the King of the Old Kingdom and nowhere near as interesting. Sabriel had once been one of them. They kept looking long after Coelle had ushered the distinguished visitors through a door to the Visiting Parents' parlor, possibly the most luxuriously appointed room in the whole school.

"I trust the things we left have not been disturbed?" asked Sabriel. "What is the situation? What news?"

"Everything is as you left it," replied Coelle. "We have no real trouble yet. Felicity! Please have the Abhorsen's trunk brought up from the cellar. Pippa and Zettie . . . and whoever is hall monitor today . . . can help you. As to news, I have messages and—"

"Messages! From Ellimere or Sameth?" asked Touchstone urgently.

Coelle took two folded pieces of paper from her sleeve and passed them across. Touchstone grabbed them eagerly and stood close to Sabriel to read them, as Felicity and her cohorts surged past and disappeared through one of the heavy, highly polished doors.

The first message was written in blue pencil on a torn piece of letterhead that had the same bugle-and-scroll symbol that had adorned the side of the postal van. Touchstone and Sabriel read it through carefully, deep frowns appearing on both their foreheads. Then they read it again and looked at each other, deep surprise clear on their faces.

"One of our old girls sent that," contributed Coelle nervously, as no one said anything. "Lornella Acren-Janes, who is assistant to the Postmaster General. A copy of a telegram, obviously. I don't know if it ever went to your embassy."

"Can it be trusted?" asked Touchstone. "Aunt Lirael? Abhorsen-in-Waiting? Is this some other ploy to cloud our minds?"

Sabriel shook her head.

"It sounds like Sam," she said. "Even though I don't understand it. Clearly much has been going on in the Old Kingdom. I do not think we will quickly come to the root of it all."

She unfolded the second piece of paper. Unlike the first, this was thick, handmade paper, and there were only three symbols upon it. Quiescent Charter marks, dark on the white page. Sabriel ran her palm across them, and they sprang into bright, vivid life, almost leaping into her hand. With them came Ellimere's voice, clear and strong as if she stood next to them.

"Mother! Father! I hope you get this very quickly. The Clayr have Seen much more, too much to tell in this message. There is great danger, beyond our imagining. I am at Barhedrin with the Guard, the Trained Bands, and a Seven Hundred and Eighty-Four of the Clayr. The Clayr are trying to See what we must do. They say Sam is alive and fighting, and that whatever we do, you must get to Barhedrin by Anstyr's Day or it will be too late. We have to take the Paperwings somewhere. Oh— I have an aunt, apparently your half-sister . . . What? Don't interrupt—"

Ellimere's voice stopped mid word. The Charter marks faded back into the paper.

"An interruption mid spell," said Touchstone with a frown. "It's unlike Ellimere not to redo it. Whose half-sister? She cannot be mine—"

"The important fact is that the Clayr have finally Seen something," said Sabriel. "Anstyr's Day . . . we need to consult an almanac. That must be soon . . . very soon . . . we will have to go on immediately."

"I'm not sure you'll be able to," said Coelle nervously. "That message got here only this morning. A Crossing Point Scout brought it. He was in a hurry to get back. Apparently there has been some sort of attack from across the Wall, and—"

"An attack from across the Wall!" interrupted Sabriel and Touchstone together. "What kind of attack?"

"He didn't know," stammered Coelle, taken aback at the ferocity of the question, Sabriel and Touchstone both leaning in close to her. "It was in the far west. But there is also trouble at the Crossing Point. Apparently General Kingswold, the visiting Inspector General, has declared for the Our Country government, but General Tindall refuses to recognize it or Kingswold. Various units have taken sides, some with Tindall, some with Kingswold—"

"So Corolini has openly tried to seize power?" asked Sabriel. "When did this happen?"

"It was in this morning's paper," replied Coelle. "We haven't had the afternoon edition. There is fighting in Corvere. . . . You didn't know?"

"We've got this far by hidden ways, avoiding contact with Ancelstierrans as much as possible," said Touchstone. "There hasn't been a lot of time to read the papers."

"The *Times* said the Chief Minister still controls the Arsenal, Decision Palace, and Corvere Moot," said Coelle.

"If he holds the Palace, then he still controls the Hereditary Arbiter," said Touchstone. He looked at Sabriel for confirmation. "Corolini cannot form a government without the Arbiter's blessing, can he?"

"Not unless everything has crumbled," said Sabriel decisively. "But it doesn't matter. Corolini, the attempted coup—it is all a sideshow. Everything that has happened here is the work of some power from the Old Kingdom—our kingdom. The continental wars, the influx of Southerling refugees, the rise of Corolini, everything has been orchestrated, planned for some purpose we do not know. But what can a power from our Kingdom want in Ancelstierre? I can understand sowing confusion in Ancelstierre to facilitate an attack across the Wall. But for what? And who?"

"Sam's telegram mentions Chlorr," said Touchstone.

"Chlorr is only a necromancer, though a powerful one," said Sabriel. "It must be something else. 'Evil updug . . . I mean dug up . . . near Edge—'"

Sabriel stopped in mid sentence as Felicity and her three cohorts staggered in, carrying a long, brassbound trunk. They put it down in the middle of the floor. Charter marks drifted in lazy lines along the lid and across the keyhole. They flared into brilliant life as Sabriel touched the lock and whispered some words under her breath. There was a snick, the lid lifted a finger's breadth, then Sabriel flung it open to reveal clothes, armor, swords, and her bell-bandolier. Sabriel ignored these, digging down one side to pull out a large, leather-bound book. Embossed gold type on the cover declared the book to be *An Alamanac of the Two Countries and the Region of the Wall*. She flicked quickly through its thick pages till she came to a series of tables.

"What is today?" she asked. "The date?"

"The twentieth," said Coelle.

Sabriel ran her finger down one table and then across. She stared at the result, and her finger ran again through the numbers as she quickly rechecked it.

"When is it?" asked Touchstone. "Anstyr's Day?"

"Now," said Sabriel. "Today."

Silence greeted her words. Touchstone rallied a moment later.

"It should still be morning in the Kingdom,"

he said. "We can make it."

"Not by road, not with the Crossing Point uncertain," said Sabriel. "We are too far south to call a Paperwing—"

Her eyes flashed at a sudden idea. "Magistrix, does Hugh Jorbert still lease the school's west paddock for his flying school?"

"Yes," replied Coelle. "But the Jorberts are on holiday. They won't be back for a month."

"We can't fly in an Ancelstierran machine," protested Touchstone. "The wind is from the north. The engine will die within ten miles of here."

"If we get high enough, we should be able to glide over," said Sabriel. "Though not without a pilot. How many of the girls are taking flying lessons?"

"A dozen perhaps," said Coelle reluctantly. "I don't know if any of them can fly alone—"

"I have my solo rating," interrupted Felicity eagerly. "My father used to fly with Colonel Jorbert in the Corps. I have two hundred hours in our Humbert trainer at home and fifty in the Beskwith here. I've done emergency landings, night flying, and everything. I can fly you over the Wall."

"No, you cannot," said Magistrix Coelle. "I forbid it!"

"These are not ordinary times," said Sabriel, quelling Coelle with a glance. "We all must do whatever we can. Thank you, Felicity. We accept. Please go and get everything ready, while we get changed into more suitable clothes."

Felicity let out an excited yell and raced out, her followers close behind. Coelle made a motion as if to restrain her but did not follow through. Instead, she sat down on the closest armchair, took a handkerchief out of her sleeve, and wiped her forehead. The Charter mark there glowed faintly as the cloth passed over it.

"She's a student," protested Coelle. "What will I tell her parents if . . . if she doesn't . . ."

"I don't know," said Sabriel. "I have never known what to tell anybody. Except that it is better to do something than nothing, even if the cost is great."

She did not look at Coelle as she spoke, but out through the window. In the middle of the lawn there was an obelisk of white marble, twenty feet high. Its sides were carved with many names. They were too small to be read from the window, but Sabriel knew most of the names anyway, even when she had not known the people. The obelisk was a memorial to all those who had fallen on a terrible night nearly twenty years before, when Kerrigor had come across the Wall with a horde of Dead. There were the names of Colonel Horyse, many other soldiers, schoolgirls, teachers, policemen, two cooks, a gardener . . .

A flash of color beyond the obelisk caught Sabriel's eye. A white rabbit ran across the lawn, hotly pursued by a young girl, her pigtails flying as she vainly tried to capture her pet. For a moment Sabriel was lost in time, taken back to another fleeing rabbit, another pigtailed schoolgirl.

Jacinth and Bunny.

Jacinth was one of the names on the obelisk, but the rabbit outside might well be some distant descendant of Bunny. Life did go on, though it was never without struggle.

Sabriel turned away from the window and from the past. The future was what concerned her now. They had to reach Barhedrin within twelve hours. She startled Coelle by ripping off her blue coveralls, revealing that she was naked underneath. When Touchstone began to unbutton his coveralls, Coelle squealed and fled the room.

Sabriel and Touchstone looked at each other and laughed. Just for an instant, before they began to dress rapidly in the clothes from the trunk. Soon they looked and felt like themselves again, in good linen underwear, woolen shirt and leggings, and armored coats and surcoats. Touchstone had his twin swords, Sabriel her Abhorsen's blade, and most important of all, she once again wore her bandolier of bells.

"Ready?" asked Sabriel as she settled the bandolier across her chest and adjusted the strap.

"Ready," confirmed Touchstone. "Or as ready as I'm going to get. I hate flying at the best of times, let alone in one of those unreliable Ancelstierran machines."

"I expect it's going to be worse than usual," said Sabriel. "But I don't think we have any choice."

"Of course," sighed Touchstone. "I hesitate to ask—in what particular way will it be worse than usual?"

"Because, unless I miss my guess," said Sabriel, "Jorbert will have flown his wife out in the two-seater Beskwith. That will leave his single-seater Humbert Twelve. We are going to have to lie on the wings."

"I am always amazed at what you know," said Touchstone. "I am at a loss with these machines. All of Jorbert's flying conveyances looked the same to me."

"Unfortunately they are not," said Sabriel. "But there is no other way home that I can think of. Not if we are to make Barhedrin before the end of Anstyr's Day. Come on!"

She strode out of the room and did not pause to look back to see if Touchstone was following. Of course, he was.

Jorbert's flying school was a very small affair, not much more than a hobby for the retired Flying Corps colonel. There was a single hangar a hundred yards from his comfortable extended farmhouse. The hangar sat on the corner of Wyverley College's West Field, which, suitably lined with yellow-painted oil drums, served as the runway.

Sabriel was correct about the aeroplane. There was only one, a boxy green single-seater biplane that to Touchstone looked as if it depended far too much on its many supporting struts and wires all holding together.

Felicity, almost unrecognizable in helmet, goggles, and fur flying suit, was already in the cockpit. Another girl stood by the propeller, and there were two more crouched by the wheels under the fuselage.

"You'll have to lie on the wings," shouted Felicity cheerfully. "I forgot that the Colonel took the Beskwith. Don't worry, it's not that difficult. There are handholds. I've done it heaps of times . . . well, twice . . . and I've wing walked, too."

"Handholds," muttered Touchstone. "Wing walking."

"Quiet," ordered Sabriel. "Don't upset our pilot."

She climbed nimbly up the left side and laid herself across the wing, taking a secure hold on the two handgrips. Her bells were a nuisance, but she was used to that.

Touchstone climbed less nimbly up the right side—and almost put his foot through the wing. Disturbed to find it was only fabric stretched over a wooden frame, he lay down with extreme care and tugged hard on the handholds. They didn't come off, as he had half-expected they might.

"Ready?" asked Felicity.

"Ready!" shouted Sabriel.

"I suppose so," muttered Touchstone. Then, much louder, he called out a hearty "Yes!"

"Contact!" ordered Felicity. The girl at the front spun the propeller expertly and stepped back. The prop swung around as the engine coughed, faltered for a moment, then sped up into a blur as the engine caught.

"Chocks away!"

The other girls pulled at their ropes, dragging out to either side the chocks that held the wheels. The plane rocked forward, then slowly bumped around in a slow arc till it was lined up on the runway and facing the wind. The sound of the engine rose higher, and the plane started forward, bumping even more, as if it were an ungainly bird that needed to jump and flap a long way to get airborne.

Touchstone watched the ground ahead, his eyes watering as their speed increased. He had expected the plane to take off like a Paperwing—fairly quickly and with ease and elan. But as they sped down the field, and the low stone wall at the northern end grew closer and closer, he realized that he knew nothing about Ancelstierran aircraft. Obviously they would leap into the sky sharply at the very end of the field.

Or not, he thought a few seconds later. They were still on the ground and the wall was only twenty or thirty paces in front of them. He started to think it would be better to let go and try and jump away from the imminent wreck. But he couldn't see Sabriel on the other wing, and he wasn't going to jump without her.

The plane lurched sideways and bounced up

into the air. Touchstone sighed with relief as they cleared the wall with inches to spare, then yelled as they went back down again. The ground came up hard, and he was too winded to do anything else as they bounced again and then were finally climbing into the sky.

"Sorry!" shouted Felicity, her voice barely audible over the engine and the rush of air. "Heavier than usual. I forgot."

He could hear Sabriel shouting something on the other side but could not hear the words. Whatever it was, Felicity was nodding her head. Almost immediately the plane began to spiral back to the south, gaining height. Touchstone nodded to himself. They would need to get as high as they could in order to have the greatest gliding range. With a north wind, it was likely the engine would fail within ten miles of the Wall. So they would have to be able to glide at least that far, and preferably a bit farther. It would not do to land in the Perimeter.

Not that landing in the Old Kingdom would be easy. Touchstone looked at the fabric wing shivering above him and hoped that most of the plane was man-made. For if parts of it were not, they would fall apart too soon, the common fate of

Ancelstierran devices and machinery once they were across the Wall.

"I am never flying again," muttered Touchstone. Then he remembered Ellimere's message. If they did manage to land on the other side of the Wall, and get to Barhedrin, then they would have to fly somewhere in a Paperwing, to engage in a battle with an unknown Enemy of unknown powers.

Touchstone's face set in grim lines at that thought. He would welcome that battle. He and Sabriel had struggled too long against opponents manipulated from afar. Now whatever it was had come out in the open, and it would face the combined forces of the King, the Abhorsen, and the Clayr.

Provided, of course, that the King and the Abhorsen managed to survive this flight.

PART THREE

CHAPTER SEVENTEEN

COMING HOME TO ANCELSTIERRE

"WIND'S VEERING NOR-NOREAST, sir," reported Yeoman Prindel as he watched the arrow on the wind gauge, which was mechanically linked to the weathervane several floors above them. As the arrow swung, the electric lights overhead flickered and went out, leaving the room lit by only two rather smoky hurricane lamps. Prindel looked at his watch, which had stopped, and then at the striped time candle between the hurricane lamps. "Electric failure at approximately 1649."

"Very good, Prindel," replied Lieutenant Drewe. "Order the switch to oil and sound general quarters. I'm going up to the light."

"Aye, aye, sir," replied Prindel. He uncovered a speaking tube and bawled down it, "Switch to oil! General quarters! I say again, general quarters!"

"Aye, aye!" came echoing out the speaking tube, followed by the scream of a hand-cranked siren and the clang of a cracked handbell, both of which could be heard throughout the lighthouse.

Drewe shrugged on his blue duffel coat and strapped on a broad leather belt that supported both a revolver and a cutlass. His blue steel helmet, adorned with the crossed golden keys emblem that proclaimed his current post as the Keeper of the Western Light, completed his equipment. The helmet had belonged to his predecessor and was slightly too large, so Drewe always felt a bit like a fool when he put it on, but regulations were regulations.

The control room was five floors below the light. As Drewe climbed steadily up the steps, he met Able Seaman Kerrick rushing down.

"Sir! You'd better hurry!"

"I am hurrying, Kerrick," Drewe replied calmly, hoping his voice was steadier than his suddenly accelerating heart. "What is it?"

"Fog—"

"There's always fog. That's why we're here. To warn any ship not to sail into it."

"No, no, sir! Not on the sea! On the land. A creeping fog that's coming down from the north.

There's lightning behind it, and it's heading for the Wall. And there's people coming up from the south, too!"

Drewe abandoned his calm, drilled into him with so much care at the Naval College he'd left only eighteen months before. He pushed past Kerrick and took the rest of the steps three at a time. He was panting as he pushed open the heavy steel trap-door and climbed into the light chamber, but he took a deep breath and managed to present some semblance of the cool, collected naval officer he was supposed to be.

The light was off and wouldn't be lit for another hour or so. There was a dual system, one oil and clockwork, the other fully electric, to cater to the strange way that electricity and technology failed when the wind blew from the north. From the Old Kingdom.

Drewe was relieved to see his most experienced petty officer was already there. Coxswain Berl was outside on the walkway, big observer's binoculars pressed to his eyes. Drewe went out to join him, bracing himself for the cold breeze. But when he went out, the wind was warm, another sign that it came from the north. Berl had told him the seasons were different across the Wall, and Drewe had been at the Western Light long enough to believe him now, though he had dismissed the notion at first.

"What's going on?" Drewe demanded. The regular sea fog was sitting off the coast, as it always did, night and day. But there was another, darker fog rolling down from the north, towards the Wall. It was strangely lit by flashes of lightning and stretched to the east as far as Drewe could see.

"Where are these people?"

Berl handed him the binoculars and pointed.

"Hundreds of them, Mister Drewe, maybe thousands. Southerlings, I reckon, from the new camp at Lington Hill. Heading north, trying to get across the Wall. But they aren't the problem."

Drewe twiddled with the focus knob, clanged the binoculars against the rim of his helmet, and wished he could be more impressive in front of Berl.

He couldn't see anything at all at first, but as he got the focus right, all the fuzzy blobs sharpened and became running figures. There were thousands of them, men in blue hats and women in blue scarves, and many children dressed completely in blue. They were throwing planks onto the concertina wire, forcing their way through and cutting where they had to. Some had already made it through the No Man's Land of wire and were almost at the Wall. Drewe shook his head at the sight. Why on earth were they trying to get into the Old Kingdom? To make matters even more confusing, some of the Southerlings who had made it to the Wall were starting to run back. . . .

"Has Perimeter HQ been informed about these people?" he asked. There was an Army post down there, at least a company in the rear trenches with pickets and listening posts spread out forward and back. What were the pongoes doing?

"The phones will be out," said Berl grimly. "Besides, those people aren't the problem. Take a look at the leading edge of that fog, sir."

Drewe swung the binoculars around. The fog was moving faster than he'd thought, and it was surprisingly regular. Almost like a wall itself, moving down to meet the one of stone. Strange fog, with lightning illuminating it from the inside . . .

Drewe swallowed, blinked, and fiddled with the focus knob on the binoculars again, unable to believe what he was seeing. There were things in the forefront of the fog. Things that might have once been people but now were not. He'd heard stories of such creatures when he was first posted to shore duty in the north, but hadn't really believed them. Walking corpses, inexplicable monsters, magic both cruel and kind. . . .

"Those Southerlings won't stand a chance," whispered Berl. "I grew up in the north. I seen what happened twenty years ago at Bain—"

"Quiet, Berl," ordered Drewe. "Kerrick!"

Kerrick poked his head out the door.

"Kerrick, get a dozen red rockets and start firing them. One every three minutes."

"R-red rockets, sir?" quavered Kerrick. Red rockets were the ultimate distress signal for the lighthouse.

"Red rockets! Move!" roared Drewe. "Berl! I want every man but Kerrick assembled outside in five minutes, number-three rig and rifles!"

"Rifles won't work, sir," said Berl sadly. "And those Southerlings wouldn't have got across the Perimeter unless the garrison was already dead. There was a whole Army company down there—"

"I've given you an order! Now get to it!"

"Sir, we can't help them," Berl pleaded. "You don't know what those things can do! Our standing orders are to defend the lighthouse, not to—"

"Coxswain Berl," Drewe said stiffly. "Whatever the Army's failings, the Royal Ancelstierran Navy has never stood by while innocents die. It will not start doing so under my command!"

"Aye, aye, sir," said Berl slowly. He raised one brawny hand in salute, then suddenly brought it crashing down on Drewe's neck, under the rim of the officer's helmet. The Lieutenant crumpled into Berl's arms, and the coxswain laid him gently down on the floor and took his revolver and cutlass.

"What are you looking at, Kerrick! Get those bloody rockets firing!"

"But—but—what about—"

"If he comes to, give him a cup of water and tell him I've taken command," ordered Berl. "I'm going down to prepare the defenses."

"Defenses?"

"Those Southerlings came from the south, straight through the Army lines. So there's something already on this side, something that fixed the soldiers good and proper. Something Dead, unless I miss my guess. We'll be next, if they aren't here already. So get going with the bloody rockets!"

The big petty officer shouted the last words as he climbed through the hatch and slammed it behind him.

The clang of the hatch was still echoing as Kerrick heard the first shouts, somewhere down in the courtyard. Then there was more shouting, and a terrible scream and a confusing hubbub of noise:

yelling and screaming and the clash of steel.

Trembling, Kerrick opened the rocket store and wrestled one out. The launcher was set up on the balcony rail, but though he'd done it a hundred times in training, he couldn't get the rocket to sit in it. When it was finally home, he pulled too quickly on the cord to ignite it, and his hands were burned as the rocket blasted into the sky.

Sobbing from pain and fear, Kerrick went back to get another rocket. Above his head, red blossoms fell from the sky, bright against the cloud.

Kerrick didn't wait three minutes to fire the next one, or the next.

He was still firing rockets when the Dead Hands came up through the hatch. The fog was all around the lighthouse by then, only Kerrick, his rockets, and the light room above the wet, flowing mass of mist. The fog looked almost like solid ground, so convincing that Kerrick hardly thought twice when the Dead creature came smashing through the glass door and reached out to rend him with hands that had too many fingers and ended in curved and bloody bone.

Kerrick jumped, and for a few steps the fog did seem to support him, and he laughed hysterically as he ran. But he was falling, falling, all the same.

The Dead Hands watched him go, a tiny spark of Life that all too soon went out.

But Kerrick had not died in vain. The red rockets had been observed to the south and east. And in the light room, Lieutenant Drewe came to and staggered to his feet as Kerrick fell. He saw the Dead and, in a flash of inspiration, pulled the lever that released the striker and the pressurized oil.

Light flared atop the lighthouse, light magnified a thousandfold by the best lenses ever ground by the glass masters of Corvere. The beam shone out on two sides, bracketing the Dead on the balcony. They screeched and shielded their decaying eyes. Desperately, the young naval officer slammed the clockwork gear into neutral and leaned on the capstan, to turn the light around. It had been designed for this, in case of total mechanical failure, but not to be pushed by one man.

Desperation and fear provided the necessary strength. The light turned to catch the Dead full in its hot white beam. It didn't hurt them, but they hated it, so they retreated, taking Kerrick's way, out into the fog. Unlike Kerrick, the Dead Hands survived the fall, though their bodies were smashed. Slowly they pulled themselves upright and, on jellied, broken limbs, began the long climb back up the stairs. There was Life there, and they wanted the taste of it, the annoyance of the light already forgotten.

Nick woke to thunder and lightning. As always in recent times, he was disoriented and dizzy. He could feel the ground moving unsteadily beneath him, and it took him a moment to realize that he was being carried on a stretcher. There were two men at each end, marching along with their burden. Normal men, or normal enough. Not the leprous pit workers Hedge called the Night Crew.

"Where are we?" he asked. His voice was hoarse, and he tasted blood. Hesitantly he touched his lips, and he felt the dried blood caked there. "I'd like a drink of water."

"Master!" shouted one of the men. "He's awake!"

Nick tried to sit up, but he didn't have the strength. All he could see above was thunderclouds and lightning, which was striking down somewhere ahead. The hemispheres! It all came back to him now. He had to make sure the hemispheres were safe!

"The hemispheres!" he shouted, pain spiking in his throat.

"They're safe," said a familiar voice. Hedge suddenly towered above him. He's got taller, Nick thought irrationally. Thinner, too. Sort of stretched out, like a toffee being fought over by two children. And he had seemed to be balding before, and now he had hair. Or was it shadow, curling across his forehead?

Nick shut his eyes. He couldn't think where he was or how he had got here. Obviously he was still sick, more seriously ill than before, or they wouldn't have to carry him.

"Where are we?" Nick asked weakly. He opened his eyes again, but he couldn't see Hedge, though the man answered from somewhere close by.

"We are about to cross the Wall," replied Hedge, and he laughed. It was an unpleasant laugh. But Nick couldn't help laughing, too. He didn't know why, and he couldn't make himself stop till he choked and had to.

Beyond Hedge's laugh and the constant boom of thunder, there was another noise. Nick couldn't identify it at first. He kept listening as his stretcher bearers stolidly carried him forward, till at last he thought he knew what it was. The audience at a football game or a cricket match. Shouting and yelling at a win. Though the Wall would be an odd

321

place to have a game. Perhaps the soldiers at the Perimeter played, he thought.

Five minutes later Nick could hear screaming in the crowd noise, and he knew it was no football game. He tried to sit up again, only to be pressed back down by a hand that he knew was Hedge's, though it was black and burnt-looking, and there were red flames where the fingernails should be.

Hallucinations, Nick thought desperately. Hallucinations.

"We must cross quickly," said Hedge, instructing the stretcher bearers. "The Dead can keep the passage for only a few more minutes. As soon as the hemispheres are through, we will run."

"Yes, sir," chorused the stretcher bearers.

Nick wondered what Hedge was talking about. They were passing between two lines of his strange, afflicted laborers now. Nick tried not to look at them, at the decaying flesh held together by torn blue rags. Fortunately, he couldn't see their ravaged faces. They were all facing away, like some sort of back-to-front honor guard, and they had linked their arms.

"The hemispheres are across the Wall!"

Nick didn't know who spoke. The voice was strange and echoing, and it made him feel unclean.

But the words had an immediate effect. The stretcher bearers began to run, bouncing Nick up and down. He gripped the sides and, on the peak of one of the bounces, used its extra momentum to sit up and look around.

They were running into a tunnel through the Wall that separated the Old Kingdom and Ancelstierre. A low, arched tunnel cut through the stone. It was packed with the Night Crew from beginning to end, great lines of them with their arms linked and only a very narrow passage in between the lines. Every man and woman was glowing with golden light, but as Nick got closer, he saw that the glow was from thousands of tiny golden flames, which were spreading and joining, and the people farther inside the wall were actually on fire.

Nick cried out in horror as they entered the tunnel. There was fire everywhere, strange golden fire that burnt without smoke. Though the Night Crew were being consumed by it, they did not attempt to flee, or cry out, or do anything to stop it. Even worse than that, Nick realized that as individuals were consumed by the fire, others would step into their places. Hundreds and hundreds of blue-clad men and women were pouring in from the far side, to maintain the lines.

Hedge was struggling ahead, Nick saw. But it was not exactly Hedge. It was more a Hedge-shaped thing of darkness, limned with red fire that fought against the gold. Every step he took was clearly an effort, and the gold flames seemed almost a physical force that was trying to prevent his crossing through the tunnel in the Wall.

Suddenly a whole group of the Night Crew ahead blazed, like candles collapsing into a final pool of wax, and disappeared completely. Before the people on either side could relink arms or new Night Crew rush in, the golden fire took advantage of the gap and roared out all the way across the tunnel. The stretcher bearers saw it, and they swore and screamed, but they kept on running. They hit the fire like swimmers running from the shore into surf, diving through it. But though the stretcher and its bearers made it through, Nick was plucked off the stretcher by the fire, wrapped in flame, and tumbled down onto the stone floor of the tunnel.

With the golden fire came a piercing cold pain in his heart, as if an icicle had been thrust through his chest. But it also brought a sudden clarity to his mind, and sharper senses. He could see individual symbols in the flames and the stones, symbols that moved and changed and formed in new combinations. These were the Charter marks he'd heard about, Nick realized. The magic of Sameth . . . and Lirael.

Everything that had happened recently rushed back into his head. He remembered Lirael and the winged dog. The flight from his tent. Hiding in the reeds. His conversation with Lirael. He had promised her that he would do whatever he could to stop Hedge.

The flames beat at Nick's chest but did not burn his skin. They tried to attack what was in him, to force the shard from his body. But it was a power beyond the magic of the Wall, and that power chose to re-assert itself even as Nick tried to embrace the Charter fire, grabbing at flames and even attempting to swallow flickers of golden light.

White sparks spewed out of Nick's mouth, nose, and ears, and his body suddenly uncurled, went ramrod straight, and flipped upright, elbows and knees vertically locked. Like some inflexible doll, Nick tottered forward, the golden flames raging at every step. Deep within his own mind he knew what was happening, but he was only an observer. He had no power over his own muscles. The shard had control, though it didn't know how to make him walk properly.

Joints locked, Nick lumbered on, past countless ranks of burning Night Crew, as more and more of them poured into the tunnel from the far end. Many of them hardly looked like Night Crew at all but could almost be normal men and women, their skin and hair fresh and alive. Only their eyes proclaimed their difference, and somewhere deep inside, Nick knew that they were dead, not just sick. Like their more putrescent brethren, these new arrivals also wore blue caps or scarves.

Ahead of him Hedge burst out of the tunnel and turned back to gesture at Nick. He felt the gesture like a physical grasp, dragging him forward even faster. The golden fire reached out to him everywhere it could, but there were too many Night Crew, too many burning bodies. The fire could not reach Nicholas, and finally he staggered out of the tunnel, away from the golden flames.

He had crossed the Wall and was in Ancelstierre. Or rather in the No Man's Land between the Wall and the Perimeter. Normally this would be a quiet, empty place of raw earth and barbed wire, made somehow peaceful by the soft whisper of the wind flutes that Nick had always presumed to be some sort of weird decoration or memorial. Now it was wreathed in fog, fog eerily underlit by the low, red glow of the setting sun and flashes of lightning. The fog thinned in places as it rolled inexorably south, revealing scenes of awful carnage. The white mass was like the curtain of a horror show, briefly drawing back to show piles of corpses, bodies everywhere, bodies hanging on the wire and piled on the ground. They were all blue capped and blue scarved, and Nick finally recognized that they were slain Southerling refugees, and that in some horrible way, that was who Hedge's Night Crew had also been.

Lightning crackled above him, and thunder rumbled. Fog billowed apart, and Nick caught a glimpse of the hemispheres a little way ahead, roped onto the huge sleds that Nick knew had been waiting for them when they off-loaded the barges at the Redmouth. But he couldn't remember that happening, or anything between talking to Lirael in the reed boat and his awakening just before crossing the Wall. The hemispheres had been dragged here, obviously by the men who were dragging them now. Normal men, or at least not the Night Crew. Men dressed in strange, ragged combinations of Ancelstierran Army uniforms and Old Kingdom clothes, khaki tunics contrasting with hunting leathers, bright colored breeches, and rusty mail.

The force that had propelled him through the tunnel suddenly retreated, and Nick fell at Hedge's feet. The necromancer was at least seven feet tall now, and the red flames burning around his flesh and in his eye sockets were brighter and more intense. For the first time, Nick was frightened of him, and he wondered why he hadn't been all along. But he was too weak to do anything but crouch at Hedge's feet and clutch at his chest, where the pain still throbbed.

"Soon," said Hedge, his voice rumbling like the thunder. "Soon our master will be free."

Nick found himself nodding enthusiastically and was as frightened by this as he was by Hedge. He was already drifting back into that dreamy state where all he could think about was the hemispheres and his Lightning Farm, and what had to be done—

"No," whispered Nick. What must *not* be done. He didn't know what was happening, and until he did know, he wasn't going to do anything. "No!"

Hedge recognized that Nick spoke with an independent voice. He grinned, and fire flickered in his throat. He lifted Nick up like a baby and cradled him to his chest, against the bandolier of bells.

"Your part is nearly done, Nicholas Sayre," he said, and his breath was hot like steam and smelled of decay. "You were never more than an imperfect host, though your uncle and father have proved to be more helpful than even I could have hoped, albeit unwittingly."

Nick could only stare up at the burning eyes. Already he had forgotten everything that had come back to him in the tunnel. In Hedge's eyes he saw the silver hemispheres, the lightning, the joining that he knew once again was the single high purpose of his own short life.

"The hemispheres," he whispered, almost ritually. "The hemispheres must be joined."

"Soon, Master, soon," crooned Hedge. He stalked over to the waiting bearers and laid Nicholas down on the stretcher, stroking his chest just above his heart with a blackened, still-burning hand. What little was left of Nick's Ancelstierran shirt dissolved at Hedge's touch, showing bare skin that was blue with deep bruising. "Soon!"

Nick watched dully as Hedge walked away. No independent thought was left to him. Only the burning vision of the hemispheres and their ultimate joining. He tried to sit up to look at them but didn't have the strength, and in any case the fog was thickening once again. Wearied by the effort, Nick's hands fell to the ground on either side of the stretcher, and one finger touched a piece of debris that sent a strange feeling through his arm. A sharp pain and a gentle, healing warmth.

He tried to close his hand on the object, but his fingers refused. With considerable effort Nick rolled over to see exactly what it was. He peered down from the stretcher and saw it was a piece of broken wood, a fragment of one of the smashed wind flutes, like the one whose stump he could see a few feet away. The fragment was still infused with Charter marks, which flowed over and through the wood. As Nick watched them, something stirred in the recesses of his mind. For a moment he remembered who he really was once more, and recalled the promise he had given to Lirael.

His right hand would not obey him, so Nicholas leaned over even more and tried to pick up the wooden fragment with his left hand. He succeeded for a few seconds, but even his left hand was no longer his to command. His fingers opened, and the piece of the wind flute fell on the stretcher, between

Nick's left arm and his body, not quite touching on either side.

Hedge did not walk far from Nicholas. He strode through the fog, which parted before him, straight to the largest pile of Southerling corpses. They had been killed by the Dead that Hedge had raised earlier that day from the temporary cemeteries around the camps. He was amused by the notion of using Southerling Dead to kill Southerlings. They had also killed the soldiers in the quaintly named Western Strongpoint, and the sailors in the lighthouse.

Hedge had crossed the Wall three times that day. Once to set the initial attacks in motion in Ancelstierre, which was no great task; second to go back to prepare the crossing of the hemispheres, which was much more difficult; and the third time with the hemispheres and Nicholas. He would never need to cross again, he knew, for the Wall would be one of the first things his master would destroy, along with all other works of the despised Charter.

All that remained to be done here was to go into Death and compel as many spirits as he could find to return and inhabit these bodies. Though Forwin Mill was less than twenty miles away and they should be able to reach it by morning, Hedge knew the Ancelstierran Army would attempt to prevent their breaking out of the Perimeter. He needed Dead Hands to fight the Army, and most of the ones he'd brought from the north and those created earlier that day in the Southerling camp cemeteries had been consumed in the crossing of the Wall, used up in order to get the hemispheres across.

Hedge drew two bells from his bandolier. Saraneth, for compulsion. Mosrael, to wake the spirits who slumbered here in No Man's Land, now freed from the chains of the hated Abhorsen's wind toys. He would use Mosrael to rouse as many as possible, though use of that bell would send him far into Death himself. Then he would come back through the gates and precincts, using Saraneth to drive any other spirits he could find into Life.

There would be plenty of bodies for all.

But before he could begin, he sensed something coming through the darkness. Ever careful, Hedge put Mosrael away, lest it sound of its own accord, and drew his sword instead, whispering the words that set the dark flames running down the blade.

He knew who it was, but he did not trust even the bounds and charms he had laid upon her. Chlorr was one of the Greater Dead now. In Life she had come under the sway of the Destroyer, but in Death she was somewhat beyond that control. Hedge had forced her obedience by other means, and as always with a necromancer's control over such a spirit, this obedience could be tenuous.

Chlorr appeared as a shape of darkness that was only vaguely human, with misshapen appendages upon a bulky torso that suggested two arms, two legs, and a head. Deep fires burned where eyes should be, though the fires were too large and too widely set apart. Chlorr had crossed the Wall with Hedge the first time and had led the surprise attack on the Ancelstierran Army garrison, in their Western Strongpoint. They had not expected an assault from the south. Chlorr had reaped many lives and was all the more powerful for it. Hedge watched her warily and kept a firm grip on Saraneth. The bells did not like to serve necromancers, and even a bell that an Abhorsen would find steady had to be shown who was master at all times.

Chlorr bowed, somewhat ironically in Hedge's estimation. Then she spoke, a misshapen mouth forming in the cloud of darkness. The words were a gibberish, slurred and broken. Hedge frowned and raised his sword. The mouth firmed up, and a tongue of blood-red fire flickered from side to side in the hideous maw.

"Your pardon, Master," said Chlorr. "Many soldiers are coming on a road from the south, riding horses. Some are Charter mages, though they are not adept. I slew those who came first, but there are many more behind, so I returned to warn my master."

"Good," said Hedge. "I am about to prepare a new host of Dead, which I will send to you when they are ready. For now, gather here all the Hands that you can and attack these soldiers. The Charter Mages in particular must be slain. Nothing must delay our lord!"

Chlorr bent her great, shapeless head. Then she reached back behind her and dragged forward a man who had been hidden by the fog and her dark bulk. He was a thin, little man, his coat ripped off his back to show a classic clerk's white shirt, complete with sleeve protectors. She held him by the neck just with two huge fingers, and he was almost dead from terror and lack of air. He fell to his knees in front of Hedge, gasping for breath and sobbing.

"This is yours, or so he says," said Chlorr. Then she strode off, her hands reaching out to touch any Dead Hands that were close by. As she touched them, they shuddered and jerked, then slowly began to follow her. But there were surprisingly few Hands left, and none at all in the tunnel through the Wall. Chlorr was careful not to go near the brooding mass of stone that still shimmered every now and then with golden light. Even she did not take crossing the Wall lightly, and possibly could not have done it without Hedge's help and the sacrifice of many lesser Dead.

"Who?" demanded Hedge.

"I'm . . . I'm Deputy Leader Geanner," sobbed the man. He proffered an envelope. "Mister Corolini's assistant. I've brought you the treaty letter . . . the permission to cross . . . to cross the Wall—"

Hedge took the envelope, which burst into flame as he touched it and was consumed, grey flakes of ash falling from his blackened hand.

"I do not need permission," whispered Hedge. "From anyone."

"I've also come for the . . . the fourth payment, as agreed," continued Geanner, staring up at Hedge. "We have done all you asked."

"All?" asked Hedge. "The King and the Abhorsen?"

"D . . . d . . . dead," gasped Geanner. "Bombed

and burnt in Corvere. There was nothing left."

"The camps near Forwin Mill?"

"Our people will open the gates at dawn, as instructed. The handbills have been printed, with translations in Azhdik and Chellanian. They will believe the promises, I'm sure."

"The coup?"

"We are still fighting in Corvere and elsewhere, but . . . but I'm sure Our Country will prevail."

"Then everything I need has been done," said Hedge. "All save one thing."

"What's that?" asked Geanner. He looked up at Hedge but barely had begun to scream before the burning blade came down and took his head from his shoulders.

"A waste," croaked Chlorr, who was returning with a string of Hands shambling behind her. "The body is useless now."

"Go!" roared Hedge, suddenly angry. He sheathed his sword all bloody and drew Mosrael again. "Lest I send you into Death and summon a more useful servant!"

Chlorr chuckled, a sound like dry stones rattling in an iron bucket, and disappeared off into the night, a line of perhaps a hundred Dead Hands shambling after her. As the last one crossed into the forward trenches, Hedge rang Mosrael. A single note issued from the bell, starting low and gradually increasing in both volume and pitch. As the sound spread, the bodies of the Southerlings began to twitch and wriggle, and the mounds of corpses became alive with movement. At the same time, ice formed on Hedge. Still Mosrael sounded, though its wielder was already stalking through the cold river of Death.

CHAPTER EIGHTEEN

CHLORR OF THE MASK

LIRAEL AWOKE WITH a start, her heart pounding and her hands scrabbling for bells and sword. It was dark, and she was trapped in some chamber . . . no, she realized, coming fully awake. She was sleeping in the back of one of the noisy conveyances—a truck, Sam called it. Only it wasn't noisy now.

"We've stopped," said the Dog. She thrust her head out the canvas flap to look around, and her voice became rather muffled. "I think rather unexpectedly."

Lirael sat up and tried to banish the sensation of being recently clubbed on the head and made to drink vinegar. She still had her cold. At least it was no worse, though the Ancelstierran spring had yet to fully flower and winter had not given up its grip on nighttime temperatures.

The stop certainly seemed unexpected, judging from the amount of swearing coming from the driver up front. Then Sam drew back the flap completely from the outside, narrowly escaping a welcoming full-face lick from the Disreputable Dog. He looked tired, and Lirael wondered if he'd been able to sleep after hearing the terrible news about his parents. She'd fallen asleep almost as soon as they'd got in the . . . truck . . . though she had no idea how long she'd been asleep. It didn't feel long, and it was still very dark, the only light coming from the Dog's collar.

"The trucks have stalled," reported Sam. "Though the wind's practically a westerly. I think we're getting too close to the hemispheres. We'll have to walk from here."

"Where are we?" Lirael asked. She stood up too quickly, and her head hit the canvas canopy, just missing one of the steel struts. There was a lot of noise outside now—shouting and the crash of hobnailed boots on the road—but behind all that there was also a constant dull booming. In her half-asleep state, it took a moment for her to understand it wasn't thunder, which she half-expected, but something else.

The Dog jumped out over the tailgate, and

Lirael followed, somewhat more sedately. They were still on the Perimeter road, she saw, and it looked like early morning. The moon was up, a slim crescent rather than the nearly full moon of the Old Kingdom. It was subtly different in shape and color, too, Lirael noted. Less silver, and more a pale buttercup yellow.

The booming noise was coming from farther south, and there was a faint whistling with it. Lirael could see bright flashes on the horizon there, but it was not lightning. There was thunder as well, to the west, and the flashes from that direction were definitely lightning. As she looked, Lirael thought she caught the faintest whiff of Free Magic, though the wind was indeed a southerly. And she could sense Dead somewhere up ahead. Not more than a mile away.

"What is that noise, and the lights?" she asked Sam, pointing south. He turned to look but had to step back before he could answer, as soldiers started to trot past the trucks.

"Artillery," he said after a moment. "Big guns. They must be far enough back, so they aren't affected by the Old Kingdom or the hemispheres and can still fire. Um, they're sort of like catapults that throw an exploding device several miles, which hits the ground or blows up in the air and kills people."

"A total waste of time," interrupted Major Greene, who had come puffing up. "You can't hear any shells exploding, can you? So all they're doing is lobbing what might as well be big rocks over, and even a direct hit with an unexploded shell won't do anything to the Dead. It'll just be a big mess for the ordnance people to clear up. Thousands of UXBs, and most of them white phosphorus. Nasty stuff! Come on!"

The Major puffed on past, with Lirael, the Dog, and Sam following. They left their packs in the trucks, and for a moment Lirael thought Mogget was still asleep in Sam's. Then she saw the little white cat up ahead behind the first double-timing platoon, dashing along the roadside as if he were chasing a mouse. As he pounced, she recognized that was exactly what he was doing. Hunting something to eat.

"Where are we?" asked Lirael as she easily caught up to Major Greene. He looked at her, took a coughing breath, and nodded his head at Lieutenant Tindall, who was up ahead. Lirael got the hint. She ran forward to the younger officer and repeated her question.

"About three miles from the Perimeter's Western Strongpoint," replied Tindall. "Forwin Mill is about sixteen miles south of there, but hopefully we'll be able to stop this Hedge at the Wall—First Platoon, halt!"

The sudden order surprised Lirael, and she ran on a few steps before she saw the soldiers in front had stopped. Lieutenant Tindall barked out some more orders, repeated by a sergeant at the front, and the soldiers ran off to either side of the road, readying their rifles.

"Cavalry, ma'am!" snapped Tindall, taking her arm and urging her to the side of the road. "We don't know whose."

Lirael rejoined Sam and drew her sword. They stared down the road, listening to the beat of hooves on the metaled road. The Dog stared, too, but Mogget played with the mouse he'd caught. It was still alive, and he kept letting it go, only to snap it up after it had run a few feet, holding it frantic and terrified in his partly open mouth.

"Not Dead," pronounced Lirael.

"Or Free Magic," said the Disreputable Dog with a loud sniff. "But very afraid."

They saw the horse and rider a moment later. He was an Ancelstierran soldier, a mounted infantryman, though he had lost his carbine and saber. He shouted as he saw the soldiers.

"Get out of the way! Get out of here!"

He tried to ride on, but the horse shied as soldiers spilled out on the road. Someone grabbed the bridle and brought the horse to a halt. Others dragged the man roughly from the saddle as he tried to slap the horse on with his hands.

"What's going on, man?" asked Major Greene roughly. "What's your name and unit?"

"Trooper 732769 Maculler, sir," replied the man automatically, but his teeth chattered as he spoke, and sweat was pouring down his face. "Fourteenth Light Horse, with the Perimeter Flying Detachment."

"Good. Now tell me what's going on," said the Major.

"Dead, all dead," whispered the man. "We rode in from due south, through the fog. Strange, twisty fog . . . We caught them with these big silver . . . like half oranges, but huge . . . They were putting them on carts, but the draft horses were dead. Only they weren't dead, they moved. The horses were pulling the carts even though they were dead. Everyone dead . . ."

Major Greene shook him, very hard. Lirael

put her hand forward as if to stop him, but Sam held her back.

"Report, Trooper Maculler! The situation!"

"They're all dead but me, sir," said Maculler simply. "Me and Dusty fell in the charge. By the time we got up, it was all over. Something made us sick. Maybe there was gas in the fog. Everyone in the reconaissance troop went down, the horses, too, or running free. Then there were these things lying all around the carts. Bodies, we thought, dead Southerlings, but they got up as we fell. I saw them, swarming over my mates . . . thousands of monsters, horrible monsters. They're coming this way, sir."

"The silver hemispheres," interrupted Lirael urgently. "Which way did the carts go?"

"I don't know," mumbled the man. "They were headed south, straight at us, when we ran into them. I don't know after that."

"Hedge is across and the hemispheres are already on their way to the Lightning Farm," said Lirael to the others. "We have to get there before they do! It's our last chance!"

"How?" asked Sam, his face white. "If they're already across the Wall . . ."

Lieutenant Tindall had the map out and was trying the switch on a small electric flashlight, which failed to work. Suppressing a curse with an apologetic glance at Lirael, he held the map to the moonlight.

As he did, Lirael felt her Death sense twitch, and she looked up. She couldn't see anything down the road ahead, but she knew what was coming. Dead Hands. A very large number of Dead Hands. And there was something else, too. A familiar cold presence. One of the Greater Dead, not a necromancer. It had to be Chlorr.

"They're coming," she said urgently. "Two groups of Hands. About a hundred in front, and a lot more farther back."

The Major barked out orders and soldiers ran in all directions, mostly forward, carrying tripods, machine-guns, and other gear. A medical orderly led Trooper Maculler away, his horse following obediently behind. Lieutenant Tindall shook the map and squinted at it.

"Always on the bloody folds, or where a map joins!" he cursed. "It looks like we could head southeast from the crossroads back there, then cut southwest and loop up to Forwin Mill from the south. The trucks might work if we do it that way. We'll have to push them back to start with."

"Get to it then!" roared Major Greene. "Take

your platoon to push. We'll hold out here as long as we can."

"Chlorr leads them," said Lirael to Sam and the Dog. "What should we do?"

"We cannot reach the Lightning Farm before Hedge on foot," said Sam quickly. "We could take that man's horse, but only the two of us could ride, and it is sixteen miles in the dark—"

"The horse is done in," interrupted Mogget. He was chewing, and the words weren't very clear. "Couldn't carry two if it wanted to. Which it doesn't."

"So we'll have to go with the soldiers," said Lirael. "Which means holding off Chlorr and the first wave of the Dead long enough to get the trucks pushed back to where they'll work."

She looked down the road past the soldiers, who were kneeling behind a tripod-mounted machine-gun. There was just enough moon- and starlight to make out the road and the stunted bushes on either side, though they were stark and colorless. As she watched, darker shapes blotted out the lighter parts of the landscape. The Dead, shambling close together in an unplanned and unorganized mob. A larger, darker shape was at the fore, and even from several hundred yards away, Lirael could see the fire that burned inside the shadow.

It was Chlorr.

Major Greene saw the Dead, too, and suddenly shouted right near Lirael's ear.

"Company! Two hundred yards at twelve o'clock, Dead things en masse in the road, fire! Fire! Fire!"

His shouts were followed by the mass clicking of triggers, loud even after the shouts. But nothing else happened. There was no sudden assault of sound, no crack of gunfire. Just clicks and muttered exclamations.

"I don't understand," said Greene. "The wind's westerly, and the guns usually work long after the engines stop!"

"The hemispheres," said Sam, with a glance at the Dog, who nodded. "They are a source of Free Magic on their own, and we are close to them. Hedge has probably also worked the wind. We might as well still be in the Old Kingdom, as far as your technology goes."

"Damn! First and Second Platoon, form up on the road, two ranks on the double!" ordered Greene. "Archers at the rear! Gunners, take your bolts and draw your swords!"

There was a sudden bustle as the machine-gunners took the bolts out of their weapons and drew their swords. Lirael drew her sword, too, and after a moment's hesitation Saraneth. She wanted to use Kibeth for some reason—it felt more familiar to her touch—but to deal with Chlorr she would need the authority of the bigger bell.

"I thought it was later than twelve o'clock," she said to Sam as they moved up to take a position in the forward line of soldiers. There were about sixty of them in two lines across the road and out into the fields on either side. The front line all wore mail, and their rifles were fixed with long sword bayonets that shone with silver. The second rank were archers, though Lirael could tell by looking at the way they held their bows that only half of them really knew what they were doing. Their arrows were silvered, too, she noticed with approval. That would help a little against the Dead.

"Um, Major Greene's 'twelve o'clock' meant 'straight ahead'; the time is about two in the morning," replied Sam, after a glance at the night sky. Obviously he knew the Ancelstierran stars as well as the Old Kingdom ones, for the heavens here meant nothing to Lirael.

"Front rank kneel!" ordered Major Greene. He stood at the front with Lirael and Sam and cast a sideways glance at the Disreputable Dog, who was growing to her full fighting size. The soldiers next to the hound shifted nervously, even as they knelt and set their bayoneted rifles out at a forty-five degree angle, so the front rank was a thicket of spears.

"Archers stand ready!"

The archers nocked arrows but did not draw. The Dead were approaching at a steady pace, but they were not close enough for Lirael and Sam to make out individuals in the dark other than Chlorr. The clicking of their bones could be heard, and the shuffle of many misshapen feet upon the road.

Lirael felt the tension and fear in the soldiers around her. The drawn-in breaths that were not released. The nervous shifting of feet and the fussing with equipment. The silence after the Major's shouted orders. It would not take much to set them fleeing for their lives.

"They've stopped," said the Dog, her keen eyes cutting through the night.

Lirael peered ahead. Sure enough, the dark mass did seem to have stopped, and the red glint from Chlorr was moving sideways rather than ahead.

"Trying to outflank us?" asked the Major. "I wonder why."

"No," said Sam. He could sense the much larger group of Dead farther back. "She's waiting for the second lot of Dead. Close to a thousand, I'd say."

He spoke softly, but there was a ripple among the nearer soldiers at his last words, a ripple that went slowly through both lines as his words were repeated.

"Quiet!" ordered Greene. "Sergeant! Take that man's name!"

"Sir!" confirmed several sergeants. Most of them had just been whispering themselves, and none made even a show of writing something in their field notebooks.

"We can't wait," said Lirael anxiously. "We have to get to the Lightning Farm!"

"We can't turn our backs on this lot either," said Greene. He bent close, the Charter Mark on his forehead glowing softly as it responded to the Charter Magic in the Dog, and whispered, "The men are close to breaking. They're not Scouts, not used to this sort of thing."

Lirael nodded. She gritted her teeth, marking a moment of indecision, then stepped out from the front rank.

350

"I'll take the fight to Chlorr," she declared. "If I can defeat her, the Hands may wander off or go back to Hedge. They'll fight badly, anyway."

"You're not going without me," said the Dog. She stepped forward, too, with an excited bark, a bark that echoed out across the night. There was something strange about that bark. It made everyone's hair stand on end, and the bell in Lirael's hand chimed quietly before she could still it. Both sounds made the soldiers even jumpier.

"Or me," said Sam stoutly. He stepped forward as well, his sword bright with Charter marks, his cupped left hand glowing with a prepared spell.

"I'll come and watch," said Mogget. "Maybe you'll scare a couple of mice out of their holes."

"If you'll let an old man fight with you—" Greene began, but Lirael shook her head.

"You stay here, Major," she said, and her voice was not that of a young woman but of an Abhorsen about to deal with the Dead. "Protect our rear."

"Yes, ma'am," said Major Greene. He saluted and stepped back into the line.

Lirael walked ahead, the gravel of the road crunching under her feet. The Disreputable Dog was at her right hand and Sam on her left. Mogget, a swift white shape, ran along the roadside, darting backwards and forwards, presumably in search of more mice to torment.

The Dead did not move towards Lirael as she marched on, but as she got closer, she saw they were spreading out, moving into the fields to present a broader front. Chlorr waited on the road, a tall shape, darker than the night save for her burning eyes. Lirael could feel the Greater Dead's presence like a chill hand upon the back of her neck.

When they were about fifty yards away, Lirael stopped, the Dog and Sam a half step behind her. She held Saraneth high, so the bell shone silver in the moonlight, the Charter marks glowing and moving upon the metal.

"Chlorr of the Mask," shouted Lirael, "return to Death!"

She flipped the bell, catching it by the handle and ringing it at the same time. Saraneth boomed out across the night, the Dead Hands flinching as the sound hit them. But it was for Chlorr the bell sounded, and all Lirael's power and attention were focused on that spirit.

Chlorr raised her shadow-bladed sword above her head and screamed back in defiance. Yet the scream was drowned in the continued tolling of the bell, and Chlorr took a step back even as she brandished her sword.

"Return to Death!" ordered Lirael, walking forward, swinging Saraneth in slow loops that were straight out of a page of *The Book of the Dead* that now shone so brightly in her mind. "Your time is over!"

Chlorr hissed and took another step backwards. Then a new sound joined the bell. A peremptory bark, impossibly sustained, stretching on and on, sharper and higher pitched than Saraneth's deep voice. Chlorr raised her sword as if to parry the sounds but took two more steps back. Confused Dead Hands staggered out of her way, gobbling their distress from their decayed throats.

Sam's arm circled in an overarm bowling motion, and golden fire suddenly exploded on and around Chlorr and splashed onto the Hands, who screamed and writhed as it ate into their Dead flesh.

Then a small white shape suddenly appeared almost at Chlorr's feet. A cat, capering on its hind feet, batting at the air in front of the Greater Dead spirit.

"Run! Run away, Chlorr No-Face!" laughed Mogget. "The Abhorsen comes to send you beyond the Ninth Gate!"

Chlorr swung at the cat, who nimbly leapt aside

as the blade swept past. Then the Greater Dead thing turned the swing into a leap, a great leap across thirty feet over the heads of the Dead Hands behind her. Transforming as she leaped, she became a great raven-shaped cloud of darkness that sped across the fields to the north, to the Wall and safety, pursued by the sound of Saraneth and the bark of the Dog.

CHAPTER NINETEEN

A TIN OF SARDINES

AS CHLORR FLED, the mass of Dead Hands erupted like an anthill splashed with hot water. They ran in all directions, the most stupid of them towards Lirael, Sam, and the Dog. Mogget ran between their legs, laughing, as Charter Magic fire burnt through their sinews and sent them crashing to the ground, the Dog's barking sent their spirits back into Death, and Saraneth commanded them to relinquish their bodies.

In a few mad minutes, it was all over. The echoes of bell and bark died away, leaving Lirael and her companions standing on an empty road under the moon and stars, surrounded by a hundred bodies that were no more than empty husks.

The silence was broken by cheering and yelling from the soldiers behind them. Lirael ignored it and called out to Mogget.

"Why did you tell Chlorr to run? We were winning! And what was that No-Face thing about?"

"It was quicker, which I thought was the point," said Mogget. He went up to Sam's feet and sat there, yawning. "Chlorr was always overcautious, even when she was an A— alive. I'm tired now. Can you carry me?"

Sam sighed. He sheathed his sword and picked the cat up, letting the little beast rest in the crook of his arm.

"It *was* quicker," he said to Lirael apologetically. "And I hate to mention it, but there are a lot more Dead Hands coming . . . and Shadow Hands, unless I'm mistaken. . . ."

"You're not mistaken," growled the Dog. She was looking suspiciously at Mogget. "Though like my Mistress, I am not satisfied with the Mogget's motivation or explanation, I suggest we leave immediately. We have little time."

As if in answer to her words, the sound of truck engines came from down the road. Obviously Lieutenant Tindall and his men had pushed them back far enough, and they could start again.

"I hope we can loop around," said Sam anxiously as they ran to the trucks. "If the wind changes again, we'll be stranded even farther away."

"We could try and work it . . ." Lirael began. Then she shook her head. "No, of course not. That would only make it worse for the Ancelstierran . . . what do you call it? Technologia?"

"Close enough," puffed Sam. "Come on!"

They had caught up with Major Greene and the rear platoon, who were double-timing back to the trucks. The Major beamed at them as they matched his pace, and several soldiers slapped their rifles in salute. The atmosphere was very different from what it had been only a few minutes before.

Lieutenant Tindall was waiting by the lead truck, studying the map once again, this time with the aid of a working electric flashlight. He looked up and saluted as Lirael, Sam, and Major Greene approached.

"I've found a road that will work," he said quickly. "I think we might even be able to beat Hedge there!"

"How?" asked Lirael urgently.

"Well, the only road south from the Western Strongpoint winds up through these hills here," he said, pointing. "It's a single lane and not even metaled. Heavily laden wagons—as Maculler described them to me—will take a day at least to get up through there. They can't possibly be at the

357

Mill before late afternoon! We can be there soon after dawn."

"Good work, Tindall," exclaimed the Major, clapping him on the back.

"Is there any other way the hemispheres could be taken to the Mill?" asked Sam. "This has all been planned so carefully by Hedge. In both the Kingdom and here . . . everything was prepared. Using the Southerlings to make more Dead, the wagons ready . . ."

Tindall looked at the map again. The flash-light beam darted in several directions over it as he thought about possible alternatives.

"Well," he said finally, "I suppose they could take the hemispheres by wagon to the sea, load them on boats, and take them south and then up the loch to the old dock at the Mill. But there's nowhere to load them near the Western Strong-point—"

"Yes there is," said the Major, suddenly grim again. He pointed at a single symbol on the map, a vertical stroke surrounded by four angled strokes. "There's a Navy dock at the Western Light."

"That's what Hedge will be doing," said Lirael, suddenly chill with certainty. "How quickly can they go by sea?"

"Loading the hemispheres would take a while," said Sam, joining the cluster of heads bent over the map. "And they'll have to sail, not steam. But Hedge will work the wind. I'd say less than eight hours."

There was a moment of silence after his words; then by unspoken consent, the huddle exploded into action. Greene snatched the map and hauled himself up into the cab of the first truck, Lirael and her companions ran to the back to jump in, and Lieutenant Tindall ran along the road waving his hand and shouting, "Go! Go!" as the trucks revved higher and slowly began to move out, their headlights flickering as the engines took the strain.

In the back of the truck, Sam put Mogget on top of his many-times-mended pack and sat down next to it. As he did, he pulled a small metal container out of his belt pouch and set it next to the cat's nose. For a few seconds, the cat appeared to be sound asleep. Then one green eye opened a fraction.

"What's that?" asked Mogget.

"Sardines," said Sam. "I knew they were standard rations, so I got a few tins for you."

"What are sardines?" asked Mogget suspiciously. "And why is there a key? Is this some sort of Abhorsen joke?"

In answer Sam tore the key off and slowly unwound the top of the tin. The rich smell of sardines spilled out. Mogget watched the procedure avidly, his eyes never leaving the tin. When Sam put it down, narrowly avoiding cutting himself as the truck went over a series of bumps, Mogget sniffed the sardines cautiously.

"Why are you giving me this?"

"You like fish," said Sam. "Besides, I said I would."

Mogget tore his gaze away from the sardines and looked at Sam. His eyes narrowed, but he saw no sign of guile in Sam's face. The little cat shook his head and then ate the sardines in a flash, leaving the tin spotless and empty.

Lirael and the Dog glanced at this exhibition of gluttony, but both were more interested in what was going on outside and behind them. Lirael pushed aside the canvas flap, and they looked past the three following trucks. Lirael could sense the second, much larger group of Dead and Shadow Hands that was advancing along the road. The Shadow Hands, which were both more powerful than the Dead Hands and unconstrained by flesh, were moving very swiftly, some of them leaping and gliding like enormous bats ahead of the main body of their shambling, corpse-dwelling brethren. They would undoubtedly wreak great trouble somewhere, but she could not spare them any further thought. The greater danger lay to the west, and already a little south, where lightning played on the horizon. Lirael noticed that the other, artificial thunder from the Ancelstierran artillery had ceased some time before, but she had been too busy to hear it stop.

"Dog," whispered Lirael. She drew the Dog closer and hugged her about the neck. "Dog. What if we're too late to destroy the Lightning Farm? What if the hemispheres join?"

The Dog didn't say anything. She snuffled at Lirael's ear instead and thumped her tail on the truck floor.

"I have to go into Death, don't I?" whispered Lirael. "To use the Dark Mirror and find out how It was bound in the Beginning."

Still the Dog didn't speak.

"Will you come with me?" asked Lirael, her whisper so low no human could have heard it.

"Yes," said the Dog. "Wherever you walk, I will be there."

"When should we go?" asked Lirael.

"Not yet," muttered the Dog. "Not until there

is no other choice. Perhaps we will still reach the Lightning Farm before Hedge."

"I hope so," said Lirael. She hugged the Dog again, then let her go and settled back onto her own pack. Sam was already asleep on the opposite side of the truck, with Mogget curled up against him, the empty sardine tin sliding about on the wooden floor of the truck. Lirael picked it up, wrinkled her nose, and wedged it into a corner where it wouldn't rattle.

"I will keep watch," said the Disreputable Dog. "You should sleep, Mistress. There are still several hours before the dawn, and you will need all your strength."

"I don't think I can sleep," said Lirael quietly. But she leaned back on her pack and closed her eyes. Her whole body felt edgy, and if she had been able to, she would have got up and practiced with her sword, or done something to try to drain the feeling off with exercise. But there was nothing she could do in the back of a moving vehicle. Except lie there and worry about what lay ahead. So she did that, and surprisingly soon crossed the line between wakeful worrying and troubled sleep.

The Dog lay with her head on her paws and watched Lirael toss and turn, and mumble in her sleep. Beneath them, the truck rattled and vibrated, the roar of the engine going up and down as the vehicle negotiated bends and rises and falls in the road.

After an hour or so, Mogget opened one eye. He saw the Dog watching and quickly shut it again. The Dog quietly got up and stalked over, pushing her snout down right against Mogget's little pink nose.

"Tell me why I shouldn't take you by the scruff of your neck and throw you off right now," whispered the Dog.

Mogget opened one untroubled eye again.

"I'd only run behind," he whispered back. "Besides, She gave me the benefit of the doubt. Can you do anything less?"

"I am not so charitable," said the Dog, showing her teeth. "Let me remind you that should you turn, I will make it my business to see that you are ended for it."

"Will you?" purred Mogget, opening his other eye. "What if you can't?"

The Dog growled, low and menacing. It was enough to wake Sam, who blinked and reached for his sword.

"What is it?" he asked sleepily.

"Nothing," said the Dog. She turned back to Lirael and plonked herself down with a frustrated sigh. "Nothing to worry about. Go back to sleep."

Mogget smiled and shook his head, the miniature Ranna tinkling. Sam yawned mightily at the sound and slipped back against his pack, asleep again in an instant.

Nicholas Sayre swam into wakefulness like a fish rising to a fly. A slow ascent that left him gasping and confused, flopping about like that same fish fresh caught on the shores of a loch—which was where he was. He sat up and looked around. Some part of his mind was comforted by the fact that he was in a twilight world made by the storm clouds above him and that lightning was crackling down less than fifty yards away. He was less interested in the pallid half sun in the east, just rising above the ridge.

Nicholas was lying on a pile of straw next to a hut, off to one side of what had once been an active wharf. Twenty yards away Hedge's men swore and cursed as they wrestled with sheerlegs, ropes, and pulleys to swing one of the silver hemispheres ashore from a small coastal trader. Another coaster stood off the wharf, several hundred yards into the loch, carefully positioned not to get close enough for the hemispheres to work their violent repulsion on each other.

Nicholas smiled. They were at Forwin Mill. He couldn't remember how they had done it, but they had got the hemispheres across the Wall. The Lightning Farm was ready, and all they had to do was join the hemispheres and everything would fall into place.

Thunder cracked, and someone screamed. A man fell away from the boat, his skin blackened and hair on fire. He lay on the dock, writhing and groaning till one of the other men stepped down and quickly cut his throat. Nick watched it all happen quite calmly. It was just the price of dealing with the hemispheres, and they were all that mattered.

Slowly, Nick got up, first to all fours, and then fully upright. It was hard work, and he had to clutch at the broken drainpipe of the hut for a while, till the dizziness passed. But slowly he grew steadier. Another man died as he stood there, but Nick didn't even notice. He had eyes only for the sheen of the hemispheres and the progression of the work. Soon the first hemisphere would be ready to be shifted into the ruined shell of the timber mill. It would be loaded into a special cradle mounted on a waiting railway wagon, one of two on the same short stretch of track.

At least that was what Nicholas had ordered. It occurred to him that he hadn't actually inspected the Lightning Farm. He had drawn the plans and paid for its construction before leaving for the Old Kingdom. That seemed like a very long time ago. He had never seen the Lightning Farm in actuality. Only in paper plans, and in his troubled dreams.

He was still weak from the illness he'd picked up across the Wall, too weak to easily walk around. He needed a stick or a crutch. There was a stretcher nearby, a simple thing of canvas and wood. Perhaps he could pull out one of the poles and use that as a staff, Nick thought. Very slowly and with infinite care, he walked over to the stretcher, cursing his weakness as he nearly fell. He knelt down and removed the pole, dragging it out of the canvas loops. It was easily eight feet long, and a bit heavy, but it would be better than nothing.

He was about to use it to stand up when he saw something glowing on the stretcher. A piece of splintered wood, painted with strange luminous symbols. Puzzled, he reached out to pick it up.

As he touched it, his body convulsed and he was violently sick. But even as he vomited, he kept one finger on what he now knew was a fragment of a wind flute. He couldn't pick it up, for his hand refused to obey him and close, but he could touch it. As long as he touched it, memory came rushing back. As long as he touched it, he was really Nicholas Sayre and not some puppet of the shining hemispheres so close by.

"Word of a Sayre," he whispered, remembering Lirael again. "I must stop this."

He stayed crouched over the pole, over his own vomit, just touching the fragment, while his mind worked fiercely at his predicament. As soon as he let the charm go, he would regress, go back to being a mindless servant. He could not pick it up or carry it in his hands. Yet there had to be some way he could keep it close enough to work its magic, to remind him who he was.

Nick inspected himself. He was both shocked and scared by how thin he had become, and by the blue and purple bruising that extended all down the left side of his chest. His shirt was merely threads and tatters, and his trousers were not much better, secured at his skinny waist not by a belt but by a piece of tarred rope. The pockets were gone, as were his underclothes.

But the cuffs on his trousers were still turned

up. Nick felt in them with his right hand, making sure they would hold. The fine woolen cloth was thinner than it had been only weeks before, but it would not easily tear.

Panting with the effort, he maneuvered his ankle as close to the wind flute fragment as he could, pulled the cuff open, and used his other hand to sweep the chunk of wood toward it. It took a couple of attempts, but finally he got it in. As he did, he forgot what he was doing, till a few seconds later the trouser cuff hit against his skin. Pain shot through his ankle, but it was bearable.

He didn't want to look at the hemispheres, but he found himself doing so anyway. The first one was on the wharf. Many people were swarming about it, tying new ropes for dragging and untying the ones used to swing it ashore. Nick saw that many of the workers grabbing the landward ropes were Night Crew again. Somewhat better-looking ones, though still rotting under their blue hats and scarves.

No, Nick thought, as the wooden charm slapped against his ankle. They were not diseased humans but Dead creatures, corpses brought into a semblance of life by Hedge. Unlike the normal men, they did not seem troubled by close proximity to the hemispheres, or by the constant lightning.

As if even thinking his name summoned Hedge, in the after-flash of the most recent lightning strike, the necromancer suddenly appeared at the side of the hemisphere. Once again Nick was surprised by how monstrous Hedge had become. Shadows crawled across his skull, twining into the fire deep in his eyes, and his fingers dripped with red, viscous flames.

The necromancer walked to the bow of the coaster and shouted something. Men moved quickly to obey, though it was clear they were nearly all wounded in some way, or sick. They cast off and raised sail, and the boat slid away from the wharf. The other, loaded coaster immediately began to make its approach.

Hedge watched it come in and raised his hands above his head. Then he spoke, harsh words that made the air ripple around him and the ground shiver. He stretched out one hand towards the waters of the loch and called again, making gestures that left after-trails of red fire in the air.

Fog began to rise out of the loch. Thin white tendrils spiraled up and up, dragging thicker trails of mist behind them. Hedge gestured to the right and left, and the tendrils spread sideways, dragging more fog up out of the water to form a wall that slowly extended down the full length of the loch. As it spread sideways, it also rolled forward, towards the wharf, the timber mill, the loch valley, and the hills beyond.

Hedge clapped his hands and turned back. His eyes fell on Nick, who instantly looked down and clutched at his chest. He heard the necromancer approach, his heels loud on the wooden planks.

"Hemispheres," mumbled Nick quickly as the footsteps stopped in front of him. "The hemispheres must . . . we must . . ."

"All progresses well," said Hedge. "I have raised a sea fog that will resist any attempts to move it, should there be any amongst our enemies skilled enough to try. Do you wish to instruct me further, Master?"

Nick felt something move in his chest. Like a panicked heartbeat, only stronger and much more frightening and repulsive. He gasped at the pain of it and fell forward, his hands scrabbling at the planks, fingernails breaking as he tore at the wood.

Hedge waited till the spasm subsided. Nick lay there panting, unable to speak, waiting for unconsciousness and the thing within him to take over.

But it did not rise, and after several minutes Hedge walked away.

Nick rolled onto his back and watched the fog roll across the sky, blanketing out the storm clouds, though not the lightning. Fog lit by lightning was not a sight he had ever expected to see, he thought, some part of him making notes at the strange effects.

But the greater part of his mind was given over to something much more important. He had to stop Hedge from using the Lightning Farm.

chapter twenty

The BEGINNING OF The END

DAWN WAS BREAKING as the truck engines began to cough and splutter once again, then ground to a halt. Lieutenant Tindall swore as his red Chinagraph pencil slipped, and the dot he was making on the map became a line, which he turned into a cross. The cross was marked on the thickly clustered contour lines that marked the descent into Forvale, a broad valley that was separated from Forwin Loch and the mill by a long, low ridge.

Lirael had fallen asleep again as the trucks had driven through the night. So she had missed the small dramas that filled the hours as the trucks sped on, not stopping for anything, the drivers pushing much faster than common sense allowed. But they had good luck, or made their own, and there had been no major accidents. Plenty of minor collisions, scrapes, and scares, but no major accidents.

Lirael was also unaware of the desertions during the night. Every time the trucks had slowed to negotiate a sharp bend, or had been forced to stop before crawling across a washed-out section of what was a very secondary road, soldiers who could not face the prospect of further encounters with the Dead leapt from the trucks and disappeared into the darkness. The company had more than a hundred men when it left the Perimeter. By the time they came to Forvale, there were only seventy-three left.

"Debus! On the double!"

The Company Sergeant-Major's shouts woke Lirael. She jerked up, one hand already scrabbling at a bell, the other on Nehima. Sam reacted in a very similar way. Disoriented and scared, he stumbled towards the tailgate, right behind the Disreputable Dog, who jumped out a moment later.

"Five-minute rest! Five minutes! Do your business and be quick about it! No brew-ups!"

Lirael climbed out of the truck, yawned, and rubbed her eyes. It was still half dark, the eastern sky light beyond the ridge but without any sign of the actual sun. Most of the sky was beginning to turn blue, save for a patch not far away that was dark and threatening. Lirael saw it out of the corner of her eye, turned swiftly, and had her worst fears realized. Lightning flashed in the cloud. Lots of lightning, more than ever before, and it was striking down across a wider area. All beyond the ridge.

"Forwin Loch, and the mill," said Major Greene. "They lie beyond that ridge. What the—"

They had all been looking across to the ridge. Now Greene pointed down into the valley that lay between them. It was lush green farmland, divided into regular five-acre fields by wire fences. Sheep occupied some of the fields. But on the southern end of the valley there was a moving mass of blue. Thousands of people, a great crowd of blue-scarved and blue-hatted Southerlings, a huge migration all across the valley.

Greene and Tindall had their binoculars to their eyes in a flash. But Lirael did not need binoculars to see which way the great crowd was heading. The leading groups were already turning to the west, to the ridge and Forwin Mill beyond. To the Lightning Farm, where from the look of the storm the hemispheres were already in place.

"We have to stop them!" said Sam. He was

pointing at the Southerlings.

"It is more important to stop the hemispheres from being joined," said Lirael. She hesitated for a second, unsure of what to do or say. Only one course seemed obvious. They had to get up on the western ridge to see what was happening beyond it, and that meant crossing the valley as quickly as possible. "We need to get up on that ridge! Come on!"

She started off down the road into the valley, jogging slowly at first but slowly increasing her speed. The Dog ran at her side, her tongue lolling out. Sam followed a half minute later, Mogget riding on his shoulders. Major Greene and Lieutenant Tindall were slower, but they were both soon bellowing orders, and the soldiers were running back from the ditch on the side of the road and forming up.

The road was more of a track, but once down the hill it cut straight through the fields, crossed the stream in the center of the valley at a concrete ford or sunken bridge, and then ran along the side of the ridge.

Lirael ran as she had never run before. A lone figure, she splashed across the ford and cut in front of the Southerlings. Closer to, she saw that they were in family groups, often of many generations. Hundreds of families. Grandparents, parents, children, babies. They all had the same scared look on their faces, and nearly everyone, no matter how old or small, was weighed down with suitcases, bags, and small bundles. Some had strange possessions, small machines and metal objects that Lirael did not know but Sam recognized as sewing machines, phonographs, and typewriters. Strangely, nearly all the adults also clutched small pieces of paper.

"They must not be allowed to cross the ridge," said the Dog as Lirael slowed to look at them. "But we must not stop. I fear the lightning is increasing."

Lirael halted for a second and turned back. Sam was about fifty yards behind, running with grim determination.

"Sam!" Lirael shouted. She indicated the Southerlings, who were starting to turn towards the ridge. Some younger men were already climbing the slope. "Stop them! I'm going on!"

Lirael began to run again, ignoring the pain from an incipient stitch in her side. With every forward step it seemed to her that the lightning beyond the ridge was spreading, and the thunder was growing louder and more frequent. Lirael left the road and began to zigzag up a long spur that ran up to the ridge. To help her along, she grabbed at stones and the branches of the white-barked trees that were dotted along the slope.

She could feel the Dead beyond the ridge as she climbed. No more than a score at first, but at least a dozen more appeared as she climbed. Obviously Hedge was bringing spirits in from Death. He must have found a source of corpses somewhere. Lirael did not think they would be Shadow Hands, for it took longer to prepare a spirit for Life if there was no flesh to house it in. At least it was supposed to take longer. Lirael was afraid that she had no idea what Hedge was capable of.

Then, without warning, she was on top of the ridge and there were no more white-barked trees, no great boulders. She could see clearly down the bare western slope to the blue waters of the loch. The hillside had been totally cleared, swept clean as if by fire and a giant broom, leaving only furrowed brown dirt. But the dirt had sprouted a strange crop. Slender metal poles, twice Lirael's height. Hundreds of them, spaced six feet apart, and joined at the roots by fat black cables that snaked down the slope and into a ramshackle stone building that had lost its roof. Parallel metal lines laid on top of many short wooden beams formed a track of some sort. They ran on the ground through the building, ending abruptly twenty yards on either side of it. There were two flatbed metal-wheeled wagons on the line, one at each end. Lirael instinctively knew that these were for the hemispheres. They would be mounted on the wagons and somehow be brought together by using the power of the lightning storm.

Lightning flashed as if to punctuate her thoughts. It came forking down all around the quay, so bright that Lirael had to shield her eyes with her hand. She knew what she would see there, because she could smell the hot-metal scent, the corrosive smell of Free Magic. It turned her stomach, and she was thankful that she hadn't eaten for hours.

One of the silver hemispheres was already on the quay. It flashed blue as the lightning struck it. The other hemisphere was on a boat out on the loch. Though most of the lightning was hitting the hemispheres, Lirael saw that it was also spreading out and up the slope, and most of the strikes hit the tall poles. They were lightning rods, the thousand lightning rods that together made up Nicholas's Lightning Farm.

As if the dark clouds above were not enough, fog was beginning to swirl off the loch. Lirael could sense this was a magical fog, built with real water, so it would be much harder to force back or dispel. She felt the Free Magic working in it, and the source of it. Hedge was somewhere down on the quay. There were Dead down there with him, moving the first hemisphere, and there were more Dead around the various small buildings that lined the quay. Lirael could sense them moving about, with Hedge at the center of everything. She felt like a fly on the edge of a cobweb, feeling the movement of the great mother spider at the center and its many offspring farther around the web.

Lirael drew Nehima, and then after a moment's hesitation her hand fell on Astarael. The Weeper. All who heard her would be thrown into Death, including Lirael. If she could get close enough, she could send Hedge and all the Dead a long, long way. Hedge, at least, would probably be able to return to Life, but there was a slim chance Lirael could return as well, and it would gain her precious time.

But as she started to draw the bell out of the bandolier, the Dog jumped up against her and pushed Lirael's hand away with her nose.

"No, Mistress," she said. "Astarael alone

cannot prevail here. We are too late to prevent the hemispheres from being joined."

"Sam, the soldiers . . ." said Lirael. "If we attack at once—"

"I do not think we would easily pass through this Lightning Farm," said the Dog, shaking her head. "The Destroyer's power is less constrained here, and the Destroyer is directing the lightning. Besides, the Dead here are led by Hedge, not Chlorr."

"But if the hemispheres join . . ." Lirael whispered to herself. Then she swallowed and said, "It's time, isn't it?"

"Yes," said the Dog. "But not here. Hedge will have noticed us, as we have noticed him. His mind is on the hemispheres for the moment, but I do not think it will be long before he orders an attack."

Lirael turned to retreat back down the eastern side of the ridge, then stopped and looked back.

"Nicholas? What about him?"

"He is beyond our help now," replied the Dog sadly. "When the hemispheres join, the shard within him will burst from his heart to become part of the whole. But he will know nothing of it. It will be a swift end, though I fear Hedge will enslave his spirit."

"Poor Nick," said Lirael. "I should never have let him go."

"You had no choice," said the Dog. She nudged Lirael behind the knee, anxious to make her move. "We must hurry!"

Lirael nodded and turned back to retrace her path down the slope. As she hurried down, sliding and almost falling in the steeper parts, she thought of Nicholas and then of everyone else, including herself. Perhaps Nick would have the easiest path. After all, it was likely he would be only the first to die, unknowing. Everyone else would be only too aware of their fate, and they would probably all end up serving Hedge.

Lirael was halfway down when an enormously loud, booming voice filled the valley. It shocked her for a second, till she recognized it was Sam, his speech greatly magnified by Charter Magic. He was standing on a large boulder only a hundred yards or so farther down the spur, his hands cupped around his mouth, his fingers glowing from the spell.

"Southerlings! Friends! Do not go beyond the western ridge! Only death awaits you there! Do not believe the papers you hold—they offer only lies! I am Prince Sameth of the Old Kingdom, and I promise to give land and farms to everyone who stays in the valley! If you stay in the valley, you will be given farms and land beyond the Wall!"

Sam repeated his message as Lirael panted to a stop next to his boulder. Below it, Major Greene's men were strung out in a long line along the bottom of the ridge. The Southerlings were gathered beyond that line, overlapping it by several hundred yards at the southern end. Most of them had stopped to listen to Sam, but a few were still climbing up the ridge.

Sam stopped talking and jumped down.

"Best I can do," he said anxiously. "It might stop some of them. If they even understood what I was saying."

"Nothing else we can do," said Major Greene. "We can't shoot the beggars, and they'd overwhelm us if we tried to stop them with just the bayonet. I'd like a word with the police who were supposed to be—"

"One of the hemispheres is already ashore, and the other is close behind," interrupted Lirael, her news provoking instant attention. "Hedge is there, and he is raising a fog and creating many more Dead. The Lightning Farm is also beginning to work, and the Destroyer is calling down and directing the lightning."

"We'd best attack at once," said Major Greene. He started to take a breath to shout, but Lirael interrupted him again.

"No," she said. "We can't get through the Lightning Farm, and there are too many Dead. We cannot stop the hemispheres from joining now."

"But that's . . . that means we've lost," said Sam. "Everything. The Destroyer—"

"No," snapped Lirael. "I'm going into Death, to use the Dark Mirror. The Destroyer was bound and broken in the Beginning. Once I find out how it was done, we can do it again. But you will have to protect my body until I can come back, and Hedge is sure to attack."

As she spoke, Lirael looked firmly into Sam's eyes, then Major Greene's and the two Lieutenants', Tindall and Gotley. She hoped some sort of confidence was being transferred. She had to believe that there was an answer in Death, in the past. Some secret that would let them defeat Orannis.

"The Dog is coming with me," she said. "Where's Mogget?"

"Here!" said a voice near her feet. Lirael looked down and saw Mogget in the shadow of the boulder, licking the second of two empty sardine tins.

"I thought he might as well have them," said

Sam quietly, with a shrug.

"Mogget! Help in any way you can," ordered Lirael.

"Any way I can," confirmed Mogget with a sly smile. His confirmation sounded almost like a question.

Lirael looked around, then strode to the middle of a ring of lichen-covered stones, where the spur rose slightly again after coming down the ridge. She checked that the Dark Mirror was in her belt pouch. Then she drew Nehima and Saraneth. This time she held the bell by the handle, straight down. It could sound more easily by accident but also could be more quickly used.

"I'll go into Death here," she said. "I'm depending on you to protect me. I'll be back as soon as I can."

"Do you want me to come with you?" asked Sam. He took out the panpipes and gripped the hilt of his sword. Lirael could tell he meant what he said.

"No," said Lirael. "I think you'll have enough to do here. Hedge is not going to leave us alone on his doorstep. Can't you feel the Dead on the move? We will be attacked here soon, and someone has to protect my living self while I am in Death. I charge you with that, Prince Sameth. If you have time, cast a diamond of protection."

Sam nodded gravely and said, "Yes, Aunt Lirael."

"Aunt?" asked Lieutenant Tindall, but Lirael hardly heard him. She carefully squatted down and hugged the Disreputable Dog, fighting back the terrible feeling that it might be the last time she would feel soft dog hair against her living cheek.

"Even if I do find out how the Seven bound the Destroyer, how can *we* do it?" she whispered in the Dog's ear, so softly no one else could hear. "How can we?"

The Disreputable Dog looked at her with sad brown eyes but didn't answer. Lirael matched her gaze and then smiled, a rueful, bittersweet smile.

"We've come a long way from the Glacier, haven't we?" she said. "Now we're going farther still."

She stood up and reached out to Death. As the chill sank into her bones, she heard Sam say something, and a distant shout. But the sounds faded, as did the light of day. Lifting her sword, Lirael strode into Death, her faithful hound at her heels.

Sam's death sense twitched. Lirael's breath steamed out, and frost formed on her mouth and nose. The Disreputable Dog stepped forward at her side and disappeared, leaving a momentary outline of golden light that slowly faded into nothing.

"Nick! What about Nick!" Sam suddenly called. He hit himself in the head and swore. "I should have asked!"

"Movement on the ridge!" someone called out, and there was a general flurry of activity. Tindall and Gotley ran to their platoons, and Major Greene shouted orders. The Southerlings, who had sat down to listen to Sam, stood up. Individual Southerlings began to climb up the ridge; then there was a general surge forward by the whole huge crowd of people.

At the same time, there was a sudden increase of lightning beyond the ridge, and the thunder rolled in, louder and more constant.

"I'm going to close the company in," shouted Greene. "We'll form an all-around defense here."

Sam nodded. He could sense Dead moving beyond the ridge. Fifty or sixty Dead Hands, headed their way.

"There are Dead coming," he said. He looked up at the ridge, then back at Lirael and at the Southerlings beyond. They were all starting to trudge forward, towards the ridge, not farther back

386

into the valley. The soldiers were already running back towards the spur, the line contracting. There was nothing between the Southerlings and their doom.

"Damn!" swore Greene. "I thought you'd stopped them!"

"I'm going to talk to them!" declared Sam, making an instant decision. The Dead were at least five minutes away, and Lirael had charged him earlier to stop the Southerlings. She would not be in danger if he was quick. "I'll be back in a few minutes. Major Greene, do not leave Lirael! Mogget, protect her!"

With that, he ran down towards a particular group of Southerlings he'd seen before but hadn't really registered as important till a moment before, when he was struck by a sudden thought. The group was led by an ancient matriarch, white haired and much better dressed than everyone around her. She was also supported by several younger men and women. It was the only group that was not obviously a family, without children and without baggage. The matriarch was the leader, Sam thought. He knew that much about the Southerlings. Someone who might be able to turn back the human tide.

If only he could convince her in the next few

minutes. When the Dead attacked, anything could happen. The Southerlings might panic, and many would run the wrong way and be trampled. Or they might refuse the evidence of their own eyes and continue blindly on over the ridge, driven by optimism and hope that finally they would find somewhere to call home.

chapter twenty-one

Deeper into Death

LIRAEL DIDN'T PAUSE to look around as she entered Death and the current gripped her, trying to drag her under in that first shocking instant of total cold. She pushed forward at once as the Disreputable Dog bounded ahead, sniffing the river for any hint of lurking Dead.

As Lirael waded, she anxiously ran through the key lessons she had learned from *The Book of the Dead* and *The Book of Remembrance and Forgetting*. Their pages shone in her mind, telling her about each of the Nine Precincts and the secrets of the Nine Gates. But knowing these secrets—even from a magical book—was not the same as having experienced them. And Lirael had never been past the First Precinct, never even crossed the First Gate.

Nevertheless, she strode forward confidently,

forcing her doubts as far back in her mind as they would go. Death was no place for doubts. The river would be quick to attack any weakness, for it was only strength of will that kept the current from sucking away Lirael's spirit. If she faltered, the waters would take her under, and all would be lost.

She came to the First Gate surprisingly quickly. One minute it had been a distant roar and a far-off wall of mist that stretched as far as she could see to the left and right. Now, what seemed only a moment later, Lirael was standing close enough to touch the mist, and the roar of the rapids on the other side was very loud.

Words came to her then, words of power impressed on her mind by both books. She spoke them, feeling the Free Magic writhe and sizzle on her tongue and lips as the words flew out of her mouth.

The veil of mist parted as she spoke, slowly rolling aside to reveal a series of waterfalls that seemed to drop down forever into a dark and endless chasm. Lirael spoke again and gestured to right and left with her sword. A path appeared, cut deep into the waterfall, like a narrow pass between two liquid mountains. Lirael stepped onto the path, the Dog so close that she was almost tangled up in

Lirael's legs. As they walked, the mist closed up, and the path faded behind them.

After they'd gone on, a very small, sneaking spirit rose from the water near the First Gate and began to walk towards Life, following an almost invisible black thread connected to its navel. It twitched and gibbered as it walked, anticipating the reward its master would give for news of these travelers. Perhaps it would even be allowed to stay in Life and be given a body, that greatest and most treasured delight.

The passage through the First Gate was deceptive. Lirael couldn't tell how long it took, but soon the river had once again become a flat and endless expanse as it resumed its flow through the Second Precinct. Lirael began to probe the water ahead with her sword as soon as she left the path, checking the footing. This precinct was similar to the First, but it had deep, dangerous holes as well as the ever-present current. It was made even more difficult by a blurring effect that made the grey light fuzzy and indistinct, so Lirael couldn't see much farther than she could touch with her sword held out at full stretch.

There was an easy way through, a path charted by previous Abhorsens and recorded in *The Book of the Dead.* Lirael took it, though she didn't trust her book learning enough to give up probing with her sword. But she did count out her steps as the Book instructed, and she took the memorized turns at each point.

She was so intent on doing that, lost in the cadence of her steps, that she almost fell into the Second Gate. The Dog's quick grab for her belt pulled her to safety as she took one step too many, counting "Eleven" even as her brain said "Stop at Ten."

As quick as that thought she tried to draw back, but the Second Gate's grip was much stronger than the normal current of the river. Only her valiant Dog anchor saved her, though it took all the strength of both of them to drag Lirael back from the precipice of the gate.

For the Second Gate was an enormous hole, into which the river sank like sinkwater down a drain, creating a whirlpool of terrible strength.

"Thanks," said Lirael, shaking as she looked into the whirlpool and contemplated what might have happened. The Dog didn't reply at once, as she was untangling her jaws from a sadly battered piece of leather that had previously been a serviceable belt.

"Take it steady, Mistress," the Dog advised quietly. "We will need haste elsewhere, but not here."

"Yes," agreed Lirael, as she forced deep, slow breaths into her lungs. When she felt calmer, she stood up straight and recited further words of Free Magic, words that filled her mouth with a sudden heat, a strange glow against her deeply chilled cheeks.

The words echoed out, and the spiraling waters of the Second Gate slowed and then stopped completely, as if the whole whirlpool had been snap frozen. Now each swirl of current had become a terrace, making up one long spiral path down to the vortex of the Gate. Lirael stepped down to the start of the path and began to walk. Behind her, and above, the whirlpool began to swirl again.

It seemed she would have to circle around a hundred times or more to reach the bottom, but once again Lirael knew it was deceptive. It took only a few minutes to traverse the Second Gate, and she spent the time thinking about the Third Precinct and the trap it held for the unwary.

For the river there was only ankle deep, and a little warmer. The light was better, too. Brighter and less fuzzy, though still a pallid grey. Even the current wasn't much more than a tickle around the ankles. All in all, it was a much more attractive place than the First or Second Precincts. Somewhere ill-trained or foolish necromancers might be tempted to tarry or rest.

If they did, it wouldn't be for long—because the Third Precinct had waves.

Lirael knew it, and she left the Second Gate at a run. This was one of the places in Death where haste was necessary, she thought as she pushed her legs into an all-out sprint. She could hear the thunder of the wave behind her, a wave that had been held in check by the same spell that calmed the whirlpool. But she didn't look and concentrated totally on speed. If the wave caught her, it would crash her through the Third Gate, and she would drift on, stunned and unable to save herself.

"Faster!" shouted the Dog, and Lirael ran even harder, the sound of the wave so close now, it seemed certain to catch them both.

Lirael reached the mists of the Third Gate only a step or two in front of the rushing waters, frantically calling out the necessary Free Magic spell as she ran. This time the Dog was in front, the spell only just parting the mists ahead of her snout.

As they halted, panting, in the mist door created by the spell, the wave broke around them, hurtling its cargo of Dead into the waterfall beyond. Lirael waited to catch her breath and a few seconds more for the path to appear. Then she walked on, into the Fourth Precinct.

They crossed this precinct rapidly. It was relatively straightforward, without holes or other traps for the unwary, though the current was strong again, stronger even than in the First Precinct. But Lirael had grown used to its cold and cunning grip.

She remained wary. Besides the known and charted dangers of each precinct, there was always the possibility of something new, or something so old and infrequent, it was not recorded in *The Book of the Dead*. Besides such anomalies, the Book hinted at powers that could travel in Death, besides the Dead themselves, or necromancers. Some of these entities created odd local conditions, or warped the usual natures of the precincts. Lirael supposed that she herself was one of the powers that altered the nature of the river and its gates.

The Fourth Gate was another waterfall, but it was not cloaked in mist. At first sight it looked like an easy drop of only two or three feet, and the river appeared to keep on flowing after it.

Lirael knew better, from *The Book of the Dead*. She stopped a good ten feet back, and spoke the spell that would let her pass. Slowly, a dark ribbon began to roll out from the edge of the waterfall, floating in the air above the water below. Only three feet wide, it seemed to be made of night—a night without stars. It stretched out horizontally from the top of the waterfall into a distance Lirael couldn't make out.

She stepped onto the path, moved her feet a little to get a better balance, and began to walk. This narrow way was not only the path through the Fourth Gate, it was also the sole means of crossing the Fifth Precinct. The river was deep here, too deep to wade, and the water had a strong metamorphic effect. A necromancer who spent any time in its waters would find both spirit and body altered, and not for the better. Any Dead spirit who managed to wade back this way would not resemble its once-living form.

Even crossing the precinct by means of the dark path was dangerous. Besides being narrow, it was also the favored means for the Greater Dead or Free Magic beings to cross the Fifth Precinct themselves—going the other way, towards Life. They would wait for a necromancer to create the path, then rush down it, hoping to overcome the pathmaker with a sudden, vicious attack.

Lirael knew that, but even so, it was only the Dog's quick bark that warned her as something came ravening down the path ahead, seemingly out of nowhere. Once human, its long sojourn in Death had transformed it into something hideous and frightening. It scuttled forward on its arms as well as legs, moving all too like a spider. Its body was fat and bulbous, and its neck jointed so it could look straight ahead even when on all fours.

Lirael only had an instant to thrust her sword forward as it attacked, the point piercing one blobby cheek, bursting out the back of its neck. But it still pushed on, despite the blaze of white sparks that fountained everywhere as Charter Magic ate into its spirit-flesh. It thrust itself almost up to the hilt, red-fire eyes focused on Lirael, its too-wide mouth drooling spit and hissing.

Lirael kicked at it to try to get it off her sword, and rang Saraneth at the same time. But she was unbalanced, and the bell didn't ring true. A discordant note echoed out into Death, and instead of feeling her will concentrated on the Dead thing, and the beginnings of domination, Lirael felt distracted. Her mind wandered, and for an instant she forgot what she was doing.

A second or a minute later she realized it, and

a shock ran through her, fear electrifying every nerve in her body. She looked, and the Dead creature was almost off her sword, ready to attack again.

"Still the bell!" barked the Dog, as she made herself smaller and tried to get between Lirael's legs to attack the creature. "Still the bell!"

"What?" exclaimed Lirael; then the shock and the fear ran through her again as she felt her hand still ringing Saraneth, without her being aware of it. Panicked, she forced it to be still. The bell sounded once more and then was silent as she fumbled it back into its pouch.

But once again she was distracted—and in that moment the creature attacked. This time it leapt at her, planning to crush her completely beneath its ghastly, pallid bulk. But the Dog saw the monster tense, and she guessed its intention. Instead of slipping between Lirael's legs, she threw herself forward and planted two heavy forepaws on Lirael's back.

The next thing Lirael knew, she was on her knees, and the creature was flying over her. One barbed finger grasped a lock of her hair as it passed, tearing it out by the roots. Lirael hardly noticed, as she frantically turned herself around on the narrow path and stood up. All her confidence was gone, and she didn't trust her balance, so it wasn't a fast maneuver.

But when she turned, the creature was gone. Only the Dog remained. A huge Dog, the hair on her back up like a boar-bristle hairbrush, red fire dripping from teeth the size of Lirael's fingers. There was a madness in her eyes as she looked back at her mistress.

"Dog?" whispered Lirael. She'd never feared her friend before, but then she'd never walked this far into Death, either. Anything could happen here, she felt. Anyone and . . . anything could change.

The Dog shook herself and grew smaller, and the madness in her eyes subsided. Her tail began to wag, and she worried the base of it for a second before walking up to lick Lirael's open hand.

"Sorry," she said. "I got angry."

"Where did it go?" asked Lirael, looking around. There was nothing on the path as far as she could see, and nothing in the river below them. She didn't think she'd heard a splash. Had she? Her mind was addled, still resonating with the discord of Saraneth.

"Down," replied the Dog, gesturing with her head. "We'd best hurry. You should draw a bell, too. Perhaps Ranna. She is more forgiving here."

Lirael knelt and touched noses with the Dog.

"I couldn't do this without you," she said, kissing her on the snout.

"I know, I know," replied the Dog distractedly, her ears twitching around in a semicircular motion. "Can you hear something?"

"No," replied Lirael. She stood up to listen, and her hand automatically freed Ranna from the bandolier. "Can you?"

"I thought someone . . . something was following before," said the Dog. "Now I'm certain. Something is coming up behind us. Something powerful, moving fast."

"Hedge!" exclaimed Lirael, forgetting about the crisis of confidence in her balance as she turned and hurried along the path. "Or could it be Mogget again?"

"I do not think it is Mogget," said the Dog with a frown. She stopped to look back for a moment, her ears pricked forward. Then she shook her head. "Whoever it is . . . or whatever . . . we should try to leave it behind."

Lirael nodded as she walked and took a firmer grip on both bell and sword. Whatever they met next, from in front or behind, she was determined not to be surprised.

chapter twenty-two

junction boxes and southerlings

The fog had hidden the quay and was drifting inexorably up the slope. Nick watched it roll and watched the lightning that shot through it. Unpleasantly, it made him think of luminous veins in partly transparent flesh. Not that there was anything living that had flesh like that. . . .

There was something he had to do, but he couldn't remember what it was. He knew the hemispheres were not far away, through the fog. Part of him wanted to go over to them and oversee the final joining. But there was another, rebellious self that wanted exactly the opposite, to stop the hemispheres from joining by whatever means possible. They were like two whispering voices inside his head, both so strident that they mixed and became unintelligible.

"Nick! What have they done to you?"

For a moment Nick thought this was a third voice, also inside his head. But as it repeated the same words, he realized it wasn't.

Laboriously, Nick staggered around. At first he couldn't see anything through the fog. Then he spotted a face peering out from behind the corner of the nearest shed. It took a few seconds for him to work out who it was. His friend from the University of Corvere. Timothy Wallach, the slightly older student who he'd hired to oversee the construction of the Lightning Farm. Usually Tim was a debonair and somewhat languid individual, who was always impeccably dressed.

Tim didn't look like that now. His face was pale and dirty, his shirt had lost its collar, and there was mud all over his shoes and trousers. Crouched down behind the hut, he constantly shook, as if he had a fever or was scared out of his mind.

Nick waved and forced himself to take a few shambling steps to Tim, though he had to clutch at the wall in the last second to stop himself from falling.

"You have to stop him, Nick!" Tim exclaimed. He didn't look at Nick but everywhere else, his eyes flickering fearfully from side to side. "Whatever he's doing . . . you're both doing . . . it's wrong!"

"What?" asked Nick wearily. The walk had tired him, and one of the internal voices had become stronger. "What are we doing? It's a scientific experiment, that's all. And who is the him I have to stop? I'm in charge here."

"Him! Hedge!" blurted Tim, pointing back towards the hemispheres, where the fog was thickest. "He killed my workmen, Nick! He killed them! He pointed at them and they fell down. Just like that!"

He mimicked a spellcasting movement with his hand and started to sob, without tears, his words tumbling out in a mixture of gasps and cries.

"I saw him do it. It was only—only . . ."

He looked at his watch. The hands were stuck in place, stopped forever at six minutes to seven.

"It was only six to seven," whispered Tim. "Robert saw the coasters coming in, and woke us all up, so we could celebrate the completion of the work. I went back to the hut for a bottle I've been saving. . . . I saw it all through the window—"

"Saw what?" asked Nick. He was trying to understand what had upset Tim so much, but there was an awful pain in his chest, and he simply couldn't think. He couldn't put the concept of Hedge together with Tim's murdered workers.

"There's something wrong with you, Nick," Tim whispered, crawling back away from him. "Don't you understand? Those hemispheres are pure poison, and Hedge killed my workmen! All of them, even the two apprentices. I saw it!"

Without warning, Tim suddenly retched violently, coughing and gasping, though nothing came out. He had already thrown everything up.

Nick watched dumbly, as something inside him reveled at this news of death and misery and an opposing force writhed against it with feelings of fear, revulsion, and terrible doubt. The pain in his chest redoubled, and he fell down, clawing at his heart and his ankle.

"We have to get away," said Tim, wiping his mouth with the back of one shaking hand. "We have to warn somebody."

"Yes," whispered Nick. He had managed to sit up but was still hunched over, one pale hand over his heart, the other clutching the fragment of wind flute through his trouser cuff. He fought against the pain in both places and the pressure in his head. "Yes—you go, Tim. Tell her . . . tell them

I'll try and stop it. Tell her—"

"What? Who?" asked Tim. "You have to come with me!"

"I can't," whispered Nick. He was remembering again. Talking to Lirael in the reed boat, trying to keep the shard of the Destroyer within him at bay. He remembered the nausea, and the metallic bite on his tongue. He could feel it again now, rising up.

"Go!" he said urgently, pushing at Tim to make him go away. "Run, before I— Aah!"

He stifled a scream, fell down, and curled into a ball. Tim crawled around to him and saw Nick's eyes roll back. For a moment he contemplated picking him up. Then he saw the white smoke trickling out of Nick's slack-jawed mouth.

Fear overcame everything then, and he started to run, between the lightning rods, up the hill. If only he could get over the ridge, get out of sight. Away from the Lightning Farm and the steadily rising fog. . . .

Behind him, Nick's hand gripped his trouser cuff even more tightly. He was whispering to himself, jumbled words spilling out in a frenzy.

"Corvere capital of two million principal products manufactured banking the attraction between two objects is directly proportional to the product of the day breaks not it is my heart four thousand eight hundred and the wind shifts generally in direction white wild Father help me Mother Sam help me Lirael—"

Nick stopped, coughed, and drew breath. The white smoke drifted off into the fog, and no new smoke emerged. Nick drew in two more shaky breaths, then experimentally let go of his trouser cuff and the piece of wind flute inside it. He felt a chill run through his body as he let go, but he still knew who he was and what he must do. Using the corner of the building, he hauled himself upright and staggered off into the fog. As always, the silver hemispheres glowed in his mind, but he had forced them into the background. Now he was thinking of the blueprints of the Lightning Farm. If Tim had made it according to Nick's design instructions, then one of the nine electrical junction boxes would be just around the corner of the main mill building.

Nick almost ran into the western wall of the mill, the fog was so thick. He skirted around it to the north as quickly as he could, staying away from the southern end, where the Dead labored to lift the first hemisphere onto a flatbed railway wagon.

The hemispheres. They glowed in Nick's mind

brighter than the lightning flashes. He was suddenly struck with a compulsion to make sure that they were properly lifted into the cradles, that the cables were correctly joined, the track sanded for traction in this wet fog. He had to see to it. The hemispheres had to be joined!

Nick fell to his knees on the railway, and then forward, to lie curled up across the cold steel and the worn wooden sleepers. He clutched at his trouser cuff, fighting against that overwhelming urge to turn right and go over to the hemisphere on its railway wagon. Desperately he thought of Lirael lifting him into the reed boat, of his promise to her. His friend Sam, picking him up after he'd been knocked out by a fast ball playing cricket. Tim Wallach, bow tied and dapper, pouring him a gin and tonic.

"Word of a Sayre, word of a Sayre, word of a Sayre," he repeated over and over again.

Still mumbling, he forced himself into a crawl. Across the track, ignoring the splinters from the old railway sleepers. He crawled to the far side of the mill, and used the wall to half crawl, half stumble down to the junction box, which was actually a small concrete hut. Here, hundreds of cables from the lightning rods fed into one of the nine master cables, each as thick as Nick's body.

"I'll stop it," he whispered to himself as he reached the junction box. Deafened by thunder, half blind from the lightning, and crippled by pain and nausea, he reached up and tried to open the metal door that was marked with a vivid yellow lightning bolt and the word "DANGER."

The door was locked. Nick shook the handle, but that small act of defiance did nothing but use up his last store of energy. Exhausted, Nick slid back down and sprawled across the doorway.

He had failed. Lightning continued to spread up the slope, accompanied by fog and booming thunder. The Dead continued to struggle with the hemispheres. One was on its railway wagon, which was being moved along the rails to the far end of the line, even as the Dead who pushed it were struck again and again by lightning. The other hemisphere was swinging off the coaster—till lightning burned the rope and it came crashing down, crushing several Dead Hands. But when the hemisphere was raised, the crushed Hands came slithering out. No longer recognizable as anything remotely human, and no use in the work, they squirmed their way east. Up the ridge, to join the Dead that Hedge had already sent to make sure that the final triumph of the Destroyer was not delayed.

"You have to believe me!" exclaimed Sam in exasperation. "Tell her again that I promise on the word of a Prince of the Old Kingdom that every single one of you will be given a farm!"

A young Southerling was translating for him, though Sam was sure that like most Southerlings, the matriarch understood at least spoken Ancelstierran. This time she interrupted the interpreter halfway through and thrust the paper she held out to Sam. He took it and quickly scanned it, acutely aware that he had only a minute or two left before he had to go back to Lirael.

The paper was printed on both sides, in several languages. It was headed "Land for the Southerling People" and then went on to promise ten acres of prime farmland for every piece of paper that was presented to the "land office" at Forwin Mill. There was an official-looking crest, and the paper supposedly came from the "Government of Ancelstierre Resettlement Office."

"This is a fake," Sam protested. "There is no Ancelstierre Resettlement Office, and even if there were, why would they want you to go to some-where like Forwin Mill?"

"That is where the land is," replied the young translator smoothly. "And there must be a Resettlement Office. Why else would the police let us leave the camps?"

"Look at what's happening over there!" screamed Sam, pointing at the thunderclouds and the constant forks of lightning, all of which were now easily visible, even from the valley floor. "If you go there, you will be killed! That is why they let you out! It solves a problem for them if you all get killed and they can say it wasn't their fault!"

The matriarch straightened her head and looked at the lightning playing along the ridge. Then she looked at the blue sky to the north, south, and east. She touched the interpreter's arm and said three words.

"You promise us on your blood?" asked the interpreter. He pulled out a knife made from the ground-down end of a spoon. "You will give us land in your country?"

"Yes, I promise on my blood," said Sam quickly. "I will give you land and all the help we can so you can live there."

The matriarch held out her palm, which was

marked with hundreds of tiny dotted scars that formed a complex whorl. The interpreter pricked her skin with the knife and twisted it around a few times, to form a new dot.

Sam held out his hand. He didn't feel the knife. All his concentration was behind him, his ears straining to hear any sound of an attack.

The matriarch spoke quickly and held her palm out. The interpreter gestured for Sam to hold his palm against hers. He did so, and she gripped his hand with surprising strength from her bony old fingers.

"Good, excellent," babbled Sam. "Have your people go back to the other side of the stream and wait there. As soon as I can, we will . . . I will arrange for you to be given your land."

"Why do we not wait here?" asked the interpreter.

"Because there's going to be a battle," said Sam anxiously. "Oh, Charter help me! Please go back beyond the stream! Running water will be the only protection you have!"

He turned and ran away before any more questions could be asked. The interpreter called after him, but Sam did not answer. He could feel the Dead coming down this side of the ridge, and he was terribly afraid he had been away from Lirael too long. She was up there on the spur, and he was her main protector. There was only so much Ancelstierrans could do, even those who had some slight mastery of Charter Magic.

Sam did not see, because he was sprinting for all he was worth, but behind him the interpreter and the matriarch spoke heatedly. Then the interpreter gestured back towards the center of the valley and the stream. The matriarch looked once more towards the lightning, then tore up the paper she held, threw it to the ground, and spat on it. Her action was mimicked by those around her, and then by others, and a great paper tearing and spitting slowly spread throughout the vast crowd. Then the matriarch turned and began to walk east, to the middle of the valley and the stream. Like a flock following its bellwether, all the other Southerlings turned as well.

Sam was panting up the spur, three quarters of the way back, when he heard shouts ahead.

"Halt! Halt!"

Sam couldn't sense the Dead so close, but he found extra speed from somewhere, and his sword leaped into his hand. Startled soldiers stepped aside as he ran past them and up to Lirael. She was still standing frozen in the ring of stones. Greene and two soldiers were in front of her. About ten feet in front of them, two more soldiers were standing over a young man with their bayonets to his throat. The youth was lying still on the ground and was shrieking. His clothes and skin were blackened, and he had lost most of his hair. But he was not a Dead Hand. In fact, Sam saw that this scorched fugitive was not much older than he was.

"It's not me, it's not me, I'm not them, they're behind me," he shrieked. "You have to help me!"

"Who are you?" asked Major Greene. "What is happening over there?"

"I'm Timothy Wallach," gasped the young man. "I don't know what's happening! It's a nightmare! That . . . I don't know what he is . . . Hedge. He killed my workmen! All of them. He pointed at them and they died."

"Who's behind you?" asked Sam.

"I don't know," sobbed Tim. "They were my men. I don't know what they are now. I saw Krontas struck directly by lightning. His head was on fire, but he didn't stop. They are—"

"The Dead," said Sam. "What were you doing at Forwin Mill?"

"I'm from the University of Corvere," whispered Tim. He made a visible effort to get himself under control. "I built the Lightning Farm for Nicholas Sayre. I didn't . . . I don't know what it's for, but it's nothing good. We have to stop it being used! Nick said he'll try, but—"

"Nicholas is there?" snapped Sam.

Tim nodded. "But he's in bad shape. He hardly knew who I was. I don't think there's much chance of him doing anything. And there was white smoke coming out of his nose—"

Sam listened with a sinking heart. He knew from Lirael that the white smoke was the sign of the Destroyer taking control. Any faint hope he'd had that Nick might escape was dashed. His friend was lost.

"What can be done?" asked Sam. "Is there any way to disable the Lightning Farm?"

"There are circuit breakers in each of the nine junction boxes," whispered Tim. "If they were opened . . . But I don't know how many circuits are actually needed. Or . . . or you could cut the cables from the lightning rods. There are a thousand and one lightning rods, and since they're already being struck by lightning . . . you'd need very special gear."

Sam didn't hear Tim's last few words. All thoughts of Nick's plight and the Lightning Farm were swept away as a cold sensation froze the hair on the back of his neck. His head snapped up, and he pushed past Tim. The first wave of Dead were almost upon them, and any question of doing something to any junction boxes was academic.

"Here they come!" he shouted, and jumped up on a rock, already reaching into the Charter to prepare destructive spells. He was surprised by how easy it was. The wind was still blowing from the west, and it should have been harder this far from the Wall. But he could feel the Charter strongly, almost as clear and present as it was in the Old Kingdom, though it was somehow inside him as much as it was outside.

"Stand ready!" shouted Greene, his warning repeated by sergeants and corporals in the ring of soldiers around Lirael's frozen form. "Remember, nothing must get through to the Abhorsen! Nothing!"

"The Abhorsen." Sam closed his eyes for a second, willing that pain away. There was no time to grieve or think about the world without his parents. He could see the Dead Hands lumbering down the slope, gathering speed as they sensed the Life ahead.

Sam readied a spell and quickly looked around. All the bowmen had arrows nocked, and they were teamed with pairs of bayonet men. Greene and Tindall were next to Sam, both ready with Charter spells. Lirael was several paces behind them, secure with soldiers all around her.

But where was Mogget? The little white cat was nowhere to be seen.

CHAPTER TWENTY-THREE

LATHAL THE ABOMINATION

THE FIFTH GATE was a reverse waterfall: a waterclimb. The river hit an unseen wall and kept on flowing up it. The dark ribbon path that crossed the Fifth Precinct ended short of this waterclimb, leaving a gap. Lirael and the Dog stared up from the end of the path, their stomachs crowding their throats. It was very disorienting to see water rising where it should fall, though fortunately it blurred into grey fuzziness before it went too far up. Even so, Lirael had the unpleasant feeling that she was no longer subject to normal gravity and might fall upwards, too.

That feeling was fueled by the knowledge that this was actually what was going to happen when she spoke the Free Magic spell to cross the Fifth Gate. There was no path or stair here—the spell simply made sure the waterclimb didn't take you too far.

"You'd better hold my collar, Mistress," said the Dog, eyeing the rising water. "The spell won't include me otherwise."

Lirael sheathed her sword and grabbed the Dog's collar, her fingers feeling the warmth and comfortable familiarity of the Charter marks that made it up. She had a strange sense of déjà vu as she pushed her fingers through, as if she knew the Charter marks from somewhere else—somewhere relatively new, not just from the thousand times she had held the collar. But she had no time to follow that feeling to some conclusion.

Holding the Dog tight, Lirael spoke the words that would carry them up the waterclimb, once again feeling the heat of Free Magic through her nose and mouth. She would likely lose her voice from it eventually, she thought, but it also seemed to have cured her Ancelstierran cold. Though she might still have a cold in her real body, out in Life. She didn't know enough about how things like that in Death would affect her in Life. Of course, if she were slain in Death, her body would die in Life as well.

The spell was slow to start, and for a moment Lirael contemplated saying it again. Then she saw a sheet of water reach out of the surface of the water-climb, moving like a strange, very thin, very wide tentacle. It crossed the gap to the ribbon path in a series of shuddering extensions and wrapped around Lirael and the Dog like a large blanket, without actually touching them. Then it began to rise up the waterclimb, moving at the same rate as the vertical current—taking Lirael and her closely gripped hound with it.

They rose steadily for several minutes, till the precinct below was lost in the fuzzy grey light. The waterclimb continued upwards—perhaps forever—but the extension that held Lirael stopped. Then it suddenly snapped back into the face of the water-climb—throwing its passengers out the other side.

Lirael blinked as she hurtled into what her common sense told her should be a cliff, but the back of the waterclimb no more followed common sense than the waterclimb acknowledged gravity. Somehow, it had pushed them through to the next precinct. The Sixth, a place where the river became a shallow pool and there was no current at all. But there were lots and lots of Dead.

Lirael felt them so strongly, they might have

been standing next to her—and some probably were, under the water. Instantly, she let go of the collar and drew Nehima, the sword humming as it sprang from its scabbard.

The sword, and the bell she held, were warning enough for most of the Dead. In any case, the great majority were simply waiting here till something happened and they were forced to go on, since they lacked the will and the knowledge to go back the other way. Very few were actively struggling back towards Life.

Those that were saw the great spark of Life in Lirael, and they hungered for it. Other necromancers had assuaged their hunger in the past and helped them back from the brink of the Ninth Gate—willingly or not. This one was young, and should thus be easy prey for any of the Greater Dead who chanced to be close.

There were three who were.

Lirael looked out and saw that huge shadows stalked between the apathetic lesser spirits, fires burning where once their living forms had eyes. There were three close enough to intercept her intended path—and that was three too many.

But once again *The Book of the Dead* had advice upon such a confrontation in the Sixth

Precinct. And, as always, she had the Disreputable Dog.

As the three monstrous Greater Dead thrust their way towards her, Lirael replaced Ranna and drew Saraneth. Carefully composing herself this time, she rang it, joining her indomitable will with its deep call.

The Dead creatures hesitated as Saraneth's strong voice echoed out across the Precinct, and they prepared to fight, to struggle against this presumptuous necromancer who thought to bend them to her will.

Then they laughed, awful laughter that sounded like a great crowd of people caught between absurdity and sorrow. For this necromancer was so incompetent that she had focused her will not upon them, but on the Lesser Dead who lay all around.

Still laughing, the Greater Dead plunged forward, greedy now, each warily eyeing the others to gauge if they were weak enough to push out of the way. For whoever reached this necromancer first would gain the delight of consuming the greater part of her life. Life and power, the only things that were of any use for the long journey out of Death.

They didn't even notice the first few spirits who clutched at their shadowy legs or bit at their ankles, shrugging them off as a living person might ignore a few mosquito bites.

Then more and more spirits began to rise out of the water and hurl themselves at the three Greater Dead. They were forced to stop and swat these annoying Lesser Dead away, to rip them apart and rend them with their fiery jaws. Angrily, they stomped and threshed, roaring with anger now, the laughter gone.

Distracted, the Greater Dead closest to Lirael hardly noticed the Charter Spell that revealed its name to her, and it didn't see her as she walked almost right up to where it fought against a churning mass of its lesser brethren.

But Lirael gained the creature's full attention when a new bell rang, replacing Saraneth's strident commands with an excitable march. This bell was Kibeth, close by the thing's head, sounded with a dreadful tone specifically for its hearing. A tune that it couldn't ignore, even after the bell had stopped.

"Lathal the Abomination!" commanded Lirael. "Your time has come. The Ninth Gate calls, and you must go beyond it!"

Lathal screamed as Lirael spoke, a scream that carried the anguish of a thousand years. It knew that voice, for Lathal had made the long trek into Life twice in the last millennium, only to be forced back into Death by others with that same cold tone. Always, it had managed to stop itself being carried through to the ultimate gate. Now Lathal would never walk under the sun again, never drink the sweet life of the unsuspecting living. It was too close to the Ninth Gate, and the compulsion was strong.

Drubas and Sonnir heard the bell, the scream, and the voice, and knew that this was no foolish necromancer—it was the Abhorsen. A new one, for they knew the old and would have run from her. The sword was different, too, but they would remember it in future.

Still screaming, Lathal turned and stumbled away, the Lesser Dead tearing at its legs as it staggered and tumbled through the water and constantly tried to turn back without success.

Lirael didn't follow, because she didn't want to be too close when it passed the Sixth Gate, in case the sudden current took her, too. The other Greater Dead were moving hastily away, she noted with grim satisfaction, clubbing a path through the clinging spirits who still harassed them.

"Can I round them up, Mistress?" asked the Dog eagerly, staring after the retreating shapes of darkness with tense anticipation. "Can I?"

"No," said Lirael firmly. "I surprised Lathal. Those two will be on their guard and would be much more dangerous together. Besides, we haven't got time."

As she spoke, Lathal's scream was suddenly cut off, and Lirael felt the river current suddenly spring up around her legs. She set her feet apart and stood against it, leaning back on the rock-steady Dog. The current was very strong for a few minutes, threatening to drag her under; then it subsided into nothing—and once again the waters of the Sixth Precinct were still.

Immediately, Lirael began to wade through to the point where she could summon the Sixth Gate. Unlike the other precincts, the Gate out of the Sixth Precinct wasn't in any particular place. It would open randomly from time to time—which was a danger—or it could be opened anywhere a certain distance away from the Fifth Gate.

Just in case it was like the previous gate, Lirael clutched the Disreputable Dog's collar again, though it meant sheathing Nehima. Then she recited the spell, wetting her lips between the phrases to try to ease the blistering heat of the Free Magic.

As the spell built, the water drained away in a

circle about ten feet wide around and under Lirael and the Dog. When it was dry, the circle began to sink, the water rising around it on all sides. Faster and faster it sank, till they seemed to be at the base of a narrow cylinder of dry air bored into three hundred feet of water.

Then, with a great roar, the watery sides of the cylinder collapsed, pouring out in every direction. It took a few minutes for the waters to pass and the froth and spray to subside; then the river slowly ebbed back and wrapped around Lirael's legs. The air cleared, and she saw that they were standing in the river, the current once again trying to pull them under and away.

They had reached the Seventh Precinct, and already Lirael could see the first of the Three Gates that marked the deep reaches of Death. The Seventh Gate—an endless line of red fire that burned eerily upon the water, the light bright and disturbing after the uniform greyness of the earlier precincts.

"We're getting closer," said Lirael, in a voice that revealed a mixture of relief that they'd made it so far and apprehension at where they still had to go.

But the Dog wasn't listening—she was looking

back, her ears pricked and twitching. When she did look at Lirael, she simply said, "Our pursuer is gaining on us, Mistress. I think it *is* Hedge! We must go faster!"

CHAPTER TWENTY-FOUR

MOGGET'S INSCRUTABLE INITIATIVE

NICK DRAGGED HIMSELF up and leaned against the door. He'd found a bent nail on the ground, and armed with that and a dim memory of how locks worked, he tried once more to get into the concrete blockhouse that housed one of the nine junction boxes that were vital to the operation of the Lightning Farm.

He could hear nothing but thunder now, and he couldn't look up, because the lightning was too close, too bright. The thing inside him wanted him to look, to make sure the hemispheres were being properly loaded into the bronze cradles. But even if he gave in to that compulsion, his body was too weak to obey.

Instead he slipped back down to the ground and dropped the nail. He started to search for it, even though he knew it was useless. He had to do something. However futile.

Then he felt something touch his cheek, and he flinched. It touched it again—something wetter than the fog, and rasping. Gingerly, he opened his eyes to narrow slits, bracing himself for the white flash of lightning.

He got that, but there was another, softer whiteness as well. The fur of a small white cat, who was delicately licking his face.

"Go away, cat!" mumbled Nick. His voice sounded small and pathetic under the thunder. He made a flapping motion with his hand and added, "You'll get struck by lightning."

"I doubt it," replied Mogget, close to his ear. "Besides, I've decided to take you with me. Unfortunately. Can you walk?"

Nick shook his head and found, to his surprise, that he did have tears left after all. He wasn't surprised by a talking cat. The world was crumbling around him, and anything could happen.

"No," he whispered. "There is something inside me, cat. It won't let me leave."

"The Destroyer is distracted," said Mogget. He could see the second hemisphere being fitted into its cradle on the railway wagon, the burnt and broken Dead Hands laboring on with mindless devotion. Mogget's green eyes reflected a tapestry of lightnings, but the cat didn't blink.

"As is Hedge," he added. Mogget had already done a careful reconnaissance, and had seen the necromancer standing in the cemetery that had once served a thriving timber town. Hedge was covered in ice, obviously engaged in gathering reinforcements in Death and sending them back. With great success, Mogget knew, from the many rotten corpses and skeletons that were already digging themselves out of their graves.

Nick somehow knew that this was his last chance, that this talking animal was like the Dog of his dream, connected with Lirael and his friend Sam. Summoning his last reserves of strength, he pushed himself up to a sitting position—but that was all. He was too weak and too close to the hemispheres.

Mogget looked at him, his tail waving to and fro in annoyance.

"If that's the best you can do, I suppose I'll have to carry you," said the cat.

"H . . . how?" mumbled Nick. He couldn't even begin to wonder how the little cat intended to carry a grown man. Even one as reduced as he was.

Mogget didn't answer. He just stood up on his back paws—and began to change.

Nick stared at the spot where the little white cat had been. His eyes watered from the glare of the constant lightning. He had seen the animal change, but even so he had trouble believing what he saw.

For instead of a small cat, there was now a very short, thin-waisted, broad-shouldered man. He wasn't much taller than a ten-year-old child, and he had the white-blond hair and translucently pale skin of an albino, though his eyes weren't red. They were bright green, and almond shaped—exactly like the cat's had been. And he had a bright red leather belt around his waist, from which hung a tiny silver bell. Then Nick noticed that the white robe this apparition wore had two wide bands around the cuffs, dusted with tiny silver keys—the same silver keys he'd seen on Lirael's coat.

"Now," said Mogget cautiously. He could sense the fragment of the Destroyer inside Nick, and even with the greater part intent on its joining, he knew he had to be careful. But trickery might serve where strength would not. "I'm going to pick you up, and we're going to go and find a really good place where we can watch the hemispheres join."

At the mention of the hemispheres, Nick felt a

burning, white-hot pain through his chest. Yes, they were close, he could feel them. . . .

"I must oversee the work," he croaked. He shut his eyes again, and the vision of the hemispheres burned in his mind brighter than any lightning.

"The work is done," soothed Mogget. He picked Nick up and held him in his unnaturally strong arms, though he was careful not to touch Nick's chest. The albino looked somewhat like an ant, carrying a load larger than himself slightly away from his own body. "We're only going somewhere to have a better view. A view of the hemispheres when they join."

"A better view," mumbled Nick. Somehow that quietened the ache in his breast, but it also let him think again with his own mind.

He opened his eyes and met the green ones of his bearer. He was unable to decipher the emotions there. Was it fear—or excited anticipation?

"We have to stop it!" he wheezed, and the pain came back with such force that he screamed, a scream drowned in thunder. Mogget bent his head down closer, as Nick continued in a whisper. "I can show you . . . ah . . . unscrew the junction boxes . . . disconnect the master cables . . ."

"It's too late for that," said Mogget. He began to head up between the lightning rods, ducking and weaving with a foresight that indicated he could predict where and when the lightning would strike.

Behind and below Mogget and his burden, one of the last of Hedge's living workers connected the master cables into the cradles that held the hemispheres atop the railway trucks. The trucks were positioned fifty yards apart on the short stretch of railway line, and the hemispheres had been set up so their flat bottoms faced each other and projected out from the cradles. The cables fed into the bronze framework that held each hemisphere. There was no sign of anything that would drive the railway trucks—and the hemispheres—together, but clearly that was the intention.

Many of the lightning rods were being hit and already were feeding power into the hemispheres. Long blue sparks were crackling around the railway cars, and Mogget could feel the greedy sucking of the Destroyer, and the stir of the ancient entity within the silver metal.

The albino began to move faster, though not as fast as he could, in order not to alarm the shard inside Nick. But the young man lay quiet in his arms, one part of his mind content that it was too late to stop the joining, the other part grieving that he had failed.

Soon there was visible evidence that Orannis flexed against its bonds. The lightning ceased around the hemispheres themselves and began to move outwards, as if pushed back by some unseen hand. Instead of a concentrated series of strikes in and around the railway cars, the lightning began to hit more and more of the lightning rods that dotted the hillside. There was also more lightning coming down from the storm. Where there had been nine bolts every minute in a small area around the hemispheres, now there were ninety across the hill-side, then several hundred, as the storm above roiled and thundered, spreading across the entire Lightning Farm.

Within a few minutes, there was no lightning at all in the center of the storm. But down below, the hemispheres glowed with newfound power, and every time Mogget glanced back, he could see dark shadows writhing deep inside the silver metal. In each hemisphere, the shadows moved to darken the side closest to the other, raging against the repul-sion that still kept them apart.

More lightning struck, the crash of the thunder

shaking the ground. The hemispheres glowed brighter still, and the shadows grew darker. With a shriek of protesting metal from long-disused wheels, the railway cars began to roll together.

"The hemispheres join!" shouted Mogget, and he ran faster up the hillside, zigzagging between the lightning rods, his body hunched over to protect his burden from the violent energies that struck down all around them.

Inside Nick's heart, a small sliver of metal quivered, feeling the attraction of its greater whole. For an instant, it moved against the heart wall, as if to burst forth in bloody glory. But the attractive force was not yet strong enough and was too far away. Instead of erupting out through flesh and bone, the shard of the Destroyer caught the flow out through a bright artery, and began to retrace the passage it had made almost a year before.

Sam lowered his hand as a Dead Hand fell shrieking, golden Charter fire eating away at every sinew. Flopping and writhing, it crawled behind two burning trees. Smoke from the fires rose up in spirals, looking like outriders for the huge bank of fog that was rolling over the top of the ridge above.

"Wish my arrows did that," remarked Sergeant

Evans. He'd put several silver arrows into that same Dead Hand, but they had only slowed it down.

"The spirit is still there," said Sam grimly. "Only the body is useless to it now."

He could feel many more Dead, climbing up the other side of the ridge, advancing with the fog. So far, Sam and the soldiers had managed to repel the first attack. But that had been only a half dozen Dead Hands.

"They're making us keep our distance while they prepare for the main attack, I reckon," said Major Greene, tipping back his helmet to wipe a sheen of sweat from his forehead.

"Yes," agreed Sam. He hesitated, then quietly said, "There are about a hundred Dead Hands out there, and more appearing every minute."

He looked behind him to where Lirael's ice-encrusted body stood between the rocks, and then around the ring of soldiers. Their ranks were thinner than before. None had been slain by the Dead, but at least a dozen or more of them had simply run away, too scared to stand and fight. The Major had reluctantly let them go, muttering something about not being able to shoot them when the whole company shouldn't be there anyway.

"I wish I knew what was happening!" Sam

burst out. "With Lirael—and those Charter-cursed hemispheres!"

"The waiting's always the worst," said Major Greene. "But I don't think we'll be waiting long, one way or another. That fog is coming down. We'll be under it in a few minutes."

Sam looked ahead again. Sure enough, the fog was moving faster, long tendrils pushing down the slope, with the bulk of the fog behind. At the same time, he felt a great surge of the Dead rise all along the ridge.

"Here they come!" shouted the Major. "Stand fast, lads!"

There were too many to blast with Charter spells, Sam realized. He hesitated for a moment, then got out the panpipes Lirael had given him and lifted them to his mouth. He might not be the Abhorsen-in-Waiting anymore, but he would have to act the part now in the face of the onrushing Dead.

Then Sam lost sight of the Major, his whole attention on the advancing Dead and the panpipes. He put his lips to the Saraneth pipe, drew a great breath in through his nose—and blew, the pure, strong sound cutting through the thunder and the damping fog.

With that sound, Sam exerted his will, feeling it stretch across the battleground, encompassing more than fifty Dead Hands. He felt their downward rush slow, felt them fight against him, their spirits raging as dead flesh struggled to keep moving forward.

For an instant, Sam held them all in his grip, and the Dead Hands slowed to a halt, till they stood like grim statues, wreathed in wisps of fog. Arrows plunged at them, and some of the closer soldiers dashed forward to hack at legs or pierce their knees with bayonets.

Still the spirits inside the dead flesh fought, and Sam knew he could not gain total domination. He left Saraneth echoing on the hillside and switched his mouth to the Ranna pipe. But he had to draw breath again, and in that brief moment, the sound of Saraneth faded and Sam's will was broken. He lost control, and all along the line, the Dead shivered into movement and once more charged down the spur, hungry for Life.

CHAPTER TWENTY-FIVE

THE NINTH GATE

LIRAEL AND THE Dog crossed the Seventh Precinct at a run, not even pausing as Lirael sang out the spell to open the Seventh Gate. Ahead of them, the line of fire shivered at her words, and directly in front, it leapt up to form a narrow arch, just wide enough for them to pass.

As she ducked through, Lirael glanced back— and saw a man-shaped figure rushing after them, himself a thing of fire and darkness, holding a sword that dripped red flames the match of those in the Seventh Gate.

Then they were through to the Eighth Precinct, and Lirael had to quickly gasp out another spell to ward off a patch of flame that reared up out of the water towards them. These flames were the main threat in the precinct, for the river was lit with many floating patches of fire that moved according to strange currents of their own or flared up out of nowhere.

Lirael narrowly averted another, and hurried past. She felt a tiny muscle above her eye start to twitch uncontrollably, a symptom of nervous fear, as individual fires roared everywhere in sight, some moving fast, some slow. At the same time, she expected Hedge to suddenly come up from behind and attack.

The Dog barked next to her, and a huge thicket of fire swerved aside. She hadn't even seen it beginning to flare, her mind so much occupied by the ones she could see and the threat of what might be coming from behind.

"Steady, Mistress," said the Dog calmly. "We'll be through this lot soon."

"Hedge!" gulped Lirael, then immediately shouted two words to send a long snake of fire twirling into another, the two joining in a combustionary dance. They seemed almost alive, she thought, watching them twirl. More like creatures than burning patches of oily scum, which is what they looked like when they didn't move. They also differed from normal fires in another way, Lirael realized, because there was no smoke.

"I saw Hedge," she repeated once the immediate threat of immolation had passed. "Behind us."

"I know," said the Dog. "When we get to the Eighth Gate, I'll stay here and stop him while you go on."

"No!" exclaimed Lirael. "You have to come with me! I'm not afraid of him . . . it's . . . it's just so inconvenient!"

"Look out!" barked the Dog, and they both jumped aside as a great globe of fire swung past, close enough to choke Lirael with its sudden heat. Coughing, she bent over—and the river chose that moment to try to pull her legs out from under her.

It almost worked. The current's sudden surge made Lirael slip, but she went down only as far as her waist, then used her sword like a crutch to lever herself up again with a single springing leap.

The Dog had already plunged under to haul her mistress out, and the hound looked very embarrassed when she emerged, soaking, to find Lirael not only still vertical but mostly dry.

"Thought you went in," she mumbled, then barked at a fire, as much to move the conversation on as to divert the intruder.

"Come on!" said Lirael.

"I'm going to wait and ambush—" the Dog started to say, but Lirael turned on her and grabbed her by the collar. The mulish Dog set her haunches down at once, and Lirael tried to drag her.

"You're coming with me!" ordered Lirael, her tone of command watered down by the quaver in her voice. "We'll fight Hedge together—when we have to. For now, let's hurry!"

"Oh, all right," grumbled the Dog. She got up and shook herself, splashing copious amounts of the river onto Lirael.

"Whatever happens," Lirael added quietly, "I want us to be together, Dog."

The Disreputable Dog looked up at her with a troubled eye but didn't speak. Lirael almost said something else, but it got choked up in her throat, and then she had to ward off another incursion by floating fires.

When that was done, they strode off side by side and, a few minutes later, stepped confidently into the wall of darkness that was the Eighth Gate. All light vanished, and Lirael could see nothing, hear nothing, and feel nothing, including her own body. She felt as if she had suddenly become a disembodied intelligence that was totally alone, cut off from all external stimuli.

But she had expected it, and though she couldn't feel her own mouth and lips, and her ears could hear no sound, she spoke the spell that would take them through this ultimate darkness. Through to the Ninth and final Precinct of Death.

The Ninth Precinct was utterly different from all other parts of Death. Lirael blinked as she emerged from the darkness of the Eighth Gate, struck by sudden light. The familiar tug of the river at her knees disappeared as the current faded away. The river now only splashed gently round her ankles, and the water was warm, the terrible chill that prevailed in all other precincts of Death left behind.

Everywhere else in Death always had a closed-in feeling, due to the strange grey light that limited vision. Here it was the opposite. There was a sensation of immensity, and Lirael could see for miles and miles, across a great flat stretch of sparkling water.

For the first time, she could also look up and see more than a grey, depressing blur. Much more. There was a sky above her, a night sky so thick with stars that they overlapped and merged to form one unimaginably vast and luminous cloud. There were no distinguishable constellations, no patterns to pick out. Just a multitude of stars, casting a light as bright as but softer than the living world's sun.

Lirael felt the stars call to her, and a yearning rose in her heart to answer. She sheathed bell and sword and stretched her arms out, up to the brilliant sky. She felt herself lifted up, and her feet came out of the river with a soft ripple and a sigh from the waters.

Dead rose, too, she saw. Dead of all shapes and sizes, all rising up to the sea of stars. Some went slowly, and some so fast they were just a blur.

Some small part of Lirael's mind warned that she was answering the Ninth Gate's call. The veil of stars was the final border, the final death from which there could be no return. That same small conscience shrieked about responsibility, and Orannis, and the Disreputable Dog, and Sam, and Nick, and the whole world of Life. It angrily kicked and screamed against the overwhelming feeling of peace and rest offered by the stars.

Not yet, it cried. Not yet.

That cry was answered, though not by any voice. The stars suddenly retreated, became immeasurably far away. Lirael blinked, shook her head, and fell several feet to splash down next to the Dog, who still gazed up at the luminous sky.

"Why didn't you stop me?" Lirael asked, made cross by the scare she'd had. Another few seconds and she would have been unable to return, she knew. She would have gone beyond the Ninth Gate forever.

"It is something that all who walk here must face themselves," whispered the Dog. She still stared up and did not look at Lirael. "For everyone, and everything, there is a time to die. Some do not know it, or would delay it, but its truth cannot be denied. Not when you look into the stars of the Ninth Gate. I'm glad you came back, Mistress."

"So am I," said Lirael nervously. She could see Dead emerging all along the dark mass of the Eighth Gate. Every time one came out, she tensed, thinking it must be Hedge. She could feel more Dead than she could see, but they were all simply coming through and immediately falling skywards, to disappear amongst the stars. But Hedge, who must have been only a few minutes behind Lirael and the Dog, did not come through the Eighth Gate.

Still the Dog looked up. Lirael finally noticed, and her heart nearly stopped. Surely the Dog wouldn't answer the summons of the Ninth Gate?

Finally, the Dog looked down and made a slight woofing sound.

"Not yet my time, either," she said, and Lirael let out her breath. "Shouldn't you be doing what we came here for, Mistress?"

"I know," said Lirael wretchedly, all too conscious of the time wasted. She touched the Dark Mirror in her pouch. "But what if Hedge comes while I'm looking?"

"If he hasn't come through now, he probably won't," replied the Dog, sniffing the river. "Few necromancers risk seeing the Ninth Gate, for their very nature is to deny its call."

"Oh," said Lirael, much relieved by this advice.

"He will certainly be waiting for us somewhere on the way back, though," continued the Dog, bursting that small bubble of relief. "But for now, I will guard you."

Lirael smiled, a troubled smile that conveyed her love and gratitude. She was twice vulnerable, she thought, with her body out in Life guarded by Sam, and now her spirit here in Death, guarded by the Dog.

But she had to do what must be done, regardless of the risk.

First of all she pricked the point of her finger with Nehima before sheathing the sword again. Then she took out the Dark Mirror and opened it with a decisive snap.

Blood dripped down her finger, and a drop fell. But it flew up towards the sky instead of down to the river. Lirael didn't notice. She was remembering pages from *The Book of Remembrance and Forgetting*, concentrating as she held her finger close to the Mirror and touched a single bright drop to its opaque surface. As the drop touched, it spread, to form a thin sheen across the dark surface of the glass.

Lirael lifted the Mirror and held it to her right eye, while still looking out on Death through her left eye. The blood gave the Mirror a faint red tinge, but that quickly faded as she focused, and the darkness began to clear. Once again, Lirael saw through the Mirror into some other place, but she could still also see the sparkling waters of the Ninth Precinct. The two visions merged, and Lirael saw the swirling lights and the sun fleeing backwards somehow through the waters of Death, and she felt herself falling faster and faster into some incredibly distant past.

Now Lirael began to think of what she wanted to see, and her left hand fell to unconsciously touch each of the bells in her bandolier in turn.

"By Right of Blood," she said, her voice growing

stronger and more confident with each word, "by Right of Heritage, by Right of the Charter, and by Right of the Seven who wove it, I would see through the veil of time, to the Beginning. I would witness the Binding and Breaking of Orannis and learn what was and what must become. So let it be!"

Long after she spoke, the suns still ran backwards, and Lirael fell farther and farther into them, till all the suns were one, blinding her with light. Then the light faded, and she gazed out to a dark void. There was a single point of light within the void, and she fell towards that, and soon it was not a light but a moon and then a huge planet that filled the horizon, and she was falling through its sky and gliding in the air above a desert that stretched from horizon to horizon, a desert that Lirael somehow knew encompassed this whole world. Nothing stirred upon the baked, parched earth. Nothing grew or lived.

The world spun beneath her, faster and faster, and Lirael saw it in earlier times, saw how all life had been extinguished. Then she fell through the suns again and saw another void, another single, struggling world that would become a desert.

Six times, Lirael saw a world destroyed. The seventh time, it was her own world she saw. She knew it, though there was no landmark or feature that told her so. She saw the Destroyer choose it, but this time others chose it, too. This would be the battleground where they would confront the Destroyer; this was where sides must be chosen and loyalties decided for all time.

The vision Lirael saw then seemed to last for many days, and many horrors. But at the same time, through her other eye she saw the Dog pacing backwards and forwards, and Lirael knew that little time had passed in Death.

Finally, she saw enough, and could bear to see no more. She shut both eyes, snapped the mirror shut, and slowly sank to her knees, holding the small silver case between her clasped hands. Warm water lapped around her, but it offered no comfort.

When she opened her eyes a moment later, the Dog licked her on the mouth and looked at her with great concern.

"We have to hurry," said Lirael, pushing herself upright. "I didn't really understand before. . . . We have to hurry!"

She started back towards the Eighth Gate and drew both sword and bell with new decisiveness. She had seen what Orannis could do now, and it was far worse than she had ever imagined. Truly,

It was aptly named the Destroyer. Orannis existed solely to destroy, and the Charter was the enemy that had stopped It doing so. It hated all living things and not only wanted to destroy them—It had the power to do so.

Only Lirael knew how Orannis could be bound anew. It would be difficult—perhaps even impossible. But it was their one chance, and she was full of single-minded determination to get back to Life. She had to make it happen. For herself, for the Dog, Sam, Nick, Major Greene and his men, for the people of Ancelstierre who would die without even knowing their danger, and for all those in the Old Kingdom. Her cousins of the Clayr. Even Aunt Kirrith . . .

Thoughts of them all, and her responsibility, filled her head as she approached the Eighth Gate, the words of the opening spell on her lips. But even as she opened her mouth to speak the words, there was a gout of flame from the darkness of the Gate, directly opposite Lirael and the Dog.

Wreathed in that flame, Hedge lunged through. His sword cut at Lirael's left arm, and he struck so hard that she dropped Saraneth, its brief jangle quickly swallowed by the river. The clang of ensorcelled steel on gethre plates echoed across the water.

The armor held, but even so Lirael's arm beneath was badly bruised—for the second time in only a few days.

Lirael barely managed to parry the next cut for her head. She leapt back and got in the way of the Dog, who was about to leap forward. Pain coursed through Lirael's left arm, shooting up through her shoulder and neck. Nevertheless, she reached for a bell.

Hedge was quicker. He had a bell in his hand already, and he rang it. Saraneth, Lirael recognized, and she steeled herself to resist its power. But nothing came with the peal of the bell. No compulsion, no test of wills.

"Sit!" commanded Hedge, and Lirael suddenly realized that Hedge had focused Saraneth's power upon the Disreputable Dog.

Growling, the Dog froze, halfway back on her haunches, ready to spring. But Saraneth had her in its grip, and she was unable to move.

Lirael circled around the Dog, moving to try to cut at Hedge's bell arm, as he had cut hers. But he moved, too, circling back the other way. There was something odd about his fighting stance, Lirael noted. She couldn't think what it was for a moment. Then she realized that he kept his head angled down, and he never looked up. Clearly, Hedge was afraid to see the stars of the Ninth Gate.

He started to move towards her, but she circled back again, keeping the motionless Dog between them. As she passed in front, Lirael saw the hound wink.

"You have led me a long chase," said Hedge. His voice was flavored with Free Magic, and he sounded much more like something Dead than a living man. He looked like it, too. He towered over Lirael, and there were fires everywhere within him, glowing red in his eyes and mouth, dripping from his fingers and shining through his skin. Lirael wasn't even sure he was a living man. He was more like a Free Magic spirit himself, only clad in human flesh. "But it is finished now, here and in Life. My master is whole again, and the destruction has begun. Only the Dead walk in the living world, to praise Orannis for Its work. Only the Dead—and I, the faithful vizier."

His voice had a hypnotic quality about it. Lirael realized he was trying to distract her while he went for a killing blow. He hadn't tried the bell upon her, which was curious—but then, she'd broken free of Hedge and Saraneth before.

"Look up, Hedge," she answered, as they circled again. "The Ninth Gate calls. Can't you feel the summons of the stars?"

She lunged at him on "stars," but Hedge was ready, and more practiced with a sword. He parried, and his swift riposte cut the fabric of her surcoat directly above her heart.

Quickly, she backed off again, this time circling away from the Dog. Hedge followed, his head still bent, watching her through hooded eyes.

Behind him, the Dog stirred. Slowly, she raised one paw from the shallow river, careful not to make a splash. Then she began to sneak after the necromancer as he stalked towards Lirael.

"I don't believe you about the Destroyer, either," said Lirael as she backed away, hoping her voice would cover the sound of the Dog's advance. "I would know if anything had happened to my body in Life. Besides, you wouldn't bother with me if It were already free."

"You are an annoyance, nothing more," said Hedge. He was smiling now, and the flames on his sword grew brighter, feeding off his expectation of a kill. "It pleases me to finish you. There is no more to it than that. As my Master destroys that which displeases, so do I!"

He slashed viciously down at her. Lirael barely managed to parry and push his sword aside. Then they were locked together, body to body, his head bent over hers and his metallic, flame-ridden breath hot upon her cheek as she turned away.

"But perhaps I will play a little with you first." Hedge smiled, disengaged, and stepped back.

Lirael struck at him with all her strength and anger. Hedge laughed, parried, stepped back once more—and tumbled over the Disreputable Dog.

He dropped his sword and bell at once, and clapped his hands to his eyes as he struck the water with the hiss and roar of steam. But he was an instant too late. He saw the stars as he fell, and they called to him, overcoming the weight of spells and power that had kept him in the living world for more than a hundred years. Always postponing Death, always searching for something that could let him stay forever under the sun. He thought he had found it, serving Orannis, for he cared nothing about anyone else or any other living thing. The Destroyer had promised him the reward of eternal life and even greater dominion over the Dead. Hedge had done everything he could to earn it.

Now, with a single glimpse of those beckoning stars, it was all stripped away. Hedge's hands fell back. Starlight filled his eyes with glowing tears, tears that slowly quenched his internal fires. The coils of steam wafted away, and the river grew quiet. Hedge raised his arms and began his own fall towards the sky, the stars, and the Ninth Gate.

The Disreputable Dog picked up Lirael's bell from the river and took it to her, careful not to let it sound. Lirael accepted it in silence and put it away. There was no time to savor their triumph over the necromancer. Lirael knew that he was only ever a lesser enemy.

Together they crossed the Eighth Gate, both filled with a terrible fear. The fear that though Hedge's words were lies, they would become the truth before they could get back to Life.

Lirael was further burdened by the weight of knowledge. Now she knew how to bind the Destroyer anew, but she also knew it couldn't be done just by her. Sam would need to be the heir of the Wallmakers in truth and not just be entitled to wear their silver trowel on his surcoat.

Others of the Blood would be needed, too, and they just weren't there.

Even worse, the binding was only half of what must be done. Even if Lirael and Sam could somehow manage that, there was the breaking, and that would require more courage than Lirael thought she had.

CHAPTER TWENTY-SIX

SAM AND THE SHADOW HANDS

AS THE DEAD broke free of Saraneth's hold, Sam blew on the Ranna pipe. But the soft lullaby was too late, and Sam's breath too hasty. Only a half dozen of the Dead lay down to sleep under Ranna's spell, and the bell caught several soldiers, too. The other ninety or more Dead Hands charged down out of the fog, to be met by swords, bayonets, silver blades, and the white lightning of the Charter Mages.

For a furious, frenzied minute of hacking and dodging, Sam couldn't see what was happening. Then the Hand in front of him collapsed, its legs cut away. Sam was surprised to see that he'd done that himself, the Charter marks on his sword blazing with blue-white fury.

"Try the pipes again!" shouted the Major. He

stepped in front of Sam to engage the next broken-jawed apparition. "We'll cover you!"

Sam nodded and brought the pipes to his lips again with new determination. The Dead had driven the defenders back with their charge, and now Lirael was only a few feet behind him, a frozen statue who would be totally vulnerable to attack.

Most of the Dead Hands were fresh corpses, still clad in their workers' overalls. But many were inhabited by spirits that had lain long in Death, who quickly transformed the dead flesh they now occupied, making it less human and more like the dreadful shapes they'd assumed in Death. One came at Sam now, wriggling like a snake between Major Greene and Lieutenant Tindall, its lower jaw unhinged for a larger bite. Reflexively, Sam stabbed it through the throat. Sparks flew as the Charter marks on the blade destroyed dead flesh. It wriggled and threshed but couldn't free itself from the sword, so the thing's spirit began to crawl out of its fleshy husk, like a worm of darkness leaving a totally rotten apple.

Sam looked down at it and felt his fear replaced by a hot anger. How dare these Dead intrude upon the world of Life? His nostrils flared, and his face reddened, as he drew breath to blow upon the pipe.

This was not the Dead's path, and he would make them choose another.

Lungs expanded to the full, he chose the Kibeth pipe and blew. A single note sounded, high and clear—but then it somehow became a lively, infectious jig. It cheered the soldiers and even made them smile, their weapons moving with the rhythm of Kibeth's song.

But the Dead heard a different tune, and those with working mouths and lungs and throats let out terrible howls of fear and anguish. But howl as they would, they couldn't drown out Kibeth's call, and the Dead Spirits began to move against their will, thrust out of the decaying flesh they occupied and back into Death.

"That's shown them!" shouted Lieutenant Tindall, as the Dead Hands fell all along the line, leaving empty corpses, the guiding spirits driven back into Death by Kibeth.

"Don't get too excited," growled the Major. He looked swiftly around and saw several men on the ground, clearly dead or dying. There were many wounded heading back to the aid post set up at the base of the spur, some of them supported by far too many able-bodied companions. Considerably more men were simply fleeing down the hill, back towards the Southerlings and the relative protection of the stream.

Most of the company had fled, in fact, and Greene felt a pang of disappointment in what he knew would be his last command. But the great majority of the men were conscripts, and even those who'd served on the Perimeter for a while would never have seen so many Dead.

"Damn them! Just when we're winning, the fools!"

Lieutenant Tindall had noticed the fleeing men at last, with all the indignation of his youth. He made as if to start after them, but Major Greene held him back.

"Let them go, Francis. They're not the Scouts, and this is too much for them. And we need you here—that was probably only the first wave. There will be more."

"Yes, and soon," confirmed Sam hurriedly. "Major—we need to bring everyone in closer to Lirael. I'm afraid if even one Dead creature gets past—"

"Yes!" agreed the Major fervently. "Francis, Edward—close up, everyone, quick as you can. See what you can do for the wounded, too, but I don't want to lose any more effectives. Go!"

"Yes, sir!" the two Lieutenants snapped in unison. Then they were shouting orders, and the sergeants were relaying them with extra flavor. There were only thirty or so soldiers left, and within a minute they were almost shoulder to shoulder in a tight ring around Lirael's iced-over form.

"How many more of the Dead are coming?" asked the Major, as Sam stared up into the fog. It was still spreading, and growing thicker, wisps winding around them as it rolled downhill. There was more lightning beyond the ridge, too, and the storm clouds had spread across the sky like a great inky stain, in parallel with the white fog below.

"I'm not sure." Sam frowned. "More and more of them keep emerging into Life. Hedge must be in Death himself, and is sending them out. He has to have found an old graveyard or some other supply of bodies, because they're all Dead Hands so far. Timothy said he only had sixty workers, and they were all in the first attack."

Both glanced over at Tim Wallach as Sam spoke. He had taken a dead soldier's rifle, sword bayonet, and helmet and now stood in the ring—much to everyone's surprise, perhaps including his own.

"It's always better to be doing," said Sam, quoting the Disreputable Dog. As he said it, he realized that he actually believed it now. He was still scared, still felt the knot of apprehension in his guts. But he knew it wouldn't stop him from doing what had to be done. It was what his parents would expect, Sam thought, but he did not dwell on that. He could not think of Sabriel and Touchstone, or he would fall apart—and he could not, must not, do that.

"My philosophy exactly—" the Major began to say; then he saw Sam shiver and reach for his panpipes.

"Shadow Hands!" Sam exclaimed, pointing with his sword as he put the pipes to his lips.

"Stand ready!" roared the Major, reaching into the Charter for marks of fire and destruction, though he knew they would be of little use against Shadow Hands. They had no bodies to burn or flesh to break. The Charter Magic the soldiers knew might slow them, but that was all.

Up on the ridge, four vaguely human shapes of utter darkness came down through the fog, rippling across rock and thorn. Silent as the grave, they ignored the arrows that passed straight through them and glided inexorably forward—directly towards Lirael and the gap between the boulders where Sam, Major Greene, and Lieutenant Tindall stood to bar their way.

When they were only twenty yards away, one Shadow Hand paused—and pounced upon a wounded soldier who'd been overlooked, lying under the overhang of a large rock. Frantically, he tried to stand and get away, but the Shadow Hand wrapped all around him like a shroud and sucked his life away.

As the soldier's dying scream gurgled into nothing, Sam took a breath and blew desperately on the Saraneth pipe. He had to dominate the Shadow Hands, bend them to his will, for he and his allies had no other weapons that would work. His sword, and the marks it bore, would hurt them, but no more.

So he blew, and prayed to the Charter that he would have the strength to overcome the Shadow Hands.

Saraneth's strong voice cut through even the thunder. Immediately, Sam felt the Shadow Hands resist his dominion. They raged against his will, and sweat broke out all over his body from the effort. It was all he could do just to stop them in place. These spirits were old, and much stronger than the Dead Hands Sam had sent walking into Death with

Kibeth. It took all his strength to stop them moving forward, as they constantly pushed against the bonds Saraneth had—oh so lightly—woven around them.

Slowly, the world narrowed for Sam, till all he could sense was the four spirits and their struggle against him. Everything else was gone—the dampness of the fog, the soldiers around him, the thunder and lightning. There was only him and his opponents.

"Bow down to me!" he shouted, but it was with his mind and will, not a shout any human ears could hear. Sam heard the voiceless spirits answer back the same way, a chorus of mental howls and hissing that clearly defied him.

They were clever, these Shadow Hands. One would pretend to falter, but as Sam concentrated his will against that one, the others would counterattack, almost breaking his hold.

Gradually, Sam became aware that they were not only resisting him, they were actually eroding the binding. Every time he shifted his concentration, they would shuffle forward a little. Just a few steps, but gradually the gap was closing. Soon they would be able to leap past him, drain the life from the soldiers at his side—and attack the defenseless body of Lirael.

He also became aware that only a few seconds had actually passed since he had started blowing through the Saraneth pipe—and he had yet to take another breath. Though the sound of the pipe continued, it was weakening. If only he could pause, refill his lungs, and sound Saraneth again, he could greatly strengthen the binding. Sam knew he was close to total command of these spirits, yet not close enough. He also knew that if he shifted his full concentration away from the four Shadow Hands to take a breath, they would be upon him.

Given that, all he could do was continue the battle of wills and try to slow them down even more. Lirael could return at any moment and banish them with the bells. Sam just had to hold them for long enough.

He stopped even trying to take a breath, shunting his body's urgent demands for air into a corner of his mind. Nothing was as important as stopping the Shadow Hands. He would concentrate every last particle of his mind and power upon them and every last wisp of air into the pipe. They would not reach Lirael. They must not. She was the last hope for the entire world against the Destroyer.

Besides, she was his blood kin, and he had promised.

The Shadow Hands took another step closer, and Sam's entire body shuddered with effort as he tried to force them back, his muscles reflecting the struggle of his mind. But he was growing weaker, he knew, and the Dead stronger. He was also close to passing out from lack of breath, and an almost overpowering urge to step back was rising inside him. Get out of the way! Take a breath! Let these monsters past!

But as he fought the Dead, he fought his own fears, pushing them away into the same distant corner of his mind that so badly wanted to draw air into his lungs. They would stay there, and he was determined to fight well beyond his last breath. At the same time, he tried desperately to think of some stratagem or cunning ploy.

Nothing came to him, and though he hadn't seen or felt them move, the Shadow Hands had stolen some ground. They were now only just out of sword's reach, tall columns of inky blackness, spreading a chill colder than the coldest of winter days.

The two on the outside were moving around

him, Sam realized, though not by much. Clearly they intended to surround and smother him with their shadow stuff, to wrap him in a cocoon of four hungry spirits. Then they would move on to Lirael.

Fire suddenly burst out around the head of the closest Shadow Hand, a fist-sized globe of pure blue flame. But the Dead creature didn't so much as flinch, and the fire spluttered out into the individual marks that had made it, and these vanished into the fog.

Another Charter-spell struck, to no effect, save to set one of the stunted trees alight as the fire rebounded off the shadowy form of the Dead. Sam realized that Major Greene and Lieutenant Tindall were trying to help him with these spells, but he could spare neither thought nor breath to warn them of the uselessness of fire against such an enemy.

All Sam's attention was on the Dead. In turn, all their attention was focused back on him, and on the struggle between them.

So neither noticed the fog suddenly swirl around them, as if disturbed by some mighty gust of air, nor the shouts and cries of the soldiers behind them.

That is, till they heard the bell. A strong, ferocious chime that fell from the air above them. It gripped the four Shadow Hands like a puppet master picking up marionettes to put back in the box. Unable to resist, they bent down, their shadowy heads raised to beg wordlessly for mercy.

No mercy was forthcoming. Another bell rang, building an angry, violent dance over the broad shout of the first. The Shadow Hands jerked upright at its sharp song, their shadow stuff stretching into thin lines, as if they were being sucked through a narrow hole.

Then they were gone, summarily executed, this time for good.

Sam fell to his knees as the Dead disappeared and drew a long, shuddering breath into his desperate lungs. Above him, a bright blue and silver Paperwing hovered for a moment, like a giant hawk over its prey. Then it fell quickly and circled down to the valley floor, where the ground was level and clear enough to land. Sam stared at it and at the two other Paperwings that were gliding down in front of the Southerlings.

Three Paperwings. The craft that had passed overhead was blue and silver, and that was the Abhorsen's color. The second was of green and silver, for the Clayr. The third was the red and gold of the royal line. Two of the three paperwings had a passenger as well as a pilot.

"I don't understand," whispered Sam. "Who wields the bells?"

Mogget was just short of the top of the ridge, zigzagging between Dead Hands and lightning rods, when he heard the bells. He smiled and paused to shout at the single Dead Hand who stood in his way.

"Hear the full voice of Saraneth! Flee while you still can!"

As a ploy, it didn't work. The Dead Hand was too newly returned to Life, too stupid to understand Mogget's words, and it didn't have Mogget's unnaturally keen hearing. It hadn't heard the bells through the thunder, and it had no sense of the power unleashed beyond the ridge. As far as it was concerned, living prey had just stopped in front of it. Close enough to grab.

Rotting fingers leapt out, clutching the little albino's leg. Mogget yowled and kicked back, the dry bones of his captor snapping with the force of the blow. But still it hung on, and other Dead were lumbering towards Mogget now, drawn by the prospect of Life to feast on.

Mogget yowled again and put Nick down. Then

he whipped around, his long-nailed fingers scratching and his sharp-toothed mouth fastening on the Dead Hand's wrist.

If it still had human intelligence, the Hand would have been surprised, because no man ever fought like this one, with an arched back and a wild combination of hissing, biting, and scratching.

Mogget bit through the Dead creature's wrist, severing it completely. Instantly, he sprang back, picked up Nick, dodged around the Hand, and sprinted off with a triumphant yowl.

The creature ignored its missing hand and tried to follow them. Only then did it discover that its strange opponent had clawed through its hamstrings as well. It took two uncertain steps and fell, the Dead spirit that inhabited it already looking desperately around for some other body to inhabit.

By then, Mogget was on the other side of the ridge. He held Nick's arm out to one side as he ran, keeping it well away from his own body. That arm shook and shivered, muscles twitched under the skin, and dark bruises blossomed all around the elbow and forearm.

Behind Mogget, the lightning storm began to

abate and the thunder to lessen. The fog was still lit with electric blue around the edges—but at the center, both the fog and the storm clouds above it had become a bright, bright red.

CHAPTER TWENTY-SEVEN

WHEN THE LIGHTNING STOPS

SAM PICKED HIMSELF up. He felt very weak, washed out, and confused. Slowly he turned to look down at the three Paperwings in the valley, several hundred yards away. They looked very small in front of the crowd of Southerlings. Magical flying craft made from laminated paper and Charter Magic, they were rather like large, brilliantly feathered birds.

The pilots and passengers from the three Paperwings were already climbing out of their craft. Sam stared at them, unable to believe who he was seeing.

"That's the King and the Abhorsen, isn't it, Prince Sameth?" asked Lieutenant Tindall. "I thought they were dead!"

Sam nodded and smiled and shook his head at the same time. He felt an irresistible spring of relief flow up through every part of his body. He didn't know whether to laugh or cry or sing, and was unsurprised to find that tears were running down his cheeks and laughter had come unbidden and was leaping out of his mouth. Because the people climbing out of the blue and silver Paperwing were indisputably Touchstone and Sabriel. Alive and well, all tales of their demise proven false in that single joyous sight.

But the surprises did not end there. Sam wiped the tears away, calmed his laughter before it became hysterical, and caught his breath as he saw a young, raven-haired woman vault out of the red and gold craft and run to catch up with his parents, her sword already out and flashing. Behind her, two very blond, brown-skinned, and willowy women were leaving the green and silver Paperwing, a little more sedately but also in a hurry.

"Who's that girl?" asked Lieutenant Tindall, with more than professional interest in their saviors. "I mean, who are those ladies?"

"That's my sister, Ellimere!" exclaimed Sam. "And two of the Clayr, by the look of them!"

He started to run down to them but stopped after only two paces. They were all hurrying up, and his place was here, by Lirael. She was still frozen in place, still somewhere in Death, facing who knew what dangers. That realization brought Sam back to the current situation. The Dead had fled from Saraneth as wielded by the Abhorsen. But they were only lesser minions of the real Enemy.

"The lightning has stopped," said Tim Wallach. "Listen—there's no thunder now."

Everyone turned back to the ridge. Sam's feelings of relief vanished in an instant. The thunder and lightning had faded away to nothing, sure enough, but the fog was as thick as ever. It was no longer lit with blue flashes but by a steady, pulsing red that grew brighter as they watched—as if an enormous heart of fire grew in the valley beyond.

Something was coming down from the ridge, a shape that seemed to have too many arms, an awful silhouette backlit by the blood-red glow from behind the ridge.

Sam raised his sword and felt for the panpipes. Whatever this was didn't seem to be Dead—or at least he couldn't sense it. But it carried the hot stench of Free Magic with it—and it was coming straight towards him.

Then the thing shouted, with the voice of Mogget.

"It's me—Mogget! I've got Nicholas!"

The fog eddied, and Sam saw that the voice came from the strange little man with the pale hair and skin who he had last seen on the hill above the Red Lake. He was carrying an emaciated body that just might be Nick. Whoever it was, Mogget held the man's right arm out to the side, where it writhed and twitched with a life of its own, all too like a tentacle.

"What is that?" asked Major Greene quietly as he signaled his men to close up again around Lirael.

"It's Mogget," replied Sam with a frown. "He had that shape in my grandfather's time. And that . . . that is my friend Nick."

"Of course it is!" shouted Mogget, who hadn't stopped walking down. "Where is the Abhorsen? And Lirael? We must hurry—the hemispheres have almost joined. If we can get Nicholas farther away, the fragment will not be able to join and the hemispheres will be incomplete—"

He was interrupted by a terrible scream. Nick's eyes flashed open and his whole body jerked into rigidity, one arm pointed back towards the loch valley like a gun. Something brighter than the sun flared at his fingertip for a moment, then it flashed over the ridge, too fast to follow.

"No!" Nick screamed. His mouth frothed with bloody foam, and his fingers clutched uselessly at empty air. But his scream was lost in another sound, a sound that welled up from the red heart of the fog beyond the ridge. An indescribable shout of triumph, greed, and fury. With that shout, a column of fire boiled up to the sky. It climbed up and up till it loomed high above the ridge. The fog swirled around it like a cloak and began to burn away.

"Free!" boomed the Destroyer. The word howled across the watchers like a hot wind, stripping the moisture from their eyes and mouths. On and on the sound carried, echoing from distant hills, screaming through far-off towns, striking fear into all who heard it, long after the word itself was lost.

"Too late," said Mogget. He laid Nick carefully down on the rocky ground and crouched himself. His pale hair began to spread down his neck and face, and his bones contracted and tightened under the skin. Inside a minute, he was once again a little white cat, with Ranna tinkling on his collar.

Sam hardly noticed the transformation. He hurried up to Nick and bent over him, already reaching for the strongest Charter marks he knew for healing, assembling them in his mind. There was no question that his friend was dying. Sam could feel his spirit slipping through to Death, see the terrible pallor of Nick's face, the blood on his mouth, and the deep bruises on his chest and arm.

Golden fire grew in Sam's gesturing hands as he pulled marks from the Charter with ferocious haste. Then he gently laid his palms on Nick's chest and sent the healing magic into his damaged body.

Only the spell wouldn't take hold. The marks slid away and were lost, and blue sparks crackled under Sam's palms. He cursed and tried again, but it was no use. There was still too strong a residue of Free Magic in Nick, and it repulsed all Sam's efforts.

All it did do was bring Nick back into consciousness—of a sort. He smiled as he saw Sam, thinking himself back at school again, struck down by a fastball. But Sam was in some weird armor, not in cricket whites. And there was thick fog behind him, not bright sunshine, and stones and stunted trees, not new-mown grass.

Nick remembered, and his smile disappeared. With memory came pain, everywhere in his body, but there was a welcome lightness as well. He felt clear and unrestricted, as if he were a prisoner freed from a lifetime locked in a single room.

"I'm sorry," he gasped, the blood in his mouth choking him as he spoke. "I didn't know, Sam. I didn't know . . ."

"It's all right," said Sam. He wiped the bloody froth away from Nick's mouth with the sleeve of his surcoat. "It's not your fault. I should have realized something had happened to you. . . ."

"The sunken road," whispered Nick. He closed his eyes again, his breath coming in choking gasps. "After you went into Death on the hill. I can remember it now. I ran down to see what I could do and fell into the road. Hedge was waiting. He thought I was you, Sam. . . ."

His voice trailed off. Sam bent over him again, trying to force the healing marks into him by strength of will. For the third time, they slid off.

Nick's lips moved and he said something too faint to hear. Sam bent still closer, his ear to Nick's mouth, and he took his hand and held it as if he might physically drag his friend back from Death.

"Lirael," whispered Nick. "Tell Lirael I remembered her. I tried . . ."

"You can tell her yourself," Sam said urgently. "She'll be here! Any moment. Nick—you have to fight it!"

"That's what she said," coughed Nick. Specks

of blood stained Sam's cheek, but he didn't move. He didn't hear the soft bark of the Dog as she returned to Life, or the cracking of ice, or Lirael's exclamation of surprise. For Sam, there was only the space he and Nicholas occupied. Everything else had ceased to exist.

Then he felt a cold hand on his shoulder, and he looked around. Lirael was standing there. She was still covered in frost. Ice flaked from her as she moved. She looked at Nick, and Sam saw a fleeting expression that he could not place. Then it was gone, visibly repressed by a hardness that reminded Sam of his mother.

"Nick's dying," said Sam, his eyes bright with tears. "The healing spells won't— The shard flew out of him— I can't do anything!"

"I know how to bind and break the Destroyer," said Lirael urgently. She turned her gaze away from Nick and looked directly at Sam. "You have to make a weapon for me, Sam. Now!"

"But Nick!" protested Sam. He didn't let go of his friend's hand.

Lirael glanced at the column of fire. She could feel its heat now, could gauge the state of the Destroyer's power by its color and the height of the flames. There were still minutes left—but very few of them. Even twice as many would not be enough for Nick.

"There's . . . there's nothing you can do for Nick," she said, though the words came out with a sob. "There's no time, and I need . . . I need to tell you what must be done. We have a chance, Sam! I didn't think we would, but the Clayr did See who was needed and they're here. But we have to act now!"

Sam looked down at his best friend. Nick's eyes were open again, but he was looking past Sam, at Lirael.

"Do what she says, Sam," Nick whispered, attempting a smile. "Try and make it right."

Then his eyes lost their focus, and his ragged breath bubbled away to nothing. Both Sam and Lirael felt his spirit slip away, and they knew that Nicholas Sayre was dead.

Sam opened his hand and stood up. He felt old and tired, his joints stiff. He was bewildered, too, unable to accept that the body at his feet was Nick's. He had set out to save him, and he had failed. Everything else seemed doomed to failure, too.

Lirael grabbed him as he swayed in front of her, his eyes unfocused. The shock broke through the distance he felt around him, and he reluctantly met her gaze. She swung him around and pointed to Sabriel, Touchstone, Ellimere, and the two Clayr, who were moving rapidly up the spur.

"You need to get a drop of blood from me, your parents, Ellimere, and Sanar and Ryelle, and bind it with yours into Nehima with the metal from the panpipes. Can you do that? Now!"

"I haven't got a forge," Sam replied dumbly, but he accepted Nehima from Lirael's hand. He was still looking down at Nick.

"Use magic!" shrieked Lirael, and she shook him, hard. "You're a Wallmaker, Sam! Hurry!"

The shaking brought Sam all the way back to the present. He suddenly felt the heat of the fiery column, and the full dread of the Destroyer filled his bones. Turning away from Nick, he used the sword to cut his palm, wiping the blood along the blade.

Lirael cut herself next, letting the blood flow down the blade.

"I'll remember," she whispered, touching the sword. Then in the next breath, conscious of how little time they had, she shouted at the soldiers.

"Major Greene! Get all your people back to the Southerlings! Warn them! You must all stay on the other side of the stream and lie down as low as you can. Do not look towards the fire, and when it suddenly brightens, close your eyes! Go! Go!"

Before anyone could respond, Lirael was shouting again, this time at the group led by Sabriel, which was almost upon them.

"Hurry! Please hurry! We have to make at least three diamonds of protection here within the next ten minutes! Hurry!"

Sam rushed down to meet his parents, his sister, and the two Clayr, holding the bloody sword flat, ready to take more contributions. As he walked, he built a spell of forging and binding in his mind, knitting the marks together into one long and complex net. When the blade was fully blooded, he would lay the pipes upon it and the spell over it all entire. If it worked, blood and metal would join in the making of a new and unique sword. If it worked . . .

Behind him, the Dog slunk over to the sprawled, silent body of Nicholas. She looked around to make sure no one was paying any attention, then barked softly in his ear.

Nothing happened. The Dog looked puzzled, as if she expected an immediate effect, and licked his forehead. Her tongue left a glowing mark. Still nothing happened. After a moment, the Dog left the corpse and bounded across to join Lirael, who was casting the Eastmark of a very large diamond of protection. It was to be the outermost of three, if there was time to cast them. If there was not, they would not survive.

Beyond the ridge, the huge column of fire burned with increasing heat, though it stayed a terrible, disturbing red. The red of bright blood, fresh from a wound.

chapter twenty-eight

the seven

"SAMETH, WHAT HAVE you done now!" were the first words out of Ellimere's mouth. But she belied her speech with an attempt to hug him, which Sam had to shrug away.

"No time to explain!" he exclaimed as he held out the bloodied Nehima. "I need some of your blood on the blade; then you have to go and help Aunt Lirael."

Ellimere immediately complied. In earlier times, Sam would have been surprised by his sister's instant cooperation. But Ellimere was no fool, and the towering column of fire beyond the ridge was clearly only the beginning of something terrible and strange.

"Mother! Father! I'm . . . I'm so glad you're not dead!" Sam cried as Ellimere ran past, her cut palm still dripping blood, and Sabriel and

Touchstone clambered up.

"Likewise," said Touchstone, but he wasted no time either, holding out his hand so Sam could make the cut. Sabriel put hers out at the same time, but she ruffled Sam's head with her other hand.

"I have a sister, or so the Clayr tell me, and a new Abhorsen-in-Waiting," said Sabriel as they wiped their palms on the steel, the marks glowing as they felt the kinship of Blood to Charter. "And you have found a different path but one no less important. I trust you have been helpful to your aunt?"

"Yes, I suppose," replied Sam. He was trying to keep all the spell for the forging in his head, and he didn't have time to talk. "She needs help now. Three diamonds of protection!"

Sabriel and Touchstone were gone before Sam finished speaking. The two Clayr stood in front of him, holding out their hands. Wordlessly, Sam cut gently into their palms, and they also marked the blade with blood. Sam hardly saw them do it, so many Charter marks were whirling around in his head. He didn't feel them take his elbows, either, and lead him back up the hill. He couldn't think of such mundanities as walking. He was lost in the Charter, dredging up marks he hardly knew.

Thousands and thousands of Charter marks that filled his head with light, spreading inwards and outwards, ordering themselves into a spell that would join with Nehima and the seven pipes to replicate a weapon that was as deadly to its wielder as to its target.

There was no time for greetings farther up the ridge, either. Lirael simply snapped out orders as Ellimere, Sabriel, and Touchstone arrived. She sent them to help make the first three marks of each diamond of protection, saving the last mark till everyone was inside and the diamonds could be completed. For a moment, Lirael had stumbled over her instructions, fearing that they might protest, for who was she to give orders to the King and the Abhorsen? But they didn't, quickly going to their tasks, building the diamonds jointly to save time, each taking a cardinal mark.

Major Greene hadn't questioned her orders either, Lirael noticed with relief. What was left of his company was running pell-mell across the valley, the able-bodied carrying the wounded, with the Major's shouts speeding them on the way. They were shouting at the Southerlings, too, telling them to lie down and look away. Lirael hoped the Southerlings would listen, though the sight of the whirling column of fire had the power to entrance as well as terrify.

Sam staggered up between Sanar and Ryelle, who smiled at Lirael as they brought him to the center of the incipient diamond. Lirael smiled back, a brief smile that took her back for a moment to the twins' words the day she had left the Glacier. "You must remember that, Sighted or not, you *are* a Daughter of the Clayr."

Lirael closed the outer diamond with a cardinal mark and stepped inside the next incomplete diamond. As she passed him, Touchstone let the Northmark flow down his sword to close the second diamond behind her. He smiled at Lirael as they stepped back inside the third and final diamond, and she saw the strong resemblance between him and his son.

Sabriel herself closed the inner diamond. In only a few minutes they had raised magical defenses of triple strength. Lirael hoped it would be enough and they would survive to do what must be done. She had a momentary panic then, and had to quickly count on her fingers to make sure they had the necessary seven. Herself, Sameth, Ellimere, Sabriel, Touchstone, Sanar, Ryelle. That was seven, though she was not sure it was really the right seven.

The lines of the diamond shone golden but were pallid in comparison with the fierce light of the column of fire. Vast as that roaring column was, Lirael knew it was only the first and least of the nine manifestations of the Destroyer's power. Worse was to come, and soon.

Sam knelt over sword and panpipes, weaving his spell. Lirael checked that the Dog and Mogget were safely inside the diamond, and noticed that Nick's body was inside, too, which somehow seemed right. There was also a large thistle bush, which was annoying and showed her haste. She hadn't had time to think about where the diamonds should be.

Everyone within the diamonds, save Sam, was stiff and awkward for a moment, in that strange calm before impending disaster. Then Sabriel took Lirael into a loose embrace and kissed her lightly on the cheek.

"So you are the sister I never knew I had," said Sabriel. "I would wish that we had met earlier, and on a more auspicious occasion. We have had many revelations thrust upon us, more than my tired mind can take in, I fear. We have gone by boat and van and aeroplane and Paperwing to come here, almost without rest, and the Clayr have Seen a great deal very suddenly. They tell me that we face a great spirit of the Beginning, and that you are not only heir to my office but a Remembrancer, too, and you have Seen the past as other Clayr See the future. So please tell us—what must we do?"

"I'm so glad you're all here now," replied Lirael. It was terribly tempting to just fall apart during this brief lull, but she could not. Everything depended upon her. Everything.

She took a deep breath and continued, "The Destroyer is building up to Its second manifestation, which I hope . . . I hope the diamonds will save us from. Afterwards, It will diminish for a little time, and it is then we must go down to It, warding ourselves against the fires that the second manifestation will leave behind. The binding spell we will use ourselves is simple, and I will teach it to you now. But first, everyone must take a bell from me . . . or from the Abhorsen."

"Call me Sabriel," said Sabriel firmly. "Does it matter which bell?"

"There will be one that feels right, one that will speak to your blood. Each of us will be standing for one of the original Seven, as they live on in our bloodline and in the bells," stammered Lirael, nervous about instructing her elders. Sabriel was quite frightening up close, and it was hard to remember

489

that she was her own sister, not just the near-legendary binder of the Dead. But Lirael did know what she was doing. She had seen in the Dark Mirror how the binding had been done and how it must be done again, and she could feel the affinities between the bells and the people.

Though there was something strange about Sanar and Ryelle. Lirael looked at them, and her heart almost stopped as she realized that as twins, their spirits were intertwined. They could wield only one bell between them. There would only be six of the needed seven.

She stood frozen and horrified as the others stepped forward and took their bells from Sabriel.

"Saraneth for me, I think," said Sabriel, but she left the bell in the bandolier. "Touchstone?"

"Ranna for me," replied Touchstone. "The Sleeper seems very appropriate, given my past."

"I will take a bell from my aunt, if I may," said Ellimere. "Dyrim, I think."

Lirael mechanically handed the bell to her niece. Ellimere looked very like Sabriel, with the same sort of contained force inside her. But she had her father's smile, Lirael saw, even through her panic.

"We will hold Mosrael together," said Sanar and Ryelle in unison.

Lirael shut her eyes. Maybe she hadn't counted right, she thought. But she could feel who should have which bell. She opened her eyes again and with shaking hands started to undo a strap on her bandolier.

"Sam will have Belgaer, and . . . and I will wield both Astarael and . . . and Kibeth, to make the seven."

She spoke as confidently as she could, but there was a quaver in her voice. She could not wield two bells. Not for this binding. There had to be seven wielders, not just seven bells.

"Hmmph," woofed the Dog, standing up and wriggling her hindquarters in a somewhat embarrassed fashion. "Not Kibeth. I shall stand for myself."

Lirael's hand fumbled on the strap that held Astarael silent, and she only just managed to prevent the bell's mournful call, which would send all who heard it into Death.

"But you said you weren't one of the Seven!" Lirael protested, though she had long suspected the truth about the Dog. She just hadn't wanted to admit it, even to herself, for the Dog was her best and oldest friend, long her only friend. Lirael could not imagine *Kibeth* as her friend.

"I lied," said the Dog cheerily. "That's one of the reasons I'm the Disreputable Dog. Besides, I'm only what's left of Kibeth, in a roundabout, hand-me-down sort of way. Not quite the same. But I'll stand against the Destroyer. Against Orannis, as one of your Seven."

As the Dog spoke the Destroyer's name, the column of fire roared higher still and punched through the remnants of the storm clouds. It was more than a mile high now, and dominated all the western sky, its red light defeating the yellow of the sun.

Lirael wanted to say something, but the words were choked by incipient tears. She did not know whether they were of relief or sadness. Whatever was to come, she knew nothing would ever be the same with her and the Disreputable Dog.

Instead of speaking, she scratched the Dog's head. Just twice, running her fingers through the soft dog hair. Then she quickly recited the binding spell, showing everyone the marks and words they would have to use.

"Sam is making the sword that I will use to break the Destroyer once It is bound," Lirael finished. At least she hoped he was. As if to reinforce her hope, she added, "He is a true inheritor of the Wallmaker's powers."

She gestured to where Sam was bent over Nehima, his hands moving in complex gestures, the names of Charter marks tumbling from his mouth as his hands wove the glowing symbols into a complex thread that tumbled out of the air and spilled down upon the naked blade.

"How long will it take?" asked Ellimere.

"I don't know," whispered Lirael. Then she repeated herself more loudly. "I don't know."

They stood and waited, anxious seconds stretching out awfully into minutes as Sam called forth his Charter marks and Orannis rumbled beyond the ridge, both of them building very different spells. Lirael found herself looking down into the valley every few seconds, where it looked like Major Greene might be having some success at making the Southerlings lie down; then she would look at Sam; then at the Destroyer's fire; and then start all over again, full of different anxieties and fears everywhere she looked.

The Southerlings were still too close, Lirael knew, though they were considerably lower in the valley than they had been. Sam did not seem to be getting any nearer to finishing. The Destroyer was growing taller and stronger, and any minute Lirael knew it would assume its second manifestation, the one for which it was named.

The Destroyer.

Everyone jumped as Sam suddenly stood. They jumped again as he spoke seven master marks, one after the other. A river of molten gold and silver flame fell from his outstretched hands down upon Lirael's bloody sword and the panpipes, which he'd separated into individual tubes and laid along the length of the silvered blade.

Moments later, the Destroyer flashed brighter and the ground rumbled beneath their feet.

"Look away and close your eyes!" screamed Lirael. She threw one arm across her face and crouched, facing down towards the valley. Behind her a shining silver globe—the joined hemispheres—ascended to the sky atop the column of fire. As it rose, the sphere grew brighter and brighter till it was more brilliant than the sun had ever been. It hovered high in the air for a few seconds, as if surveying the ground, then sank back out of sight.

For nine very long seconds, Lirael waited, her eyes screwed shut, her face pushed into her very dirty sleeve. She knew what was to come, but it did not help her.

The explosion came as she counted nine, a blast of white-hot fury that annihilated everything in the loch valley. The mill and the railway were vaporized in the first flash. The loch boiled dry an instant later, sending a vast cloud of superheated steam roaring to the sky. Rocks melted, trees became ash, the birds and fishes simply disappeared. The lightning rods flashed into molten metal that was hurled high into the air, to fall back as deadly rain.

The blast sheared the top of the ridge completely off, destroying earth, rocks, lightning rods, trees, and everything else. Anything left that could burn did, till it was extinguished seconds later by the wind and the steam.

The outermost diamond of protection took what was left of the blast after it destroyed the protective earth of the hill. The magical defense flared for an instant, then was gone.

The second diamond had the hot wind and the steam that could strip flesh from bone. It lasted only seconds till it too gave way.

The third and final diamond held for more than a minute, repelling a hail of stones, molten metal, and debris. Then it also failed, but not until the worst had passed. A hot—but bearable—wind rushed in as the diamond fell and washed around the Seven as they crouched on the ground, their eyes still shut, shaken in body and mind.

Above them, a huge cloud of dust, ash, steam, and destruction rose, climbing thousands of feet till it spread out like a toadstool top, to cover all in shadow.

Lirael was the first to recover. She opened her eyes to see ash falling all around like blackened snow, and their little diamond-shaped patch of unharmed dirt an island in a wasteland where all color had drained away under a sky that was like a cloudy night, with no hint of sun. But it was not the shock it could have been. She had seen it already in the past, and her mind was fully occupied, racing ahead to what they must do. To what she would have to do.

"Protect yourselves against the heat!" she shouted, as the others slowly stood and looked around, shock and horror in their eyes. Quickly, she called the marks of protection into being, letting them flow out of her mind and across her skin and clothing. Then she looked for the weapon she hoped Sam had made.

Sam held it by the blade and looked puzzled, as if uncertain what he'd wrought. He offered it to Lirael, and she took the hilt, not without a stab of fear. It was not Nehima anymore, and it was not the same sword. It was longer than it had been, with a much broader blade, and the green stone was gone from the pommel. Charter marks ran everywhere through the metal, which had a silvery-red sheen, as if it had been washed in some strange oil. An executioner's sword, Lirael thought. The inscription on the blade seemed the same. Or was it? She couldn't recall exactly. Now it simply said, "Remember Nehima."

"Is that it?" asked Sam. He was white-faced with shock. He looked past her to the valley, but he could not see anything of the Southerlings or Major Greene and his men. There was too much dust and there was little light. But he couldn't hear anything either. No screams or shouts for help, and he feared the worst. "I did what you said."

"Yes," croaked Lirael, her throat dry. The sword was heavy in her hand, and even heavier on her heart. When . . . if . . . they bound Orannis, this was what she would use to break It in two, for no binding could long contain the Destroyer if It was left entire. This weapon could break Orannis, but only at the cost of the wielder's life.

Her life.

"Does everyone have a bell?" she asked quickly, to distract herself. "Sabriel, please give Belgaer to Sam, and tell him the binding spell."

She didn't wait for an answer but led the way across the blasted ridge, down through the fires and the broken hillside, the pools of ash and the cooling metal. Down to the shores of the dry loch, where the Destroyer momentarily rested before its third manifestation, which would unleash even greater powers of destruction.

A grim party followed her, each holding a bell, the binding spell Lirael had taught them repeated over and over in every head.

As they got closer, the stench of Free Magic overcame the smoke, till its acid reek cut at their lungs and waves of nausea struck. It seemed to eat at their very bones, but Lirael would not slow her pace for pain or sickness, and the others followed her lead, fighting against the bile in their throats and the cramps that bit inside.

The steam had fallen back as fog, and the cloud above brought a darkness close to night, so Lirael had little to guide her but instinct. She chose the way by what felt worst, sure that this would lead them to the sphere that was the core of the Destroyer. She knew that if they slowed to try to pick a path by more conventional means, they would soon see a new column of flame, a beacon that would only signal failure.

Then, quite suddenly, Lirael saw the sphere of liquid fire that was the current manifestation of the Destroyer. It hung in the air ahead of her, dark currents alternating with tongues of fire upon its smooth and lustrous surface.

"Form a ring around It," commanded Lirael, her voice weak and small in this abyss of destruction, amidst the darkness and the fog. She drew Astarael in her left hand, wincing at the pain. In all the rush, she'd forgotten about Hedge's blow. There was still no time to do anything for it, but then the thought flashed through her mind that soon it wouldn't matter. The sword she rested on her right shoulder, ready to strike.

Silently, her companions—her family, old and new, Lirael realized with a pang—spread out to form a ring around the sphere of fire and darkness. Only then did Lirael realize that she had not seen Mogget since the destruction, though he had been inside the diamonds of protection. She could not see him now, and another little fear flowered in her heart.

The ring was complete. Everyone looked to Lirael. She took a deep breath and coughed, the corrosive Free Magic eating at her throat. Before she could recover and begin the spell, the sphere began to expand, and red flames leapt out from it, towards the ring of Seven, like a thousand long tongues that sought to taste their flesh.

As the flames writhed, Orannis spoke.

CHAPTER TWENTY-NINE

THE CHOICE OF YRAEL

"SO HEDGE HAS failed me, as such servants do," said Orannis, its voice low like a whisper but harsh and penetrating. "As all living things must fail, till silence rings me in eternal calm, across a sea of dust.

"And now another Seven comes, all a-clamor to lock Orannis once more in metal, deep under earth. But can a Seven of such watered blood and thinner power prevail against the Destroyer, last and mightiest of the Nine?"

Orannis paused for a moment of terrible, absolute silence. Then it spoke three words that shook everyone around it, striking them like a harsh slap across the face.

"I think not."

The words were said with such power that no

one could move or speak. Lirael had to start the binding spell, but her throat was suddenly too dry for speech, her limbs too heavy to move. Desperately, she fought against the force that held her, drawing on the pain in her arm, the shock of seeing Nick's dying face, and the awful and total destruction all around.

Her tongue moved then, and she found a hint of moisture in her mouth, even as Orannis swelled towards the ring of Seven, its tongues of flame reaching out to wrap around the fools who sought to fight it.

"I stand for Astarael against you," croaked Lirael, sketching a Charter mark with the tip of her sword. The mark hung there, glowing, and the fiery tongues recoiled from it—a little.

It was enough to free the others and begin the spell of binding. Sabriel drew a mark with her sword, and said, "I stand for Saraneth against you." Her voice was strong and confident, lending hope to all the others.

"I stand for Belgaer against you," said Sam, his voice growing in strength and anger as he thought of Nick, his bloodless face looking up as he told him to "make it right." Quickly, he drew his Charter mark, fingers almost flinging it in front of him.

"I stand for Dyrim against you," Ellimere pronounced proudly, as if it were a challenge to a duel. Her mark was drawn deliberately, like a line in the sand.

"As I did then, so do I now," said the Disreputable Dog. "I am Kibeth, and I stand against you."

Unlike the others, she didn't draw a Charter mark, but her body rippled, brown dog skin giving way to a rainbow of marks that moved across her in strange patterns and conjunctions of shape and color. One of these marks drifted in front of her snout, and she blew on it, sending it out in front to hang in the air.

"We stand as one, for Mosrael, against you," intoned Sanar and Ryelle in unison. They drew their mark together, in bold strokes with their clasped hands.

"I am Torrigan, called Touchstone, and I stand for Ranna against you," declared Touchstone, and his voice was that of a king. He drew his mark, and as it flared, he was first to sound his bell. Then the Clayr added Mosrael's voice, the Dog began a rhythmic bark, Ellimere swung Dyrim, Sam rang Belgaer, and Sabriel let Saraneth call deep and low over them all.

Finally, Lirael swung Astarael, and her mournful tone joined the ring of sound and magic that surrounded Orannis. Normally, Weeper would throw all who heard her into Death. Here, combined with the other six voices, her sound evoked a sorrow that could not be answered. Together, the bells and Dog sang a song that was more than sound and power. It was the song of the earth, the moon, the stars, the sea, and the sky, of Life and Death and all that was and would be. It was the song of the Charter, the song that had bound Orannis in the long ago, the song that sought to bind the Destroyer once again.

On and on the bells went, till they seemed to echo everywhere inside Lirael. She was saturated with their power, like a sponge that can take no more. She could feel it inside her and in the others, a welling up that filled them all and then had to go rushing out.

It did, flowing into the mark she'd drawn, which grew bright and spread sideways to become a strand of light that joined the next mark, and then the next, to form a glowing ring that closed around the globe of Orannis, a shining band in orbit around the dark and threatening sphere.

Lirael spoke the rest of the binding spell, the words flying out of her on a flood tide of power. With the spell, the ring grew brighter still and began to tighten, forcing back the tongues of flame. It sent them writhing in retreat, back into the sphere of darkness that was Orannis.

Lirael took a step forward, and all the seven did the same, closing the human ring behind the magic one of light. Then they took another step, and another, as the spell-ring tightened further, constricting the sphere itself. All around, the bells rang on in glory, the Dog's bark a rhythm the bellringers followed without conscious thought. A great feeling of triumph and relief began to swell in Lirael, tempered with the dread of the sword on her shoulder. Soon she would wield it and, all too soon, would walk once more to the Ninth Gate, never to return.

Then the spell-ring stopped. The bells faltered as the ringers halted behind it in mid step. Lirael flinched, feeling a backlash of power, as if she'd suddenly walked into an unexpected wall.

"No," Orannis said, its voice calm, devoid of all emotion.

The spell-ring shivered as Orannis spoke, and

began to expand again, forced outwards by the growing sphere. The tongues of fire re-appeared, more numerous than before.

The bells still rang, but the ringers were forced to step back, their faces showing emotions that ranged from grim despair to doomed determination. The spell-ring faded as it opened out, stretched too thin by the growing power of Orannis.

"Too long did I linger in my metal tomb," spoke Orannis. "Too long have I borne the affront of living, crawling life. I am the Destroyer—and all will be destroyed!"

With the last word, the flames lashed out and gripped the spell-ring with a thousand tiny fingers of dark fire. They twisted and wrenched at it every way, hastening its destruction.

Lirael saw it happen as if she were far away. All was lost now. There was nothing else to do or try. She had seen the Beginning, and seen Orannis bound. Then, the Seven had prevailed. Here, they had failed. Lirael had known and accepted the certainty of her own death in this venture, and thought it a fair price for the defeat of Orannis and the saving of all she loved and knew.

Now, they would all merely be the first of a multitude to die, till Orannis brooded on a world of ash and cinders, kept company only by the Dead.

Then, in the midst of despair, Lirael heard Sam speak and saw a flash of brilliant light flow up next to him, to form a tall shape of white fire that was only vaguely human.

"Be free, Mogget!" shouted Sam, as he held a red collar high. "Choose well!"

The shape of fire grew taller. It turned away from Sam towards Sabriel, and its head descended as if it might suddenly bite. Sabriel looked up at it stoically, and it hesitated. Then it flowed over to Lirael, and she felt the heat of it, and the shock of its own Free Magic that mixed with the lung-destroying impact of Orannis.

"Please, Mogget," whispered Lirael, too soft to be heard by anyone at all.

But the white shape did hear. It stopped and turned inwards, to face Orannis, changing from a pillar of fire to a more human shape, but one with skin as bright as a burning star.

"I am Yrael," it said, casting a hand out to throw a line of silver fire into the breaking spell-ring, its voice crackling with force. "I also stand against you."

The spell-ring tightened again, and everyone automatically stepped forward. This time, it didn't stop but contracted again. As the ring tightened, the tongues of flame blew out, and the sphere grew darker. Then it began to glow with a silver sheen, the silver of the hemispheres that had bound Orannis for so long.

Lirael stepped forward again, her eyes fixed on the shrinking sphere. Dimly she was aware that Astarael still rang in her hand, as she was even more faintly aware that Yrael was singing now, singing over the bells and the barking, his voice weaving into the song.

The sphere contracted still further, the silver spreading through it like mercury spilt in water, traveling in slow coils. When it became fully silver, Lirael knew she must strike, in the few moments when Orannis was completely bound. Bound not by the Seven, but by the Eight, she realized, for Mogget—Yrael—could be nothing else but the Eighth Bright Shiner, who was himself bound by the Seven in the long ago.

Bells rang, Yrael sang, Kibeth barked, Astarael mourned. The silver spread, and Lirael moved in closer and raised the weapon Sam had made for her from blood and sword and the spirit of the Seven in the panpipes.

Orannis spoke then, in bitter, cutting tones.

"Why, Yrael?" it said, as the last of the dark gave way to silver, and the shining sphere of metal sank slowly to the ground. "Why?"

Yrael's answer seemed to travel across a great space, words trickling into Lirael's consciousness as she raised her sword still higher, body arching back, preparing for the mighty blow that must cut through the entire sphere.

"Life," said Yrael, who was more Mogget than it ever knew. "Fish and fowl, warm sun and shady trees, the field mice in the wheat, under the cool light of the moon. All the—"

Lirael didn't hear any more. She gathered up all her courage and struck.

Sword met silver metal with a shriek that silenced everything, the blade cutting through in a blaze of blue-white sparks that fountained up into the ashen sky.

Even as it cut, the sword melted and red fire streaked up into Lirael's hand. She screamed as it hit, but hung on, putting all her weight and strength and fury into the blow. She could feel Orannis in the fire, feel it in the heat. It was seeking its last revenge on her, filling her with its destructive power, a power that would burn her into ash.

Lirael screamed again as the flames engulfed

the hilt, her hand now no more than a lump of pain. But still she held on, to complete the breaking.

The sword broke through, the sphere split asunder. Even knowing she would fail, Lirael tried to let go. But Orannis had her, its spirit kept momentarily whole by the thin bridge of her sword, the last remnants of the blade between the hemispheres. A bridge to her destruction.

"Dog!" screamed Lirael instinctively, not knowing what she said, pain and fear overwhelming her intention to simply die. Again she tried to open her hand, but her fingers were welded to the metal, and Orannis was in her blood, spreading through to consume her in its final fire.

Then the Dog's teeth suddenly closed on Lirael's wrist. There was a new pain, but a clean one, sharp and sudden. Orannis was gone from her, as was the fire that threatened to destroy her. A moment later, Lirael realized that the Dog had bitten off her hand.

All that remained free of Orannis's vengeful power was directed at the Disreputable Dog. Red fire flowered about her as she spat out the hand, throwing it between the hemispheres, where it writhed and wriggled like a dreadful spider made from burned and blackened flesh.

A great gout of flame erupted and engulfed the Dog, sending Lirael stumbling back, her eyebrows frizzled into nothing. Then, with a long, final scream of thwarted hope, the hemispheres hurtled apart. One narrowly missed Lirael, tumbling past her into the loch and the returning sea. The other flew up past Sabriel, to land behind her in a flurry of dust and ash.

"Bound and broken," whispered Lirael, staring at her wrist in disbelief. She could still feel her hand, but there was nothing there save a cauterized stump and the burnt ends of her sleeve.

She started to shake then, and the tears came, till she couldn't see for crying. There was only one thing she knew to do, so she did it, stumbling forward blindly, calling to the Dog.

"Here," called the Dog softly, in answer to the call. She was lying on her side where the sphere had been, upon a bed of ash. Her tail wagged as she heard Lirael, but only the very tip of it, and she didn't get up.

Lirael knelt by her side. The hound didn't seem hurt, but Lirael saw that her muzzle was now frosted white, and the skin was loose around her neck, as if she had suddenly become old. The Dog raised her head very slowly as Lirael bent over her, and gave her a little lick on the face.

"Well, that's done, Mistress," she whispered, her head dropping back. "I have to leave you now."

"No," sobbed Lirael. She hugged her with her handless arm and buried her cheek against the Dog's snout. "It was supposed to be me! I won't let you go! I love you, Dog!"

"There'll be other dogs, and friends, and loves," whispered the Dog. "You have found your family, your heritage; and you have earned a high place in the world. I love you, too, but my time with you has passed. Goodbye, Lirael."

Then she was gone, and Lirael was left bowed over a small soapstone statue of a dog.

Behind her, she heard Yrael speak, and Sabriel, and the brief chime of Belgaer, so strange after the massed song of all the bells, its single voice freeing Mogget from his millennia of servitude. But the sound was far away, in another place, another time.

Sam found Lirael a moment later, curled up in the ash, the carving of the Dog nestled in the crook of her handless arm. She held Astarael—the Weeper—with her remaining hand, her fingers clenched tight around the clapper so it could not sound.

NICK STOOD IN the river and watched with interest as the current tugged at his knees. He wanted to go with that current, to lie down and be swept away, taking his guilt and sorrow with him to wherever the river might go. But he couldn't move, because he was somehow fixed in place by a force that emanated from the patch of heat on his forehead, which was very strange when everything else was cold.

After a time that could have been minutes or hours or even days—for there was no way to tell whether time meant anything at all in this place of constant grey light—Nick noticed there was a dog sitting next to him. A large brown and black dog, with a serious expression. It looked kind of familiar.

"You're the dog from my dream," said Nick. He bent down to scratch it on the head. "Only it wasn't a dream, was it? You had wings."

"Yes," agreed the dog. "I'm the Disreputable Dog, Nicholas."

"Pleased to meet you," said Nick formally. The Dog offered a paw, and Nicholas shook it. "Do you happen to know where we are? I thought I—"

"Died," replied the Dog cheerily. "You did. This is Death."

"Ah," replied Nick. Once he might have wanted to argue about that. Now he had a different perspective, and other things to think about. "Do you . . . did they . . . the hemispheres?"

"Orannis has been bound anew," announced the Dog. "It is once again imprisoned in the hemispheres. In due course, they will be transported back to the Old Kingdom and buried deep beneath stone and spell."

Relief crossed Nick's face and smoothed out the lines of worry around his eyes and mouth. He knelt down beside the Dog to hug her, feeling the warmth of her skin in sharp contrast to the chill of the river. The bright collar around her neck was nice, too. It gave him a warm feeling in his chest.

"Sam and . . . and Lirael?" asked Nick hopefully, his head still bowed, close to the Dog's ear.

"They live," replied the Dog. "Though not without scathe. My mistress lost her hand. Prince

Sameth will make her one, of course, of shining gold and clever magic. Lirael Goldenhand, she'll be forever after. Remembrancer and Abhorsen, and much else besides. But there are other hurts, which require different remedies. She is very young. Stand up, Nicholas."

Nicholas stood. He wavered a little as the current tried to trip him and take him under.

"I gave you a late baptism to preserve your spirit," said the Dog. "You bear the Charter mark on your forehead now, to balance the Free Magic that lingers in your blood and bone. You will find Charter mark and Free Magic both boon and burden, for they will take you far from Ancelstierre, and the path you will walk will not be the one you have long thought to see ahead."

"What do you mean?" asked Nick in bewilderment. He touched the mark on his forehead and blinked as it flared with sudden light. The Dog's collar shone, too, with many other bright marks that surrounded her head with a corona of golden light. "What do you mean, far from Ancelstierre? How can I go anywhere? I'm dead, aren't—"

"I'm sending you back," said the Dog gently, nudging Nick's leg with her snout, so he turned to face towards Life. Then she barked, a single sharp sound that was both a welcome and a farewell.

"Is this allowed?" asked Nick as he felt the current reluctantly release him, and he took the first step back.

"No," said the Dog. "But then I am the *Disreputable* Dog."

Nick took another step, and he smiled as he felt the warmth of Life, and the smile became a laugh, a laugh that welcomed everything, even the pain that waited in his body.

In Life, his waking eyes looked up, and he saw the sun breaking through a low, dark cloud, and its warmth and light fell on a diamond-shaped patch of earth where he lay, safe amidst ruin and destruction. Nick sat up and saw soldiers approaching, picking their way across an ashen desert. Southerlings followed the soldiers, their just-scrubbed hats and scarves bright blue, the only color in the wasteland.

A white cat suddenly appeared next to Nicholas's feet. He sniffed in disgust and said, "I might have known"; then he looked past Nick at something that wasn't there and winked, before trotting off in a northerly direction.

The cat was followed a little later by the weary footsteps of six people, who were supporting the seventh. Nick managed to stand and wave, and in the space of that tiny movement and its startled response, he had time to wonder what all the future held, and think that it would be much brighter than the past.

The Disreputable Dog sat with her head cocked to one side for several minutes, her wise old eyes seeing much more than the river, her sharp ears hearing more than just the gurgle of the current. After a while a small, enormously satisfied rumble sounded from deep in her chest. She got up, grew her legs longer to get her body out of the water, and shook herself dry. Then she wandered off, following a zigzag path along the border between Life and Death, her tail wagging so hard, the tip of it beat the river into a froth behind her.